THE BILLIONAIRE'S BABY SWAP

BY
REBECCA WINTERS

First Published in Great Britain 2016
By Mills & Boon, an imprint of HarperCollins*Publishers*
1 London Bridge Street, London, SE1 9GF

© 2016 Rebecca Winters

ISBN: 978-0-263-91975-2

23-0416

Our policy is to use papers that are natural, renewable and recyclable products and made from wood grown in sustainable forests. The logging and manufacturing processes conform to the legal environmental regulations of the country of origin.

Pri
by

Rebecca Winters lives in Salt Lake City, Utah. With canyons and high alpine meadows full of wildflowers, she never runs out of places to explore. They, plus her favorite holiday spots in Europe, often end up as backgrounds for her romance novels, because writing is her passion, along with her family and church. Rebecca loves to hear from readers. If you wish to email her, please visit her website at www.cleanromances.com.

To my wonderful father, who brought
over 15,000 babies into the world.

At his funeral, our family was besieged
with grateful mothers who loved their OB.

I miss him terribly.

CHAPTER ONE

AT FIVE TO three in the afternoon, Valentina Montanari finished her timed online engineering test and sent it into the testing site at the University of Naples Federico II. She could now forget her graduate studies for a semester and concentrate on the baby.

The strange backache that had come on during the test hadn't stopped. She got up from the table on the terrace, where she'd been working with her laptop and walked inside the villa to the kitchen for a drink. Maybe because of the way she'd been sitting, she'd developed a cramp.

"What's wrong, Valentina?"

She darted a glance at her brother's ever-watchful housekeeper, Bianca. "Oh, just a backache."

"When did it start?"

"While I was taking my test. Don't worry about it." She poured herself a glass of freshly made lemonade. Bianca was a fifty-year-old treasure who cooked and cleaned for Valentina's older brother, Rinieri, who was still a bachelor. She watched her like a hawk.

"A backache this close to the due date could mean your baby is ready to come."

"I'm due July 6. That's four days from now. At my

checkup last week, Dr. Pedrotti said the baby hadn't dropped yet and I might even go past my due date."

"All my babies started with a backache that never went away." The widowed mother of three no doubt knew what she was talking about. Right now Valentina wished her own mother were alive and here to talk to.

"The doctor said some backache was to be expected." She drank half a glass. "I'll walk around for a few minutes to work it off." But she'd only made it to the doorway of the kitchen when the pain reached around, gripping her like a pair of giant tongs.

"Caspita!" Valentina exclaimed. She braced herself against the door frame, surprised by the degree of pain.

Bianca nodded. "I *knew* it! I'm calling your doctor."

"I hate bothering him yet, Bianca."

The housekeeper ignored her and made the call. After a quick conversation, she hung up. "He says this could be the beginning of labor. First babies generally take a long time to be born, and your water hasn't broken yet. But he suggests you leave for the hospital. He'll check you out there. If it's a false alarm, no harm is done and you can come home. Rinieri said he'd be in Milan today, so I'll phone Carlo to drive you."

Before she could stop her, Bianca had made the call to Valentina's married brother, Carlo, who was two years younger than thirty-two-year-old Rini. After she got off the phone, she said, "Luckily he flew home early from Naples. He said he'd come for you right away."

"You shouldn't have called him. The pain is easing."

"Yes. But it will come back again and again. You get your things together."

"My bag is already packed," she called over her shoulder on her way to her bedroom to freshen up. Rini had already seen to that.

His nature to be in charge and have everything under control was the reason he'd been catapulted to CEO of the renowned Montanari Corporation at such a young age. Seven months ago her oldest brother had been the one to take care of her when she'd discovered she was pregnant. He'd talked her into moving out of the family villa in Naples and brought her to his villa a few kilometers from the vertical town of Positano.

Valentina adored both her brothers, but it was Rini who'd provided her with the emotional support she'd needed when she'd found out the father of her baby didn't want children or responsibility. Being abandoned by Matteo had damaged her confidence, and Rini had recognized that fact by being protective.

Once her relationship with Matteo was over, it was Rini who'd insisted she live with him instead of their father, who'd been grieving since the death of their mother in a car accident. He'd grown weak and needed a wheelchair more and more. He slept poorly. All he would need was a baby around the family villa in Naples.

Carlo had invited her to live with him, but she didn't want to intrude when he had a wife and child. She was blessed to have such wonderful brothers, but throughout her pregnancy she would have given anything if her mother had still been alive. They'd been so close. Now she was gone, and a grieving Valentina was going to have a baby without her mother's loving kindness and help.

A few minutes later she heard Carlo's voice talking to Bianca. Grabbing her purse and overnight bag, she walked to the foyer of the villa. He broke into a big smile and took the bag from her. "You're going to be a *mamma* in a little while. Let's get you to the hospital."

"I'm fine now."

"That's what Melita said before our little Angelica was born. Bianca was right to call me."

"Please don't tell Papà yet. He'll just worry."

"I agree."

She thanked the housekeeper and followed Carlo out to the courtyard, where his Mercedes was parked. As he opened the front passenger door, another pain took over. This one actually stung.

"Take some deep breaths until it passes, Valentina."

Carlo had been through this before with his wife. He had a calming effect on her. In a minute the pain subsided enough for her to get in the front seat. After some effort, he helped fasten the seat belt below her swollen belly. He patted her tummy. "Angelica's going to have a little cousin before long."

"I can't believe it's really coming."

"Don't be scared."

"I'm in too much pain to be scared."

He shut the door and walked around to the driver's side. Once behind the wheel, he started the car and they left the villa that was perched like an eagle's nest above the dizzying landscape of the Amalfi Coast.

The evening summer traffic impeded their progress to the main road leading to the Positano hospital. Valentina could see Bianca's wisdom in calling Carlo to come and get her. It would have taken Rini too long to get there.

Another pain, harder than the others, had taken over. She had a feeling this was really it. Her brother knew what was happening and let out a few epithets because someone was blocking the road.

"I should have brought you in the helicopter."

Normally unflappable, Carlo was showing a surprising amount of angst. If she weren't in so much pain, she'd smile because he seemed to be the one who was scared.

He honked the horn, but it did no good. At least a dozen cars were backed up with more cars lined up behind them. It took forever to reach the turnoff. The loud, blaring sound of a siren was getting closer. Another pain had started worse than the others. Valentina had always heard a woman comes close to death giving birth. If it was from the pain, she believed it.

"Carlo—my water just broke!"

"Hang in there. I'll have you at the hospital in a few minutes."

Suddenly there was a collision and the sound of twisting metal.

"Signor Laurito?"

What did his private secretary want now?

"*Si*? I'm just walking out the door to fly home to Ravello. Can't it wait until tomorrow?"

"This is an emergency. Signora Corleto is on line two."

His pulse raced. He knew his pregnant ex-wife could go into labor anytime now. He turned on the speaker to talk to his former mother-in-law. "Violeta? What's going on with Tatania?"

"Oh, Giovanni, the most terrible thing has happened! She started bleeding and we sent for an ambulance. On the way to the Positano hospital it was involved in an accident with two other cars. My precious *figlia*—" She was crying so hard he could hardly make out her words.

"How bad is she?" The baby? His heart plunged to his feet. Had she lost it?

"The collision caused her to deliver the baby in the ambulance. Both are at the hospital on the third floor east wing. I don't care what she says. She *needs* you."

Giovanni needed answers, but she was too distraught to give him details. "I'll be right there."

He alerted his helicopter pilot, then raced out of the office and took the steps two at a time to reach the roof of the Laurito Corporation in downtown Naples. The flight to Positano took twenty minutes. After the short trip, his pilot set them down on one of the two helipads.

Giovanni waved him off and hurried inside the hospital. He reached the east wing and approached a doctor putting information into a computer at the nursing station. "*Scusi*—who can tell me the status of Signora Corleto and her baby?" When they'd divorced, she'd taken back her maiden name of Corleto.

The doctor looked up. "You are…?"

"Her ex-husband, Giovanni Laurito."

"*Ah.*"

"Signora Violeta Corleto, her mother, phoned and told me she'd been in an accident."

"That's correct. She's in with her daughter now. By

some miracle she wasn't injured, but she had the baby in the ambulance before they could get her here. I'm glad you've come. I understand your ex-wife doesn't want to see the baby or keep him."

"That's right. It's been settled in court."

"Then that means you are the sole parent to your son."

"Si."

"Why don't you talk to the pediatrician in the nursery? I just came from there. Your baby is doing fine."

"And my ex-wife?"

"She lost some blood, but is recovering nicely."

"So she's out of danger?"

"Si."

Grazie a Dio.

"If her mother looks for me, tell her I'll be in the nursery." Violeta had never given up hope the two of them would be reconciled. That would be an impossibility.

"Go down the other end of the hall and through the doors. You can't miss it. Congratulations."

"Thank you."

Giovanni was still reeling with shock when he reached the nursery. The clerk alerted the pediatrician, who came out of his office to greet him.

"Signor Laurito, I'm Dr. Ferrante. Your ex-wife's doctor told me to expect you. You have a fine boy, who is doing well. Twenty-one inches long, seven pounds and five ounces."

"That's wonderful to hear. How soon can I see him?"

"Right now. Come in this other room and wash your hands. While you do that, I'll have the nurse wheel him in here, where you can hold him and inspect him all you want. Later she'll show you how to bathe and feed him."

Giovanni's heart started to pound hard. He'd played with the nieces and nephews from his two sisters' marriages, but he'd rarely held a tiny baby. To think this newborn was his own son!

When Tatania had first learned she was pregnant, she'd threatened to have it aborted. No doubt she'd wanted to punish Giovanni because of their failed marriage that she'd blamed on him. But her father, Salvatore, had threatened to disown her if she went through with it. His will had prevailed, *grazie a Dio*.

After removing his suit jacket and tie, Giovanni washed his hands and dried them with the automatic blower. The moment was surreal for him as the nurse pushed the cart through the door and smiled up at him.

"You have a beautiful *bambino*, Signor Laurito. Here. Put this cloth over your shoulder and you can hold him. He's asleep, but he'll soon wake up for his bottle."

He did as she said, but his eyes had fastened on the baby wrapped up in a crib blanket. His boy lay on his back. He had a beautiful face, almost angelic. Since Giovanni had black hair and Tatania was a brunette, the wisp of gold hair came as a surprise. His heart melted at the sight of him.

"Vitiello, *mi figlio*." That was an old family name he'd decided to give him after he learned they were having a boy. He'd call him Vito for short.

Without hesitation Giovanni picked him up and put him against his shoulder. The warmth of his tiny body seeped through him. "To think your first experience in life happened inside an ambulance. That's a story the whole family will talk about for the rest of your life." He kissed his cheek and neck.

Giovanni might not have given birth, but his paternal instincts had taken over, and he was filled with a joy he hadn't known in years. His marriage to Tatania had never taken. Since the divorce he'd felt relief, but was pretty much devoid of any other feelings. She'd gone through the greater part of her pregnancy without Giovanni's help. To be united suddenly with his son thrilled him to the core of his being.

He couldn't comprehend that Tatania didn't want to coparent with him. According to the doctor, she hadn't asked to see the baby. If he knew Violeta, she would work on her daughter, but Giovanni didn't hold out hope. Every child needed a mother and father, but during their marriage, Tatania had shut down. It was as if every motherly instinct had been drained out of her. Psychiatric counseling hadn't helped.

Eager to examine his son, he put him on the changing board and unwrapped him down to his shirt and diaper. Being uncovered had wakened him. His eyes opened. Giovanni couldn't tell their color. Maybe a muddy slate blue.

He kissed him on either cheek. "I'm your *papà*. Welcome to my world." He checked his legs and feet that were wiggling. Those tiny hands had fingers that curled around his finger. Before long he would pull him up slightly to discover how strong he was. Laughter came out of Giovanni.

In a minute the pediatrician walked in the room and smiled. "It looks like father and son are doing well. The nurse will bring you a bottle and teach you how to feed him."

"Thank you, Doctor."

The rest of the night turned out to be pure delight as he fed and bathed Vito. By 11 o'clock Giovanni felt like an old hand, but he was exhausted. He arranged for his pilot to pick him up. He'd go home to sleep, then come back in the morning.

Once the baby was released, they'd fly home, where Stanzie and her husband, Paolo Bruno, were waiting for him. The attractive couple in their early forties had been managing the Bruno Advertising agency under their uncle Ernesto Bruno. Giovanni had become acquainted with the dynamic couple three years earlier through business. But months ago their uncle let them go because the business was failing.

Giovanni had stepped in to help them out and asked if they'd take care of his villa and garden for a temporary period. He believed in them and planned to set them up in their own advertising business a little later down the road that would benefit the three of them. Until that could be accomplished, he'd hired them to work for him, an arrangement that suited everyone. They'd been hoping to have children, but it hadn't happened yet and they could hardly wait for the arrival of the baby.

He'd spent the past month turning one of the guest rooms into a nursery with everything the baby would need. But nothing had prepared him for the sheer wonder of being a father. This tiny infant was his heart's blood. Already those protective feelings had taken root. He could tell his life had changed in ways he'd never dreamed of.

* * *

Two weeks had passed since the birth of the baby. Valentina looked down at her handsome son while he slept on his back. She was still trying to breast-feed, but the baby wasn't getting enough milk so she supplemented with formula.

She'd also struggled trying to decide on the right name for him before he was born. But once she'd laid eyes on him, she felt Riccardo suited him best. She'd called him Ric from that moment on.

"Did you name him after our grandfather?" Carlo questioned while they were gathered round in the nursery. Everyone was crazy about the baby, who luckily slept soundly.

"Yes, but let me ask you a question. I want your opinion on something. Because Matteo was blond, and I am, too, I didn't expect to have a baby with black hair. Dark hair does run in our family, but Ric's hair is a stark black. I don't know. Do you think Ric looks like our grandfather Riccardo?"

Carlo shook his head. "No. Not at all." Other than the dark hair, Valentina didn't see any similarities, either, but she'd had to ask. "This little guy has a distinct widow's peak."

"Papà noticed it immediately when he came to visit and thought it odd. Now I'm going to ask another question. Do you think he looks like me?"

Rini's eyes narrowed on her. "No."

"But he doesn't look anything like Matteo. He was blond and blue-eyed. My baby's eyes are dark already."

"Now that you mention it, Melita thought it strange he doesn't look like you."

At Carlo's comment a sick feeling grew in the pit of her stomach, and she turned away from the crib. "Let's not talk about it anymore."

"He could be a throwback to an ancestor, but none of it matters. Don't worry about it." Carlo kissed her cheek. "I've got to go home. Melita is waiting for me to help put Angelica to bed. Talk to you later." His footsteps faded down the hall.

Rini stayed in the nursery with her. "Valentina? Look at me." She was afraid to. "I know what has been going through your mind since you brought Ric home from the hospital. At first I didn't dwell on it, but tonight I have to admit I'm puzzled that I see no signs of you or our family in the baby. Before you turn yourself inside out, there's a simple way to learn the truth."

"I know," she whispered. "Get a DNA test done."

"Exactly. Then you'll know the baby is yours and you can stop driving yourself mad with worry."

Her breath froze in her lungs. "You wouldn't suggest my doing that if you didn't have doubts, too." Nothing got past her successful brother who was known for his genius in the business world. She held herself taut. "What if the baby isn't mine? I love little Ric with all my heart and soul. He's so gorgeous and so sweet."

They stared at each other for an overly long moment.

"Find out the truth first before you tear yourself apart."

Tears filled her eyes. "If he isn't my son, then it means that someone else went home from the hospital with *my* baby. Things like this just don't happen!" she cried out. The baby stirred before growing relaxed again.

"I agree switched babies are very rare, but it does happen. That's not to say that it happened to you, but to remove all doubt, call the doctor and have the DNA test done. I'll take you to the hospital in the morning and we'll get this thing settled."

Though she wanted to be more independent, she didn't know how she could do this alone and was grateful for Rini's loving support.

They hugged good-night and she went to her room, leaving the doors open so she could hear Ric when he woke up for his next bottle. Unable to sleep, she got on the internet and researched switched-baby stories. The latest one had come out of France. But the switch hadn't been discovered until twenty years later.

How horrible that must have been for both sets of parents. If Valentina's baby was given to the wrong mother, then she wanted her own baby back as soon as possible. But she wanted Ric, too. He was her very heart. How could she possibly give him up? They'd already bonded. Tears streamed down her cheeks.

Was there a mother out there who was worried that her baby didn't look like her, either, and wondered if some terrible mistake had been made? If so, then she'd already bonded with Valentina's birth baby. Valentina could hardly bear it.

She spent the rest of the night in agony. Instead of sleeping, she went in the nursery and sat in the rocker, holding Ric. The nursing just didn't give him enough milk. She fed him bottles to satisfy him at two different times during the night. Morning couldn't come soon enough. There wasn't any time to lose getting to the hospital to learn the truth!

Giovanni fed Vito his early-morning bottle before turning him over to Stanzie. He hadn't expected her to be a babysitter to Vito and had decided to hire a nanny. But when Stanzie heard that, she begged to do the honors.

In two weeks his boy was filling out and so much fun to play with, Giovanni had a hell of a time leaving the villa to put in a day's work at his office. He'd had visits from his parents and sisters since he'd brought the baby home. Violeta had begged to see him. He could hardly refuse her.

Giovanni realized she was a doting grandmother and could understand her pain over her daughter's refusal to see Vito. His son would be lucky to have the love of two grandmothers who already worshipped him.

After his flight to work, he met with Ernesto Bruno over a working lunch in his office conference room. The man's company did advertising for major companies, including the Montanari Corporation. For the last little while Giovanni had been working to buy Bruno's failing advertising business. He'd settled on a price that would be very lucrative for him. A win-win situation.

But by the end of the meeting, it became clear that Signor Bruno was still stalling. Maybe Giovanni had underestimated his loyalty to the Montanari family. It appeared the new CEO Rinieri Montanari, a shrewd entrepreneur, wanted to make Bruno Advertising a part of *his* company. Giovanni realized that in order to get to the root of the problem, he needed to go through Rinieri himself to settle this one way or the other.

He and Ernesto agreed to look at numbers and meet again in a week. After the other man left, Giovanni went back to his office to look over last month's accounts. He should have done it before, but Vito's arrival had consumed him.

Giovanni told his secretary to hold all calls. To his surprise she walked in on him, disturbing his concentration. "Signor Laurito? Forgive me, but there's a call for you on line two. It's Signor Conti, the administrator of the hospital in Positano. He said it was extremely urgent."

The administrator? Why?

He thanked his secretary and got on the phone. "This is Giovanni Laurito. You wished to speak to me?"

"I realize you're an important man, but something has come up I need to discuss with you. Could you come to the hospital this afternoon? Because of confidentiality, I can't talk about this over the phone."

Giovanni's brows knit together. Maybe this was about Tatania. But if she'd changed her mind about seeing the baby, she'd go through her attorney surely, not to mention her mother. "I'll be there as soon as I can." He hung up and alerted his pilot. Before leaving his office, he called the villa to inquire about Vito.

"He's being a perfect boy and is taking his nap."

"That's good. Thank you, Stanzie. I'll be home for dinner. *Ciao*."

A half hour later he was invited in the administrator's office. "Thanks for getting here so quickly."

They shook hands and he sat down, but Giovanni was on edge. "Tell me what's wrong."

"I won't beat around the bush. Today we discovered that two babies from the hospital's nursery went home with the wrong mothers."

Giovanni felt his gut twist.

"This is the kind of mistake every parent dreads. One *I* dread. Someone in the nursery put the wrong band on the wrong babies. It is a terrible thing to have happened."

"How did you find out?" Giovanni's voice grated.

"One of the mothers came to the hospital with questions about her baby. He didn't look like her or the father. We had her DNA tested with her baby's DNA. The result proved that the baby couldn't be *her* baby."

Shock brought Giovanni to his feet. "Are you saying the baby I took home isn't mine and my ex-wife's?"

"No. We're having DNA tests on every baby boy that was in the nursery before this particular mother went home. Your baby is the last one on the list of eight we need to check. If you'll go to the lab, a technician will draw your blood and the necessary tests will be done along with your ex-wife's and son's blood to prove paternity. We need to do this process immediately so the babies can be returned to their rightful birth parents before any more time goes by."

"Let's do it now," he bit out, horrified that Vito might not belong to him after all. He thought of all the parents involved. Sixteen people were traumatized by the realization that their sons might have been one of the two to be switched. He swallowed hard. Was it Vito?

"I'll walk you to the lab."

They left the office together. "How long will this take?"

"In three days we'll know all the facts. The lab is rushing everything. Believe me when I tell you we'll move heaven and earth to make this right."

Giovanni grimaced. "Nothing could make it right."

"I know, and I can't tell you how sorry I am this has happened."

The administrator was taking this hard, as he should. Giovanni sensed that. But the thought of having to give Vito back to another set of parents was unbearable. If that happened, it meant his birth son was out there somewhere. Giovanni couldn't imagine having to give up the precious son he'd taken to his heart. But if his birth son was out there, naturally he couldn't wait to see him and hold him. This was a nightmare of impossible proportions.

After the blood was drawn, he flew back to Ravello. The second he entered the kitchen, Stanzie took one look at him and let out a cry. "What has happened to you? You're as white as a sheet!"

He looked her in the eye. If the impossible had happened, this was going to be hard on her and Paolo, too, not to mention his whole family and Violeta. Everyone was crazy about Vito. "There's a possibility that the wrong baby was sent home from the hospital with me."

"No—" She put her hands to her mouth.

"In three days I'll know the truth."

Tears rushed down her cheeks…the same invisible tears he'd shed from the moment the administrator had explained his reason for the unexpected call. While he stood there in agony, she rushed out of the kitchen, no doubt running to tell Paolo the dreadful news.

Giovanni hurried through the villa to the nursery. Vito was awake. The minute he saw Giovanni, his arms and legs grew animated. His love for this child went so deep it could never be rooted out. He changed his diaper before carrying him to the terrace that overlooked the Mediterranean, where the scent of the roses was especially strong and sweet.

He kissed his cheeks. "I couldn't possibly give you up, Vito. We're going to forget that a mistake was made. You belong to me."

CHAPTER TWO

"SIGNORINA MONTANARI?"

Valentina recognized Signor Conti's voice. She gripped her cell phone tighter. *"Si?"*

"We have located your baby, even without the birth father's DNA. The DNA tests have proved that the baby you took home is a match for the blood tests of the couple whose baby was born on the same day as yours."

"Oh, no—" she cried out in pain. So it *was* true. The babies had been switched.

"I'm so sorry, *signorina*. You have no idea how terrible I feel about this, too. It should never have happened."

She wiped her eyes that kept dripping. "How was it possible?"

"I've learned that they were born within ten minutes of each other. After a full investigation is carried out, we'll learn the reason why the babies were tagged with the wrong mothers."

"Don't you know I'm dying inside?"

"Of course you are. That's why you need to be united with your son as soon as possible."

"And give up the one I already love?" she cried out in anger.

"Signorina—"

Weak from emotion, she sank down on one of the kitchen chairs. Valentina had been waiting for this day, yet dreading it. She felt guilty over her fear that she'd see the baby she'd given birth to and she wouldn't love it the way she loved Ric. It was a horrible thing to admit to herself, let alone her family.

Her birth baby had been loved and taken care of by another mother who had to be going through this same agony. The pain was so unbearable, Valentina could hardly breathe.

"Signorina?"

"I—I'm here." Shock that this day had come made her slow to respond. If she hadn't pursued this—if she hadn't said anything, then she wouldn't have to give up this little boy she adored. Her heart was torn into pieces.

"Since time is of the essence, if you can be at the hospital by noon with your baby, then the exchange can take place and your birth baby will be turned over to you. You need to be united with him as soon as possible."

She moaned. "I'm devastated, Signor Conti."

"I have no doubt of it. Do you have someone to help bring you to the hospital? You need to come to the outpatient entrance. When you sign in, you'll be told where to go."

"I—I don't know if I can do this." It took a minute to quiet her sobs. "Will I be able to talk to the mother who has been taking care of my baby?"

"It's not hospital policy."

"But that's cruel!"

"I'm sorry, but we have to treat this like a closed

adoption process. Everything sealed. Your privacy has been insured. The other parents don't know your name, and you don't know theirs."

"I understand the legalities, but there are little things they should know about Ric."

"Of course. Why don't you write down your routine and any medicines and formula you're using, anything the other parent needs to know."

Sobs still shook her body.

"Signorina?"

"I'm here."

"I'll see you at noon. I realize this is very traumatic for you. It would be for anyone. The hospital will have a counselor on hand to help you deal with your grief. We'll do everything we can for you."

Can you make it all go away?

"Again, I'm so sorry, *signorina.*"

She clicked off, unable to say another word. It was already eight in the morning. Only a few more hours before she had to give him up. Valentina hurried through the house to the nursery, where she found Rini holding Ric. He was dressed to go to work, but he loved the baby and sought him out at every opportunity.

"I just got the call. Ric isn't my baby. Your suspicions were right, too. I'm supposed to be at the hospital at noon to pick up my birth baby."

Rini grimaced. "I'll drive you."

"But you have work. I know you're having a problem with Signor Bruno and should be there to put out another fire."

"That can wait. Nothing's more important than helping you."

"I wish to heaven I'd never asked for a DNA test."

"You were acting on a mother's intuition that turned out to be inspired."

"But to pay this price—I don't think I can do it."

"Yes you can. Your birth baby is out there waiting for you. You're the strongest woman I know. Don't forget I'll be there for you."

She stared at the brother who'd been such a bulwark. "I know. You've always stood by me. I love you so much." Valentina had never done anything on her own and felt shame that she'd always been dependent on family. In showing such bad judgment with Matteo, she felt a failure, but her family had never made her feel like one. Right now she had to prove to herself how strong she really was.

"I love you, too, Valentina. More than you know. Can I help you pack up some things?"

"I'm not sure what to take, but I'll wrap him in the quilt I made."

Rini patted the baby's back. "The other mother will have everything Ric needs."

Tears filled her eyes. "You're right. I need to write down instructions for the parents since we won't be meeting. If you're willing to play with Ric, I'll get myself ready and make the list they'll need."

At eleven they left for the hospital in Rini's BMW. When they walked into the outpatient department and she'd checked in with her baby, she turned to her brother. "The woman at the desk said my family has to wait in the reception area."

He nodded. "I'll be right here."

"I'm glad no one in the family knows about this yet. I need time to deal with it first, then I'll tell Papà."

Rini gave her a hug before she turned away from him in pain. Signor Conti met her inside the double doors.

"Come down the hall to this room." Valentina clutched Ric to her heart while she followed him to a small room with chairs and a table. "Again, I'm devastated, *signorina*. This is a terrible situation, and I will do whatever I can to help."

She nodded in a daze. "What happens next?"

The second she'd asked the question, a nurse appeared at the door. Signor Conti looked at Valentina with anxious eyes. "If you'll give the baby to the nurse, then yours will be brought to you."

But Ric is mine.

Valentina's pain had reached its zenith. She broke down sobbing. "I don't know if I can do this, but I h-have to," she stammered. "If the other parents want to know, I named him Riccardo. Here's the list of information to give them."

Signor Conti took it from her. Valentina kissed Ric's cheeks, then gave him up to the nurse. She thought she'd die when the three of them left the room.

Is this really happening? Her body felt like ice.

In a minute the head of the hospital returned with the nurse, who carried a baby wrapped in a darling blue-and-white quilt. Valentina could hardly breathe as she walked over and put the infant in her arms. Signor Conti said, "I was told his name is Vitiello, but his nickname is Vito. I'll give you a few minutes to get acquainted, then I'll be back." He put a list made by the other woman on the table, and they both left the room.

Taking a deep breath she looked into the face of her birth son.

A cry escaped her lips.

Without doubt his facial bone structure was Valentina's. She saw shades of her mother, as well. Her beloved mother who was no longer here to turn to for love and advice. The baby had deep blue eyes. His pale blond hair—the way it grew—was hers and Matteo's. She carefully unwrapped him to check his toes.

He'd been dressed in a cute one-piece polo suit in navy and white. She could tell he'd been given perfect care and was thriving, but his little chin had started to wobble, tugging at her heartstrings. Valentina was a stranger to him, but she realized he belonged to her. All of a sudden he started to cry, wrenching her heart.

"Oh—my precious baby. I'm your real mommy, Vito. I know you're confused, but I already love you to pieces."

She put him over her shoulder. "You dear, dear little thing." She stood up and walked around, whispering endearments to comfort him. Right now she prayed that her darling Ric was feeling the same love from his birth mother. But the more she tried to quiet him down, the more he resisted, filling her with panic.

The head of the hospital came in Giovanni's room accompanied by a nurse. With the door open, he could hear a baby crying at the top of his lungs from another room. It was Vito! But Giovanni couldn't do anything about it because the nurse placed the baby in his arms. Then she left.

"His name is Riccardo," Signor Conti informed him. He put a list made by the other mother on the table. "I'll be back in a few minutes." The closed door shut off most of the sound.

Giovanni looked down at the baby. The second he saw his face and those dark eyes peering from the edges of an exquisite hand-stitched quilt in blue, yellow and white, he didn't need the proof of a DNA test to know it was his son. The telltale black hair and widow's peak proclaimed him a Laurito. His nose and mouth had the look of Tatania. He had long fingers, a trait of the Laurito men.

He could tell the mother had taken meticulous care of him. The one-piece navy body suit had four white sailboats. Giovanni was thrilled beyond belief at the sight of his son, but the baby wasn't happy to be with him and began to cry.

"Riccardo—*figlio mio*—I know you're frightened, but we'll become friends. You'll see." He raised him to his shoulder and ran his hand over his back. "I know you miss the mother who took care of you, but now you're home with me where you belong."

How shocking to feel this instant affection when he'd felt the same way about Vito. Seeing his own flesh and blood was like a miracle. He kissed his head and cheek while he walked around patting his little back to quiet him down. His son smelled wonderful.

But no amount of loving helped. If anything, the crying was getting worse. Vito had never cried this hard with him. Anyone hearing Riccardo would think something was terribly wrong.

Unable to stand it another minute, he scanned the list given him to find out if Riccardo had been nursed or drank formula. What he did see was the mention of formula. It was the same kind he'd given Vito.

Anxious to comfort him, he pulled out one of

Vito's bottles and tried to get his son to drink it, but the baby was too upset and fought him.

Frantic because nothing was working, he opened the door to take him for a walk, anything to help him stop crying. Once out in the hallway, he heard Vito, who was crying hysterically. The sound came from another room around the corner and a long way down the hall. That was where Giovanni headed because two screaming babies needed comfort, rules or no rules.

As he reached the closed door ready to knock, it opened unexpectedly.

"Oh—" The mother cried to see Giovanni standing right there.

"*Mi scusi, signora.* I was just coming to find you."

"That's what *I* was about to do."

Despite the fact that both babies were crying at the top of their lungs, for a moment his gaze took in the angelic-looking woman. At first she seemed so familiar to Giovanni he couldn't understand. Then it struck him that it was because the son he'd taken home from the hospital and adored was a tiny replica of her, down to her blond hair. Good heavens, what a gorgeous woman!

But he couldn't go on staring at her when something needed to be done quickly to quiet the babies. "Let me take Vito."

"Yes. He doesn't want me," her voice trembled.

Giovanni felt her pain and grasped him in his other arm while handing a tearful Riccardo back to her. Without hesitation the exchange took place in the hallway. He didn't care if they weren't supposed to meet. Apparently she didn't care, either. It told him this terrible situation had nearly destroyed her, too. Already he felt a bond with her as she crushed Ric to her, yet never took her eyes off Vito.

After a few seconds their children quieted down and eventually blessed peace reigned. She looked up at him. Suddenly they both laughed in relief. In that instant he felt a tug on his emotions to discover this woman could find humor at such a precarious moment. She appealed to him in ways he couldn't begin to explain.

"Thank you for coming to our rescue." She sounded a little breathless as their eyes clung.

"I didn't know what else to do."

"I hear you. Where's your wife?"

"I'm divorced. She gave up her mother's rights."

Her incredible sapphire-blue eyes clouded. "I'm so sorry."

"It's past history. Is your husband here?"

She kissed his son—her son. "We never married. Our relationship ended a long time ago."

At this historic moment he had too many questions, but the hall wasn't the place for the kind of conversation they needed. "Why don't I grab the diaper bag out of the room I was in and join you in here so we can talk."

"Please hurry—"

That pleading in her eyes got to him. He understood the urgency and was gone and back in a flash. After closing the door, he dug inside the bag and handed her Vito's bottle.

She did the same with her bag. "Here's one for Ric."

He liked the shortened version. In a minute both

babies had settled down and were drinking, totally happy to be in familiar arms.

Signor Conti poked his head in the room, shocked to see the four of them together. "So *this* is where you went, *signor*. It seems your babies found you."

"Our children don't understand hospital rules," Giovanni muttered. "But it wouldn't have mattered how this was handled, the babies need time to adjust."

He cleared his throat. "Under the circumstances, let me introduce you. Signorina Valentina Montanari, please meet Signor Giovanni Laurito."

Giovanni's body quickened. Such a prominent name in Italy's business world made him wonder if she was any relation to Rinieri Montanari, the new head at Montanari's. He was a hard man to do business with, forcing him to hold talks with Ernesto Bruno when he needed to meet with the CEO himself.

"I can see you two have a lot to talk about. This is a situation no one is prepared for. Since you've met, stay here as long as you need to. Remember we provide counseling if you feel that you need it."

They thanked him. Giovanni closed the door behind the administrator and sat down with Vito slumped against his shoulder.

She sat in the other chair and kissed Ric with all the love of a doting mother. He admired her for going through this whole experience without a husband to help her.

"Ric's hungry. I tried to nurse him, but I didn't have enough milk so he's been getting used to the formula."

"It looks like both babies have been on the same brand sent home by the hospital." He had dozens of questions but asked the first one on his mind. "How soon did you decide Ric wasn't your son?"

She darted him a glance. "From the first moment I saw him, I was surprised he didn't look at all like me. In the beginning I didn't say anything to my family, but after two weeks everyone agreed he didn't look like anyone on our side of the family. In the case of the baby's father, I saw no resemblance to him, either.

"My oldest brother knew I was worried and suggested I get a DNA test done so I could be absolutely certain one way or the other. My fear turned into a nightmare when the results came back, letting me know he wasn't my baby."

Giovanni nodded. "*Nightmare* is the right word, but I was the last person to be contacted by the hospital, so I haven't had as much time as you to be torn apart."

She smiled sadly. "No matter the length of wait, it has been a hideous experience loving our children, yet knowing we would have to give them up." Her gaze centered on him. "Now that I've met you, there's no question Ric is your son. His hairline and coloring match yours."

Giovanni was still trying to grasp the fact that their babies had been switched. "How much did he weigh?"

"The chart said eight pounds, four ounces. He was twenty-two inches long. He'll be tall like you. My baby's father was five foot ten. It explains why he's a little lighter and smaller."

His eyes lingered on her features. "Vito has so much of you in him, it's uncanny. I thought it odd that he was born with blond hair, but I never considered that he wasn't mine."

"My brother told me it was my mother's intuition."

Giovanni nodded. "If my wife hadn't refused to see him, she would probably have felt something wasn't right."

She expelled a deep sigh. "The mystery has now been solved."

"But not the agony," he finished the thought she hadn't spoken. "Our situation is so unique, there's no precedent to follow. I've read that out of four million babies born every year, twenty-eight thousand are switched temporarily, or permanently."

"I read the same article and was surprised it was that high," she murmured. "The doctor told me the car accident caused both myself and your ex-wife to deliver while we were in the ambulances taking us to the hospital. The mistake must have happened after we arrived at the ER."

His eyes found hers. "Were you injured?"

"No. I was already in labor. Everything happened so fast, I guess the impact sped up the process."

"The same thing happened to Tatania. She'd started bleeding, so her family called an ambulance for her. But she got the help she needed in time to recover with no aftermath of problems."

"Thank heaven."

"It's a miracle the accident didn't do more damage. I'm afraid my ex-wife's family will probably sue the hospital. Signor Conti hasn't said as much, but you know it's what he's fearing."

Valentina lifted the baby to her shoulder to burp him. "I can tell he's really sorry. He even offered counseling to help us. But as far as a lawsuit goes, I don't want to sue anyone. A ghastly mistake was made, but today it's been rectified. Surely whoever put the wrong bracelet on the boys had no idea what he or she had done. It happened." She kissed his little head. "No one's perfect."

"You're right." In a sue-happy world, Giovanni found her attitude not only amazing, but refreshing. In fact she appealed to him so much, he wanted to spend the rest of the day with her so they could really get to know each other.

"I'd better get going."

"Please don't leave yet." His mind raced ahead to prevent her from leaving. "I can understand why there's a rule that parents don't meet under a situation like this. The sooner we get our birth babies home, the sooner we can bond with them. But you and I *have* met. I'm not sorry."

After a slight pause she admitted, "Neither am I."

"Thank heaven you said that because I have to tell you I love Vito from the bottom of my soul. To forget him would be impossible. I want, need, to stay in touch with you."

Tears glistened in those fabulous blue eyes. "You've taken the words right out of my mouth. Ric is the most precious thing in my life. I held him all night, not wanting to let him go. Seeing the two of them together like this is tearing me apart. I know I have to give Ric up, but I can't bear it. If only there were a way to share them, but of course that's impossible."

He clasped Ric a little tighter. This was a place in Hell he didn't know existed. No way was he going to let her and his son just walk out of his life! He stared at her. "Maybe there is a way."

Her startled gaze met his. "What do you mean?"

"Since we both feel the same, I have a suggestion. After what happened today, it's clear we need time to spend together with both children so they get used to both of us. When they've learned to trust us and be happy with both of us, then we'll decide when we can safely make the separation, knowing it won't traumatize them."

"But how would that work?"

"You could stay at my villa with Vito for a few days. I'd get an extra crib. Then I could stay at your home for a few days with Ric. After a time we could separate and take one of them home with us and see how they handle being away from us overnight."

She averted her eyes. "According to everything I've read, that's exactly what we shouldn't do."

"Does it matter? We're talking about you and me and our babies."

Valentina bit her lip. "Even if it were possible, I'm living with my brother, so the idea of your staying at his house isn't possible." Giovanni Laurito had been a thorn in her brother's side. To consider getting involved with him when she knew how Rini felt made the whole situation precarious. Valentina couldn't believe the coincidence of both families having been brought together under such bizarre and astonishing circumstances.

"Where do you live?"

"Here in Positano."

"I live in Ravello. My home is open to you for as long as is needed. Why don't you fly home with me now so we can talk and make plans?"

She stirred restlessly. Much as she wanted to go

with this man, Rini would never condone it. "People would think we were out of our minds."

"I don't particularly care. They would have to be in our shoes to understand how we feel. We're alone in this and we love both boys. Their welfare is all that matters. Don't you agree?"

"My brother would never permit it."

"Forget your brother for a minute."

He didn't know what he was asking.

"What is it *you* want? I caught you in the doorway wanting to find me, though you shouldn't have. I heard Vito crying and couldn't stay away from your door, either. Nothing about this situation has gone according to the book."

"I know," she whispered. "I—I need to think about it." Valentina was so tempted to go with him, it was killing her. The babies' needs aside, she felt an overpowering attraction to this man, who made her think and want things she'd thought were dead inside her.

"Then let's do this. We'll program our phone numbers into our cells. Since both babies are asleep, let's exchange them now. I'll take Ric home with me. You take Vito. We'll see how it goes tonight. In the morning we'll talk again. How does that sound?"

Valentina had to admit it sounded wonderful.

Though she didn't say anything, she reached in her purse with her free hand and pulled out her phone. He did the same. Once the programming was done she said, "My brother is waiting for me. I'll leave first before Vito wakes up and finds out he's with a stranger. Please keep the quilt I made for Ric. He's used to it."

"Did you make it?"

"Yes. My mother made beautiful quilts. I learned from her."

His eyes traveled over her face with an intensity that made her heart race. "You're remarkable, and can make something this beautiful and be a loving mother, too. I hope you know I'm in awe of you, and for going through this whole experience alone."

She felt his sincerity. His words boosted her confidence and thrilled her in a way he couldn't possibly understand. "I—I'd better get going." Her voice faltered.

"Be expecting my phone call in the morning."

Valentina knew herself very well. She was already hoping to hear from him. He could have no idea how much.

Her glance strayed to Ric. Her first impulse was to kiss him, but after a slight hesitation, she left the room, taking Giovanni's son with her in the quilt he'd bought him.

She walked out to the lounge of the outpatient department in a complete daze. The reality of Giovanni Laurito being Ric's father was stunning.

The *man* was stunning.

More than that, he was breathtakingly handsome, charming, reasonable and so loving to both babies it brought tears to her eyes. In a word, he was wonderful.

To think that all this time the famous CEO at Laurito's had been fathering Vito, *her* son. All this time Valentina had been mothering *his* son, Ric. The whole thing made reason stare.

She found her brother pacing the floor while he did business on his phone. As soon as he saw her, he put it away. How to tell him the true facts? She needed to think about it for a while first because she knew it would be a shock to him when he learned Giovanni Laurito was Ric's father.

"Sorry I was so long."

"Don't apologize for anything. Are you going to let me see my nephew?"

She nodded and turned the sleeping baby around so he could get a good look. "His name is Vito. He's so precious I can't believe it."

After a minute, her brother stared at her with a somber expression. "He's yours all right. Genes don't lie."

"No. They definitely don't."

"I know this is hard on you."

"You have no idea. Let's go. I want to get him home before he wakes up."

"I'll bring the car around the entrance."

"Thank you."

In a few minutes she got in the backseat with the diaper bag and settled Vito in the car seat. So far he hadn't stirred. She felt Rini's piercing gaze through the rearview mirror. If he knew what she and Signor Laurito had talked about, he'd quash the idea in a heartbeat.

No one had a greater right to an opinion than Rini. She owed him everything. But Vito's father had asked her a salient question. Is it what *you* want?

It didn't take long to reach the villa. She hurried inside with Vito and went straight to the nursery. Bianca followed her and grew misty-eyed. She'd loved Ric, too, but now that she could see Vito, she marveled over the likeness to Valentina and was smitten with him.

After putting him in the crib, she leaned against the

bars and looked down at him. He truly was adorable, but she could never forget that this had been Ric's bed several hours before.

By now he was probably at his new home in Ravello. Signor Laurito's villa was a little over an hour away from Positano. Had Ric awakened and discovered she was gone? Her pain went so deep she broke down sobbing.

She felt Rini's arm close around her. He pulled her into him, where she buried her face against his shoulder. "I wish I could comfort you."

"You've done everything for me any human could ask for, but this is a problem not even King Solomon could make right. The truth is I want both babies." She lifted her head, aware that she'd soaked his shoulder. "They're both mine."

He kissed her forehead before releasing her. "I admire you more than you know for handling this with such grace and dignity."

For her brother to say that went a long way to make her feel better about herself as a capable person and mother. "I'm trying to, but I'm afraid Signor Conti is expecting the hospital to be sued." That was Signor Laurito's opinion.

"I suppose it's possible," he reasoned. "Look at the turmoil this has cost because someone made a serious mistake by not following the hospital rules. Everything about this has been handled wrong."

"I've been thinking about that." She sank down in the rocking chair, her eyes focused on her baby. "But everyone makes mistakes. Mine was worse for getting involved with Matteo when I knew better. He'd fed my ego and look what happened. But the person

who put the wrong wristbands on the babies didn't
do it willingly."

"That's one of the things I love most about you,
Valentina. You have a generous heart. I can't think of
another mother who wouldn't want justice after what
has happened."

She flicked her gaze to him. "But what good would
it do now? The damage has been done. Our mother
would say the same thing. All I can do is love my
birth baby and pray that God takes my pain away for
losing Ric. It's so strange. I feel like I gave birth to
both of them."

"I feel your sadness. What can I do to help?"

Valentina grasped his hand. "You're helping right
now by listening to me. I couldn't have gotten through
all this without your love and encouragement. But
right now I'm exhausted. I think I'll lie down for a
few minutes and ask Bianca to let me know when he
wakes up for another bottle."

"I'll stay in here with him."

"I love you, Rini." She got up and kissed his cheek.
Another glance at Vito and she went to her bedroom
down the hall. Her body felt like it weighed a thousand
pounds. She sank down on the bed and cried herself
to sleep while visions of Ric and his striking father
played in her mind.

When she was next aware of her surroundings, the
baby was crying. She sat up. "I'm coming, Ric!" Valentina flew out of the bedroom, but when she reached
the nursery, she discovered Rini holding Vito and she
realized her mistake in thinking it was Ric. He was
crying his little heart out.

She reached for him. "It's all right, Vito. I'm here,

darling." She put him against her shoulder and walked around the room patting his back. To her surprise it was dark outside. She must have been asleep for hours. Her life had been turned around and upside down. Rini looked as tired and frustrated as she felt.

"How long has he been this upset?"

He flashed her a wry smile. "Almost from the moment he woke up and saw me looking at him. He needs you."

"I wish I were the person he wanted."

"Before long you'll be the mother he turns to."

Now was the time to tell Rini the truth of the matter. Valentina had made the mistake of getting involved with Matteo without the benefit of her family's knowledge until it was too late. If she planned to have any more contact with Signor Laurito, she didn't want to hide it from her brother, no matter if he didn't approve.

"Rini? There's something you should know. I found out Vito's mother gave him up at birth."

He frowned. "Is she mentally ill?"

"Maybe. She and his father are divorced, so it's the father I met at the hospital. His name is… Giovanni Laurito."

Her brother's eyes narrowed in reaction. "You must be joking."

She shook her head. "Signor Conti introduced us when he discovered we'd gotten together to quiet the babies. Nothing about this situation has been normal. But the point is, the children will have a hard time adjusting. Signor Laurito has made a suggestion that I've been considering to help the babies adjust."

A long quiet ensued. "What might that be?" he

asked in a cool tone. When she told him, he took his time before responding. "Signor Laurito doesn't recognize boundaries."

Valentina swallowed hard. "Has he done something criminal?"

"No."

"Then what is it you have against him?"

"Ernesto did work for our company before Laurito discovered him. Now he wants to buy him out."

"Is that wrong?"

"No."

"Isn't that business? Invading someone else's boundaries?"

Her brother lifted his head. "Yes."

"But you don't have to like it."

"No."

"Thank you for being honest with me. In this particular case, I'm afraid I don't care about boundaries, either, not when it comes to our babies. Don't worry. I'm not making any decisions yet, but I wanted you to know everything." She hugged her brother. "Thank you for taking care of Vito while I slept."

"We managed to get acquainted," he said without referring to the other matter. "Right now he hasn't got any use for his uncle, but that will change. Bianca has your dinner ready whenever you want to eat."

"Thanks, but I'll wait until I can get Vito to quiet down. You go. You've lost a whole day to help me. I'm fine now."

"The family has called. I told them about the switch and said you'd get back to everyone in the morning."

"That's good. I'm not up to dealing with anything except my baby. Please plan to go to work tomorrow."

"If you're sure."

"I knew this would be hard, but I'll get through it. Bianca will help me."

"Okay." He kissed her cheek and left the nursery. She knew the revelation about Ric's father and his idea for getting the babies together had shocked Rini. But it was better he knew everything so Valentina wouldn't have to take on more guilt for remaining quiet.

She walked a whimpering Vito through the villa and out to the back terrace and the swimming pool beyond. "This is your home now, sweetheart." *But only for the time being.*

Then she would have to make arrangements to live on her own.

Valentina had intruded on her brother's life long enough. Though her father would do anything for her, she didn't want to put that burden on him. She needed to be on her own and take care of her baby and herself. Behaving like a grown-up was a start in the right direction.

"I'm a mother now, the head of my own family. We'll make it work somehow, Vito."

She kissed his wet cheeks. But no matter how much she tried to comfort him, he was unhappy. Maybe a bath would help. Unfortunately he didn't like it and cried throughout the whole ordeal. When he finally went to sleep with a bottle, it was two in the morning.

Valentina stole to the kitchen and warmed up the dinner Bianca had made for her. She needed food. If Vito woke up again and cried uncontrollably, she would need the energy to deal with him.

For the rest of the night she sat in the rocker. The baby woke up and cried several times. He drank his bottle but fussed through most of it. Around eight in the morning her cell rang just as she was holding Vito, who fought the bottle because he was crying too hard. *Please be Ric's father.*

CHAPTER THREE

VALENTINA CLICKED ON. *"PRONTO?"*

"Signorina Montanari?"

That deep male voice wound deep inside her body. Her heart thumped in reaction because she'd wanted to hear it again. In the background she could hear Ric crying.

"Yes." She was too breathless to say anything else.

"It sounds like you didn't get any more sleep than I did. Ric has been crying so hard, he's running a slight temperature."

"Oh, no—as you can tell, Vito's every bit as bad."

"We need to meet, if only to quiet the children for a few hours."

"I thought Vito would start to accept me, but it hasn't happened yet."

"I'm not Ric's *mamma*. What would you say if I came by for you in a few minutes and drove us to that park near the hospital? I've installed another car seat in the back. We can spread some blankets on the grass while we talk." Her pulse raced. "But if you don't want to do that, I'm going to the hospital and have Dr. Ferrante examine Ric in case something else is wrong."

"I'd rather meet you first to talk before we both lose our minds." She gave him directions to the villa and they hung up.

Valentina knew her brother would never condone it, but Vito's continual crying had made her frantic. As for Ric, she'd heard him wailing in the background. With Ravello more than an hour away, it meant Signor Laurito had been desperate for help. Something had to be done. So far nothing was working for either of them.

She put Vito in the crib and left him crying while she took a quick shower and opted to wear a skirt and blouse. After putting on lipstick and brushing her hair, she was ready. Before she left the room, she phoned her brother and left him a message that she was meeting with Signor Laurito today. Rini wouldn't like it, but at least she was being honest with him.

Once she'd packed the diaper bag, she lifted Vito out of the crib and carried him into the kitchen in his carry-cot. "Bianca? Ric's birth father is coming for me. We're going to the park by the hospital in order to discuss our situation. I don't know when I'll be home. You can always phone if you need to."

"Does Rini know where you'll be in case he phones?"

"Yes. I told him Vito is so unhappy I've got to do something."

"That's true. The poor *bambino*."

"All he's done is cry. I've learned that Ric is just as miserable, so we're going to try and work something out. The exchange was too abrupt."

The older woman nodded. "The switch should have

been caught before you ever left the hospital. Now that they've been home with you, they're used to you."

"I know. That's why we've got to come up with a plan."

"Vito's *mamma* is having the same problem?"

"Not Vito's *mamma*."

"What do you mean?"

"His *mamma* gave him up. His *papà* is raising him."

Bianca's hands clapped to her own cheeks. "The mother doesn't want him?"

"No. Poor Signor Laurito is frantic. During the call I could hear the baby crying in the background. He said Ric is running a temperature and needs to be checked by the doctor."

"Then you go on. When Riccardo sees you, he will calm down."

"Vito is suffering just as terribly." She went to the fridge and pulled out two bottles of formula. After putting them in the diaper bag, she said goodbye and hurried through the house to the front door.

When she emerged into the courtyard, she saw Signor Laurito waiting for her outside his dark gray Maserati sedan, wearing a black polo and stone-gray pants. This was the first time she'd looked at him in broad daylight and realized she hadn't been wrong about Ric's father. He was without question the most attractive man she'd ever seen in her life. He'd haunted her dreams last night. No wonder Ric was so handsome.

He reached for Vito and kissed him, then he put him in the back next to Ric and fastened him in.

"Where did you get another car seat?"

"When I brought Vito home from the hospital, I'd

already bought a car seat for this car and one for Paolo and Stanzi's car—they're a couple who help me out around the house. This morning I installed it in mine, just in case you were amenable to going to the park with me."

After stowing the carry-cot in the trunk, he helped Valentina into the front seat. In less than a minute they were off to the park, with two infants crying at the top of their lungs.

Valentina happened to glance at him just as he looked at her. The situation was so crazy they both started laughing like they'd done at the hospital. He shared her sense of humor, something she loved. Between the noise all four of them were making, she couldn't seem to stop. The much-needed release from tension had affected him, too.

There wasn't much traffic. Before she knew it, they came to the park. He pulled the car to a stop near a copse of trees that provided shade. Valentina jumped out and plucked Ric from his car seat. "It's okay, darling." She pressed her cheek to his and could tell he was too warm. He snuggled against her.

Giovanni spread some blankets on the grass before claiming Vito from the backseat. "Hey, Tiger. What are all the tears for?"

Slowly but surely quiet reigned. They laid the babies on the blanket and sat next to them. Two pairs of eyes, one blue and one black, stared at both of them.

Ric's father said, "Do you get the feeling they're sizing us up?"

Valentina wiped the tears from her eyes. "I can hear them saying, 'Why are you torturing us like this?'"

Their gazes met. "Before this goes any further, may

I call you Valentina, or should I continue to call you Signorina Montanari?"

This tall, hard muscled male had a charisma she couldn't ignore. How was it that his marriage hadn't worked? His wife didn't want her own child? She couldn't comprehend it. Except that she couldn't comprehend Matteo not caring that she was going to have his baby.

"Please call me Valentina. And you?"

"I prefer Giovanni." He studied her features. "Does Vito's father *know* he's a father?"

"Yes." She played with Ric's fingers before scooping him up to hug him. "I was always a serious student and didn't date often. Much more important to me was to be like my brilliant engineering brothers and father. Because I'm a woman, I wanted to prove myself in a household of male geniuses."

His head lifted. "So you *are* from the famous Montanari engineering family."

Something in his demeanor let her know the revelation had shocked him in the same way it had shocked Rini. "Yes. I'm close to getting my graduate degree in chemical engineering. Matteo, Vito's father, was one of my engineering professors."

"Ah. Tell me about him."

"I took two classes from Matteo before he asked me to come into his office to discuss the direction I wanted to go with my studies. I believed him to be gender blind and was flattered that my revered professor was showing so much interest in my future career. I accepted a lunch date so we could talk more without interruption.

"That led to other lunch dates. I admired his intellect and looked up to him so much, naive me couldn't see that all he wanted was to take me to bed, nothing more."

She saw Giovanni grimace.

"Reflecting back on last year, I'm positive he slept with other students from time to time. No wonder he has remained single. My attraction to him hadn't been physical. Since I've come from a family of engineers, I was determined to get my graduate degree. Matteo was the one who'd seemed to take me seriously and listened to my ideas. He fed my ego by saying all the right things to make me feel important.

"When he told me how much he needed me and started kissing me, I succumbed even though it went against the morals of my upbringing. But after being with him one time, I couldn't do it again and told him I hadn't felt right about it. Not without marriage.

"He told me he never planned to marry. With that remark I knew I'd made a huge mistake. We parted company and I never planned to see him again. So no one could have been more shocked than I to learn I was pregnant even though he'd used protection. I notified him immediately. Not because I was hoping for a proposal, but to let him know he was going to be a father.

"Matteo told me a baby was the last thing he wanted and hoped I didn't expect anything from him. He thought I'd understood that from the beginning." She took a deep breath. "So unless he suddenly discovers he has a paternal instinct, I'll never hear from him again."

His jet-black eyes looked at her between black

lashes. "What if he changes his mind and comes back wanting to start over and help you raise your son?"

"It's way too late for that. His utter selfishness killed any ounce of feeling I once had for him. If he were to show up demanding to see our son, I couldn't stop him from having visitation, but I can tell you right now he'll never come back. He's too in love with himself. It's an ugly story that happens far too often in society.

"One day I'll have to tell Vito the truth about his birth father. He'll think less of me of course, but hopefully the knowledge won't ruin his life."

This man was so easy to talk to it shocked her that she'd confided in him to this degree. It was time to change the subject. "What if your ex-wife decides *she* wants to be a part of Ric's life?"

By this time he'd picked up Vito and held him to his chest. "She won't. I'm the reason our marriage didn't work. I didn't love her the way she deserved to be loved, and I take full responsibility. When our divorce became final, she signed away all rights to the baby."

Her eyes widened. "Even though she was pregnant?"

"Yes. She conceived during a brief period of reconciliation, but we both knew our marriage wasn't going to make it. She moved back to her parents'."

"Where do they live?"

"Here in Positano. Two months after the divorce she called to tell me she was going to have a baby. Though she'd been on birth control, we discovered there'd been an antibiotic interference. The news couldn't have come at a worse moment, but I was overjoyed to think I was going to be a father."

She moaned. "How hard for both of you. So for seven months you haven't been together?"

He shook his head. "We've only been in touch through our attorneys. I was at my office in Naples when her mother called to tell me she'd gone to the hospital. Tatania doesn't want to hear my voice."

"How could that be?"

"She's angry with me for not being the man she thought she was marrying."

"I suppose it's human nature to want to change the things you don't like. I've never married, so I can't speak from experience. Did that make you angry?"

"Not angry, only frustrated with myself for getting married when I knew my deepest feelings weren't involved."

She shook her head. "Then why *did* you propose to her?"

He sucked in his breath. "That's a long story for another day. Right now I want to concentrate on our babies."

Valentina didn't dare press for more answers. "To think your ex-wife and I were both involved in that accident and gave birth on the spot is absolutely uncanny. Carlo told me the police gave the ambulance driver the citation for not taking more precautions no matter the emergency. But my brother is still upset and wishes he'd flown me to the hospital in the helicopter."

"It's water under the bridge now," he murmured. "We can thank providence there were no injuries."

Valentina nodded and reached in the diaper bag

for a bottle to feed Ric. He made a lot of noise when he drank and wouldn't stop unless she pulled the bottle away to burp him. The second she put him to her shoulder, Vito let out the loudest burp she'd heard him make. His father burst in deep rich male laughter she felt coil inside her.

When she kissed his cheek before feeding him the rest of his formula, he felt cooler. There was nothing wrong with him that being with her again couldn't fix. He was so precious she didn't know how she could ever say goodbye to him. In her heart she knew Giovanni Laurito had those same feelings.

"Perhaps in time your ex-wife will come to you, desperate to see her son. If she did, I don't see you as the kind of man who would turn a deaf ear."

His brows met in a frown. "You don't even know me." He'd reached in his bag for a bottle and started to feed Vito.

"That's true, but I've seen you with your son. The way you love him tells me what kind of a person you are. You love him so much, you came to find him when you heard him crying. The hospital rules meant nothing to you. I'm sure you'd fight to the death for him. It's just something I know inside of me."

"Then we've met our match," he said in a low husky tone, "because you were willing to forget protocol, too. Otherwise you wouldn't have agreed to come to the park with me today when I know your brother would have forbidden it."

She blinked. "What does my brother have to do with my decision?"

"Possibly more than you think."

"What do you mean?"

"I've been putting two and two together. Your brother's name is Rinieri. Correct?"

"Yes." She averted her eyes. "But—"

"He and I have been undeclared business enemies for over a year. There was a time when I had a certain advertising agency in my sights that was in financial difficulty. I made an offer to buy out the owner because I like their work. But I found out he did work for your brother's company. I decided to make the man an offer to come to work for our company exclusively, and he said he was considering it.

"But your brother dangled a counteroffer in front of him, and now negotiations are at a standstill. Because of this, I do know your brother will never agree to the suggestion I proposed to you at the hospital about our spending time together with the boys."

Valentina felt a chill run down her spine. "When Signor Conti introduced us, I realized who you were. The Laurito logo is everywhere." She'd just put Ric down because he'd fallen asleep. "The one with the laurel wreath like the emperors wore."

His half smile quickened her pulse.

"I thought, 'You're *that* Laurito!'"

"I'm one of them. Our earliest ancestors came from Laurito near Salerno. In the early eighteen hundreds, one of my ancestors who was head of obstetrics in Naples came up with a stethoscope to hear the fetal heartbeat. Thus began the manufacture of medical instruments. It developed into major hospital equipment.

"Today that includes all types of machines to carry out research in medical and scientific laboratories. I've worked for some time on creating new advertising strategies for our company."

"How incredible."

"The advertising part is where your brother comes in to the conversation."

"I love and respect my brother, but he doesn't interfere with my making my own decisions."

"So if I asked you to come home with me today and stay as my guest for a few days while the four of us get acquainted, you wouldn't be worried how your brother will react? I wouldn't want to be the person to create friction between the two of you."

There was nothing she'd love more than to go with him. But at this moment she didn't know what to do, let alone what to say. While she sat there in a daze, he got to his feet. Vito had finished his bottle and slept against Giovanni's shoulder.

"At least this meeting has quieted the babies for now," he murmured. "I've found out there's nothing wrong with Ric except that he misses you. While they're both asleep, I'll run you back to your brother's villa. If Vito is inconsolable later and you decide you want to try the experiment we've talked about, then give me a call. If I don't hear from you, then I'll know you've decided that getting together isn't a good idea, after all. I'll respect whatever you decide."

He was such a good man, Valentina marveled. The thought of not seeing him again was unthinkable.

She eventually stood up and carried Ric to the car. Giovanni brought Vito along with the diaper bags and blankets. In a minute both babies were strapped in so they could leave the park.

He drove her home in silence and retrieved the carry-cot from the trunk.

She put Vito in it. Luckily he was still in a sound sleep. The knowledge that Ric was in the car was killing her, but what could she do?

"Our meeting did settle them down. Maybe it was all they needed and they won't be as upset from now on. Thank you for making it possible," she whispered and started toward the house. "I've enjoyed this morning."

"So have I. More than you know." His voice sounded husky.

The last thing she'd wanted to do was leave. Her attraction to Ric's father was so strong, it frightened her how much she could care for him after just two meetings with him. What was wrong with her?

Giovanni watched the lovely woman with the creamy blond hair and beautiful figure disappear behind the door. The double irony here was that he feared Ric wasn't the only male in the Laurito household who was going to miss her.

What were the odds of a baby switch that had thrown a Montanari and a Laurito together? She would have to be strong in her own right to go up against her brother, especially when he'd learned the name of Ric's birth father.

Giovanni could imagine their conversation. He'd tell her to forget another meeting. The baby would soon adapt. In truth, if Giovanni had a sister who'd been put in the same circumstance, he would tell her the same thing.

But Giovanni was the one embroiled in this cruel twist of fate. He loved both children and could hardly tear himself away from the villa when he knew Vito was inside. Since he'd told Valentina she would have to be the one to contact him, he had no choice but to drive back to Ravello without her.

He had hopes that if Ric woke up on the way home, he'd like the ride enough not to cry. The more he thought about it, the more he worried that he might have seen the last of his other son and the mother who'd given birth to him. He felt a sense of loss that was acute.

To his surprise Ric was awake by the time he reached his villa. When Giovanni removed him from the car, he didn't cry. *Grazie a Dio.*

"Oh—" When Stanzie saw them in the foyer she rushed over to kiss the baby's cheek. "His temperature is gone."

"We spent a few hours at the park. I think he liked it."

"Of course he did. He's much happier now."

"I'm going to change his diaper and put him in his baby swing on the terrace."

"Shall I prepare another bottle?"

"Thank you, but he probably won't want it for a while." Giovanni needed to call his assistant and tell him he wouldn't be in the office for a few days. Ric needed him even if his little son didn't want him yet. He wanted the mother who'd taken him home from the hospital. *So did Giovanni.*

Their lives had been turned upside down. He couldn't help but wonder what Valentina Montanari was going through right now. If Vito was being as difficult as Ric had been to this point, she was in for another sleepless night, too.

* * *

At 11 o'clock Rini entered the nursery while Valentina was giving Vito his last bottle. He'd been inconsolable all day. But for the moment he was so worn out from crying, he'd stopped fighting her and began drinking.

"How's he doing?" he whispered. "I had business in Genoa that made me late."

Vito heard his voice and his eyes opened before he stopped drinking. Then he started crying again. She put the bottle down and hugged him to her shoulder to quiet him.

"Sorry," Rini mouthed the word. "Why don't I hold him for a while so you can go to bed?"

"It won't work, Rini. He thought you were his daddy, whom he adores. He's still looking for him. If you'd seen them together today, you'd realize how difficult this is."

"Which is why you shouldn't have gotten together with him." Lines darkened her brother's face. "How can you expect Vito to forget?"

"I can't." She shifted Vito to her other shoulder in an effort to calm him down. "I need to talk to you about this, but it will take a while."

Rini pulled up a chair and sat down. "I'm listening."

"As you know, he's raising the baby himself because his ex-wife gave up her parental rights. She's never seen her birth son and doesn't want to."

Rini rubbed the back of his neck. "That's tragic."

"I agree. He called me this morning because Ric had been crying so much he was running a temperature. His plan was to take him back to the hospital to see if something else was wrong. We talked briefly and decided to meet because I haven't been able to comfort Vito, either. He came by the villa and drove us to the park near the hospital."

Her brother got up from the chair and stood there with his hands on his hips. All the while Vito kept whimpering. "He should never have called you."

"We exchanged phone numbers at the hospital in case of an emergency. It was a horrible moment. Vito was in one room, Ric in another. Both children cried hysterically after the exchange. I was frantic and opened the door to discover an equally frantic father standing there holding a red-faced Ric. We reached for our children and held them until they settled down."

Rini shook his head. "Whatever happened to rules?"

"I knew that was what you would say. As Signor Laurito stated, the children didn't recognize rules. Nothing about this situation has been normal. His ex-wife and I both gave birth before our ambulances reached the hospital where the switch took place. He loves Vito as much as I love Ric, and we find the situation impossible. I think his plan for us to spend a few days together will work."

"You think?" he blurted with uncustomary harshness. "You do realize who he is—"

"Yes. He's a brilliant CEO of his own company, just like you." In fact they were a lot alike. That was probably what was wrong. Within a few minutes she'd told him details about how Giovanni's company had gotten started. "I explained that I couldn't do this here at the villa, so he has invited me to stay at his villa with Vito for a few days, no more."

Her brother paced the floor for a moment, then

stopped. "Despite the fact that I think the idea is a mistake, why did you rule out my villa?"

"Because this isn't my home. You've been wonderful to me, but I would never ask that of you. Especially when he told me the two of you are on opposite sides of a business transaction."

Rini looked surprised. "He told you *that*?"

"Yes. He's forthright and honest, exactly like you. I trust him. If Vito hasn't settled down by tomorrow, I'm considering doing it. I know I don't need your approval, but I want it more than anything."

A bleak expression crossed over his face.

"I want my baby to be happy. Vito didn't ask for this. Neither did Ric. His father is in agony just like I am. If we can give our children a better start by getting them to trust both of us, then we can separate them and it won't be such a horrible shock. What would be the harm in doing this?"

His head went back and he closed his eyes. "I don't have an answer for that. It sounds like your mind is made up. I love you, Valentina, and I'll support your decision, but I can't answer for the rest of the family."

"The rest of the family hasn't been here for me every day and night since you moved me here. I'm blessed to have a brother like you."

Vito was crying hard again. She got up from the rocking chair and walked around the room with him. Rini's gaze met hers.

"I'll leave so you can get him to sleep. I've an early-morning meeting at the office. Phone me when you know your plans."

Her eyes smarted. "I promise." She watched her brother's retreating back. There was so much he could have said, but he'd kept silent. Because he was wise and had so much integrity, that's why he was the head of Montanari.

A half hour passed and Vito finally fell asleep. Valentina went to her room and slept until she heard him crying around four. After that there was no comforting him. At eight in the morning she reached for her phone and called the one person who could end this nightmare.

"Valentina?" Giovanni answered on the second ring. "I trust your night was as bad as mine." His voice sounded an octave lower than usual, telling its own tale of another sleepless night.

"Vito's been awake since four."

"Ric finished off his three o'clock bottle and fussed off and on until ten minutes ago. He's sleeping, but before long he'll wake up looking for you. I don't want to live through another day like yesterday."

"I—I talked to Rini," she stammered. "He thinks getting the babies together is a mistake, but he said he'd support me in whatever decision I make. If you meant it, I'll take you up on your invitation to stay with you for a few days."

"You just said the words that saved my life. Ric and I will come for you. I should be there by 10 a.m."

"We'll be ready."

"*A presto*, Valentina."

After rushing to shower and wash her hair, she dressed in another blouse and skirt. Next she got busy packing for herself and some of the outfits she'd bought for Ric. Bianca was in the kitchen when Valentina went downstairs and poured herself a cup of coffee.

The first thing she needed to do was phone Rini. His voice mail was on. She left the message that she would be in Ravello and be staying for several nights. "Call me anytime, Rini. Love you," she said before hanging up, then drank most of the hot liquid.

"How can I help you?"

"I've got everything packed, Bianca. Thank you so much for all you do. You've been wonderful. All I can hope is that this experiment will help the four of us get acquainted. Hopefully the next time Signor Laurito brings me and Vito home, my baby won't be so unhappy."

She kissed Bianca's cheek and carried a suitcase and the diaper bag to the front door.

When she went back up to the nursery, Vito was crying again. She dressed him in another outfit and put him in the carry-cot with the blue-and-white quilt Giovanni had bought him with one of Mondrian's composition-type designs. He had wonderful taste.

"In just a minute you're going to be with your *papà*, Vito." She kissed his hot cheeks and carried him downstairs to the foyer.

Bianca had already opened the door. "The *signor* has arrived."

Yes. He certainly had. Today he'd come dressed in a white polo crewneck and jeans that molded to his powerful thighs. To her chagrin she realized she felt an excitement that didn't have anything to do with getting the children together. The man himself stood a class apart from other men. She'd scoffed all her life about the idea of love at first sight, but she hadn't met Giovanni…

For the first time in her life she'd been struck by

a physical and emotional attraction so strong, she astounded herself. The fact that he was Ric's father only added to the attraction.

"*Buongiorno*, Valentina."

"*Ciao*! It has to be a better day than yesterday."

"Is there any doubt?"

No. There wasn't, not now that he was here.

She felt his jet-black eyes wander over her, bringing heat to her cheeks, before he picked up the carry-cot and gave Vito a kiss. She followed with the suitcase and diaper bag. Once he'd settled Vito in the car seat, he stowed everything else in the trunk.

Valentina would have opened the rear door to give Ric a kiss, but caught herself in time. He wasn't crying right now. If he didn't see her, that would be better. She climbed in front and fastened the seat belt without a struggle.

"I see a smile on your face."

Valentina studied his rugged male profile. "Almost three weeks ago I struggled to get the seat belt around me on my way to the hospital."

Before he started the car he said, "No one would ever know you gave birth less than a month ago."

"Though you're a liar, I thank you."

His kind of deep male laughter excited her. He drove them out to the road leading to the coastal highway headed for Ravello. "Have you noticed there's no noise coming from the backseat?"

"Yes. I'm afraid to talk about it for fear I'll break the spell."

"Both my sisters have told me that when their children were babies, they often took them for a drive to get them to sleep."

Valentina nodded. "I heard the same thing from my sister-in-law. Since it's working right now, I couldn't be happier."

They followed the Amalfi Coast road beneath a golden Mediterranean sun. The car meandered five hundred meters above a turquoise sea. She could smell the fragrance from the lemon groves. Around each curb perched pastel-hued villas on the mountainside. No sight on earth could match it.

"You've got another smile on your face." He noticed everything.

"Though I was born and raised in Naples, I've always thought this is the most beautiful place on earth."

Giovanni nodded. "The locals call it 'the footpaths of the gods.' In my teens I rode my bike here with some friends from Naples. When we reached Ravello, I decided it was where I would live one day. Naples has a stifling effect on me."

"You're like Rinieri, who's also allergic to the crowded city. Early on he loved to rock climb and dive with his friends. They explored the Amalfi Coast and climbed to the top of the cliffs. He saw the turn-of-the-last-century villa he lives in now and decided he'd buy it one day. I never saw anyone work so hard to make that dream a reality." She looked away from him. "You must be a workhorse, too."

By now they'd reached the town of Amalfi. To Valentina it was a beguiling combination of mountains plunging to the sea with crags of picturesque villas and lush forests that took her breath.

"You've just described my ex-wife's reason for wanting a divorce." The unexpected revelation could explain one of the major reasons why their marriage had failed, but there had to be more to it than that. "Now that I have a son to raise, I've got to take another look at my life. I don't want him to grow up accusing me of never being there for him."

She bit her lip. "Was your father absent a lot?"

"Almost constantly. I see him more at work."

"I grew up in a family where the men were married to their work. Having observed my brothers, it's apparent to me that successful men have a hard time balancing their lives. Business has a way of consuming them."

"But it shouldn't," he bit out. "Since I'm going to be raising Ric alone, I'm going to have to change the way I do business."

"The fact that you want to be a more involved father is commendable."

He darted her a glance. "But you're not holding your breath."

"You've already been an amazing father to Vito or he would never have cried his heart out when he had to leave you. At the park his eyes followed you every second. Your bond with him is so strong, I'll admit I've been jealous."

"Then it shouldn't shock you that I've felt the same way about Ric's attachment to you. But if our plan works, our problems will go away."

Heaven willing. "Does your family know I'll be staying with you for a few days?"

"No. I've decided to proceed on a need-to-know basis. Of course, everyone knows about the switch."

"Are you worried that my staying with you will get back to your ex-wife?"

"Not at all, but for the time being it's no one else's business. My two older sisters have a bad habit of getting nosy."

Valentina chuckled. "My family is like that, too."

"Then we understand each other."

"Definitely."

"I take it your brother knows you're here with me."

"Yes. We talked last night."

CHAPTER FOUR

GIOVANNI DIDN'T COMMENT. Instead he made a left turn onto another road that climbed higher up the mountain. At the top sprawled the refined jewel town of Ravello with its dreamy gardens and magnificent views. Royals as well as composers like Wagner had stayed in the spectacular villas dotting the landscape. Valentina could understand why.

They kept climbing through a grove of green olive and lemon trees. He slowed down at the side of a stunning two-story white villa with burnt red tiles built in the Mediterranean style. Pale blue shutters adorned the windows. She'd thought there could be nothing more fabulous than her brother's ochre colored villa, but this place was spectacular.

Deep purple and red bougainvillea draped over the several terraces. A rock garden with palm trees formed a backdrop for the rectangular swimming pool. The profusion of flowers created poetry of such perfection, she wished she were an artist. Turning toward the sea, she gasped softly. "You live in heaven, Giovanni."

"That's what I thought when I first explored this spot years ago."

"Your darling Ric will grow up in a virtual wonderland."

Giovanni shut off the engine and levered himself from the car with a masculine grace he wasn't aware of. She slid out her side and they both opened the rear doors to get the children. Ric was still asleep, but Vito had awakened. His gaze fastened on Giovanni.

She smiled at him. "See how he searches for you?"

While he kissed her son, she plucked Ric from the car seat and followed his father across a patio into a fabulous sunroom. She gasped softly. It was circular in design with a tall ceiling and tall rounded windows filled with light that looked out on the gardens and sea below.

He kept moving through the breathtaking house to the curving staircase inlaid with stone tiles, enhancing the earth-toned colors of the surrounding landscape. Once they reached the second floor, he walked down a hall with a balustrade that overlooked a portion of the villa below.

"Your room is right here with its en suite bathroom." He opened the door and they entered a bedroom on the right. The moment she entered, she fell in love with the decor: oranges and yellows with cream walls and dark timbers overhead. An old armoire and an antique queen-size bed delighted her.

Over in another corner she spied a beautiful walnut crib all made up for the baby. She turned to him. "When did you get this?"

"After you phoned me this morning, I asked Paolo to run into town and get one that matches Ric's. He bought all the things to go with it. While I was gone, he put it together.

"As you know, he and his wife are here temporarily, looking after the house. They fell in love with Vito and now they love Ric."

"That's because he's made in your image," she broke in on him. Ric was still asleep. One day he'd be a heartbreaker like his arresting father.

"I'll bring up your things from the car and be right back."

She put Ric on the bed and changed his diaper, and then explored the room. The dresser had a hand-painted flowered design in the citrus tones. On the wall above the dresser was a large reproduction of the *Procession of the Magi* in marvelous colors, a famous fresco by Gozzoli. If Giovanni was the one who chose the art work, then it told her he was a man with many admirable facets, not the least of which were his parenting skills.

To think Matteo didn't even want to be told when the baby was born. For whatever deep-seated reason, Giovanni's ex-wife hadn't wanted to see her son. Both parents were missing out on the greatest joy of life and didn't know it.

Giovanni was still holding Vito when he arrived with her suitcase and purse. "Bring Ric with you and I'll show you the nursery. It adjoins my room."

She picked up the baby and followed him down the hall past the staircase. His room was clearly a man's bedroom. Through the open paneled doors she could see the charming nursery and an adult rocking chair.

The crib had a cute mobile of colorful fish. "How darling!"

"My mother helped decorate."

"It's wonderful."

He put Vito in the crib and changed him. Out of the corner of her eye she saw a minifridge propped against the wall to hold the bottles. With Ric in the crook of her arm, she looked at the baby furniture and stuffed animals. She loved the little walnut rocking chair with Giovanni the Bear sitting inside it. In the bookcase several baby books were displayed, including her favorite, *Papa Piccolo, the Cat.*

"Oh, look, Ric. Elmer the Patchwork Elephant!" She drew it from the shelf and showed it to him. The toy seemed to distract him. "He's pink and yellow and blue. And he's soft." She nudged his cheek with it, then walked over to the mobile and wound up the little music box. It started to turn and played "*Giro Giro Tondo,*" a cute tune. Both babies watched the little fish go round and round. The music stimulated them and their bodies grew animated.

"You've learned to like that, haven't you, sweetheart." She kissed Ric's neck and cheek.

Giovanni's smile filled her universe with sunshine. He moved closer. In a low voice he said, "Do you know how great it is to be in here with no noise except the sound of the music box?"

Her heart pounded hard in her chest. With the stress lines gone from his striking face, he was too gorgeous. She averted her eyes before he could catch her staring at him.

"Stanzie has fixed lunch and served it on the table in the sunroom. Let's take the children downstairs and put them in the playpen while we eat. There's a bathroom off the sunroom where you can freshen up."

Together the four of them left the nursery. "I love

the layout of your home. How long have you lived here?" They started down the stairs.

"Three years. Tatania and I were married soon after."

She followed him past the living and dining rooms to the sunroom and put Vito in the playpen. "I'll be back in a minute." Valentina found the bathroom and freshened up. Once she'd washed her hands, she returned to see Giovanni leaning over the playpen. He was talking to their sons who appeared to be listening to him. The precious moment seized her by the throat and she fought tears.

This plan to help their babies get used to the change was a good plan. Everyone was happier. He must have sensed her standing there and turned around. "I finally have a chance to welcome you. The boys have told me they're glad to be here."

Giovanni... "I am, too." She was filled with so many new emotions bombarding her, she could hardly talk.

"Our plan is working, Valentina. You feel it, too. I know you do."

How could she possibly deny it?

When she would have found her voice, an elegantly dressed woman probably in her fifties with dark hair appeared outside the screen of the open double doors of the sunroom. "Giovanni? May I come in? I've brought a toy for the baby."

He looked over his shoulder. "Violeta— By all means, come in. I didn't know you were coming." In a few long strides he opened the screen door so she could enter.

"I tried to reach you, but your phone was on voice mail." She handed him a gift bag.

"I'm afraid I was too busy with the babies to check my messages. Violeta Corleto, I'd like to introduce you to Valentina Montanari. She's the mother whose baby was switched with mine and Tatania's."

The lovely older woman was obviously shocked to see Valentina there.

"How do you do, Signora Corleto?" Valentina crossed the expanse to shake her hand.

Ric's grandmother studied her with unsmiling eyes. Then she looked at Giovanni for an explanation. "I don't understand."

"The babies grew hysterical when we made the first exchange, so we decided to get together for a few days in order for them to get used to both of us."

Her dark brown eyes looked haunted. "I can't believe the hospital allowed you to meet each other."

"The hospital director handled things the best way he knew how. But the babies were so upset, Valentina and I sought each other out so we could comfort them."

"My husband is suing the hospital for what has happened."

Valentina took a steadying breath. "I heard your daughter had a hard time. Is she getting better?"

"Yes."

"I'm so glad. The odds of both of us being in a crash on the way to the hospital are astronomical. We just have to be thankful the babies are fine and thriving."

Giovanni picked up Ric and showed him to his ex-mother-in-law. "Valentina named him Ric."

Tears filled the older woman's eyes. "Oh, Giovanni—he looks so much like you and Tatania." She touched his face, but Ric didn't like it and his chin wobbled.

"Tatania needs to see him. Once she does, she won't be able to resist him."

Instead of a response Giovanni asked, "Do you want to stay to lunch? Hold him? Valentina and I were just about to sit down."

"No. I only came by to see him and bring a gift, but I've upset him. I'll call you later."

"Let me walk you out to your car."

"I'm so glad we met," Valentina called after her. She nodded and left. Valentina's heart sank to her feet to see the sorrow on the face of Tatania's mother. When Giovanni came back inside, she said, "I feel so sorry for her. There've been too many shocks."

"You were very sweet to her, Valentina. Seeing her daughter in the baby made it all the more difficult to accept the fact that Tatania doesn't want anything to do with Ric."

"It's so sad."

"Time will heal the wounds." He put Ric in the playpen. "Shall we eat? Stanzie is a great cook."

The rest of the day and evening turned out to be pure pleasure as they ate and played with the babies.

"How did Stanzie and Paolo come to work for you?"

"It's an interesting story. Their last name is Bruno."

"You're talking about the same Bruno as my brother."

He nodded. "They managed an advertising agency for his uncle Ernesto," he explained. "Over several years I often ate lunch with them while we discussed ideas to expand the advertising for Laurito's. They're some of my favorite people.

"But Ernesto wasn't a visionary man and the business was failing. Paolo had some brilliant ideas. Unfortunately his uncle wouldn't listen and it reached a point where he let them go."

"He did that to his own family?"

"Afraid so. I asked them to work for me at the villa until I get them set up in another advertising business I plan to run."

"So that's why you were in competition with Rini?"

"Yes. I wanted to buy out Ernesto so Paolo and Stanzie could go back to managing the business the way they wanted. But your brother saw a great business opportunity, and it's still up in the air which way Ernesto will go. Please don't say anything to your brother, who would have his own ideas about the people he wants to hire. It's a private matter."

"I wouldn't interfere, but I admire you very much for trying to help."

"Paolo and his wife are amazing people with real talent. While they're living with me, I've arranged for someone to rent their house in Naples."

"And I have to tell you that Paolo and Stanzie are darling with the babies."

"It's a shame they couldn't have children of their own."

"Maybe there's still hope. I know people who had babies in their forties."

"I've told them the same thing."

By the time they decided to take the babies upstairs and bathe them, Valentina felt like they were a family.

The nursery had its own en suite bathroom. They took turns giving the babies their baths. Giovanni put Ric in the water first. "You like this, don't you?" He washed his dark hair with the baby shampoo. Valentina handed him a big fluffy towel after he lifted him out of the water.

"It's your turn, Vito." She filled the sink with fresh water and then gave him his bath. He didn't like his head shampooed, but he didn't actually cry. "See. This feels good. You and your brother are being very brave."

Valentina realized her mistake before Giovanni handed her a matching towel. His eyes were smiling at her slip. "That just came out." She hugged him to her and carried him into the nursery.

Giovanni diapered Ric and put him in a white baby-gro for bed. Then he flicked her a glance. "If you want to know the truth, when we were in that hospital room, I kept thinking they were like our nonidentical twins."

Our twins. Her breath caught at the thought.

"Well, tonight should be a lot of fun for them. Their first slumber party." She heard him chuckle before she put a little blue babygro on Vito. After sitting in the rocking chair, she fed him his last bottle. Giovanni brought a chair in from his bedroom and did the same with Ric.

As long as they were both in the room with the babies, there were no tears. Only the sounds of the boys drinking rather noisily disturbed the peace and quiet. After being burped, Vito fell asleep first. She left him on her shoulder. He was her little angel. At this point she loved both babies so much she could hardly stand it.

Ric finally passed out with his bottle. Giovanni put him in his crib, then signaled Valentina to follow him into the bedroom. He patted the bed. She lay down on one side and put Vito in the middle. Giovanni stretched out on the other side. They turned toward the sleeping baby and smiled.

This was like playing house, except this wasn't a dollhouse and none of them were dolls.

Giovanni was a full-grown, breathtaking male. Her bones melted with the way his eyes devoured her.

"Do you know this is the first time I've felt this content in years? How about you?"

She nodded. "Once I started undergraduate school, I put pressure on myself to succeed. The stress increased when I got into graduate school. Then I lost my mother, and her death devastated the whole family for a long time."

"I can only imagine," he commiserated.

"I could go to her about anything, Giovanni. She knew I suffered from an inferiority complex and told me I had to believe in myself no matter what." Her eyes smarted. "I'm wondering now if she hadn't died, would I have gotten involved with Matteo?"

Giovanni reached across to give her arm a squeeze. "But if you hadn't, we wouldn't be lying here with our little boy who has brought so much joy into our lives. It's why I can't be sorry about my marriage to Tatania even though it ended. Ric is a living miracle."

"They both are," Valentina whispered.

"Thank you for accepting my invitation." His voice throbbed.

"I'm thrilled to be here, but it's getting late so I'll say good-night and take Vito with me." She was loving this way too much. Using every bit of willpower, she rolled off the bed before gathering Vito in her arms.

Giovanni followed her out of his room to her bedroom down the hall. She felt his eyes on her as she put Vito in the crib. "Please remember this house is yours while you're here."

"I will. If you need help, I'll hear the crying and come."

"That works both ways, Valentina. *Buonanotte.*"

After this wonderful evening, she didn't want to say good-night, but to have stayed on his bed any longer would increase her desire to stay with him all night. She wanted to lie in his arms and be kissed senseless by him. How crazy was that!

"Good night."

Giovanni groaned to have to walk away from her. He wanted to stay and make slow, passionate love to her. In all his adult life he'd never known desire like this. But it was too soon to show her how he felt. She needed time to get to know and trust him.

Though the babies were the reason they were together at all, it was the woman herself he'd also been drawn to from the first moment she'd opened the door at the hospital. He loved the way she loved the babies with a fullness of heart.

Valentina had been fearless in defying hospital policy in order to make them happy. When it came down to the wire, she'd forgotten herself in the need to protect her children. Those actions told him reams about her character.

He got ready for bed and slept with one ear open. At ten after three he heard Ric start crying. Throwing on his robe, he hurried into the nursery to change his diaper and feed him. As he reached for a bottle from the fridge and put it in the microwave to warm it up, Valentina came in the room with a fussy Vito. She was a vision in a nightgown and pale yellow robe.

Her eyes searched his. "I'm glad you're up. Vito must have awakened at the same time as Ric. Vito's still looking for you. I heard Ric fussing and thought we'd join you."

Giovanni grinned. If she only knew, he'd willed her to come. *"Benvenuta al Caffetteria Laurito, signorina."*

Laughter bubbled out of her as she sat down to feed Vito. He plucked Ric from the crib and sat next to her, thinking this was the way marriage should be. Two parents who'd lost sleep, but were crazy about each other and their babies.

The children could hear both their voices. Long after the babies had dozed off again, he and Valentina were deep in conversation about his life. "Did you always want to work for the family business?"

"Not in the beginning. I went to Sapienza University in Rome, thinking I might pursue medicine."

"What changed?"

"My father's constant urging that I join the company."

"Because he needed his son behind him."

"My mother and sisters said as much."

Valentina eyed him thoughtfully. "Are you sorry you didn't become a doctor?"

"No. I've found there's a strong bent for business in my blood. I derive a certain excitement from winning over a new account."

"You're probably sick of my asking you all these questions."

"No, Valentina. You couldn't be more wrong about

that. It's so easy to talk to you, I feel like I've known you all my life."

"I feel the same way, but I'd better take Vito back to bed before I wear out my welcome."

Lines darkened his striking features. "Don't you know you could never do that?"

She looked away quickly and hurried out of the room with Vito, leaving him bereft. He went back to bed and slept till seven when Ric needed another bottle.

After showering and dressing, he took the baby downstairs and walked out on the patio, where he found his guest with Vito. She saw him coming.

"Good morning. I couldn't resist coming out here this morning. All this lavender wisteria thrives in such huge clumps, it's fantastic. And the smell is so heavenly, Giovanni. I've always heard that Ravello is the garden town of the Amalfi Coast, but in my opinion it could be the Garden of Eden. You should charge admission."

He chuckled. "The last thing I want is a stream of people invading my inner sanctum."

"I know that." She smiled. "I was only teasing you."

"The garden and sunroom are the reasons I bought this place. I spend most of my time in the sunroom, where I can wander outside on a whim. Every flower has its season to bloom. I'm constantly delighted myself."

"I think you have an artist's soul."

"What makes you say that?"

"The painting in my bedroom by Gozzoli."

"At Christmas our mother used to read to us from a storybook about the Magi with that same painting on the cover. I was always fascinated by it. Last year I happened to see the reproduction in a store, taking me back to my childhood. I bought it on the spot and put it in the guest room."

"I love it. I love the way the room is decorated, the colors. The nursery is adorable with its charming touches. I love your villa, the setting, everything! Forgive me for going on and on about it, but I just can't help it."

"Your opinion means a lot to me. Shall I bring your breakfast out here?"

Color filled her cheeks. "You've done too much for me already by allowing me to mother your son a little longer." The tremor in her voice tugged on his heartstrings. She swept past him and entered the house. It took every ounce of self-control not to reach out and pull her into his arms.

She put Vito in his carry-cot and sat down at the table. "Another feast," she exclaimed when they'd finished eating.

"Wait till you eat the lunch Stanzie has prepared for us."

Valentina's gentle laughter warmed his insides. "You're still hungry?"

"I will be because I'm taking you and the babies out for a picnic."

"Where?"

"It's a surprise. On the way we'll stop in town for another carry-cot stroller so we can push the babies around."

They went upstairs to get the children ready. While he dressed Ric in a yellow sunsuit, he flicked her a glance. "Do you know I'm having the time of my life?"

She'd put Vito in shorts and a blue-and-white-striped shirt. "Can you believe these are the same unhappy little boys of a few days ago? Vito isn't fighting me this morning. I think you were inspired to suggest we work together to help them adjust." She flicked him another glance. "You do know that your unorthodox methods explain why you're running your family's company. You get results!"

"Let's hope it continues."

"So far so good. Vito's going to help me get my purse, then we'll meet you downstairs."

Before long they left the villa, loaded with a hamper full of food and bottles. Giovanni drove them along a road that led to town. After they'd made their purchase, they got back in the car and wound their way to the famous site of the Villa Rufolo.

"I've heard of this place."

"An Englishman built a strange concoction of structures, cultural elements and mixed styles, but it's the villa's garden you'll fall in love with. We'll enter through the tower, then walk around first. Later we'll come back to eat near the temple over there."

Valentina couldn't wait to get started. Once they fastened the babies' carry-cots in their strollers, they were ready to go. The whole property filled with statues, fountains and an ancient cloister enchanted her. Giovanni was better than any tour guide and incredibly patient as she asked question after question.

Eventually they reached a terraced garden that offered fantastic views of the Church of the Annunziata and the brilliant blue water of the Mediterranean below. "According to Gore Vidal, this is the most beautiful spot on earth."

"It's certainly one of them."

They walked back to the car. Giovanni got out the hamper and carried it to a grassy spot while she pushed both strollers behind him. He spread out a blanket, and they let the boys lie down on their backs while she and Giovanni ate.

Her gaze swerved to him. "Tell me something. You don't mind showing me around when you've probably done this before with your ex-wife?" Valentina didn't want to be jealous of her; still, she couldn't help that she would have loved to know him a long time ago.

"If she came here, it wasn't with me. She preferred my apartment in Naples when I had to stay there for business. She often told me how isolated she felt here in Ravello."

"Some people need a big city."

His dark eyes pierced hers. "What about you?"

"I'm a lot like my brothers. We love being on top of the mountains looking down to the sea."

She changed the babies' diapers, then got out two more bottles. Together she and Giovanni fed them while they soaked in the heavenly atmosphere. When her cell rang, it startled her. She drew the phone out of her skirt pocket. It had to be one of her family. Her dad's caller ID showed up. She clicked on. "Papà?"

"How's my daughter?"

"I'm great. How are you?"

"Missing you."

"I've missed you, too." More than he could know.

"When am I going to see my grandson?"

"Very soon."

"Carlo and Rinieri told me about the switch. They say he looks exactly like you. You always were our most beautiful baby."

Tears filled her eyes. "Papà... I promise I'll come to Naples."

"Rinieri said he'd bring you and the baby tomorrow."

Uh-oh. If Rini said that, then he was holding Valentina to her assurance that she'd only spend two days away to help the children adjust to the change.

"If all goes well, I'll see you then. I love you, Papà."

Until she hung up she didn't realize Giovanni had gotten to his feet. His nearness and male potency assaulted her senses. "Is everything all right?"

She took a big breath. *No.* The thought of leaving him in the morning had disturbed her more than she wanted to admit. "Yes," she lied. "It was my father. Rini told him he was flying me to Naples tomorrow so he could meet his grandson."

His jaw hardened perceptibly. "So you've already talked to your brother?"

"No. But when I told him our plan about the babies, I said I would only be away a couple of days. Apparently he took me at my word and let my father know I'd be bringing Vito."

He stood there with his powerful legs slightly apart. The light breeze disheveled his black hair. His coloring and olive skin made him too gorgeous. "I see. Naturally you don't want to disappoint your father. In that case I'll drive you back to Positano first thing in the morning. But until then, let's enjoy the time we have."

She lifted her eyes to him. "I *am* enjoying it." Way too much. "So are the babies."

He walked over to the hamper and pulled out a soda. "Do you want one?"

"Just water. Thank you."

"Do you think our boys are going to handle another separation so soon?" He handed her the bottle and sat down by her.

"Probably not, but in all honesty, will there ever be a good time?"

Giovanni took a long swallow. "I've been asking myself the same question and the answer comes up no."

They needed to make the decision to separate for good and get on with their individual lives, but the thought upset her too much. "Still, we don't have to worry about it today. You've gone to a lot of trouble to make it possible for us to enjoy this fabulous time together."

"Give me a minute to carry the hamper back to the car, then I'll help you put the babies back in the strollers so we can leave."

By nine that evening, the day out for the picnic had come to an end. They'd returned to the villa, where the babies had been bathed, fed and put to bed. After thanking Stanzie for the delicious packed lunch and the dinner she'd served upon their return, Valentina said good-night to Giovanni.

When she reached her room, she texted her brother.

Rini—I'll be home tomorrow around ten. Spoke to Papà. I've told him to expect me and Vito tomorrow. Lov u.

She'd kept the message short. Rini would vet her on the flight to Naples.

Valentina looked around the bedroom and decided to get packed. Afterward she showered and washed her hair. A day at the Villa Rufolo meant she'd picked up some sun. It felt good.

Once she'd blow-dried her hair, she put on a nightgown and got ready for bed. A knock on the door prompted her to slip on her robe. She tied the sash and walked over to open it. Giovanni's dark gaze drifted over her, sending her heart palpitating.

"I didn't realize you were ready for bed."

"We'll both be up in the night. I thought I'd better catch as much sleep as I can."

Lines darkened his handsome features. "When do you want to leave in the morning?"

I never want to leave.

"I texted my brother and told him I'd be back around ten."

"Then we ought to get away by eight thirty." She nodded. "Valentina?"

"Yes?"

"I had a wonderful time with you. It was an extraordinary day." He stood too close.

"I agree. I've been hoarding the memories."

"I don't want it to end." His voice grated.

She put her hands in her robe pockets in order to hide her nervousness. "I don't, either, but now that the babies aren't so upset, we know we have to make that final break."

"Says who?" he challenged.

Valentina averted her eyes. "Says everyone. Conventional wisdom."

"I've been doing things all my life to please other people. For once I want to do something *I* want to do."

She let out a sigh. "When I was thirteen, one of my teachers was lecturing our class about the rules. She said you can do whatever you want in here as long as it doesn't hurt you or anyone else. It made a lot of sense."

"I had a teacher who said the same thing, but we're talking about our children. They had a different start than most children. Why don't we capitalize on what has happened?"

If her heart pounded any harder, he'd be able to hear it. She lifted her head. "What are you suggesting?"

"That we go on seeing each other."

"It won't work, Giovanni. If we don't stop this now, Vito will always be looking for you. That's not fair to him or Ric."

"Even if it will make them happy?"

"They'll be happy. Give them a few days away from us and they won't remember us anymore."

His eyes flashed. "You want to make a bet?"

"Giovanni—" She shook her head.

"Let's give it two more days and then see how they react apart from us. I don't want you to leave." He unexpectedly cupped her face in his hands and kissed her lips.

His mouth on hers sent a bolt of electricity through her body. With a soft gasp she moved away from him. "We mustn't do this. It won't work. We have to say a final goodbye tomorrow."

"You could rearrange the time with your father."

"I could, but I won't and you know why. Now I'm going to say good-night."

She closed the door and leaned against it, terrified she'd give in to anything he had to say. Valentina touched her lips. He'd awakened a new longing in her.

If she did what he was asking, then she'd be putting her own selfish need ahead of her son's needs. What Giovanni was asking just wasn't possible.

Rini had warned her it wasn't a good idea to see Giovanni again. She'd thought she could handle it. She'd wanted to handle it for the babies' sake, but she hadn't counted on caring for Giovanni to this extent. After Matteo, she thought she'd learned her lesson and couldn't imagine ever getting close to another man again. The love for her baby would be all that mattered to her.

After another minute, Valentina opened the door again so she could listen for Ric. Then she turned off the light and slipped out of her robe. Once in bed, she buried her face in the pillow. That way she could smother her tears. Tomorrow she would have to be strong. Tonight she couldn't help but give in to the emotions roiling inside of her.

Giovanni's kiss was all she could think about. Ever since the hospital, he'd infiltrated her thoughts. Her Vito had gotten his start with the kind of exceptional man she hadn't known existed. It was all turned around. Now there were two babies she loved with every atom of her body. Worse, she'd fallen deeply in love with Giovanni. There was no other explanation for the reason he'd taken up lodgings in her heart.

CHAPTER FIVE

A WEEK LATER when Giovanni saw the name on the caller ID, he picked up. "Stanzie?"

"Forgive me for disturbing you at work. I know I've done it every day this week, but I don't think Riccardo likes me or Paolo. If you want to hire a nanny, maybe you should." He could hear in her voice she was close to tears.

There was only one woman Ric wanted when Giovanni wasn't there. This business couldn't be allowed to go on. "Of course he likes you, but he's still not used to the change. I'll be home early and we'll talk."

After he got off the phone, he alerted his pilot, then told his assistant to reschedule any appointments because he was leaving for the day. A half hour later he'd hired a limo with a car seat for an infant to drive him from the helipad in Positano to the Montanari villa. He told the chauffeur to wait.

Giovanni used the wrought-iron knocker to bring someone to the door. If it was Rinieri himself who answered, so be it, though he imagined he was still at work. With no results the first time, he knocked again.

When the door opened, he heard a gasp.

"Giovanni—" Valentina held Vito in her arms. She sounded like she was out of breath and had hurried to the door.

"I had to see you, but if I'd phoned, I feared you wouldn't pick up."

The sound of his voice must have brought Vito's head around. The second he saw Giovanni he made jerky arm movements and started to cry. Though she held him fast, he kept looking at Giovanni instead of hiding against her and cried harder.

"He wants you," she murmured. "He's been looking for you all week. Go ahead and hold him."

Giovanni didn't need an invitation. He drew him into his arms and cuddled him against his chest and shoulder. "It's only been a week, but you've grown!" Vito cried a little longer, then rested peacefully against him. "I've missed you, too, Tiger."

He glimpsed tears in Valentina's eyes. She looked tired but beautiful in a sleeveless top and shorts. "Your bonding with him was so strong. Rini doesn't fill the bill, wonderful as he is."

Rejoicing that she'd admitted it, he tried to give Vito back to her, but he clung to him. "I'll tell you why I'm here. Stanzie called me at work a little less than an hour ago and said I needed to hire a nanny because Ric doesn't like her or Paolo. I told her I was coming home. After we hung up I flew straight here, knowing what needs to be done. Ric misses you terribly. Nothing has been the same since you left the villa."

She wiped her eyes. "Maybe you could bring Ric here and I'll take care of both babies for a few days. Then I'll take Vito there and you can watch both of them for a few days. It would mean rearranging your work schedule."

He shook his head. "That won't work and you know it. I'm as exhausted as you are trying to comfort Ric, so I've come to ask you to move in with me. For how long I have no idea. Unfortunately the babies had just enough time to get attached to both of us, so instead of trying to fight the obvious, let's get together for the sake of their happiness and our sanity."

Valentina eyed Vito. "It's true that if I tried to take him from you right now, he'd have a meltdown."

"Ric was having one when Stanzie called."

An anxious expression broke out on her face. "If we get together now, it can't be for too long. Otherwise it would cause too much damage to the children and I wouldn't be able to handle it. But there's another risk. You know how people talk. I was never married. People would say I was a loose woman using you for what I could get out of you."

"People could say I got rid of Tatania because I'm a womanizer who wanted you and that's why we're divorced. None of it's true."

"You admit it could create a scandal both our families would have to live with."

"My parents learned a long time ago I make my own decisions."

"But your mother-in-law—"

"No matter what, she wants to be a grandmother to Ric. I say to hell with what anyone else thinks! Our babies were switched at birth and nothing has been normal about it."

After a pause, she said, "I know what Carlo would say. Get over it and lead your own lives."

"And Rini?"

She looked away. "He hasn't said anything, but he's aware of how Vito has behaved. H-he knows how much I mourn the loss of Ric," she said, her voice faltering.

"If you asked your father, what do you think he'd say?"

"To follow my heart. That has always been his advice."

"Did you ask his advice about Matteo?"

"No. I already knew he wouldn't approve of my getting involved with a professor so much older."

That was news to Giovanni. "How much older?"

"Twenty years."

That explained a lot about the engineering professor having a midlife crisis with a student as utterly delectable as Valentina. No doubt it fed his ego to seduce the daughter of one of the celebrated Montanari engineering family.

Giovanni nuzzled Vito's neck and kissed him. Her fragrance went where the baby went. "He gave you a beautiful son."

She swallowed hard. "He did."

"So what *does* your heart say now?"

There was an interminable silence while he waited for her answer. When she looked at him, he saw more tears. "You already know the answer or I would have closed the door on you before Vito got the chance to realize who it was."

Relief swept through him in waves. "I have a limo waiting. Go ahead and do what you have to do to get ready. I want time to play with Vito. We'll walk around out here."

"I'll have to leave a message for Rini and a note for Bianca. She went to the market."

"Take your time. You don't have to bring everything yet. There'll be other days to come back for more things. We're in no hurry."

He wandered around the courtyard, admiring the explosion of flowers and Rinieri's exquisite taste in buying this two-story villa. Its design reflected a bygone era of elegance and refinement. Like Giovanni, Rinieri had his own helipad at the rear of the estate, but he wouldn't have been so presumptuous as to use it.

When he saw Valentina come out the front door, he strapped Vito in the car seat, then helped her put her things inside. She disappeared once more for the carry-cot. While he'd waited for her, she'd changed into white pants and a top of navy-and-white stripes that outlined her womanly figure. The sight of her ignited all his senses.

Once everything and everyone were installed, he instructed the driver to take them back to the Positano helipad. He let Vito cling to his finger. She studied the two of them. "Look how excited he is to be with you."

"If you think he's happy, wait till Ric discovers you on the premises." Their eyes met. Her tears were gone.

"I pray we're doing the right thing, Giovanni. Down the road—"

"Don't think about that," he interrupted her. "Let's enjoy the here and now. The future will take care of itself." He had plans for them, but after her experience with Matteo, he didn't want to make a wrong move.

Within minutes they lifted off for the short flight to his villa in Ravello. Though he'd bought it and made it his own, he'd never felt like he'd really come home until the helicopter set them down.

Paolo and Stanzie were out in the garden that bordered the swimming pool, tending Ric. They waved when they saw him climb out. But he hadn't come alone. When they caught sight of Valentina, Stanzie cried with excitement and hurried toward her with Ric.

"Welcome, Valentina!"

"It's good to be back, Stanzie."

Ric heard her voice. Just like Vito, he started wiggling to get to her. This time Giovanni's eyes filled to see the way he cried and burrowed into her neck. His son knew exactly where he wanted to be. He took after Giovanni in that department. This moment was one he'd treasure all his life.

Valentina rocked Ric in her arms. Over his little head with its black hair she looked at Giovanni. Without being able to resist he said, "Remember that bet I made you a week ago?"

She nodded. "They *do* remember us and it's been a lot longer than two days."

"If you hadn't been such a terrific mother, Ric wouldn't have suffered so much. I say we all go for a swim."

"Won't the water be too cold for them?"

"We'll pull them around on the rafts."

Her blue eyes lit up. "That sounds fun. I'll hurry inside and change. Come on, Ric. You can help me."

Stanzie wasn't ready to give up Vito.

Giovanni followed Valentina into the house with her suitcase. After he set it inside her room, he headed for his own room to change. He threw off his suit and tie, so anxious to get outside he didn't care about anything else. After pulling on a pair of brown-and-white trunks, he grabbed some towels and hurried out to the back patio.

A couple of children's toy plastic rafts rested against the wall. He tossed them in the water.

"Come on, Vito. We're going for our first pool ride."

He smiled at Stanzie, who gave him up. Hugging him to his chest, he carried him into the pool. After settling him on his back in the middle of one of the rafts, Giovanni started moving it around at the shallow end.

"Don't be scared. Your mommy's going to be out here in a minute with your brother." That was the second time the word had slipped out. While he moved him around he caught sight of Valentina walking toward the pool with Ric. Her long legs and the way she filled out her white one-piece bathing suit knocked the wind out of him. She walked down the steps into the pool and put Ric on his back on the other raft.

Giovanni pulled the raft over to her. "I told you guys this was going to be fun."

The babies were so shocked by what was happening, they forgot to cry. Valentina saw their expressions and laughed so hard it infected him. From the beginning they'd shared the same sense of humor. It was just one of the many things he loved about her. If there was heaven on earth, this was the place.

The next half hour of play was pure delight. As long as the babies could see both of them, they were mesmerized. Valentina had put him in the same condition. When he saw those eyes glittering like sapphires above the water as she watched him, he almost had a heart attack.

He swam over to her. "What do you say we take them in and feed them?"

"I was just going to suggest it. One dark head and one blond. Aren't they adorable?"

Giovanni's emotions were running all over the place. He grabbed Ric while she reached for Vito. Together they took the babies inside and up the stairs. Then she carried Vito and headed for the nursery in the pants and top she'd worn earlier. Giovanni had slipped into his room to put on shorts and a shirt.

They sat down and fed the babies. Ric finished first. His eyes were closed as Giovanni placed him in the crib with the fish mobile and turned it on. Very soon after Vito had finished, too. As she left the nursery to put him down, she said in a hushed voice, "We'll have to get a mobile for Vito so he won't feel left out."

"Shall we drive into town and get one? While Stanzie and Paolo keep watch, let's eat dinner out."

"Maybe we shouldn't leave the children yet."

"We won't be gone long, and I'm the one starving now."

"So am I," she confessed. "Give me a minute to change into something more appropriate."

Valentina freshened up and decided to wear one of her sundresses with cap sleeves in a pale pink. She met him at the Maserati parked at the side of the villa where a garden of white moonflowers gave off a beguiling scent.

"I feel like I'm wandering in a fantastic dream."

Her eyes had fastened on Giovanni. He looked incredible in charcoal trousers and a silky dark vermilion sport shirt. Open at the neck, she could see the dark hairs on his well-defined chest. She wanted to be in his arms so badly it was killing her.

"I'm taking you to my favorite restaurant at a hotel where Grieg stayed during his travels here. It's rumored he never wanted to leave Ravello."

"Of course he didn't. I adore Grieg. During my pregnancy I must have listened to his first piano concerto dozens of times."

He drove them out to the main road past flowered terraces and hanging gardens to the village center and pulled into the parking area reserved for the hotel patrons. Twilight had descended.

The maître d' showed them out to a patio with candlelit tables overlooking the spectacular villa gardens. Sculptured topiary trees surrounded the fountain playing below. The sight took her breath. Grieg's music, "Wedding Day at Troldhaugen," could be heard in the background, adding to her sense of entrancement.

Giovanni's eyes gleamed like jet between black lashes as he reached for her hand across the table. "Will you let me order for you?"

"I'd love it."

"Some women wouldn't like that."

"I'm not some women."

"No, you're not." He squeezed her hand before letting it go.

Soon they were feted with swordfish *piccata*, a dish wrapped in ham and roasted almonds. The sumptuous meal came with kale, polenta and risotto.

After one bite, she exclaimed, "I've never tasted anything so delicious. The presentation looks too good to eat, but I plan to devour everything anyway."

Giovanni's laughter warmed her heart. They lingered over the predessert and the dessert served at the end with coffee. She passed on the wine, too drunk on the atmosphere with a man like Giovanni to get any more euphoric, but he fed her the last chocolate petit four. Her lips tingled as they brushed his fingers, causing her to hunger for his kiss.

Quite a few of the diners who recognized him nodded and stopped to shake hands. He introduced Valentina, but made no explanations about her. One of the men who'd come to their table assessed her in a way that made her blood curdle. Giovanni noticed and cut the other man off. The gossip would already be starting, but Giovanni didn't worry about lighting his own fires and made no excuses.

Female heads turned everywhere they walked. His striking features, not to mention his tall, well-honed physique made her the envy of the evening. With hands clasped, they strolled through the winding alleyways filled with flowers and shops. Valentina had reached a new high with this incredible man.

Before they left the town, they visited a children's shop. The young woman at the counter where they bought a mobile and some toys for the boys to chew on couldn't take her eyes off Giovanni.

Before heading back to the car, they stopped at another shop for two bottles of *limoncello*, a favorite product in this land of lemons. "One of these is for Paolo and Stanzie. The other is for us."

"I had it once years ago."

"From the lemons here in Ravello?"

"I'm sure not."

"Then you're in for a treat. Tonight is a special occasion. After we get home, I thought we'd drink a toast to our time together. May it last."

If only that were possible.

Right now Valentina couldn't relate to the life she'd led before meeting Giovanni. She felt like she'd been brought to an enchanted mountain by a prince right out of a fairy tale. Everywhere she looked, bursts of flowers in every color hid exquisite villas and palazzi. Cypress trees formed picturesque silhouettes against the night sky. From dizzying heights she looked down the many sloping gardens to the sea and breathed in the delightful fragrance of citrus and rose.

But the most tantalizing fragrance of all came from the soap Giovanni used, combined with his own male scent. She was drawn to it the way a bee zoomed in on an orange blossom, wanting its nectar, the food of the gods.

He could be a Roman god, but she was thankful he wasn't. Otherwise he wouldn't have brought her to dinner or fed her dessert from his own hand. The contact had sent spirals of desire through her body.

As they reached the villa, she noticed a thumbnail moon climbing in the velvet sky. "This has been a perfect day and a perfect night, Giovanni."

"Almost perfect," he muttered. "I'm sorry Claudio made you uncomfortable. He's a gossip, and he's known as a womanizer, who wished he'd been the one sitting next to you tonight."

"Please don't apologize for his behavior. It—"

"It happens all the time?" he finished her words.

"I know. A man wouldn't be a man if he didn't notice you. I'm the lucky one."

She sucked in her breath. "You're very good for a woman's ego. Thank you for tonight. It's one I'll never forget." She heard her own voice quiver from emotion.

"It's not over yet."

They went inside the sunroom. "Stay here. I'll get two aperitif glasses." He took one of the *limoncello* bottles with him.

She put their sack of purchases down on the table while she waited.

Soon he returned. "I checked on the children. They're sound asleep. Stanzie and Paolo are happy with our gift and have gone off to have their own celebration." He opened the other bottle and poured them each some liqueur. She took one, he picked up the other.

"I'd like to make a toast." He stared into her eyes. "To our partnership, which I've wanted since the first day at the hospital." He clicked her glass and drank.

His admission caused her hand to tremble as she sipped her drink that looked like liquid sunshine. "Giovanni, I—"

He stopped the flow of words with a touch of his finger to her lips, fanning the flame he'd ignited at dinner. "Can you imagine a time when we won't be partners? Not every baby switch has a happy ending as we've learned after reading all the research. Our children deserve the very best from both of us. We owe it to them and each other for the rest of our lives."

She pondered what he'd said. *Partners* had been an interesting choice of words. When he'd asked her to move in, he'd said he didn't know for how long. Giovanni was used to thinking in business terms. In the metaphoric sense she agreed they'd be partners for a lifetime because of the link to the children. But in a literal sense she didn't see them staying together longer than a month.

By then Ric would have grown attached to Giovanni. Vito would be old enough for the separation, since she planned to move back to Naples to finish her studies. The winter semester would be starting in September. There were good day-care centers suggested by the university. Valentina would make inquiries and find the one that suited her best.

Thank goodness for student loans. After she graduated and got a good job with an engineering firm, she'd pay it off. Knowing that Giovanni worked in Naples, she expected he'd come to see Vito, so that bond wouldn't be broken. She'd see him and Ric from time to time. It could all work.

"I'll think about everything you've said. Thanks again for the lovely evening." She put the glass down. *Get out of here, Valentina, before you can't.* "Now I'm headed for bed."

"Buonanotte."

Valentina's heart thundered in her chest all the way to her room. There'd be little sleep for her tonight. But to her surprise, she did sleep until Vito awakened for his bottle at four.

Around seven she got up and dressed in jeans and a top, expecting that Giovanni would have left for work. But when she carried Vito down the hall to the nursery, she found him feeding Ric. He was clean shaven and wore another pair of jeans and a creamy colored crewneck shirt. It didn't matter what he wore, he was a sensational-looking man.

She reached for a bottle and put it in the microwave. "Don't you need to get to your office?"

His dark gaze swept over her, making her far too aware of him. "I've arranged for some time off. How would you like to go out on my cruiser? I thought we'd visit several places and be gone for two or three nights. You can do night duty for me at some point. It's true I've been a *cavallo di battaglia* too long."

"But don't forget that being a workhorse put you in the reins of your family's company in the first place."

"I'm not sure if I like it. Right now I find that I'm loving to be on vacation and don't want it to end."

She knew how hard he worked, but this baby had forced him to take a break. No invitation could have thrilled her more. "The boat is the perfect way to enjoy ourselves with the children without having to take them in the car."

"My thinking exactly. Unless there's anything else you need to do, we'll leave after breakfast."

They worked together to pack up the children and their things. Valentina hurried to her room to do some packing. Before long they went downstairs with all their paraphernalia to eat.

After breakfast, they packed up the car. The Brunos waved them off.

Giovanni drove along a road that wound lower and lower to a private area of beach where he kept his boat tethered to the pier.

"What a wonderful cruiser!"

"When Paolo and Stanzie moved in the villa, I told

them they could take it out whenever they wanted, so they've kept it in top condition."

"It's nice to see that a couple who work together are so much in love. You can tell by their glances and smiles at each other."

"No one could ever say that about Tatania and me. The secret is to fall in love first. Those lucky enough for that to happen have love going for them when they marry."

"I'm sorry your marriage didn't work. I know you've told me it's all your fault, but I know that's not true. Did she really not know you were a hard worker? I bet if you asked her, she would have to admit she looked past that trait in you. If she could have been honest with herself, she might have decided to follow her own instincts to find a man who wasn't a workaholic."

"Hindsight is a wonderful thing."

"Don't I know it," she said with a wry smile. "If I hadn't felt like such a failure, I would have realized why Matteo had so much influence over me by telling me what I needed to hear."

He shook his dark head. "A failure? When you've almost received your graduate degree in engineering at the age of twenty-five?"

"Looking back, I realize how odd that sounds now. But growing up, it felt like my brothers received all the attention and I admit I was jealous. My mother tried to help me. She said that one day I'd become my own person and those feelings would go away."

Giovanni stared hard at her. "Have they gone?"

"Now that I'm a mother, I've been forced to grow up. Somehow those feelings of jealousy I harbored seem absurd in light of the problems you and I have been forced to face."

He nodded. "Becoming a parent has been a life-changing experience for me, too. Work used to be everything. But since Vito was born, I can't get home to him at night fast enough."

"They are absolutely precious."

"We're very lucky."

"Yes," she whispered.

They got the children on board with the other items. Then he reached for the infant life preservers his siblings had used for their babies. After putting them on the children, they placed them in their carry-cots and lowered the visors to shield them from the sun. After undoing the ropes, Giovanni started the engine and they made their way at a wakeless speed into open water.

CHAPTER SIX

THE GULF OF SALERNO offered some of the most divine scenery imaginable. Along this winding coastline, steep rocky slopes rushed down to the sea, and tiny villages with colorful houses stacked on top of each other clung to the rugged cliffs.

Had Valentina ever been this happy? She couldn't remember.

While Giovanni piloted the boat, she walked to the rear of the fabulous cruiser, resting one knee on the banquette to watch birds and fish, along with the colorful sailboats off in the distance. Later, after lunch, they carried the babies below to one of the bedrooms for their nap. For the next few hours she and Giovanni were free to enjoy this pleasurable moment out of time.

"Since I've anchored the boat, will you be all right if I take a swim?"

"Of course."

"I'd ask you to join me."

"No. One of us has to stay on board. Go for it, Giovanni. The water is so inviting."

"I'll be right back." He disappeared below, leaving her alone to brood over the time when they had to say a real goodbye. She had to fight thoughts of one day being married to him. He'd only recently been divorced. To take on a new wife would be the last thing he'd want. Though they wouldn't be parting company for a while, her heart was already rebelling.

Giovanni emerged on deck in blue swim trunks. His hard-muscled body took her breath before he slid over the side into the water and started swimming around the cruiser with the speed of a torpedo. He circled maybe ten times, then trod water close to the end of the boat with his hair sleeked back.

She smiled at him. "You look like you're having a marvelous time."

"I haven't taken a day off like this in years."

"Neither have I."

"I'll get back on board so you can have a turn."

"I would, but I'm not ready to swim in the sea yet. Please stay out there as long as you want. I'm enjoying watching you."

"After we go back to my place, you can use the pool so I'm able to watch *you*."

Warmth rushed to her face that had nothing to do with the sun. "I don't want to go back. This is glorious."

"Then we won't."

She drank the rest of her water. *Don't tempt me, Giovanni.* "You have a business to run."

"Didn't you hear what I just told you? Right now my only business is to love Ric and make him feel secure. With your help it's happening."

"I don't know how I would have gotten through all this without your help. Vito is a different baby."

He flashed her a smile that melted her bones. "We do good work."

Too good. Her mind told her she shouldn't have gotten involved with him once they'd left the hospital, but that wasn't what her heart was telling her.

"Ready or not, I'm coming aboard!" He swam to the end of the boat. With stunning male dexterity he heaved himself onto the transom. She handed him one of the towels so he could dry himself off. "Before the babies wake up, come and sit by me while we drive on."

She didn't need to be urged.

He threw the towel around his shoulders and took his place at the wheel. Valentina handed him his life preserver. "Please put it back on."

"For you I'll do it."

"For Ric. He's going to want you around forever."

She couldn't decipher the look in his incredible black eyes that held hers before he turned on the engine. All she knew was that once he'd raised the anchor and they'd taken off across a calm sea, a thrill of exhilaration swept through her just to be sitting next to him.

The sight of the lemon-grove terraces of the cliffs combined with the delicious scent gave her a feeling of euphoria. When she moved to an apartment in Naples, she would always remember this time with a man who was bigger than life to her. His ex-wife could roam the earth and never meet another man like Giovanni.

"What's on your mind, Valentina? Talk to me."

"I guess I'm trying to understand the other reasons why your marriage didn't work. What else caused the strife? Ric is so dear. If your ex-wife saw him, her heart would melt."

To her surprise he brought the boat to a stop and

turned to face her. "Where to start? My parents wanted me to marry her. Tatania's father, Salvatore, was in business with mine. They're both on the board of the company. Because some of my family board members wanted to champion a second cousin of mine to take over the reins, my father didn't want that to happen.

"My mother came to me in private and told me that Tatania's father wanted our marriage. He worked hard on my father to talk to me. A marriage would bring the needed votes in my favor to put me in as head instead of my cousin. Mother begged me to do this because my father was intimidated by Salvatore and always had been.

"I realized my father had always lacked a certain confidence. He looked to me to help fight all the internal battles. That bit of knowledge about his insecurity finally persuaded me to follow through."

"Are you saying she married you because of her father's pressure?"

"To some degree, yes. I'd had various girlfriends throughout my life, but nothing serious. Because of my parents' urgings, I started spending time with her and we got on well enough. Knowing my father was pinning all his hopes on my asking Tatania to marry me, I could see that if I didn't, it could break his spirit.

"But once we were married, she complained about the hours I was working. I questioned how she could be upset since she knew what my life was like. She claimed that she'd loved me from the first time she'd met me, but she didn't know what it meant to be married to a CEO.

"It's true I worked harder than I'd ever done. Both

my father and hers had big expectations where I was concerned."

"How old are you?"

"Thirty-two."

"That's young to have so much responsibility."

He nodded. "I worried I would let my father down if I didn't do the lion's share. I told Tatania that if I did the hard work now, then I could slow down after a couple of years. But our home life did suffer. It got to the point that she said she didn't want to start a family if I didn't spend more time at home. I felt trapped."

"Did she have a job?"

"No. She led an active social life, but the day came when she said she was going to stay at her parents for a while. After two months' separation, we talked and decided to try again. I promised to stay home more. That worked for two weeks, but then there were new problems out of the country I had to see about. She refused to travel with me."

"Why?"

"Because it would mean her sitting in a hotel room all day long while I was working."

"She didn't like exploring new places?"

"Not alone."

"How sad."

"Tatania couldn't take any more of my being absent and filed for divorce. It's true that I was a willing pawn at the time of our marriage, but I'd intended to be a good husband. Unfortunately I didn't marry Tatania for the right reason. Without being in love with her, our marriage couldn't make it. You know the rest."

"But after she was pregnant—"

"That's the mystifying part. She said she didn't

want the baby even if we stayed married because then she'd be stuck raising her baby by herself because I wouldn't be around. She had every reason to believe that was true. Tatania was also convinced that another man wouldn't look at her if she had a baby in tow. As you can see, I did damage to our marriage and she became embittered."

"I'm sorry I brought up something that's so painful for you."

"Not painful anymore. Just sad. I've been thinking about Vito's father, who hasn't stayed in touch with you if only to know he had a son."

"A baby would ruin his lifestyle. He wants his pleasures without any of the responsibility. The man never grew up." She stared at him. "The past is behind us, Giovanni. We're the lucky ones to be the parents of our wonderful babies. And guess what? I think I can hear one of them fussing. I'll go down and bring them up."

"We'll feed them and put them in the playpen."

She stood up. "I'll need to get pictures with my phone." Valentina wanted some of Giovanni to keep forever.

"I want to take pictures, too," he asserted.

Did he want one of her? Fool that she was, she hoped he did.

"See you in a minute." She could hear both of them crying now. "I'm coming!"

With the babies propped in the playpen, Valentina stretched out on her back on one of the side banquettes to get a little sun and let Giovanni drive them farther along the coast. Such a gorgeous day with only a light breeze made their outing idyllic.

He turned on some music from the iPod. Suddenly

the air was filled with the sound of Pavarotti singing Italian love songs. She'd grown up on classical music and adored opera. Learning that he enjoyed it, too, added another fascinating dimension to this remarkable man.

Valentina sat up. "These love songs make me cry."

Giovanni turned off the engine and looked back at her with a satisfied expression. "I remember my mother crying over opera. It's in our Neapolitan genes, Valentina. Our family had arguments at our house over who was, or is, the better tenor—Caruso, Pavarotti or Bocelli."

She laughed. "I could add another great to that list. Mario Lanza from the American films. When I heard him sing 'Ave Maria' in the cathedral with the choir, it was so beautiful, it hurt. And after I heard Pavarotti sing 'Celeste Aida,' I felt I was listening to an angel."

Giovanni nodded. "When this is over, shall I put on the flower song he sang in *Carmen*?"

"Oh, yes! It's another aria that tears your heart apart." They looked at each other, but with him wearing sunglasses, she couldn't see what was going on in his mind. "My mother's love of classical music infected me at an early age. Her favorite opera was *Madame Butterfly*. I wasn't as enamored after I read the short story of the naval officer who used Butterfly for amusement before abandoning her."

Giovanni removed his glasses to reveal eyes filled with compassion. "You see yourself as Butterfly?"

"I didn't know I did until just now. I've lost some confidence, Giovanni."

He sat forward. "You're not alone. Tatania lost so much faith in me, she didn't want to mother our child.

I was anything but the supportive husband. Over the months during her pregnancy I'd begun to doubt my ability to be a good husband, let alone a good father."

"But you're wonderful! Can't you feel it?" she cried softly.

"Meeting you is helping me find my center, Valentina. I intend to keep working on getting better at it, but you have to know my gratitude to you knows no bounds."

His confession sank deep in her heart.

He started the engine, and once more they cruised through the calm water. The late afternoon sun shone down, reminding her to turn over. She laid her head on her arms and kept an eye on the babies while she absorbed the music like a sponge.

For the next half hour she lay there entranced. When the tape ended, she got to her feet and was surprised to find they'd come to a tiny stretch of pebbled beach along the coast. He'd pulled into a dock and shut off the engine. She had to look way up to see the top of the verdant mountains. They had a magnificence that kept her in awe.

"What's this place?"

"Laurito Beach. Few people know about it. When I was young, my friends and I would come here in the summer and build a fort in the trees. This small cove was the starting point for the pirates who used to raid the commercial boats passing by. We pretended to be pirates. The little village of Laurito I was telling you about is higher up the mountain."

Giovanni got out and tied up the boat. "The Ristorante Da Adoni a few yards off caters to anyone, a come-as-you-are spot. I'm hungry for dinner."

She was, too. They picked up the carry-cots and walked the short distance where they could eat and enjoy the view of the water. Giovanni ordered them *zuppa di cozze*, a soup of mussels freshly caught, followed by *coniglio all'Ischitana*, an exotic rabbit dish with garlic, chilli, tomato, herbs and white wine. Divine, divine.

They both held the babies on their laps while they ate. The waiter grinned at them. "So nice to see the *mamma* and *papà* out together with the *bambini*." He whispered something to Giovanni she didn't catch. After he walked away, she asked what he'd said.

"You'll blush."

"Oh, dear."

"But you want to know, right?"

Valentina chuckled.

"I thought so. He said how lucky I was that I had such a delicious-looking wife when she'd just given me two babies. What joy to make another one with her right away!"

That *did* make her blush. "You made that up."

He lifted his hands. "I swear."

If he'd take off his sunglasses, she'd be able to see if he was kidding her.

"He said something else, too, but then you'd turn red like a lobster."

"Thank you for editing his remarks."

Giovanni's low laughter resonated inside her. "Did you know the Ravello summer music festival is putting on a performance of Wagner's *Parsifal* near the end of August? I don't know who the tenor will be, but I'll get front-row tickets for us whether it's held indoors or outside."

To see that with Giovanni would be another thrill of a lifetime. The thrills were stacking up minute by minute. Though she would probably be in Naples by that date, she kept the thought to herself. Valentina didn't want to spoil their time together during this trip.

"You do too much. I can never repay you."

"Our relationship isn't based on payment."

"I know. But I still want to thank you for your unending generosity." Time to change the subject. "Where are we headed next, Captain?"

A smile broke out on his tanned face. "There's another cove five minutes away where we'll anchor for the night."

After they carried the babies back to the boat, they took them downstairs to get them ready for bed. Then Giovanni went up on deck to drive the boat to the spot where they would spend the night. As he was lowering the anchor, his cell phone rang.

He'd put it in a dashboard compartment. After reaching for it, he checked the caller ID. His father knew he'd taken some time off. He wondered what reason had prompted him to call while Giovanni was on holiday.

He clicked on. "Papà?"

"Quanto tempo, figlio mio."

It hadn't been that long since they'd seen each other. This call was about something else.

"What's the problem?"

"Claudio told me he saw you out dining last night with a very beautiful blonde woman. She's Vito's *mamma*, so don't deny it."

"I'm denying nothing. She's with me now."

"Tatania's family is outraged that you've brought that woman into your house."

His father misspoke. Only Salvatore was upset because it interfered with his plans to get Tatania back with Giovanni. "It's my business surely. Our divorce was final months ago and don't forget, she divorced me."

"They're suing the hospital. When you file suit, too, the publicity won't be good if you're involved with the Montanari woman."

Ah. Now his father had gotten to the point. "I have no intention of suing the hospital."

"Of course you will. This should never have happened."

"Valentina and I talked it over. It was a terrible mistake, but there was no malice in what happened. Therefore there's no justification in suing anyone. Since Tatania refused to see the baby after it was delivered, the switch meant nothing to her. Papà, you know full well that this is all coming from Salvatore and *not* Violeta, who is a reasonable woman and loves my birth son.

"As for Valentina and me, we've rectified the situation to our satisfaction. Now we're involved in helping our babies adjust to the switch. It's working beautifully."

"Giovanni—" He lowered his voice. "Putting the suit aside, the Montanari woman was never married. Everyone's talking about the sister of Rinieri Montanari who got pregnant out of wedlock by that amorous professor from the university. It doesn't look good for my son who's the CEO of Laurito's to be seen in her company. Your judgment should be beyond reproach."

"That's too bad, Papà, because she has moved in with me. We and the babies are very happy. I'm on vacation and won't be back in the office for a couple of days. We'll talk then if you wish. I love you and Mamma. *Ciao*."

Valentina was standing by him when he clicked off. His eyes swerved to her. "How much did you hear?"

"It's started, hasn't it? That man who stopped at our table last night, the one who kept undressing me with his eyes? He's already gone running to your father."

Giovanni nodded. Claudio might be married, but he had other women on the side. The way he'd looked at Valentina had disgusted him. "We knew this kind of trouble had to happen and have already discussed it."

"But I know you love your father," she persisted, "and you don't want to disappoint him."

"I know you love yours, but no one else is involved in this except you and me and our children."

She moistened her lips nervously. "It could get ugly for you."

"I won't let it. We're partners, remember?"

"How could I possibly forget?"

"Good. That's what I wanted to hear. Now let's go downstairs to bed."

He set the boat alarm and they went below. She changed into a pair of navy sweats he loved. Both children slept in their carry-cots in his cabin. When she would have gone to the other cabin, he said, "Stay in here with me tonight, Valentina. The queen-size bed is perfect for us. This way I can guard the three of you with no worry."

Without waiting for her response, he swung her up in his arms and laid her down on the bed. "I might want to have my way with you, but only with your permission."

"Not in front of the children," she teased, but she stayed right there. "Where are you taking us tomorrow?"

"We'll travel along the coast to the medieval village of Castellabate. It's a World Heritage Site. Later in the day we'll take the children ashore in their strollers so we can explore the small streets and alleys. You'll love it. And if we're up to it, we can walk to the thirteenth-century castle at the top for a spectacular view."

"I've never been there before."

"I seem to remember a restaurant that serves the best calamari and saffron risotto with porcini you ever tasted. My mouth is watering just thinking about it."

"One would think that's all you have on your mind."

"That's how much you know." Without hesitation, Giovanni brushed her mouth briefly with his own. He'd been needing to do that or go out of his mind. She kissed him back, then turned to face the babies.

"Where did you go?" he whispered against her neck.

"This is happening too fast."

"But I want to do it, again and again. Don't tell me you didn't like it because I wouldn't believe you."

His declaration was like a bolt of lightning penetrating her body. "I did like it. That's not the point."

"Then what is?"

"I've been attracted to you from the first day we met, and it frightens me."

"Why?"

"I never felt this way about Matteo. This is so different. I know my love for the babies has a lot to do with the strength of my feelings for you. What I can't figure out is how to separate what's really going on inside of me. All I know is, I'm a mom now and I need to concentrate on that without letting personal feelings complicate everything. Let's go to sleep."

"I'll try," he murmured.

The children woke up once in the middle of the night. They fed them in bed, then put them back in their carry-cots. Once all was quiet, he pulled Valentina against him and buried his face in her hair. "Don't think of moving away from me. Not now, not ever."

"You mustn't keep saying things like that to me."

"I can't help it. I didn't have a mad passion for Tatania. I'm afraid *you* take the honors in that department."

She squeezed her eyes together. "It's because I'm Vito's mom. You're reading too much into it."

"I agree it's because of that and a myriad of intangibles. But I can hear your next argument. Both of us have come out of unsatisfying relationships and being together is filling a void. I can add several others. I need the woman who mothered Ric for two weeks to become his nanny so I can go to work without worry. And you're a Montanari. Binding our two families will build a dynasty and—"

"Stop!"

"Relax, Valentina. We're partners. Until you want to touch me so much you can't stay away from me, I'll keep my hands and mouth off you."

Valentina lay there awake for a long time. Giovanni was a man of strong feelings and instincts that had propelled him to the kind of success most men could only dream of. To tell her he was madly attracted to her had to be an exaggeration. It was probably more of the idea that he was happy after being unhappy for so long. That described her state of mind. He'd created this fantasy world.

With the children being so content now, everything seemed perfect. It would stay that way until the real world intruded. The phone call from his father was only the beginning. Before long she'd be hearing from her family. Pretty soon everything would fall in on them, but until that happened she wanted to stay here in his arms.

When the babies started fussing, she fed them and went to the galley to make breakfast. Giovanni loved food. Because of his energy, he didn't gain weight. A little while later she called him to come and eat.

They ate at the pull-down table while the babies watched from their carry-cots. He acted so happy and was so much fun to be with, she never wanted this vacation to end. When they finished eating, she cleaned up the kitchen while he took the babies up on deck.

Their day turned out to be glorious, but the climb to the castle at the top wore her out. After a delicious fish dinner in the town, it felt good to get back to the cruiser and relax. Before long it was time to feed the babies and put them to bed.

Giovanni flashed her a compelling smile. "Now that we're alone, how about a game of *tressette*? Sit on the banquette by me." He produced a deck of cards.

Valentina eyed him with a smile. "I don't think I've played it."

"I'll teach you."

Once they got going, she didn't want to stop. "I'm going to beat you if it kills me!" But she never did and he chuckled with absolute glee. "You're cheating. You *have* to be!"

"I swear I'm not."

"Let me see your cards." Something was wrong. "Show me the palm of your hand."

He stared at her through veiled eyes. "Now, why would I do that?"

"You *are* cheating!" She grabbed his hand, but he was so strong she couldn't pry his fingers apart. Laughter rolled out of him despite her frustration. "You're terrible!" She tried again and found her shoulder against his chest.

His free arm went around her and pulled her closer. "I lied," he murmured near her ear. "I'm sorry, but you're so much fun I couldn't help myself." He undid his other hand so she could see cards he'd kept hidden. "Forgive me?" he asked and released her.

She felt his warm breath on her cheek, increasing her desire for him. To her chagrin she didn't want him to let her go.

Until you want to touch me so much you can't stay away from me, I'll keep my hands and mouth off you.

Valentina had been the one to start this intimate tug-of-war. She'd reached for his hand, not the other way around. Aware that she'd given herself away, she got up from the banquette. "It's time to check on the children."

Giovanni followed her below and they got ready for bed. Valentina looked down at them. "They're so sweet. I never knew how much I would love being a mother."

Giovanni lounged against the door. "I'm still reeling from the joy of fatherhood. I felt a deep sadness when Tatania told me she didn't want anything to do with it once she'd had the baby. But neither she nor Matteo could have any comprehension of what they're missing."

She turned to him. "I'm not sorry for what we're doing. We owe them everything we can do to give them the best start in life, even if the world says scathing things about us."

"Your children have a warrior for a mother. It's a privilege to know you, Valentina. Now let's get in bed."

His words stayed with her long after he'd wrapped his arms around her. Giovanni had a way of making her feel cherished. If she'd never met him, she would never have realized a man like him was out there in the cosmos. Twenty-eight thousand baby switches a year worldwide. What were the odds of it happening to her and Giovanni?

The next day they headed toward home. En route they went ashore at several places for a meal. Giovanni swam while she took pictures of him. By evening they'd cruised close to Ravello, but anchored near the pier to spend one more night on board. Once the babies were down, he turned on another Pavarotti track.

Valentina wanted to prolong this moonlit night because tomorrow he'd have to go to work. It wouldn't just be the babies who would miss him. But he would always come home at the end of the day because he was a devoted father.

She lay down on her stomach on one of the banquettes. "Could we sleep up here tonight? It's glorious out. We'll keep the doors open to listen for the children."

"You're reading my mind." He walked over and threw a light blanket over her. She watched him lie down on the banquette opposite her. They turned to each other, supporting their heads with their arms. "Have you ever gone camping?"

"No. Carlo used to go and I'd beg him to take me. He'd always say, 'next time.'"

"Would it interest you to go with me?"

"I can't think of anything I'd like more. We'd carry the babies on our backs in those fun-looking pouches. You're talking a campfire and a tent, right?"

Giovanni sat up suddenly. In the darkness, the sight of his arresting features excited her to the core. "Where did you come from?" His voice sounded husky.

"I've been wondering the same thing about you."

"Some of my happiest memories were out camping and fishing with my friends. I want to teach the boys to love the outdoors."

"Whenever you want to go, I'm your man."

A broad smile broke out on his handsome face. "What a man!"

She laughed.

"Being with you makes me want to become a house dad so we can do everything together."

"That would work for about a week, then you'd need the stimulation of applying that amazing brain of yours to the business you love. My mother understood that about my father. She was a very smart woman."

"You must miss her a lot."

"Oh, I do. She would have loved Vito and teaching me how to be a good mother."

"Trust me, Valentina. You already are because you've put his happiness before your own. That takes a very special person. If she were alive, she'd be tremendously proud of you."

His praise caused her throat to swell. "I could say the same thing about your fatherly virtues, even if you do love business."

"I love exploring new markets, but not the administrative duties."

"Well, your company is depending on you to go on doing great things for them."

"What about you?"

"I've made up my mind to take classes this winter semester to finish my degree."

After a long silence, he said, "You can fly to Naples with me on the days you have classes. I'll fly you home after."

She raised herself up on one elbow. "Giovanni? You and I *will* be partners forever. But when I told you I'd live with you, I didn't mean forever and neither did you. Once August is over, the boys will be better able to handle the separation. I'm planning to find an apartment in Naples near the university and put Vito in day care attached to the university. I'll always want you to come by and bring Ric, but I need to make my own way."

His brows furrowed. "If you're thinking of doing this to protect my reputation, then forget it, Valentina."

"Giovanni—this isn't about you. It's about me becoming independent. The women in the Montanari family don't have careers. I'll be the first."

"You can do that. I'll help you."

"That's the problem. I've been helped all my life. Now that I have a baby, I need to do this by myself."

"How will you finance everything?"

"A student loan. If I'm careful, I can get through school. After that I'll find a job and pay it back like thousands of other husbandless women do. You have no idea how much it would mean to me to make something of myself. Rini and Carlo have done it. So can I."

"Your brothers got help, too. With your name being Montanari, the university won't give you a loan."

"You're probably right, so I'll apply under my mother's maiden name."

"That's illegal. If you need a loan, I'll give you one."

She slid off the bench. "You're a man in a million, Giovanni. I've always been given help, and now here you are offering to pay my expenses so I can finish school. As if I'd let you do that. I *have* to do this by myself, even if I have to get an entry-level job first and take another couple of years to get my degree. Please tell me you understand."

He exhaled slowly. "I do. You're the woman born with the proverbial silver spoon in your mouth. My admiration for you just keeps growing because you want to make your own way."

Valentina hadn't expected an answer like that. He always had a way to distill a potential problem. "Thank you for taking me seriously and for offering to help me financially." She took another drink of water, then lay back down.

"You're welcome. How soon are you going to look for a job?"

"In a couple of weeks."

"Good. Then let's forget those plans and enjoy the time we have together. How does that sound?"

Giovanni was being so kind and agreeable she hardly knew what to say. "I don't deserve your kindness."

"*Deserve* is an odd word. Why do you use it?"

She bit her lip. "I went against the principles I was brought up with by getting involved with Matteo. If I try hard to be the best mother and provider I can be for the rest of my life, then maybe I'll be able to forgive myself."

"That's a lot of guilt you're carrying around. I'm sure your family doesn't make you feel that way. You're an amazing woman. You need to be kind to yourself."

"Thank you for saying that. You're a terrific listener. It explains why your family looks to you for leadership."

"I've noticed you have trouble accepting a compliment. You'd better get used to it because as I told you, I've never been so attracted to a woman."

This wave of euphoria with the children would pass for him. However Valentina feared her attachment to him went much deeper than that. She buried her face in her arms until she knew no more.

CHAPTER SEVEN

VALENTINA PROPPED THE babies in their swings by the pool while she looked for a job on her laptop. Since Giovanni had taken them down the coast on the cruiser two weeks ago, the time had flown by and she needed to get busy.

He'd gone to work each business day, but had come home early to play with the children. They'd settled down to a routine and last weekend had spent time touring the grounds of the Villa Cimbrone, for which Ravello was famous.

Their long walks and talks while they enjoyed the babies had been heavenly. But pretty soon she needed to register for school *if* she was going to go at all.

"Valentina?" She looked up to see Giovanni walking toward her. "I missed you at breakfast. What's going on?"

She was always so thrilled to see him, she could hardly breathe. "I got up early to look for a part-time job that will fit with my studies."

"I'm glad you're going ahead with your plans."

"You really mean that?"

"Of course. I know how important getting that degree is to you. Have you decided where you want to live?"

"I've already found an apartment online, but I need to see it in person and visit the day-care center I have my eye on. Rini told me he'd give me enough money until I receive my first paycheck from the job. Then I'll pay him back."

"Good for you."

"Giovanni—you have no idea how much your support means to me." Her voice caught. "You've done everything for me and I've done nothing in return."

"What are you talking about?" He gripped her upper arms, pulling her out of the deck chair. Lines had darkened his face. "You've helped me transition from being a robot into a flesh-and-blood human being and father. I couldn't have done any of this without you. Don't you understand?"

He pressed a kiss to her lips and shook her gently before his hands slid away with seeming reluctance. The contact sent her pulse racing. "A-are you leaving now?" she asked, her voice faltering.

"Yes. I'll see all of you after I get home from work and we'll talk some more about your plans." He acted like he wanted to say more, then changed his mind and walked back in the house. Before long she saw the helicopter fly off, taking her heart with him.

No sooner had he gone than she heard a voice. "Valentina?" She turned her head in time to see Giovanni's mother-in-law walking toward her.

"Violeta—how nice to see you." Both she and Giovanni's mother had come by twice in the past two weeks. Valentina had missed her mother horribly and enjoyed both women's company.

"The babies are adorable, but it's you I need to talk to."

"Please sit down, Violeta. How are you?"

"I need to tell you something because I know you are a good person and a wonderful mother."

Valentina's brows broke into a delicate frown. "I think the world of you, too. What's wrong?"

"If my husband knew I was here to tell you this, he'd have grounds to divorce me. The mood he has been in since the baby switch has been very hard on me."

"Why has it upset him so much?"

"He's convinced that if it hadn't happened, Giovanni would have been to see Tatania by now and help her to get better emotionally."

"I see." Knowing how Giovanni really felt made this uncomfortable for Valentina.

"Giovanni's preoccupation with both babies has changed him. His mind isn't on the pressures of his position as CEO. He told me he has no intention of suing the hospital for the mishandling of the babies. For that decision my husband blames you for living in this house and your influence over him."

She shook her head. "I have no influence, Violeta. He loves both babies. That love has prompted him to make certain decisions. I—I love both babies, too," she confessed. "This has been hard on everyone. We're trying to do the right thing."

"Nevertheless my husband has been in conference with Giovanni's father, and there's a groundswell from the board to ask Giovanni to step down as CEO. Were you aware of that?"

"No—" Valentina clutched the edge of the table.

She felt like she'd been shot. "But you can go home and tell your husband he has nothing more to worry about. I'll be living in Naples by the end of the week."

"You mean at Giovanni's apartment there?"

Valentina knew he kept one, but he'd never pushed it on her. He understood she wanted to be independent. Something about his calm, caring demeanor made her want to do things his way.

"No. Winter semester is starting at the university. I'll be living nearby in an apartment I've found and putting Vito in day care. I hope to graduate in the spring and get a job."

"You're going to work?"

"Yes. I plan to be an engineer like my brothers."

"Oh—" She looked shocked. "You must be very brilliant."

"I wish." She'd never felt she could measure up to her brothers, but having given birth to Vito had given her a new sense of self-worth, never mind that Giovanni had contributed to that feeling. "But the point is, I'm convinced that the babies are happy now and that they'll be able to handle the separation so Giovanni and I can get on with our lives."

She stared at Valentina through eyes reflecting torment. "So you and Giovanni—?"

"We're not lovers, Violeta," she answered the unasked question. "We're friends who've been through a terrible ordeal and are doing our best to work things out."

Violeta looked downcast. "I'm sorry. I didn't mean to pry."

"It's all right. Giovanni loves you and loves it that you're Ric's grandmother."

Her brown eyes filled with tears. "Thank you. I love him, and I love both your babies."

Now Valentina was weepy. "They're hard not to love."

"You're easy to love, too." Valentina hadn't expected that confession from Tatania's mother. "No matter what you say, I see it in Giovanni's eyes."

"What you see is a man who has fallen in love with fatherhood." He was still in that state of euphoria, and it made his gorgeous black eyes shine. "In that respect he's unique."

"I agree," she whispered and got up from the table. "I'm going to tell my husband what you said. It will give him hope that Giovanni and my daughter will get a second chance." Valentina's heart sank, but it wasn't her place to disabuse the older woman. "I know it will stop all the talk over asking Giovanni to step down."

Valentina kept a smile on her face. "That's good for the Laurito company. Now, why don't you stay for a while. You can feed Ric his bottle."

"You'd let me?"

"Of course. He loves his *nonna*."

Violeta walked around and gave her a kiss on the cheek. "I'll come again, but your news is too important. I need to get back home and talk to my husband."

Valentina walked her to her car. When she'd disappeared, Valentina found Stazie in the sunroom putting flowers in a vase.

"Stazie? I need to fly to Naples. I know this is a great imposition, but could you tend the boys until I get back? Giovanni might get home first. I'm just not sure."

"Of course I'll tend them. You rarely let me help."

"Thank you so much."

She hurried back out to the children and phoned Rini. Luckily he was in his office. "Rini? Could I ask a great favor?" So much for her independence.

"Of course. How are you?"

"I'm ready to check out the apartment and the day-care center. Could you send the helicopter here?"

"You mean now?"

"If it's convenient. I'll fly to your office. From there I'll get a taxi and check out those places. Maybe you can drop me back here this evening?"

"Tell you what. I need a break. When you arrive I'll ask my driver to take us where you need to go. We'll have dinner with Papà before we leave Naples."

"You're the best, Rini."

"Hey—I've missed you and Vito. I bet he's gained ten pounds since the last time I saw him."

She chuckled. "Not quite. Love you."

While she waited for the helicopter, she brought the babies into the sunroom and put them on the floor on a quilt. It was hard to leave them, but this was an emergency.

At 6:30 p.m. Giovanni jumped down from the helicopter, anxious to be with Valentina. He would ask Stanzie and Paolo to watch the children while he took her to a great restaurant for a night of dinner and dancing.

He'd kept his distance over the past two weeks. But while he'd been at work today, his thoughts had been totally focused on her. After the close quarters they'd shared on the cruiser, he'd go mad if he didn't get her into his arms.

This time of evening he usually found her in the

sunroom with the babies. Instead he discovered Ric
and Vito in the kitchen. Stanzie had put them in their
swings while she cooked dinner. He smiled at her and
kissed the boys. "Is Valentina upstairs?"

"No. She flew to Naples. Her brother will bring
her home tonight."

That revelation sucked all the air out of him. "Any
other news?"

"*Si.* Signora Corleto came over this morning."

Uh-oh. "What time did she come?"

"About eleven."

"What time did Valentina leave?"

"Around noon. Dinner will be ready in a few minutes."

"Thank you, Stanzie. I'm going to take the boys
for a short walk." He put them in their strollers and
left the villa.

Whatever conversation had gone on between Valentina and Violeta, it had prompted his houseguest to
take off. She didn't have to tell Giovanni her schedule, but the fact that he hadn't heard from her let him
know something had alarmed her.

Violeta was not a vindictive woman. Quite the opposite. "Hey, guys—we're on our own until Valentina comes home." He kissed their heads. "Let's go
back and eat. Stanzie has made something that smells
good."

Later that night after giving them a bath and putting them to bed, he started down the stairs just as
Valentina was coming up. In the dim light her classic features and gleaming blond hair emphasized her
beauty.

"Welcome home," he said in a quiet voice.

"Sorry I'm late."

"You don't owe me any explanation. Stanzie told me where you'd gone."

She nodded. "After Rini and I returned to the villa, he drove me here. How are the children?"

"I put them down. Why don't you tell me about your day?"

He walked with her to the nursery. After she peeked at the boys, they tiptoed out of the room and went back downstairs to the sunroom. The night called to him. She must have felt it, too, and followed him out to the garden, where the roses were in full bloom.

She leaned over to smell one. "Their scent lies heavy on the air."

"My parents have a garden in Naples, but the fragrance here is much more powerful." His gaze wandered over her. "Did you accomplish a lot today?"

"Yes. Rini went with me. I like the apartment I'm going to rent, and I was impressed with the people who run the day-care center. They only allow ten children. Two of the four workers look solely after the babies. Both have had nursing experience. I'm sure Vito will get the attention he needs."

"Have you had success finding a job?"

"Not yet, but I'm hopeful. Rini and I had dinner with my father. It was a good day."

"I heard that Violeta dropped by."

"Yes."

"Want to tell me what you two talked about, or was it confidential?"

"She said her husband is suing the hospital."

"We already knew that. What else did she say that caused you to leave so fast?"

She turned to the view of the sea. "Whatever we talked about is no longer important."

"Why? Because you're going to move to Naples, therefore you're no longer a threat? I'm not unaware that Tatania's parents would like us to get back together. With you out of my villa for good, that removes the biggest roadblock to effecting a reconciliation. Am I right?"

"Yes."

Giovanni grasped her shoulders and pulled her back against his chest. He buried his face in her hair and felt her tremble. "When I got home from work, I was planning to take you out for a night of dinner and dancing."

"At this point that would be a mistake."

"Explain what you mean." He turned her around. Their mouths were only centimeters apart.

"I can't. You're holding me too close to think."

After expelling his breath, he let go of her, but it took all his strength to do so. "Is that better?"

She backed away from him. Her shimmering blue eyes held a haunted expression. "Did you know there's a movement within your company to ask you to step down as CEO because everyone believes you and I are lovers?"

His blood ran cold. "Violeta *told* you that?"

"Yes, but she didn't say it in a mean way. We like each other. She wanted me to know the truth because she loves you and Ric. I allayed her fears by letting her know that you and I are not lovers. Furthermore I told her I'm moving to Naples by the weekend."

Maybe *he'd* misjudged the situation. "In other words, you don't have deep feelings for me."

"Of course I do," she practically shouted at him.

"But it seems not deep enough, otherwise you wouldn't have flown to Naples the moment Violeta stopped by to give you the bad news. I thought we were going to do this together. Like partners, remember?"

Valentina shook her head. "We've been through all this. You knew I was planning to leave. What she told me helped me to get on with my plans a little sooner. Giovanni—you're not just anybody. You're the head of the Laurito Corporation.

"I knew we'd have to face a lot of bad publicity while we tried to do the right thing for our babies. But what I didn't know was that the board would actually remove you from your position. You've worked so hard for everything you've achieved. I refuse to be the woman who brings you down."

"Tatania's father worked on Violeta to get his own way before she showed up here. Surely you must see that."

"All I know is, I can't stay here any longer. I'm trying to put away the guilt I suffered over my bad judgment with Matteo. But if I thought that you could be toppled by your own board members because of me, terrible guilt would consume me. This is all my fault. If I hadn't asked the hospital for a DNA test, we wouldn't know of each other's existence."

His anger flared. "If you hadn't followed your mother's intuition, we wouldn't have the joy of loving two sons. Can you honestly stand there and tell me you're sorry for discovering the truth?"

"You know I'm not," her voice shook, "but I don't want to be the one responsible for ruining your life! Violeta's visit was a blessing in disguise. Just so you know, I'm going to pack everything up tonight. Rini is going to come for me and Vito in the morning. I'll stay with him until Friday. The furnished apartment will be ready then, and he'll help me move."

Blind with anger over what was happening, he knew he had to get away from her in order to calm down. Gutted by the sudden change in their arrangement, he needed to channel his negative energy with action.

"Don't let me keep you, Valentina. *Buonanotte.*"

He raced back inside to his room and changed into his trunks. A good dozen laps in the pool wouldn't take away the rage he was feeling over Tatania's father. He'd always been the ultimate manipulator orchestrating everyone's lives, including Giovanni's father. But the physical exercise would help Giovanni clear his head before he put his plan into action and fought fire with fire.

When the next morning came, he purposely stayed in the bedroom so Valentina could feed the babies and say her goodbye to Ric before Rini Montanari came for her. From the other guest room window at the end of the hall, he saw her get in the car with Vito and drive away.

Now that she'd gone, Giovanni contacted his pilot, who would be picking him up within a few minutes. He'd called for a morning meeting of the entire Laurito board. For the occasion he'd dressed in a formal suit and tie.

On his way out, he stopped in the sunroom, where Stanzie was entertaining Ric in his swing. She looked up.

"You just missed Valentina."

"We said good-night last night." He leaned over to kiss his son. "I'll see you this evening."

"Is everything all right?"

Giovanni smiled at her. "Things couldn't be better."

"But…she said she was moving to Naples."

"That's right. She had a lot on her mind today. Don't worry about it."

Stanzie frowned at him. "I don't like it. Paolo and I enjoy her very much."

"She holds you two in the highest regard. I'll check in with you later to see how Ric is doing."

A half hour later he entered his office and checked with his assistant. "Has anyone bowed out of this morning's meeting?" It was scheduled to start in ten minutes.

"No, but your uncle Benito said he'd be a few minutes late."

He nodded. "I'll be making an announcement. When the meeting is over, I'll tell you what I want you to say to the media."

His assistant's eyes widened, but they'd worked together too long and he knew better than to question Giovanni.

"I'm headed for the conference room now." He left his office and started down the hall.

"Giovanni?" His father had just gotten off the private elevator.

"Papà—" He gave him a hug.

"I've been anxious to talk to you about something that has concerned me for the last month. After the meeting let's go to lunch."

"We'll do it."

They entered the room. Little by little most of the

members of the board had taken their seats around the long oval table. As he stood to call the meeting to order, his oldest uncle came in with Tatania's father and took their places next to Giovanni's father.

"I appreciate all of you rearranging your busy schedules to attend this emergency board meeting. I wouldn't have called for it if it weren't for the most vital of reasons. After you put me in as CEO of Laurito's two years ago, I made up my mind to bring results that would satisfy your faith in me.

"But as all of you know, I became a father very recently. The birth of our son Vitiello has been the most soul-changing experience of my entire life. I say *our son Vitiello* because he was the son I took home from the hospital to raise. But three weeks later I discovered there was a mistake made at the hospital. Vitiello was not our baby.

"The courageous mother who went home with her baby realized something was wrong, and DNA tests were done. It turns out we had each other's babies. The hospital arranged for the mistake to be rectified. Our birth son, Riccardo, was returned to me, and her son, Vitiello, was returned to her. But not without a lot of agony because the bonding between parent and child took place before the mistake was caught.

"I now feel as if I'm the father of twins. I love both babies with every fiber of my being. I never knew how wonderful it was to be a father. It has crystallized my vision of the future in a new way. In order to be the kind of father my sons deserve, I'm stepping down as CEO, effective by the end of the day."

The gasps he'd expected were louder than even he

had imagined. Both his father and Tatania's father looked like they'd had a coronary.

"What I would like to do is be the head of our marketing department, but that will be up to the new CEO." He eyed his second cousin, who'd been considered as the pick before Giovanni had been installed. "Never question that my loyalty will always be to Laurito. But it's a privilege to be a father and I want to be there to enjoy as much of it as possible.

"That's all I have to say. Thank you for coming to this meeting."

He left the room and headed for his office to talk to his assistant. "You can tell the press I've stepped down as CEO to devote more time to my family. Between you and me I hope to be given a lesser position in the corporation that suits my needs." His assistant looked so crestfallen he added, "Don't worry. If I'm given another job around here, I'll want you with me."

Before there was a stampede to his office, he texted his father.

Meet u at Alforno's, Papà. Come alone. We need to have a long talk.

Valentina set up the swing in the kitchen for Vito while she cooked dinner. Having moved out of Giovanni's villa, she felt like part of her had died. He'd done nothing to prevent her from leaving. In fact he'd stayed away while she'd gotten up this morning to feed the babies. She'd thought he might come downstairs and try to persuade her not to go, but of course he didn't do that.

The only remedy to her heartache was to keep busy.

She told Bianca to take the night off. Valentina would fix Rini's dinner herself. He liked her veal-filled cannelloni with white sauce, a recipe their mother often cooked.

She turned on the radio while she stuffed the pasta. Her favorite news station was RAI1, and she half listened to the Tuesday evening news. In the midst of cooking, she bent over to kiss her baby's precious face. She put the pacifier back in his mouth. "Next week I'll be taking you to the doctor for your next checkup. You're such a good eater he'll probably tell me you're getting too chubby."

Tears rolled down her cheeks to realize she wouldn't be living with Ric or Giovanni anymore. She knew he'd been upset over Violeta's visit, but he'd made it clear that he honored Valentina's decision to move out.

What did you want him to do? Take you upstairs and make love to you?

She didn't dare answer that question and put the dinner in the oven. The news was still on as she set the table for Rini.

"Today the country is stunned by the announcement that Giovanni Laurito, the dynamic CEO and entrepreneur of the Laurito Corporation, has stepped down from his position to devote more time to his family."

What?

With her heart thudding she rushed over to the radio to turn up the volume.

"The corporation's spokesman has shed no other light on the resignation, but already the announcement has negatively affected the stock market. Members of the board have declined comment at this time. But there's speculation that due to his divorce from Tatania Corleto, the daughter of Salvatore Corleto, one of the pillars of the company, certain internal domestic problems forced him to make this unexpected decision."

"No—"

"His two years as head of the corporation have shown unprecedented growth in a market that has catapulted Laurito to the top of medical machines technology throughout Europe. His reputation for—"

Valentina turned it off, not wanting to hear any more. Tears streamed down her face. "Oh, Giovanni— Look what I started—I can't bear it."

"Valentina?" She jerked around to see her brother walk in the kitchen. "What's wrong?"

"Have you heard tonight's news?"

Lines darkened his face. "It was on the noon segment. Everyone at Montanari's was surprised."

"It's my fault, Rini."

"Of course it isn't." He hugged her. "Whatever he did has nothing to do with you."

"Yes, it does." She pulled away from him. "None of this would have happened if I hadn't called the hospital about getting a DNA test."

"You can't blame yourself for wanting to know if Ric was your son!" He drew Vito out of the swing and hugged him. "Because of what you did, you have your birth son home with you."

"When I tell you what happened yesterday, you'll understand why I feel so fragmented by the news." Wiping the tears from her cheeks, Valentina recounted the conversation with Violeta.

After she'd finished, he said, "So because of what

she said, you think Giovanni Laurito fell on his sword because of you?" He sounded incredulous.

"Yes! I stayed with him for a few weeks and because of that, he had to step down."

Rini shook his head. "I know enough about his character to promise you he doesn't do anything unless he wants to. He asked you to live with him for the babies' sakes. It was a joint decision, Valentina."

"I should have known better."

"Where is all this guilt coming from?"

"You know," she mumbled and walked over to the oven.

"The circumstances with Matteo were entirely different."

"When I called the university to see about classes, I found out by accident that Matteo is no longer teaching there. Because of mistakes I've made, he has gone elsewhere and now it has cost Giovanni his position at Laurito's. I'm the loose, unmarried woman who—"

"Valentina—" He cut her off. "I don't ever want to hear you talk like that again."

His anger surprised her. "What are you saying?"

"I thought you made the wrong decision to go with Giovanni, but have since changed my mind. I've seen a remarkable change in you. I'm proud of you for doing what you thought was right. Anyone can see both you and Vito are thriving. Being with Giovanni has done that for you."

"You honestly believe that?"

He nodded. "I wasn't in your skin or Giovanni's. You both followed your intuition. Good for you."

She took the cannelloni out of the oven, hardly able to believe her ears. "If you'll sit down, I'll serve you."

He reached for Vito and sat on a chair at the table. "This little guy is worth everything you've gone through."

Valentina nodded. "I adore him." She put Rini's food and coffee on the table, then plucked the baby from his arms and sat down across from him.

"This tastes delicious. You're not eating?"

"I couldn't." She looked at him. "Rini? I'm so upset I can't think about going to school right now. A job is all I can handle. I don't want to work at a restaurant or a department store. There's an opening at one of the university bookstores. The hours are good and it's close to the apartment and the day-care center. I'm going to arrange for an interview tomorrow."

"At least that's an environment you're familiar with, but since you've decided not to go to school, there's no hurry for you to see about a job."

"Yes, there is. It's time you led your own life."

He shook his head. "I do."

"But there's more to life, brother dear. You need your privacy to make that happen. Excuse me while I bathe Vito and put him down with his bottle. Thank you for being my rock."

"I wish there were more I could do."

"If I can fly to Naples with you on Friday, I'll move in the apartment and leave Vito at the day care while I see about that job at the bookstore. I really do need to be on my own. This has nothing to do with you."

"Little sister? I've never been more proud of you than I am at this moment."

She stared at him, knowing in her heart he meant it.

In another hour she'd put Vito to bed and went to her room, but she was so racked with pain over

Giovanni, she couldn't stand it any longer and phoned him. It rang a long time before going to voice mail.

"Giovanni? I—I heard the news on the radio this evening," she stammered. "Please call me when you get an opportunity. Please."

She clicked off and clutched the phone in her hand. Where was he? What was he doing? Valentina could only imagine the storm he'd created at the corporation after an announcement like that. He was so young to step down from a career of such magnitude. What would he do if he left the company outright?

Absolutely sick about it, she phoned Stanzie. They'd shared phone numbers when she'd been living at the villa in case of an emergency, but Valentina had never had a reason to call her.

Not until now…

"Pronto?"

"Stanzie? It's Valentina."

"Ah—I'm so glad it's you. His family has called and called. His *mamma* is worried sick about him."

Valentina heard the anxiety in her voice. "I tried to reach Giovanni. Where is he?"

"He came home for the baby earlier and took him out on the cruiser. They aren't back yet. By the things he took, I think maybe he'll be gone for a long time. But he shouldn't be alone, not after giving up his job." Stanzie sounded shaken. "You need to come. You are the only person who makes him happy."

"That's not true."

"I know what I see. When you came in to this house, everything changed. Why did you leave?"

She could hardly swallow. "So I wouldn't be the one to cause trouble for him at his work."

"If his work were that important, he wouldn't have given up the position. Nothing is as important to him as the babies. You come tomorrow and Paolo will help you find him. All the time you were here, I heard you two talk like he has never talked before. Talking and laughing. He was a different person with you. Please come, Valentina. He needs you."

Stanzie clicked off before Valentina could say anything else.

He needs you.

She sank down on the side of the bed with her head in her hands. *Heaven help me. I need him.*

Quickly, before Rini went to bed, she hurried to his den, where he usually worked after dinner. She knocked on the door and he told her to come in.

He looked at her tearstained face. "What's wrong?"

"I just got off the phone with Stanzie. She says Giovanni has gone out on his cruiser with Ric and doesn't know when he'll be back. His family is terribly concerned about him. She wants me to come because she's worried, too."

Rini gazed at her through veiled eyes. "You're in love with him."

There was no hiding anything from her brother. "Yes."

"Has he told you he's in love with you?"

"No. We've never even kissed."

"Why not?"

"Because he knows how guilty I feel after what happened with Matteo. He promised me he wouldn't touch me unless I wanted him to."

"That's it?"

"No. He asked me not to leave. I did it so he wouldn't

have to face the board. They were going to force him to step down because of me."

"But he was one step ahead of them and faced them anyway knowing what it would cost him. What does that tell you?"

She looked down. "I don't know exactly."

"When a man like Giovanni gives up everything for his children, it says something loud and clear. I think you know what it is. In the morning I'll fly you to Ravello so you can find out for yourself."

She couldn't credit that he was saying all this to her. "You don't think I'm terrible?"

Rini got up from his desk. "For loving a good man?"

Valentina blinked in surprise. "You think that about him?"

"I do."

"He's more than good," she cried softly. "He's the most wonderful man alive."

CHAPTER EIGHT

GIOVANNI AWAKENED TO the sound of a text. Morning had come. Ric was awake, lying there in his carry-cot on the floor in his life preserver. Giovanni picked him up to hug him and change his diaper. After that he reached for the phone.

He'd ignored all his calls and texts for the past eighteen hours. Unless it was Stanzie with some emergency, he had no desire to communicate with anyone. He looked at the screen and discovered it was Paolo.

Giovanni—come home immediately. This concerns Vito.

Just the mention of Vito caused an adrenaline rush. He texted back. What's wrong? While he waited for an answer, he got dressed in jeans and a T-shirt. When there was no response, he texted him again. I'm coming.

More anxious than ever, he freshened up, then took Ric on deck and fed him a bottle. Still no response on his phone. Why hadn't Valentina phoned him about Vito? He frantically searched all the calls and saw that she *had* phoned him late last night.

He'd made another mistake by not checking the calls until now so he could call her back. Maybe she'd taken Vito to the hospital. The thought of anything being seriously wrong with the baby made him break out in a cold sweat. He'd anchored the cruiser off Amalfi. The sea was calm. If he opened the throttle full strength, he could make it back to Ravello within a half hour.

The normally short trip seemed to take hours. Relief swamped him when he reached Ravello and slowed to a wakeless speed to pull alongside the dock. He tied the rope, then removed Ric's life preserver and lifted him to the dock in his carry-cot.

He grabbed the diaper bag. "Come on, buddy. We're going to find out what's wrong with your brother."

The drive to the villa only took a few minutes. He sprang from the car with Ric and hurried into the sunroom. "Paolo? Stanzie?"

Where in the hell were they? He raced through the house with Ric. Maybe they were in their suite at the back of the villa, but he didn't find them. Since he knew they wouldn't leave, he decided they were upstairs for some reason and couldn't hear him.

He carried Ric with him and headed for the nursery. Before he reached the entrance, he heard the music box playing from the mobile. What on earth? He rushed in the room and caught sight of Vito in the other crib.

Giovanni set down the carry-cot and walked over to him. The baby saw him and started wiggling with excitement. "Vito—you don't look sick, thank heaven."

"He's not sick, but he *is* missing you."

Valentina's voice. He wheeled around. When he

saw her, he thought he was hallucinating. "You're here—"

She smiled. "Yes. Aren't you going to pick him up? He's been waiting for you. I'm dying to hold Ric." She leaned down and pulled him into her arms. "I've missed you so much. Did you have a fun overnight with your *papà* on the cruiser?*"*

While she covered him in kisses, Giovanni stood there dazed. "Where are Stanzie and Paolo?"

"I gave them the rest of the day and the night off and take full responsibility if that upsets you."

"No. They work too hard." He rocked Vito in his arms, but his eyes were a piercing black as they centered on her. "How did you persuade Paolo to text me with a message you knew would turn me inside out?"

"I honestly have no idea what he said."

"He indicated something was wrong with Vito."

"I'm sorry. When I asked them to help me find you, he said he knew how to do it."

"Paolo knows me well."

"I was cooking dinner last night when I heard about your resignation on the news. I almost fainted from shock *and* pain. To walk away from your life's work and have it go out over the news—Giovanni—when you change your mind and want to go back, the media will turn it into a circus."

The features of his handsome face were masklike. "I'll never change my mind."

She took a deep breath. "You say that now, but—"

"But nothing. While Tatania was carrying our child and refused to let me share in any of it with her, I had months to do a lot of soul-searching about my life and the things I've done wrong."

She shook her blond head. "What wrong things?"

"For starters, I should never have married her. That decision has ruined her life, but I can't do anything about that now."

Valentina moved closer to him while she held Ric. "She didn't have to marry you."

"Yes, she did. Her father had a powerful hold on her."

"Just as the love for your father persuaded you to act in a way that would make him happy."

His mouth tightened. "Our divorce has damaged her. You talk about *your* guilt, but you have no idea of mine."

"Didn't she ask for the divorce?"

"Yes."

"Did you ever have a down-to-the-bare-bones talk with her before you separated for good?"

"No. She wouldn't allow it."

"Maybe you need to find a way to reach her so you can both talk it out."

"I don't want her back, Valentina."

"I believe you, but maybe she's sorry she shut you out of her life so abruptly and wants a chance to explain why she didn't want to see the baby. Have you thought she might be too nervous to approach you after the way she cut you off?"

His head reared back. "Is that why you're here? To convince me to talk to her?" He sounded incredulous.

"Of course not," she whispered. "It hurt me that you made a decision about stepping down without telling me. I thought we were partners."

"Did it occur to you it hurt me that you left for Naples within an hour of my mother-in-law's visit?

I didn't have the luxury of knowing what she'd said to you."

His remark squeezed her heart. "After the wonderful way you've treated me since we met, that was a mistake I freely confess I made. I shouldn't have gone anywhere until you knew everything. If I'd stayed put until you came home, we could have talked everything out and it might have prevented you from making a decision that is going to have a lifetime effect on you. Please forgive me."

His black brows furrowed. "Contrary to what you're thinking, my plan to step down had its genesis the moment Tatania told me she was pregnant. Long before I knew you existed, I realized that becoming a father trumped every honor the world could bestow on me. I'd been an absent husband, but I vowed I'd turn my life around and be the best father possible. Up to the end of her pregnancy, I begged her to reconsider visitation."

Valentina prayed that what she was going to say wouldn't spell the end of their relationship. "As I said, maybe you need to make one more effort. Almost six weeks have gone by. Tatania has to be feeling much better physically. I know I am. Take Ric with you. I'm sure Violeta could arrange it. She loves you and Ric. It's possible Tatania will have a change of heart and want to see your baby."

"You're serious." Again he looked astounded.

"Yes. Because of your defining moment when you found out you were going to be a father, it's possible Tatania will have that same kind of moment when she sees his precious little face. As the years go by he's going to be curious about his own mother. He'll crave her love. Think how wonderful it would be if she changes her mind and wants to be a full-time mother to him now. It could be the making of her life and Ric's.

"If she turns down the opportunity, then you would have done everything you could and you'll be able to answer Ric honestly that you tried to do all in your power to unite mother and son."

Giovanni's gaze searched hers for at least a minute. "When did you get to be so courageous and wise?"

"When I looked in Ric's face for the first time. I didn't know he wasn't my son, but like you, I felt an overwhelming feeling of love that transcended anything else in my life. When I saw Vito for the first time, that joy doubled."

He kissed her son. "I'll think about what you've said."

"Good. Now, why don't we take the children downstairs and I'll serve us lunch. Last night I made a big casserole of cannelloni and brought it with me. Afterward we'll put the children down for their naps and talk."

"How long are you here for?"

"For as long as it takes."

His heart raced. "I thought you were moving into your apartment on Friday."

"That's still a possibility."

"But?"

"I don't know the answer yet. I'm still on vacation and I was thinking how fun it would be to drive to Laurito in your car tonight. We all want to see the town where your family came from and have dinner there. Maybe stay overnight in one of the hotels?"

"You'd better be careful what you're saying to me. I'm holding you to all of it."

"That's a relief," she tossed over her shoulder.

Valentina, Valentina... "It's high summer season. We may not be able to get separate bedrooms."

"The boys took a vote and don't see that as a problem. We're one big happy family, right?"

Excitement swept through him. If she was saying what he thought she was saying...

"As long as we're going to Laurito, I suggest we get started after lunch. There's a quaint hotel at the foot of Bulgheria Mountain in Cilento National Park. You'll love the green setting. We'll get a room right by the pool and swim tonight under the stars. How does that sound?"

"Divine."

After he took Vito downstairs to the sunroom, they put the children in the playpen. "I'm going to take a quick shower."

"Lunch will be ready when you come back down."

He paused in the doorway. "If I didn't tell you earlier, it's good to see you. Does your brother know?"

"Rini knows everything," came the cryptic response. She flashed him an intense blue glance. "It's good to see you, too. When Paolo told me he'd sent for you, I didn't know how long it would take before you came. I feared maybe you'd gone far away and wouldn't respond."

"*Vito* was the magic word to bring me back in a hurry."

"Of course. That boy changed your life and mine."

Streams of unspoken thoughts and memories passed between them before he raced up the stairs two at a time. Too much more of this emotional roller-coaster ride and his heart might not be able to stand it.

Before he headed for the bathroom, he reached for his phone and made reservations at the hotel he had in mind. A few rooms bordered the pool. The concierge said he'd arrange one for their esteemed guest Signor Laurito. Normally Giovanni didn't use his name to get what he wanted. Today was an exception because he wanted this night to be perfect.

He had one more phone call to make. Violeta picked up on the third ring. "Giovanni? Oh, how good to hear your voice. I've been out of my mind with worry over you."

"I'm sorry I haven't gotten back to you before now. How would you like to do me a favor?"

"Anything!"

"I need to sit down with Tatania and have a long talk. I'll be bringing Ric with me. Do you suppose you could arrange it without anyone else knowing? Not even Salvatore?"

After a hesitation, she said, "I'll do it. Does this mean—?"

"Violeta—" he interrupted her. "Though the divorce was final, I loved Tatania in my own way, but not the way she truly needs to be loved. I want her to marry a man who thinks the sun rises and sets with her.

"If she'll allow it, she has a son who will see her as his whole world. He needs her and she needs him. Ric already loves you."

All he heard was her weeping. Finally she said, "I'll call you tomorrow."

"Bless you, Violeta."

He hung up the phone.
And bless you, Valentina.

Valentina's breath caught when she spotted the fabulous white monastery turned resort in the middle of an enormous forest. "How big is it?"

"The forest stretches sixty thousand square meters."

"So huge! The thick pines are such a dark green, I've never seen anything like this."

"With the night falling so fast, they look almost black."

"I love it!"

With the darkening sky she could barely make out the sign as they came to the town before entering the forest.

Welcome to Laurito, with its population of a thousand souls. Its namesake is the Italian-Greek monastery established in the tenth century.

"These mountain villages are so charming, Giovanni. But you've seen all this so many times before I must drive you crazy while I gush over everything. I'm as bad as a nomad in the desert who breaks into song at the sight of an oasis."

He burst into laughter, the kind she loved to hear because it told her he sounded happy. "How do you know so much about nomadic life?"

"One of my ancient history classes on Egypt suggested reading a true account of a nomad around 600 BC."

"Did it make you long for the desert?"

She smiled. "No. Their hardships sent shudders

through me. Give me tonight's mouthwatering fish pasta dinner and the lush vegetation of these mountains any day." They drove on through the greenery until they came to the cluster of white buildings.

"We've arrived."

"I love it already."

Valentina waited in the car with the babies while he went inside to register. In another few minutes they went around to the end. When he let them inside their room with two queen-size beds, she noticed that two cribs had been set up in the corner. Giovanni had said this was a family-friendly resort.

The large window looked out on the swimming pool shaped like a giant pear. It was so close all you had to do was step out the door and dive in. Lights illuminated the water that shimmered pure aqua in the night air. A few people were out in it having fun.

She turned to Giovanni. "How did you know I've been longing for this?"

"You're not the only one."

Together they fed the babies and put them down for the night in the cribs. "Do you ever wonder if they communicate when we're not around?"

He grinned at her. "No doubt they can hear each other breathing."

"I bet it's comforting."

Giovanni kissed both of them. "I'm going to get changed and meet you in the pool."

It only took him a few seconds. After he left, she changed into her new aqua bikini. Before anything else she walked over to the cribs. Their darlings were asleep. Confident that it would be all right to leave them for a little while, she slipped out the door and stepped down into the water. Giovanni was already doing laps. With the water being the perfect temperature, she swam to the other end.

While she trod water, Giovanni's dark head emerged in front of her. "This *is* a surprise." His deep voice sent spirals of desire through her.

She loved it when he was in a playful mood. "I hoped I'd find you here."

"Did you indeed. Come here to me, darling."

No sooner had he spoken than Giovanni reached for her and drew her to the edge of the pool. He lifted her face to him. "Be very sure this is what you want."

"I want you to make love to me, but I haven't been to my doctor yet. Still, that doesn't prevent me from wanting to be close to you right now. If you don't touch me, then I'm afraid I'll be the one to die."

She heard a moan before he lowered his mouth to hers. Valentina had been wanting this for too long. She welcomed his kiss with a hunger she couldn't appease no matter how hard she tried. To be in his arms and set on fire by his passion had turned her into someone she didn't know. Every touch from him thrilled her to the marrow of her bones.

He kissed her face and neck. She did the same to him. It was as if they couldn't get enough of each other and were trying to love each other all at once. "I've been wanting to do this for weeks," he confessed.

"Then you have some idea of what it has been like for me. Whenever you've kissed the boys, I've wanted it to be my turn."

"When I look in Vito's face, I see yours. I smell your fragrance on him. From the beginning I've suffered agony because I didn't dare make a wrong move with you. I need you, Valentina."

"Don't you know that's how I feel, too?"

His kisses grew longer, deeper. She never wanted this ecstasy to end. Then she heard a groan and he tore his lips from hers. He was literally trembling. "I don't want to do this out here where anyone can see us. Let's go inside."

She'd forgotten about the other people in the pool. Giovanni had become her entire world. With her arms around his neck, he swam them to the other end and carried her up the steps into their hotel room.

Once inside the door, he backed it closed and set her down. They didn't want to let each other go. He crushed her in his arms until there was no air between them. Those rock-hard legs trapped hers. His hands smoothed over her back and hips, igniting the woman in her. This man was everything she'd ever wanted and so much more, she was lost in a frenzy of longing that had burst out of control.

At first she thought she'd imagined the ringing of his cell phone. But when Ric started to fuss, she realized someone was trying to reach Giovanni.

He was slow to respond. "Who would be calling me this time of night?"

"You'd better answer it before both babies are awake."

Giovanni gave her a swift kiss before reaching for the phone he'd left at the bedside table. When he sat down on the side of one of the beds to talk, she knew this was important. Taking advantage of the moment, she reached for her robe and hurried into the bathroom for a shower.

Not liking the smell of chlorine in her hair, she washed it and wrapped it in a towel. Once she'd thrown on her robe, she washed out her bikini, then walked into the other room. Something of importance was going on. He was still on the phone.

She wandered over to Ric's crib. He'd settled back down, thank goodness. Vito hadn't been disturbed. The sound of Giovanni's phone was familiar to the baby. That had to be the reason he'd stirred.

Valentina sat in one of the chairs and dried her hair while she waited. Her watch said ten after eleven. He kept his voice low so she couldn't make out actual words. Finally he hung up and put the phone back on the table. His head turned to her.

"Give me a minute to shower, and I'll tell you what that was about." Reality had intruded on the rapture they'd shared. It couldn't be recaptured. Not tonight. She suffered real pain. The only thing to do was counteract it.

After he disappeared, she reached for her brush to put her hair in some semblance of order and got in bed. Giovanni came back in the room a few minutes later wearing his robe. He sat on the side of her bed and reached for her hands.

"Was that your father?"

"No. Violeta. She wanted me to know that Tatania has her six-week checkup with the doctor at Positano hospital in the morning at nine thirty. She'll be driving her. Violeta believes that if I'm there with Ric waiting for her in Violeta's car when she comes out of his office, it will be the perfect time and place to talk. She'll leave the door unlocked so I can get in. Anywhere else and she might refuse to see me."

"Do you think it might be too big of a jolt for her?"

"I said the same thing to Violeta. But her mother's instinct tells her that Tatania needs a jolt to break her out of this funk she's been in. As she pointed out, her daughter has reached rock bottom. If seeing me and the baby doesn't do anything but make her angry, then what does it matter? Tatania is already angry."

Valentina lowered her head. "A mother's instinct is a powerful thing as we both know. In order for you to get there on time we need to leave here early."

He nodded. "I'll drive us back to Ravello and send for the helicopter to take me and Ric to Positano. You must realize this wasn't the way I expected our overnight to go."

She squeezed his hands tighter. "If you want to know the truth, I'm glad she phoned. You need to do this, the sooner the better. Not only for our sake, but for Ric's. Tatania has lost time bonding with him. Of course it's not too late, but I believe Violeta is right. Shock might be the one method to wake her up."

Valentina heard a sharp intake of breath before he lay down on the bed and pulled her into his arms. "What would I do without you?"

"I'm not planning on your finding out," she whispered against his cheek.

"Will you let me hold you tonight?"

"After we held each other on the cruiser, do you have to ask?"

"Yes. What other woman in the world has your ability to love and be so decent at a critical time like this? I want to deserve you."

"Oh, Giovanni." She nestled closer against him.

"You and Vito will be at the house waiting for me

when I get back? No more letting anyone else influence you to leave early?"

She burrowed against him. "No one has the power to wrench me from your side." For the rest of the night she held this incredible man in her arms.

At six in the morning after feeding the babies, they left Laurito for Ravello. Giovanni was deep in thought. Paolo and Stanzie were there to greet them when they walked across the patio to the sunroom.

Giovanni hugged them before going upstairs to get ready. Valentina put the babies on the floor and kissed their tummies until their laughter filled the room. While she played with them, she heard the helicopter. He came back to the sunroom. After kissing the boys, he kissed her fiercely.

"I'll be here when you get back," she spoke before he could say it. Their eyes clung before he put Ric in his carry-cot and wheeled away with him.

Stanzie came in after he'd gone. Her eyes looked anxious. "Is everything all right?"

Valentina sat back on her heels. "It will be, no matter what happens." In the next breath she told Stanzie where he was going and why.

The other woman sank down in a chair. "I wish he would have done this a long time ago. This is *your* doing."

"Don't give me any credit. He wanted to meet with her, but was waiting until Violeta was on board."

"It's a good woman who puts her child's happiness first."

"I couldn't agree more. Please thank Paolo for getting Giovanni back here so fast. His method worked.

Except something tells me *you* were the one who came up with the idea."

Stanzie smiled without saying anything.

The day wore on. First lunch, then dinner. By bedtime Valentina realized something important was going on, otherwise he would have been home hours ago. Not until she climbed into bed did she hear the sound on her phone. He'd sent her a text.

Will be home tomorrow. Kiss Vito for me.

Valentina suffered another sleepless night, tossing, turning and worrying. The next morning she looked out the window and discovered a cloudy sky overhead. Hoping it wasn't a bad omen, she went to the nursery to take care of Vito.

By afternoon Giovanni still hadn't arrived. Unable to stand it any longer, she put the baby in the stroller and took a long walk beyond the villa to work off her nervous energy. He slept on and off.

Maybe Giovanni had been in talks with his father about his future with the company. Many thoughts ran through her mind until she was a nervous wreck. Near five o'clock she started back to the villa beneath a darkening sky. On the way, she heard the sound of rotors in the distance. Her heart jumped to look up and see the helicopter overhead.

Giovanni—

She started running as she pushed the stroller along the road. Valentina had walked farther than she'd realized and couldn't believe how long it was taking her to get back. As she turned onto his private road leading up to the side of the villa, she saw Giovanni running toward her. If there weren't good news, he wouldn't be flying down the road to reach her.

The second she could see his eyes, she parked the stroller and ran toward him. He swung her off her feet and clutched her to him without realizing his strength. One look at his face and she saw a different man.

"Violeta's plan worked!"

"I can see that," she answered breathlessly. "Where's Ric?"

"With his mother. She's going to keep him for a few days."

Those words told her everything she needed to know. The guilt he'd been suffering for so long was gone. In its place was a man at peace. "Oh, Giovanni. I'm so happy for you."

"You have no idea."

Yes, she did.

"Violeta drove us to their villa. We talked all day and all night discussing everything, including how to handle visitation. Tatania was like a different person. When she looked at Ric for the first time, I saw a light enter her eyes. It was as if she'd come alive."

"So have you." She cupped the side of his hard jaw with her hand.

He kissed it. "Come on. Let's take Vito and spend the night on the cruiser. I need to tell you everything."

CHAPTER NINE

THE FIRST RAIN of the season hit after Giovanni anchored off Furore, the little mountain village between Ravello and Positano. He'd wanted to show Valentina the fjord where a cluster of old fishermen's houses clung to the side of the rocky gorge. But she wasn't disappointed when the weather forced them to stay below with Vito until the storm passed over. She loved the cozy feeling of having the man and son she loved so close to her.

After eating dinner in the galley, they moved into one of the cabins and put the baby in his carry-cot in the other cabin. She sat on the side of the bed. Giovanni grabbed a pillow and stretched out on the floor.

"I'd come up there with you, but if I do that, I won't be able to talk and we have a lot to discuss. What do you want to know first?"

At last she was going to have answers. "Was Tatania's father there?"

"He walked in the villa after flying in and discovered the four of us in the living room. Ric was cuddled in her arms. Before I could say anything, Tatania told her father that she and I had said our goodbyes, but she'd decided to be a mother to her son. I didn't know she had it in her to stand up to him. Naturally he was nonplussed and walked over to look at the baby."

"That must have been an amazing moment."

"Oh, it was. Tatania had changed before our very eyes. We're going to set up times during the week and every other weekend to parent him. I told her I needed to discuss the schedule with you, then I'd get back to her."

She frowned. "Me—"

"We're partners, Valentina. Everything I do, I plan to run through you first."

Partners? That word again. *Don't panic yet, Valentina.* "Did her father talk to you about your decision to step down?"

"No. His pride won't allow it, but I had a long conversation with my father earlier today. He's aware I want to run the marketing division and is probing the members of the board to see where they would stand."

"That's a beginning."

"Yes. These things take time."

"How did Ric behave with her?"

"As I expected, he started to cry, but then Violeta was there and talked to him. Soon Tatania broke in. The sweetness in her voice touched my heart and soon touched Ric's. He stopped crying and let her feed him a bottle."

Giovanni leaned forward and put his hands on either side of her legs. "It's going to be all right. Thanks to you, Ric is going to grow up with his birth mother, who loves him. If you could have seen her with him... The baby has changed her."

She nodded. "They've changed all of us. That's what babies do."

He was working up to something. "Valentina Montanari, I'm so deeply in love with you, I can't wait any longer for this. While I'm on my knees, will you tell me the thing I want most to hear in this world?"

"That I want to be your wife? As if you didn't know." Suddenly she got down on the floor and showed Giovanni how she felt about him with a kiss that sent him reeling. He rolled her over so he could look down at the beautiful vision before him.

"Right now I could eat you alive and want to get married right away. Saturday if we can work it."

"Saturday?" she half gasped. "Don't you think we need to give Tatania time to deal with the fact that I'm going to be Ric's stepmother? She's not going to like sharing your baby with me."

"Valentina—she knows we've been living together. Violeta has learned to like you very much. She's seen the loving care you've given Ric. Trust me, it's not going to be a problem."

A shadow crossed over her face. "There are other considerations."

"Name one."

"Maybe we shouldn't get married this fast."

"Why not?"

She searched his eyes. "You haven't even been divorced a year."

"It doesn't matter. No man knows our history except you and me. You know the truth of everything. That's all that's important. We fell madly in love that first day. I need you with me mentally, emotionally and physically as soon as possible."

"I want that, too. You know I do."

"If any couple ever needed a honeymoon, we do."
He kissed her again, long and hard.

When next she came up for air she said, "Don't you
know how much I want that, too? But I haven't been
for my six-week checkup yet. My doctor warned me
to refrain from intimacy until he examines me."

"How soon is your appointment?"

"Next Monday."

"I guess I can wait that long. I want your doctor's
seal of approval, too. After we leave his office, we'll
get married."

"But how can we do it so fast? Don't we have to
wait the customary three weeks?"

"I have connections that solve the problem. But I'm
being selfish. If you want a big wedding that takes
weeks and maybe months to plan, we'll do it."

She shook her head. "I think we're both way beyond that."

"Grazie a Dio."

A soft laugh escaped her lips he couldn't stop tast-
ing.

"Where do you want to be married, *adorata*?"
After he'd asked the question, he kissed her mouth
again and again. She'd become his addiction. When
she didn't answer right away he said, "I'm going too
fast for you, aren't I?"

"No." She pressed her forehead against his. "It's
what I love about you. No grass grows under your feet.
Is there a church that has special meaning for you?"

"This wedding isn't about me."

"There's a church in Naples near my parents' villa

the family has attended, but I don't have a favorite place. Something tells me you do."

"If the truth be known, I like the countryside church outside Laurito."

"The little white one hidden in the trees?"

"You remember?" He kissed her neck.

"Of course. I found it charming."

"For years I've been friends with the older priest who presides there."

She smiled at him. "Somehow that doesn't surprise me. Your ancestors came from that area."

"What would you think if he marries us in a private ceremony? Afterward we'll stay at the quaint *locanda* nearby for the night and drive home to the children the next day. Maybe two weeks after that we'll throw a party at the villa for our families to announce our marriage. When we're sure the babies can handle it, we'll take an extended honeymoon."

She wound her arms around his neck. "You know exactly what I think. I'm fathoms deep in love with you, Giovanni. My heart and soul are yours, but you've been aware of that from the first. It's embarrassing how transparent I've been."

"Embarrassing?"

"That first night when we took the babies home, I couldn't wait for morning. If you hadn't phoned, I would have phoned you. I thought to myself, 'Signor Laurito will make this all right.' Even then, I knew you had the answers for my whole life."

"I had a revelation that you were the answer to mine," he said in a half-savage tone. "Do you have any idea how long I've been waiting to hear those words?"

He reached in his pocket and pulled out a blue diamond ring mounted in white gold. Finding her left hand, he found her ring finger and slid it home. "I had this made for you two weeks ago, but needed to find the right time to give it to you."

Valentina held it up. "It's beautiful. Oh, my love—" She pressed a hot kiss to his mouth. "*You're* such a beautiful man, I can't stop looking at you."

Giovanni chuckled. "Don't let anyone else hear you say that."

"Any woman who hears me will be thinking the same thing."

He plundered her mouth once more. "We've got things to do. If you want to go to school, you know I'm behind you on that. Whatever happens we're going to do everything together. You'll have to cancel on your apartment."

"I can't think about anything right now. You've just proposed and I'm the happiest woman who ever lived."

She didn't know the half of it. "Do you think your father is still awake? I'd like to phone him and tell him how much I love his angelic daughter."

"He has trouble sleeping. I'm sure a phone call from you will bring him a lot of peace. He's been worried about me. While you do that, I'll phone Rini. I want him to know our plans. He won't say anything."

"Let's do it in a minute. I need another kiss to let me know I'm not dreaming all this."

"Papà?" It was Sunday night. Giovanni had been waiting at the villa for the important call from him. Valentina was downstairs playing with the babies on the patio. "What's the verdict?"

"Not good, *figlio mio*."

"That means Salvatore has garnered enough votes to keep me out."

"Afraid so. He's outraged that you're living with Valentina."

"So being a grandfather hasn't softened him up. For Tatania's sake, that's too bad."

"My concern is for you. What are you going to do?"

"I have something in mind I've been considering for months."

"What is that?"

"I'm going to branch out on my own, but it's a subject for another day. I'll be in touch with you again soon. Give Mamma my love."

"Giovanni—wait!"

"I have to go. *Buonanotte*, Papà."

He left the bedroom and went downstairs to the kitchen. Stanzie and Paolo were eating dinner. "I'm glad you're both here. We need to talk." He sat down at the table with them.

Stanzie's eyes lit up. "Is this what I think? I saw the diamond on her finger. It's the same blue as her eyes."

Giovanni was warmed by her excitement. "The closest match I could find. After her doctor appointment tomorrow, we'll be getting married at the church in Laurito in an evening ceremony."

A gasp of excitement came from Stanzie.

"We don't want to wait. Except for her father and brother, no one else knows but you. I've made all the arrangements. It'll be a totally private ceremony with my old friend Father Mancini officiating.

"Would you two mind tending the *bambini* overnight tomorrow night? We'll be staying at the inn near the church and come home on Tuesday. We don't plan to take a long honeymoon for several months."

"Of course we'll watch over them. We love them!" she cried.

"Thank you, Stanzie. After we get back I plan to talk business with the two of you."

Paolo stopped chewing. "What do you mean?"

"I'm not working for the family business anymore. That association has come to an end. With hindsight I can see it's a good thing to get away from all the nepotism that ties hands. A while back I purchased office space in Naples as an investment for the future. I'm glad I did because I plan to start my own advertising agency. I'd hoped your uncle would sell his business to me so you could run it, but that hope has died."

"You would have done that for us?" Paolo looked incredulous.

"Of course, but no matter. My attorney is drawing up the paperwork now for a new business. I'm calling it PSG Advertising. The letters stand for Paolo, Stanzie and yours truly. You'll be part owners with me in charge of putting all your great innovative ideas to work while I drum up business and bring in new accounts. I already have half a dozen possible clients in mind who have no association with my family's business."

The two of them sat there speechless while their eyes misted over.

"Though we'll keep your apartment here at the villa for you whenever you come to visit, I'm aware you'd love to get back to your house in Naples. All our lives have been on hold for too long.

"I want to be a full-time father and husband. Owning a business like this will require hard work, but it won't force me to give up my soul. My personal life is the most important thing to me.

"Valentina will go back to school for her degree. After she graduates, she'll find work as an engineer, but she'll make sure it doesn't interfere with being a wife and helping me raise our boys."

"Who will help you here?"

"We'll find someone from the village to come in periodically, but Valentina insists she wants to be in charge of the house. She and I are a team."

"We are," Valentina piped up. She'd entered the kitchen. Giovanni had no idea how long she'd been listening. She walked over and put her arms around his neck from behind. "You two should know you're the role model for us. Last night we talked about how amazing you are. A husband and wife who love to be together and love what they do is a rare phenomenon."

Giovanni kissed her arm. "They've agreed to watch the children until we get back on Tuesday."

"Congratulations on your coming marriage," Paolo murmured. "When Giovanni first brought you here, Stanzie and I agreed you were the angel who'd come to bless his life."

"It's the other way around. He's my prince. No woman in the world is as lucky as I am. The baby switch threw us into the darkest abyss. Only a loving man and father was able to perform the miracle that brought us into the light."

"Ready, Valentina?"

"Almost." The next time Giovanni caught sight of her, he'd see a woman who burned to become his bride.

She put on the knee-length ivory wedding dress. The color matched her strappy high heels. The slim-form chiffon swished around her legs. Three-quarter-length sleeves and the modest V-neck bodice of illusion lace gave it an ethereal look.

After giving her hair a quick brushing, she applied softshell-pink lipstick to her lips. When she'd gone shopping for a dress, she'd found some gold earrings with blue jewels. The last thing she did was pin on the corsage of creamy roses he'd left in her room.

"Hurry," he called to her.

With heart pounding she walked out in the hall and started for the staircase. The second he saw her coming down, he took several pictures with his phone before putting it back in his pocket.

Her husband-to-be looked magnificent in an expensive light gray suit. Against the white of his shirt he wore a striped silver-and-gray tie. His black eyes smoldered as she walked up to him. "I didn't know anyone so beautiful could be real," he whispered in an unsteady voice. Heat filled her cheeks.

He was so gorgeous she ached inside for him. "I can't wait to be married to you."

Giovanni sucked in his breath. "I can tell you just put on lipstick, but I have to kiss you." She was already there, leaning toward him. With a fierce hunger, she welcomed his compelling mouth.

Both of them moaned with need before he helped her into the helicopter. The heavenly scent filled the interior. For the rest of the short trip to Laurito she floated on a cloud of euphoria. He gripped her hand. "Did you say goodbye to the children?"

"I didn't dare."

He kissed her palm. "Neither did I. We have to hope they behave."

A limo was waiting for them when they reached Laurito. Giovanni directed the driver to the church and instructed him to wait until they came back out.

"Ready?" he whispered, hugging her to his side.

Breathing in the marvelous scent of him, she kissed his smooth, shaven cheek before they entered the doors. No one was inside except the priest and two church workers there to witness the marriage. They walked down the aisle to the altar. The interior of the small church with its frescoes of the saints lent a spiritual essence she would always remember.

"Father Mancini?" Giovanni shook his hand and introduced Valentina.

The older priest smiled at her. "I have known Giovanni Laurito for a long time. You have made him very happy, Signorina Montanari. He says he's in a great hurry to marry you."

"We're both impatient, Father."

"Then we won't waste any more time. Giovanni? Take Valentina by the hand and repeat after me."

Thus began the sacred ceremony. When Giovanni pledged his love and devotion to her, the words wound straight to her heart. She professed her love and devotion to him with the same solemnity. "I now pronounce you man and wife, in the name of the Father, the Son and the Holy Spirit. Amen."

He made the sign of the cross. "Do you have rings to exchange?"

"We do," Giovanni spoke up and slid the matching gold band next to her blue diamond.

Valentina took the gold ring she'd bought him from

off the finger of her right hand and slid it onto the ring finger of his left hand.

The priest nodded. "You may now kiss your bride."

"At last," Giovanni murmured before his mouth descended on hers. The first kiss from her husband thrilled her so much her legs buckled. He had to prop her up.

Father Mancini cleared his voice, reminding her they had an audience. Again she blushed before Giovanni finally let her go. "I'll follow you to the vestibule where you'll sign your name to the marriage document."

Giovanni put her arm through his and they made the trip to the entrance. Normally the church would have been overflowing with guests. Their ceremony was private, unique, and she loved every moment of it.

The priest stood by while they signed their names. Then he added his signature and dated it before rolling it up and handing it to her. "Come and worship often."

"We will, Father," Valentina assured him.

"I'm adopting her son, Vitielli. As soon as it becomes legal, we'll be coming to you to baptize him."

"Ah. And what about your son, Giovanni?"

"His mother will make the arrangements with her priest in Positano."

"Excellent."

Valentina shook his hand. "Thank you, Father."

Giovanni put his arm around her waist and ushered her out of the church to the limo. He gave the chauffeur directions to the inn where they were staying. She was relieved the drive only took about two minutes. Valentina couldn't wait to be alone with him.

They carried their overnight bags into the reception

area of the charming getaway tucked in the greenery. After obtaining the key, Giovanna cupped her arm and they walked down the hall to their room. The place was a restored farmhouse, completely enchanting. When the door shut, enclosing them, she felt that they'd entered a world from another century.

"Come here, Signora Laurito. You don't know how long I've been waiting to say that." She moved toward him. He unpinned the flowers from her dress and put them on the dresser. "There's something we haven't done yet. It's time I found out what it's like to dance with my wife. I want to feel every part of you."

He drew her into his arms. For a little while they moved in place. He kissed her neck, her ears and throat. When his lips brushed across her cheeks and temples, she couldn't stop trembling. All the time he was driving her crazy as he kissed her everywhere except her mouth, he was undoing the buttons on the back of her dress.

Her hands slid up the shirt covering his well-defined chest to undo his tie. "Kiss me, *caro*."

Their wedding night began with a giving and taking that took Valentina to a place she'd never known existed. She couldn't recall how one minute they were standing, and the next he'd taken her to bed. From the moment he touched her, desire licked through her body like flames that grew hotter and more intense.

"I love you, Giovanni. No one should love someone the way I love you."

"I love the things you say to me and the way you say them. Give me your mouth again, *innamorata*. I can't live without it."

Throughout the rest of the night they loved with

abandon. The pleasure they gave each other was exquisite beyond belief. This was her husband thrilling her. She felt sorry for every woman who would never know what it was like to be loved by him.

"Don't ever stop loving me, Valentina," he begged. "Don't ever let me go or I'd die in agony."

"Giovanni, darling—just try to get away from me and you'll see what happens. You've done something to me. I'm on fire for you. Love me again."

"I intend to. Over and over."

When morning came she awakened first, shocked to see how late it was. Her gorgeous husband lay on his side with his arm around her hip. Even in sleep he was possessive of her in a way that touched her heart.

For a while she studied his face, the way his black lashes fanned against his olive skin. The black hair she'd disheveled gave him a dashing look. He needed a shave. She rubbed her cheek against his jaw to be closer to him.

He must have felt her because his eyes opened. His black gaze enveloped her before he pulled her on top of him. "I was dreaming about you."

One corner of her mouth lifted. "While you were dreaming, I was watching you. Do you realize something amazing happened last night?"

"After what went on for hours and hours, what kind of a question is that?" Giovanni kissed a favorite spot.

"We didn't eat dinner. I've never known you not to be hungry before."

"You've cast a spell over me." His eyes burned like dark fires. "I have a different kind of hunger." He started loving her again until she felt immortal.

When next she came awake, she found her husband looking at her.

"You're incredibly beautiful, do you know that?"

"I hope you'll always be able to say that to me. I love you, Giovanni. I'm so happy to be your wife I can hardly believe we're married. I loved our wedding."

"It was perfect."

"I don't want any of this to end. How soon do we have to leave here?"

"How about never."

"I hope the babies are behaving."

"Do you miss them?"

"I'll be honest and tell you I didn't think about them until just now." She heard a knock on the door. "Who do you suppose that is?"

"I ordered breakfast." He reached for his robe and put it on to answer the door. In a few minutes he brought the tray to their bed and they ate with relish.

"Valentina? There's one subject we haven't talked about."

"What's that?"

"Actually it's all we've talked about since we met, but not in the context I'm thinking of now."

"You mean about us having our own baby?"

He nodded. "You read me like a book."

"It's been on my mind, too. Yesterday Dr. Pedrotti said he hoped he wouldn't need to see me unless I was pregnant again."

"Do you think it's possible that one day you'll want to have our baby?"

Valentina moved the tray to the floor before pushing him back against the pillows. "It hurts that you would ask that question in such a defeated tone of voice. You might as well have asked me if I thought the world was going to end tomorrow.

"Of course I want a baby with you! I know you missed out on the thrill of going through Tatania's pregnancy with her. I missed out on having a husband around while I was carrying Vito."

"But I know you want to work as an engineer one day. For you to have another baby requires a lot of sacrifice."

"Darling—I want a baby with you more than anything in the world. I was hoping we could try for one when the boys start to walk."

His eyes lit up. "You mean it? You're not just saying it to humor me?"

She kissed him for a long time. "Wouldn't it be fantastic to have a girl?"

"Fantastic," he murmured. "She'll have golden locks."

"Whatever you say, Giovanni. I know you think bigger and faster than anyone else. But for now let's concentrate on us. The only thing I want to do is make love to my husband. I've been dreaming about it for weeks."

"So have I." His smile looked wicked. "I'm waiting."

CHAPTER TEN

Two weeks later

As Valentina stepped out of the shower and wrapped a towel around herself, Giovanni walked inside the bathroom. His eyes blazed like hot black fires, scorching her everywhere he looked. "With guests arriving in the next half hour, you shouldn't be this ravishing or I'll have a heart attack and there'll be no groom for our families to congratulate on our recent wedding."

She flashed him a mysterious smile. "Should I have locked the door?"

He caught her in his arms. "It wouldn't do any good. I'd knock it down to get to you." So saying, he kissed her mouth until she felt faint with longing. When he lifted his head, he said, "I can tell you're trembling. Something tells me you're a little nervous."

Valentina lifted anxious eyes to him. "I just want everything to go all right."

Giovanni kissed the end of her well-shaped nose. "As long as you and I are all right, nothing else matters. Besides, we hold the trump card."

"What do you mean?"

"The children."

Her lips relaxed into a smile. "Of course. They look so darling in their little tuxedo outfits I can hardly stand it."

"Why don't we hold our sons so that when everyone arrives, the children will be the first thing they see and any other thoughts they had about our quick marriage will fly out the window."

"That's a perfect idea!" She pressed a kiss to his compelling mouth. "Now I need to get dressed."

"Let me help you."

"Giovanni—"

"You're blushing all over."

"Stop!"

"Ti amo, Signora Laurito."

"Ti amo, Signor Laurito."

Twenty minutes later she and Giovanni had dressed in their wedding clothes and went downstairs to the patio, where Stanzie and Paolo were tending the children in their swings. Valentina's eyes filled with happy tears to see the babies all decked out in little black tuxedo suit coats and ties with white shirts and black pants.

Giovanni had hired a videographer to come and film the entire evening. Classical music played in the background. Flowers from the garden filled the house and the tables set up outside on the terrace. Torches illuminated the pool area and fabulous banquet table overflowing with sumptuous food and champagne. He pinned a corsage of gardenias on her shoulder and kissed her once more.

Paolo gave them the heads-up that people were arriving. On cue, Valentina and Giovanni picked up their boys and stood together to start welcoming their families. Giovanni's family walked out on the patio followed by Valentina's. Rini pushed her father's wheelchair right up to Valentina so she could kiss her father. Bianca had come with them.

The minute everyone saw the babies, there was pandemonium. The younger children rushed over to play with them. Everyone wanted to hold and kiss them. Valentina glanced at her handsome husband. "Your idea was ingenious," she whispered. "Another Giovanni Laurito takeover. No one stood a chance."

His deep happy laughter traveled through her entire body. She loved this man with a passion she couldn't begin to express.

With all the attention, their babies clung to them. He grasped Valentina's hand and cleared his throat. "Welcome, everyone. Valentina and I are thrilled you could come to celebrate our marriage. We were married two weeks ago at the church in Laurito and are ecstatically happy.

"Our babies refused to be comforted unless we were both with them. You might say they were responsible for this marriage that has been founded on nothing but love from the first moment Valentina and I laid eyes on each other.

"Please enjoy yourselves for the rest of the night, but we have no idea how long our boys will last with all this excitement."

Valentina and Giovanni met each other's families and rejoiced that Vito and Ric would have so many little cousins to grow up with. Maybe twenty minutes into the evening, two more people arrived. Valentina sucked in her breath.

It was Violeta and… Tatania, Ric's beautiful, black-haired mother.

"I'm glad they came," Giovanni murmured, "but I'm not surprised Salvatore isn't with them. Excuse me for a minute."

She watched Giovanni carry Ric over to her and place him in her arms. Ric had spent enough time with his mother that he didn't fuss at being passed to her. Giovanni came back and slid his arm around Valentina's waist.

"*Grazie a Dio* you convinced me to talk to her. Tell me the truth. Does it hurt to see him respond to her?"

Valentina stared up at him with tear-filled eyes. "Not at all. She's *his* mother. I have my son, Vito, and the memories of Ric being mine for those first two and a half weeks. No one can take that away from me. And of course, I have you. What more could I want in this entire world?"

"*Bellissima*—I can't wait to get you alone tonight."

"I'm way ahead of you and have already started the countdown."

His burst of laughter caused heads to turn in their direction. Valentina's wonderful husband sounded so happy, she shared a smile with Stanzic and Paolo, who knew the pain he'd been through and were overjoyed for him.

* * * * *

MEET THE FORTUNES

Fortune of the Month: Charles Fortune Chesterfield

Age: 29

Vital statistics: Dark, sexy hair women love to tousle, seductive blue eyes. Six feet plus of honest-to-goodness princely charisma.

Claim to fame: "Bonnie Lord Charlie" is an international hottie whose TV adverts for British tourism promise visitors to England "the royal treatment."

Romantic prospects: Are you kidding?

"Social media would have me as some kind of lothario. This is not strictly true. I do enjoy feminine attention. I can't help it if women find me irresistible. I do not fear commitment; I simply choose to avoid it.

But now there's Alice. And Flynn. My son! From the moment I found out he was mine, everything changed. I've promised to do everything in my power to be a good father to my boy, and that means keeping my hands off Flynn's mum. Strictly friends, she says. It's what she wants. It's the right thing to do. And I'm bloody certain it's going to kill me."

* * *

The Fortune's of Texas:
All Fortune's Children
Money. Family. Cowboys.
Meet the Austin Fortunes!

FORTUNE'S SPECIAL DELIVERY

BY
MICHELLE MAJOR

First Published in Great Britain 2016
By Mills & Boon, an imprint of HarperCollins*Publishers*
1 London Bridge Street, London, SE1 9GF

© 2016 Harlequin Books S.A.

Special thanks and acknowledgement to Michelle Major for her contribution to the Fortunes of Texas: All Fortune's Children continuity.

ISBN: 978-0-263-91975-2

23-0416

Our policy is to use papers that are natural, renewable and recyclable products and made from wood grown in sustainable forests. The logging and manufacturing processes conform to the legal environmental regulations of the country of origin.

Printed and bound in Spain
by CPI, Barcelona

Michelle Major grew up in Ohio but dreamed of living in the mountains. Soon after graduating with a degree in journalism, she pointed her car west and settled in Colorado. Her life and house are filled with one great husband, two beautiful kids, a few furry pets and several well-behaved reptiles. She's grateful to have found her passion writing stories with happy endings. Michelle loves to hear from her readers at www.michellemajor.com.

To all the Fortunes readers. I'm thrilled to be
celebrating the 20th anniversary with you!

Chapter One

"A toast to your marriage."

Charles Fortune Chesterfield lifted his glass of deep red cabernet, unable to hide the smile that curved one corner of his mouth. "Or should I call it your unmarriage? Your remarriage?" He winked at his sister Lucie, sitting across the table from him in the trendy Austin restaurant. It was early April and the weather in Central Texas was quite fine, a welcome change from the dreary rain of a London spring. He would rather have been sitting at a table on the restaurant's spacious patio, enjoying the fresh air and the sound of the city passing by them. Unfortunately, the paparazzi hounded his family wherever they went, so Charles and Lucie were huddled in a quiet booth in the back of the restaurant.

"Don't be cheeky, Charles," Lucie answered in a clipped tone, her hazel eyes flashing. "If you came all the way to Texas to tease me, you should have stayed in London."

"I'm happy for you, Luce." Charles set down his wine-glass and grabbed his younger sister's hand, giving it a squeeze. "Truly I am. That's why Austin was my first stop on this trip."

"And…" she prompted, her smile returning.

"You and Chase make a lovely couple," he offered. "It's obvious how much he loves you." Charles hoped his sister realized he was sincere. He hadn't seen her as happy as she was now, reunited with her first love and husband, Texas oilman Chase Parker. Few had known about Lucie's impulsive wedding when she was only seventeen until the fact that she and Chase were still married came to light last month. Charles had hated watching his younger sister hounded by the press, but true love had triumphed in the end.

He'd flown in yesterday from London and gone straight to dinner with Chase and Lucie at the sprawl-ing Parker ranch outside town. Even jet-lagged, he'd been able to see how much they loved each other. His family had wasted no time in filling him in on the news from Horseback Hollow, the small Texas town the rest of his siblings called home. Lucie had also informed him that family matriarch and cosmetics mogul Kate Fortune was still in Austin and apparently meeting with their generation of Fortune children to look for someone to take over the empire built on her Fortune Youth Serum.

"Chase is perfect," Lucie agreed now, "although I wouldn't recommend calling him 'lovely' to his face. A native Texan won't appreciate that description, Charles. But I'm talking about you." She punched a few keys on her cell phone and lifted it for a better view. She'd gone to one of the online tabloid sites so popular in Britain.

The headline displayed on the small screen read Is the Third Time a Charm for Bonnie Lord Charlie? An obvious reference to Charles's two previous broken engagements. Below the headline was a grainy photo of Charles and a beautiful, thin and very regal-looking brunette.

"Lady Caterina Hayworth?" Lucie asked, her brow puckered. "Tell me you're not engaged to Conniving Cat. I know you like your women brainless and beautiful, but she's a social climber of the worst sort. You must know she wants your celebrity status as much as she wants you."

"I hate that nickname," he muttered, running his finger along the smooth screen as if he could blot out the maddening words.

"Conniving Cat?" Lucie waved a hand in the air. "Perhaps it isn't kind, but you must admit—"

"Not that one," he clarified. "Hell, Caterina loves the moniker. I think she was the one to start it. I mean 'Bonnie Lord Charlie.'" He scrubbed a hand over his face, the transatlantic time change suddenly catching up with him tenfold. "Jensen is the one with the title." Their mother, Josephine May Fortune Chesterfield, had married Sir Simon Chesterfield after ending her first, loveless marriage to Rhys Henry Hayes. "The press doesn't feel the need to give Brodie or Oliver a fake title," Charles said, referring to their two older half brothers from Josephine's first marriage. "And calling me 'bonnie' is ridiculous. I'm a twenty-nine-year-old man, not a wee lad toddling around in rompers."

"You *are* quite handsome." Lucie's smile turned sympathetic. "I'm sure it's meant as a compliment."

"It's an implied dig that I don't *do* anything, that I have nothing to offer but my face and my family's good name. No use denying it."

Her slim shoulders stiffened. "You do plenty, Charles. I think your ads single-handedly doubled the number of women vacationing in Britain over the past year."

He fought back a grimace, even though he had no one but himself to blame. The ad campaign that featured him promising visitors to England "the royal treatment" had started as a joke during a meeting he'd attended with the British Tourism Council two years ago. He'd been expected to bring ideas to the table, but had spent the night before the meeting clubbing with friends and had shown up to the meeting a half hour late with a raging headache. He'd pitched the Royal Treatment campaign as a jest, but the council had loved it. Before he knew what was happening, Charles ended up the star of a series of print and television ads, wearing a tux in front of various British monuments, giving it his best James Bond–meets–Mr. Darcy impression.

He was happy to do his part for queen and country, but lately wished his contribution could be of a more meaningful sort. Lucie, like their mother, devoted herself to various charitable organizations. Their brother Jensen was a successful financier. Everyone in his family had something of substance to offer.

Except Charles.

That, too, was his fault. For years he'd cultivated his image as a good-time guy. He'd been the charmer in his family as a kid, perpetually entertaining his parents and siblings, always good for a laugh. After Sir Simon died, it had seemed the right thing to do to make his mother smile as often as he could. So that's what people had come to expect from him—a good time. Only his father had ever seemed to want him to be something more.

"That is part of why I'm here. I have meetings set up with the Texas Tourism Board next week. We'd like to do some cross-promotions—Texans and high tea. That sort of thing." He leaned forward. "Did you know almost three million Americans are projected to visit England this year?"

"And most of them want 'the royal treatment'?" Lucie asked with a laugh.

Charles forced a smile. He had a reputation to uphold, after all. "I suppose. You're right about me needing an escape. There's work and family, but I also needed to get away from the press. Cat and I were nowhere near to being engaged. We weren't even a proper couple."

Lucie taped a finger on the cell phone screen. "Did she know that?"

"Chalk it up to selective hearing on her part," Charles said. "Don't get me wrong, she's a lovely lady." He sighed. "They're all lovely ladies."

"But what about the right woman, Charles?" Lucie took a sip of her wine and waved away the waiter who approached their table. "Now that Chase and I are together, you're officially the last man standing in the family. Brodie, Oliver, Jensen and Amelia are happy in Horseback Hollow. Even Mum seems to have found love again."

"Jensen mentioned a burgeoning romance with Orlando Mendoza." Charles was happy for his mother, although it was difficult to imagine her with anyone but his father.

"She's glowing," Lucie said with a wistful sigh.

"Then the two of you have that in common, dear sister." Charles twirled the stem of the wineglass between two fingers. "Marriage…remarriage…whatever you want to call it agrees with you. But I don't believe there's only one woman in the world for me."

"Because you haven't met her yet," Lucie argued.

"I've met plenty of women."

"And bedded most of them."

Charles took a long drink of wine. "I'm absolutely *not* having this conversation with my sister."

"If you'd only—"

At that moment, Charles's cell phone rang. He drew the device out of his coat pocket as Lucie frowned.

"Send the call to voice mail," she told him with her best sisterly glare. "I'm not finished lecturing you."

He grinned, then glanced at the display. "Sorry, sis, it's an Austin number. Might be important *royal* business." But when he accepted the call and said hello, whoever was on the other end of the line was silent. "Anyone there?" he asked into the phone.

He was about to hang up when he heard a funny squeak that might have been "hello."

A throat cleared. "Is this Charles?" a woman's voice asked.

"Who wants to know?" he responded, then met Lucie's curious gaze and shrugged his shoulders.

"Hang up," his sister whispered.

Charles understood her reaction. The caller was likely a reporter trying to track him down, or one of the frequent fame hounds who'd come after his family through the years, especially since their connection to the prominent Fortunes was revealed. Charles, like all the Fortune Chesterfields, had learned to guard his privacy—one more reason the tabloid photo with Lady Caterina irked him.

But something about the way the woman on the other

end of the phone spoke his name intrigued him. Her voice was soft, with a sweet Texas drawl and more than a hint of nerves. Charles might be a magnet for women, but the timid girls typically gave him a wide berth.

"This is Alice," the woman told him.

"Alice," he repeated, liking the way the two syllables sounded on his tongue. But he had no recognition of an Alice from his past.

"Alice Meyers," she continued, a little breathlessly. "I'm sorry to call you out of the blue. I got your number from the tourism board office."

Right. Suddenly an image—a beautiful blonde, with long legs and a shy but sexy smile—popped into his mind.

Alice cleared her throat again. "We met last year—"

"At the tourism conference here in Austin," he continued. "I remember you." Charles tried to hide his small smile from Lucie. What he remembered most about Alice was spending a blissful night with her in his hotel room after the conference ended. He'd even asked for her number, something he rarely did after a casual dalliance. But he'd liked Alice Meyers, and he'd thought she liked him. Too bad when he'd come out of the shower the next morning she'd disappeared from his hotel room and his life.

Now, more than a year later, she was ringing him. Charles felt his smile widen. Intriguing, indeed.

Alice breathed a sigh of relief that Charles remembered her. Of course, she'd known who he was before they'd met at the bar in the conference hotel last spring. Every woman between the ages of ten and ninety knew

Bonnie Lord Charlie. But she hadn't expected him to commit her to memory. Men rarely did.

She'd followed his romantic exploits in the tabloids since their encounter, and it was a wonder Charles could remember what girl he was with on any given night. The man seemed to be the British equivalent of the Energizer Bunny when it came to women.

"Alice, are you still there?" His crisp accent broke through her musings.

"I need to see you," she blurted, then bit down hard on her lip as silence greeted her outburst. He was bound to think she was a stalker for calling him out of blue and making such a bold request.

"That's a lovely offer," he said finally, sounding every bit the aristocrat he was. How was it possible for him to sound more British than before? "But I'm fairly booked on this visit."

"It's important," she whispered, swallowing back the emotion clogging her throat. "I promise I won't take much of your time."

"Can you give me a hint what this mysterious meeting might entail?"

"It's personal and…" She paused, then added, "Please, Charles."

There was another long moment of silence. Alice checked her phone to make sure Charles hadn't hung up on her. She wouldn't exactly blame him. He was handsome, rich, and famous around the world. She was nobody, yet was demanding precious time from him. But even if he said no now, Alice couldn't give up. Seeing Charles again was too important.

"Tomorrow morning," he said suddenly.

"Gr-great," she stammered, shocked that he'd agreed.

The fingers holding the phone trembled with both nerves and exhilaration. "We could meet in Zilker Park. Are you familiar with it?"

"I am."

"There's a bench under a big oak tree near the entrance of the Zilker Botanical Garden. How about ten o'clock?"

"Very good. I'll see you in the morning, Alice."

The way he spoke her name made sparks zing low in her belly. His accent made every word sound like a caress. She shook her head, needing to keep her wits about her. As good a time as she'd had with Charles, she hadn't contacted him for her sake. "Goodbye, Charles. Thank you."

As the call ended, she pulled the phone away from her head, her hand trembling as she stared at it. "I did it," she whispered, glancing at the baby sleeping in the swing in the corner of the room. Her son, Flynn, was a champion napper at four months, which was one of the few things that had made being a single mom a tiny bit easier for Alice.

"Come here and tell me everything." She turned to see her best friend, Meredith Doan, gesturing wildly from the galley kitchen in Alice's two-bedroom apartment. Meredith was the only person who knew about Charles, and Alice had confided in her friend only recently, needing an ally to bolster her confidence.

"It went well," Alice said quietly as she stepped into the small space. "We're meeting tomorrow morning."

"You look like you need this," Meredith said, handing Alice a glass of white wine. "Your face is beet red. Charles remembered you?"

"Yes, after a moment." Alice took a deep breath, her first since dialing Charles's number.

"Tell me again how you ended up having an affair with Bonnie Lord Charlie."

"It wasn't exactly an affair," Alice answered, taking a fortifying sip of wine. "It was one night. We met at the annual Texas tourism conference last spring. There was an international focus, so the board invited representatives from several European countries to attend. Charles has ties in Texas now through the Fortunes, so he came from Britain."

Meredith wiggled her eyebrows. "And you snagged yourself a royal? Nice work, Meyers. I didn't think you had it in you."

"I didn't," Alice said quickly. "I don't. It wasn't like that, Meredith. It was special."

"They all are, sweetie."

Alice knew she would have a difficult time convincing her friend. She'd met Meredith her first day working at the Texas Tourism Board, and they'd struck up an unlikely friendship. Meredith worked in the marketing department and was as outgoing off the clock as she was on the job. Since Alice had known her, Meredith had dated a number of guys and even had a few random hookups. Alice, on the other hand, had no one.

Until Charles.

When they'd met at an industry reception the last night of the conference, Alice had expected him to look right past her. Almost everyone did, so she was used to it. There'd been a flurry of Texas women vying for his attention, flirting like they did it for a living. Alice had barely been able to make eye contact when she and Charles had been introduced. He was so handsome, several inches taller than her own five foot nine. His dark hair was expensively cut but perpetually tousled from his habit of running his fingers through it. His brilliant blue eyes seemed to see right into her soul.

It had been a silly thought, and she'd spent the rest of the party watching him laugh and joke with the crowd that constantly surrounded him. He was like a fun magnet and almost exactly her opposite in every way. As the dancing started midway through the evening, with conference attendees from all different countries and backgrounds letting loose in the hotel bar, Alice had been ready to leave. Before she could, Charles had slipped into the booth next to her. He'd told her he'd been watching her all night, waiting for a moment alone with her.

It had been difficult to believe, but he'd stayed at her side the rest of the evening. They'd talked about everything and nothing, and to her surprise, Charles had seemed as happy to escape the noise and bustle of the crowd as Alice. So when he'd invited her up to his room…

"What happened to the condom?" Meredith said, pointing a finger at her. "Your first time out of the gate and you don't use protection? I thought I'd taught you better."

"We did use protection," Alice protested weakly. "I got pregnant anyway. They aren't one hundred percent effective. And I guess saving the condom for a couple years wasn't such a great idea, after all."

After one too many cosmos at a happy hour shortly after she'd met Meredith, Alice had lamented her perennial virginity to her new friend. Alice hadn't set out to still be a virgin at age twenty-five, but she'd been shy and awkward through her teen years and focused on her classes during college. She'd expected to meet Mr. Right at some point, but when he never materialized, decided she might have to settle for Mr. Right Now. She'd hoped gregarious Meredith could help her, and the first thing her new friend had done was give Alice a condom to keep in her wallet.

It had stayed there for two years, until the night with Charles. Of course, he'd had protection, but she'd insisted on using hers. It meant something to her, a rite of passage of sorts. Even though it had been only one night—well, twice in one night—when she'd left his hotel the next morning, her purse had felt ten pounds lighter on her shoulder.

Only six weeks later, when she couldn't keep down her breakfast each morning, did she realize how foolish she'd truly been.

"You know this means Flynn is a Fortune," Meredith said in an awestruck tone.

Alice set her wineglass on the quartz counter, her fingers suddenly unsteady again. "He's my baby, Mer. Mine." Flynn was everything to her.

"But you're going to tell Charles."

"He deserves to know." She crossed her arms over her chest, the implications of what she'd put into motion settling like a west Texas dust storm on her shoulders. "I doubt he'll even want to be involved. Everyone knows his reputation. I'm sure tomorrow will be the last time Flynn and I will ever see Charles."

Chapter Two

The next morning was bright and warm, the exact weather Charles was coming to expect from Austin in April. He'd booked a room at the Four Seasons Hotel for the duration of his visit, even though Lucie had invited him to stay at the Parker ranch outside town. But Charles liked the vibe of downtown Austin, and despite his social nature, he also appreciated time alone. Later, the day would turn hot and humid, but it was pleasant enough now that he'd chosen to walk the few miles from his hotel, situated on Lady Bird Lake, the reservoir in downtown Austin, over to Zilker Park.

The walkway was busy, and he enjoyed watching men and women running, mothers with small children and strollers, and the trees and flowers that lined the path. Even more, he enjoyed the anonymity. A few people did a double take when he passed, but no one stopped him.

In London, he could barely get from his flat to the corner coffee shop without a camera flashing. This was a welcome change.

By the time he spotted the striking blonde sitting on the park bench outside the Zilker Botanical Garden entrance, Charles felt more relaxed than he had in ages.

Alice Meyers.

Yes, he remembered her. She was typing something into her phone, so he had a minute to study her. She was as lovely as she'd been a year ago and perhaps a bit curvier. The change suited her. Her pale hair was pulled back into a loose bun, a few strands escaping to brush across her cheek. Her skin was smooth and pale in contrast to her lush mouth. He'd kissed those lips all night long, never tiring of the taste of her.

Charles ran a hand through his hair, surprised at the sudden rush of memories. He didn't know why Alice had contacted him after so long, and there were plenty of women who meant more to him than she did. He approached slowly, waiting for her to glance up. She wore a silk blouse in a soft pink hue, tailored jeans and the most delectable pair of intricately strappy sandals he'd ever seen. The heels she'd worn the night they met had been just as unique, and he was irrationally glad that amazing shoes seemed to be a staple for her.

He was almost in front of her when she finally looked away from her phone. Her big hazel eyes widened and color tinged her cheeks.

"Charles," she breathed, quickly standing and thrusting a hand toward him.

He had every intention of shaking her hand, but at the last minute grasped her fingers and lifted her hand to his mouth, brushing his lips across her knuckles.

He forced himself to release her hand, and took a step back.

"Good morning, Alice."

"Hello," she said. "Thank you for meeting me." The pulse in her delicate neck fluttered wildly, and she swallowed. For some reason, her agitation made him relax. Certainly someone so nervous wouldn't be preparing to blackmail him.

"I'm glad you called," he said, making his tone reassuring. Whatever her reason for wanting to see him, Alice clearly needed some encouragement right now. Charles didn't consider himself the nurturing type but this woman seemed to bring something new to the surface in him.

"You are?" She sounded dubious, and it was hard to tell whom she doubted more—herself or him.

"I am." He flashed his most charming smile. "I enjoyed our time together last year, brief as the encounter turned out to be. If you—"

A sharp cry interrupted him. Alice turned to the buggy next to the park bench. He'd been so intent on her as he approached, he hadn't noticed it before. The stroller was one of those fancy American types, not the traditional pram many mums in Britain favored. This one was dark gray with navy blue trim and seemed as sturdy as a tank with an infant seat snapped into the top. Alice pushed back the cover to reveal a small baby peering out at them.

"This is my son," she said quickly. "His binky fell out." She reached under the baby and pulled out a piece of green rubber, popping it deftly in the boy's mouth just as he opened it to cry again. He began sucking and within seconds took a deep breath and seemed to settle back to watch the morning go by from his baby stroller throne.

"A real little prince you have there," Charles said, taking a step closer to the stroller.

Alice blinked at him as if he'd just said her son was next in line to the British throne.

"Figure of speech," he clarified. "How old is the lad?"

"Four months," she whispered. "He's…he's everything to me."

"I can see why." Charles hadn't spent much time around babies until his siblings had started with their own progeny. He'd discovered he liked wee ones, assuming he could give them back to their parents when a nappy needed changing. He leaned over the stroller and the baby looked up at him, with blue eyes bright and clear like his nephew Ollie had at that age.

Charles felt a vise wrap around his chest. He stared at the dark-haired boy a few more seconds, then staggered back a step, clutching at his shirtfront. "That baby looks exactly like the boys in my family." He met Alice's gaze. "He looks like *me*."

She stared at him, a mix of emotions ranging from apprehension to relief flashing across her delicate features. One hand was wrapped around the stroller's handle, like a gust of wind was coming and she needed the buggy to ground her. "Yes," she said simply, after an awkward moment. "He's yours."

A dull roar filled Charles's head. He had a baby. A son. He was a father. It seemed impossible. Yes, he'd dated plenty of women, but he'd been careful. Always. He'd always…

"How did this happen?"

The baby made another noise, and Alice picked him

up, cradling the boy in her arms. "The usual way, I guess," she said with an almost apologetic smile. "That night at the conference—"

"I remember the bloody night," Charles yelled, then scrubbed a hand over his jaw as Alice flinched. He took a breath, made his voice lower. "But we used protection. As I remember, the first condom was yours."

As Alice nodded, her cheeks flamed bright pink. She lowered herself to the park bench, still holding the baby tight to her chest. "I'd been saving it," she told him. "For my…first time. That was a mistake."

For an instant, Charles wondered if she was referring to the old condom or choosing him to take her virginity. It had been obvious that she was inexperienced, but he hadn't realized the full extent of her innocence until he'd pushed inside her. He'd tried to be gentle, to make it good for her, but his desire and need for her had been a force like nothing he'd experienced before.

Misinterpreting his silence, she continued, "I didn't mean for it to happen. You have to believe me, Charles. If you want a DNA test, I understand."

He looked at Flynn and simply *knew* deep in his soul. This was his son. He might be shocked, but there was no doubt she was telling the truth. "No test," he told her curtly.

"It's never been my intention to trap you. I just thought you should know."

"Why now?" He paced back and forth in front of the bench, too frantic with conflicting emotions to stand still. "I should have bloody well known a year ago."

"What would you have done?"

He stopped to consider the question and turned to

Alice, who seemed to read his thoughts before even he knew them.

Her chin tipped up and her shoulders straightened. "I know who you are, Charles. I know how you live." Gone suddenly was the nervous, shy girl he'd encountered, and in her place was a fierce, formidable mother. She adjusted the infant in her arms and leaned forward. "I loved this baby from the moment I discovered I was pregnant. I was going to be his mother, no matter what anyone else thought of the decision."

Resolve mixed with tension in her gaze. Charles caught a brief glimpse of what a woman like Alice must have endured, making the choice to become a single mother. Who had supported her during the pregnancy and the baby's birth? Would he have stepped into that role if she *had* told him?

"I didn't say I don't want him," he said, the anger at not knowing disappearing as quickly as it had arrived. He sank next to her on the bench and lifted one finger to trace the top of the baby's small head. The boy had a decent amount of hair for a little one, dark and downy soft.

"You certainly didn't say you *did*," Alice countered.

Charles nodded, willing to acknowledge that, even if it wasn't the whole truth. "I'll admit this is quite a shock. I don't know you well, Alice, but I'd gather a one-night stand with a stranger isn't the way you planned to bring a child into the world."

She let out a small, tired laugh. "Nothing about this was part of my plan, but he's here now. I wouldn't change a thing."

"Does he have a name?"

Alice smiled. "Flynn. His name is Flynn Davis Meyers."

"A strong name," Charles told her. "I like it. Although

I suppose it will be Flynn Davis Fortune Chesterfield now." He closed his eyes for a moment, leaned his head back and tried to gather his roiling thoughts. "I almost understand why you didn't tell me at first, but after he was born…"

"I'm sorry, Charles. Really, I am." She placed a hand on his arm. The touch was light, but it reverberated through him. "I had a lot of resistance at first from my friends and family. Not only could no one believe I'd gotten pregnant, but they also didn't think I could handle a baby on my own. Not my coworkers, friends or even my parents." Flynn fidgeted in her arms and she drew her hand away from Charles to snuggle the baby closer, his eyes drifting shut again. "But I knew being a mother would change everything for me."

She gazed at Flynn, her eyes full of so much affection that Charles instinctively leaned closer, wanting to be a part of that kind of love.

"It did change me," she said. "It made me better and stronger, but I got used to being on my own. I started relying on myself and it felt like that was my only option. Until…"

"Until what?" Charles asked, so close now he could smell the vanilla scent of her shampoo.

"It's silly, but I was getting a haircut last month and saw a picture of you in an old tabloid magazine."

Charles grimaced. "Whatever the article said, I highly doubt it was true."

She laughed, and Charles watched as Flynn's eyes snapped open, focusing on her face. The boy seemed as fascinated by Alice as Charles felt. How did a baby form that bond so quickly? Did Charles have it in him to be any sort of father to this child?

"It was a photo of you holding your niece, Clementine. The magazine was from last year, so she was around Flynn's age in the picture. You looked so…" Alice searched his face, offered him another hopeful smile.

"Terrified out of my mind," he suggested.

"Natural," she corrected. "You looked natural holding the baby—like it made you happy."

"Little Clementine is a fine baby."

She shrugged. "It made me realize it wasn't fair to keep Flynn from you. Again, I'm sorry. For the shock and for not telling you earlier. Like I said, I don't expect anything from you."

He knew she meant the words as comfort, but they were like salt in an open wound. No one had ever expected anything from Charles. Nothing beyond a laugh, a free pint and a good time. For a long time, he'd liked it that way. But now…this was different.

"Would you like to hold him?" Alice asked gently.

He almost said no. Flynn wasn't a niece or nephew he could bounce on his knee, then hand back to a doting parent. *He* was the parent. Alice might think he looked like a natural, but he certainly didn't feel like one. Still, when she shifted toward him, Charles reached for the baby.

"Relax," Alice coached him. "You're doing fine."

Forcing his muscles to loosen, Charles held the baby close to his chest, cradled in the crook of his arm. Flynn yawned, stretched and blinked. His blue gaze, so familiar, yet all his own, met Charles's. At that moment, Charles felt his world rumble and shift. It wasn't like a lightning bolt or clap of thunder. But the energy inside him changed. Here was the meaning he'd been craving in his life, all wrapped up in one tiny, powder-scented package. He was holding *his son* in his arms.

He wrapped his arms tighter around the baby and placed a gentle kiss on Flynn's forehead.

Alice gasped when Charles kissed Flynn, her whole world suddenly spinning out of control.

Charles glanced up at her. "Did I do something wrong?"

She shook her head. "No, of course not. I just didn't think you'd to take to him so quickly. I thought…" She trailed off, knowing that everything she'd expected about Charles's reaction to finding out he had a son was insulting and, apparently, off the mark.

Obligation and a niggling sense of guilt had prompted her to call him when she'd found out he was visiting his family in Texas. But she hadn't realized what had stopped her from contacting him before that. It wasn't as much how he would respond to the knowledge of being a father, but Alice's reaction to Charles.

They'd spent only one night together, but she'd felt the overwhelming charge of attraction and longing as soon as she looked up and saw him standing in front of her today. He was just as handsome, looking almost formal and wholly British in his slim trousers, expensive loafers and dark, fitted shirt.

The temperature was beginning to rise as the sun drew higher in the sky, and Alice could feel a bead of sweat roll between her shoulder blades. Charles, on the other hand, looked as dashing and sophisticated as if he were ready to meet a foreign dignitary. He smelled delicious, expensive and spicy. The scent made her want to lean in closer to him and beg him to press his mouth to hers.

She was such a fool.

Charles likely hadn't given her a moment's thought in the past year, and she'd struggled to keep him out of her mind and, more annoyingly, her dreams. But Charles in the flesh was far more powerful than her fantasy version. To see him show such easy affection with her son—with *their* son—made Alice almost melt on the spot.

Unfortunately, it also made the future far more complicated, and she liked her simple life with Flynn.

"My father was a wonderful man," Charles told her, his gaze back on the baby. "The most honorable, good-hearted, kind person I've ever known. I couldn't ever hope to compare to him, but I want to follow his example. I'm going to do the right thing by Flynn, Alice. I promise you that much."

She nodded dumbly, unable to speak around the emotion rising thick and hot in her throat. Automatically, she reached for the baby, needing the weight of Flynn in her arms to settle her. Charles handed him to her, their fingers brushing as he did. She felt the touch all the way to her toes, her skin tingling with awareness. Needing to gain control of herself, Alice stood and gently placed Flynn back into his stroller. She strapped him into the infant seat and turned to Charles. "I should go," she said, "Thank you for meeting me and for being so good about all of this. I really don't—"

"Expect a call from me tomorrow," Charles interrupted, also standing. He slid the sunshade over Flynn and took a step toward Alice before stopping. "I have some plans to put into motion, papers to draw up." His fingers rested on the stroller handle as hers had earlier. His touch was confident, proprietary, and despite his devil-may-care attitude about life, Alice knew from

Charles's work with the tourism council that he was smart and cunning, with powerful connections on both sides of the Atlantic. Once he decided there was something he wanted, little could stop him from having it.

"If you change your mind, I understand," Alice said quickly, no longer sure what she wanted from her son's father. Afraid of both what he made her feel and the way he could change her life.

"I won't." He leaned forward, kissed her cheek in much the same way he'd kissed Flynn's forehead. The brush of his lips was gentle, sweet and utterly irresistible. Cue the melting once again. Great. Just when Alice needed to keep her wits about her, one innocent touch could turn her to mush. "Thank you, Alice," he said as he straightened. "For calling me. This morning has changed everything."

"Goodbye, Charles," she said, and gripped the stroller handle harder than necessary. He moved back and she turned for the path toward her car, his words echoing in her ears.

Yes, everything had changed. Now she wondered exactly what that would mean for her.

Chapter Three

"Why am I such an idiot?" she asked Meredith later that night. They were back in Alice's cozy apartment, and she'd just put Flynn down for the night.

"Something about a hot guy will do that to you." Meredith tipped her wineglass toward Alice. "Add a British accent to the mix, and it's no wonder your ovaries went into overdrive with Charlie Boy."

"He wants to be a father to Flynn," Alice told her friend with a small sigh. She brought her own glass to her lips but set it on the coffee table before taking a drink. Her head had been pounding since the meeting with Charles, and she didn't need anything to make it worse.

"Isn't that what you wanted?" Meredith asked, clearly confused.

"No…yes… I have no idea what I want," Alice admitted. "I'm so tired, I can't think straight."

Meredith gave her a sympathetic smile. "The transition back to work hasn't been an easy one."

"I love my job, but it's different now that I have Flynn. Everything is different." Her maternity leave had ended just over a month ago, and she'd returned to her job with the Texas Tourism Board, which was based out of Austin. She'd worked there for just over three years, and what Alice lacked in a gregarious, outgoing personality, she made up for in attention to detail, understanding the market and her ability to assess what people wanted out of a visit. But it was more difficult for those skills to shine through when she was chronically sleep deprived and always torn between being at work or at home with her son.

She'd modified her schedule so she could work from home two days a week, and had found a semiretired nanny, a sweet older woman, to watch Flynn another two days. Alice's mother took the baby one day a week. But Alice still got up before dawn most mornings to put in extra hours, and with Flynn's sometimes erratic sleeping patterns, she never felt rested. Her exhaustion was starting to take a toll, and Alice often felt like she was slogging through mud just to form a coherent thought.

"Charles had a right to know he has a child," she told Meredith, "but I never expected him to take to the idea so readily. Of course I want Flynn to know his father, but he's my son. Mine." Her voice caught, and she cleared her throat. "Flynn is my sole reason for being and now I'm going to have to share him. What if Charles wants partial custody? What if he takes Flynn to England for part of the year?" She knew she sounded irrational but couldn't help it. Being a mother was the best thing that had ever happened to her. She couldn't imagine a night when she didn't tuck Flynn in bed or a morning without a baby-scented snuggle to greet her.

"What if he wants the three of you to be a family?" Meredith asked.

Alice snorted. "Don't be ridiculous. Charles has no interest in me beyond Flynn. He barely remembered who I was at first. Just another in his long list of conquests in the bedroom." She drew her knees up to her chest and rested her chin on them. "Not that I was much of a prize."

"Don't sell yourself short, Alice. You're not an awkward teenager anymore. In case you haven't looked in a mirror in the past few years, you're gorgeous. Men stare at you everywhere we go."

"They don't—"

"They do, but you don't notice."

"I noticed Charles," Alice admitted. "We only had one night together and it's been over a year. I'm tired, stressed and still have ten pounds of baby weight to lose. The last thing on my mind is men. But I could barely form a sentence this morning because of my reaction to him. How am I supposed to remain calm and in control when all I want is to…"

"Jump his bones?" Meredith suggested with a wink.

Alice laughed at the old-school expression, a welcome break in the tension that seemed ready to consume her. "I'm a mother now, Mer."

"Last time I checked, you're still a woman."

The funny thing was, the only time Alice had felt like a woman recently was with Charles. He made her feel alive and aware of herself in a different way than normal. In a way that made her hot and itchy and longing for…more. It had to be something biological, like pheromones. There was no other way to account for her reaction to him. "Until I know how Charles wants to proceed, I can't let down my guard. Flynn is my first— my only—priority."

"Then you have to at least give Charles a chance." Meredith stood, picked up both their wineglasses. "For Flynn's sake."

Alice unfolded her legs and followed her friend to the kitchen, where Meredith set the glasses in the sink. "Thanks for listening. I needed a friend tonight."

"My pleasure, sweetie." Meredith hugged her. "I've got to go now. I'm meeting a few people for drinks at a bar downtown. Want to call a last-minute sitter and join us?"

Alice grimaced. "It's nearly nine."

"The night is young."

"Not for me. I'm exhausted and my alarm is already set for five tomorrow morning."

"I'll see you at the office, then," Meredith said.

Alice locked the door to her apartment behind her friend and sighed. Her mind drifted to Charles and what he might be doing tonight. Was he also at a bar downtown or out to dinner with a woman? He had no shortage of female companionship, and Alice knew she didn't stand a chance when compared to the women he usually favored. Of course, she'd see him again, thanks to Flynn, but Alice hated that she longed for more. Her attraction to him made her feel weak when what she needed was to be strong for her son.

She quietly let herself into Flynn's room. Her eyes adjusted to the darkness and she approached the crib. He slept on his back, his face turned toward her, and her heart swelled with love at how innocent he was. He deserved the best she could give him, which was why she worked so hard, put in extra hours and ignored her own needs. That's what mothers did for their children.

She'd wait to hear from Charles and concentrate on ignoring her feelings for the tall, handsome Englishman. Her only identity was that of a mother, and it was better for everyone if she didn't fool herself into thinking it could be anything else.

Charles lay in bed early the next morning, watching the windows of his hotel suite slowly brighten with dawn light. His sleep had been sporadic and fitful. He'd drift off, only to awake in a cold sweat minutes later. Wispy tendrils of panic had threatened to claim him in the dark, so many unspoken fears and regrets from his life coalescing into one important word.

Father.

Bloody hell.

What had he been thinking to tell Alice he wanted to be a part of Flynn's life? She'd seemed more than willing to let him off the hook. Shirking responsibility was Charles's specialty in life. He'd even made a successful career of taking the easy way out. He traveled, shook hands with dignitaries and the rich and famous. He attended parties and smiled for the cameras, and somehow that made him an asset to the British tourism industry.

His existence was so different than that of his siblings, with their businesses, philanthropic projects and seemingly endless supply of energy and work ethic. Even if the superficiality of his life had begun to chafe at his soul, it was what Charles did well. He knew he wouldn't fail at being a man about town. The stakes were too low for him to care that much. And if he didn't care, he couldn't be hurt. Wouldn't disappoint anyone.

Flynn and Alice were different. They upped the stakes in a manner that scared the hell out of him. Charles certainly knew people whose lifestyles hadn't been affected by parenthood. Friends of his from the exclusive schools he'd attended growing up hired nurses, nannies and housekeepers while they continued to party and travel with their society wives, leaving the care of the children to the hired help. It was a time-honored tradition in the British upper class but bore little resemblance to how Sir Simon and Lady Josephine had raised Charles and his siblings.

His parents had built their lives around the family, raising a tight-knit group of children with love, laughter and bucketfuls of patience.

Charles knew he'd been a particular challenge, always into mischief as a boy and usually pulling one or more of his siblings along with him. It was all in good fun, and as much as he pushed the limits of his parents' patience, he never once doubted their unconditional love.

He'd spent enough time with his siblings and their spouses to know they were raising their children with much the same philosophy. His family set the bar high, and this was the first time Charles felt the need to live up to those standards.

If only he knew how.

He didn't have the first clue about being an instant family man, and it wasn't just Flynn that scared him. The beautiful blonde from a year ago had occasionally flitted across his mind, leaving him with a satisfied smile and a trace of longing. Seeing Alice again had felt like a swift blow to the head, knocking him off his game and instantly breaking through the self-control he'd so carefully cultivated. He tried to tell himself it was simply because she was now the mother of his son, but it felt like something more. It felt as if she might be the answer to a question he hadn't even thought to pose.

He grabbed his phone off the nightstand and quickly texted Lucie. A part of him dreaded telling anyone in his family about this monumental development in his life, but they were bound to discover it sooner than later. One thing that came with having such a close family was the inability to keep anything secret.

But his younger sister had managed to keep her marriage to Chase Parker under wraps for ten years. Technically, Lucie had believed that the marriage had been annulled shortly after it had taken place, but still...

Lucie texted back almost immediately and agreed to meet him for breakfast in an hour. He forced himself out of bed, then took a hot shower in the hopes of reviving himself a bit. He was on his third cup of black coffee in the hotel restaurant when his sister sank into the chair across from him.

"To what do I owe the pleasure?" she asked, folding her hands in front of her on the table. "I thought you were heading to Horseback Hollow this morning."

"Plans changed," he said, his leg bouncing under the table. It probably hadn't been the best idea to over-caffeinate before this conversation.

"Official *royal* tourism business, I assume," Lucie said with a smirk. She took a drink of water from the goblet set at her place. None of his siblings ever tired of teasing him about the ad campaign.

"I have a son," Charles answered, the older brother in him slightly gratified when she choked and coughed, her eyes widening in shock as she lifted a napkin to her mouth.

"How... When... Who...?" Lucie looked as gob-smacked as Charles felt, but it was good to say the words out loud. Not that holding Flynn in his arms hadn't made it real, but he'd almost wondered if lightning might strike him down for actually claiming the boy as his own.

A waiter approached their table, and Charles glanced at the menu. "I'll have the eggs Benedict," he told the young man. "How about you, Luce?"

She didn't move but continued to stare at him, mouth agape.

"She'll have tea and the granola and yogurt, I believe."

With a curious glance at Lucie, the waiter nodded and walked away.

Charles picked up his coffee cup, then set it down again, as his head was still buzzing. He waved his fingers in front of his sister's face until she blinked. "Which question would you like answered first?"

Patting the napkin to her lips, she leaned forward. "How did this happen?"

He felt the corner of his mouth curve, since that was the exact question he'd first asked Alice. "The usual way."

Lucie blinked a few more times. "How old is the boy?"

"Four months."

"And the mother?"

"I don't know her exact date of birth, but I'd guess midtwenties."

"This is serious, Charles."

"Trust me, Lucie," he said, as he ran a hand through his hair, "I know that."

She gave the barest nod of acknowledgment. "Who is the mother?"

"Her name is Alice Meyers."

"The woman who called when we were out the other day?"

"Yes. She lives here in Austin and heard I was in town."

"Why hadn't she told you about the baby before now?"

He shrugged. "She didn't think I would want to be involved."

Lucie tilted her head, considering that.

"I'm not certain she even wants me involved," Charles continued. "She seems to be managing fine on her own."

"Are you sure…" Lucie trailed off as the waiter brought a small tea service to the table.

"That he's mine?" Charles finished when the waiter had left again. "Yes. His name is Flynn, and he looks just like me and quite a bit like Ollie when he was that age."

Lucie met Charles's gaze as she unwrapped a tea bag and poured steaming water over it. "Still…how well do you know this Alice Meyers? If she's one of your usual girls, you should have proof. There are tests—"

"Alice offered, but I refused." He took a deep breath as he thought about Alice's big eyes and sweet smile. "She wouldn't…there's no question. I'm the father."

"So what now?"

Charles had a minute to think about his answer as their food arrived. "I've put in a call to the family attorney," he said, then took a bite of egg. "The first order of business is making provisions for the boy."

"There's more to being a daddy than 'making provisions,' Charles." Lucie's tone was chiding.

"I understand that, but I have to start somewhere." He pointed his fork at his sister. "Cut me a bit of slack, Lucie. This was a shock, to say the least."

She nodded. "Well, if this Alice Meyers isn't asking for anything, then I suppose you have options."

"What kind of options?" Charles demanded, his breakfast suddenly churning in his stomach. He tossed his napkin over his barely eaten plate of food. "Are you suggesting that I ignore the responsibility I have to my son?" He said the words through clenched teeth, hating that they were exactly what he'd been thinking earlier. A child meant commitment, and everyone knew Charles didn't do commitment.

But he wanted to now. He wanted to be a decent father to Flynn. He wanted someone to believe he could.

"You wouldn't ignore it," Lucie said gently. "I'm fully aware of how you've lived to this point, Charles, but you are a good man in your heart. You're our father's son. You *will* make this work."

His sister's words were a salve on the wound of his self-doubt. Lucie was right. Charles might not have any idea of how to be a father, but as he'd told Alice, he'd had the best role model anyone could ask for in Sir Simon. Still, he wondered where to even begin. "He's so tiny," he said to Lucie. "Like a miniature old man. Only soft and cute."

Lucie grinned. "That's an interesting mental image. Do you have a picture?"

Charles shook his head. "I could barely remember my own name once I saw him, let alone to take a photo. But I'm staying in Austin and will get to know him."

"What about Alice?"

"I'll prove to her that I deserve to be part of Flynn's life, if that's what it takes."

"What I meant was, where does Alice fit into all of

this? Mothers and babies are kind of a package deal, you know. How do you feel about Alice?"

"Alice seems…" How did he describe his jumbled feelings for a woman he'd spent only one night with but couldn't get out of his mind? Alice was not just beautiful on the outside but a truly good person, someone who deserved to be loved and cherished. She was the kind of woman who produced thoughts of rings and bended knees and forever. Charles might be able to manage fatherhood, but that didn't make him a forever type of chap. "She's nice, Lucie. Far too nice for someone like me."

"You've always sold yourself short."

"I'm a realist," he argued. "I know who I am."

"You know who you've been up until now," she countered. "You're not in Britain, Charles. Trust me, Texas is the best place for a new start."

"One step at a time."

"Just promise me you'll get to know Alice as well as the baby."

He signaled for the check. "Of course. I'll be spending time with both of them. I can't very well take a baby gallivanting about town on my own."

"You know what I mean." Lucie rolled her eyes. "You have more walls surrounding you than the Tower of London. Get to know her, Charles, and let her know you. The real you, not only Bonnie Lord Charlie."

"Does that mean you believe there's more to me than 'the royal treatment'?" he asked. It was meant to be a joke but the question came out in an almost desperate tone.

"I know there is," Lucie answered just as gravely.

He gave a curt nod, hoping his sister was right.

Chapter Four

Alice finished giving Flynn his bottle just as the doorbell rang later that afternoon. Charles had texted in the
morning, asking if he could stop by to talk about the
next steps, and Alice had been teetering on the edge of
panic ever since.

What did that mean? She knew she had rights as
Flynn's mother, but was also aware that her meager resources were no match for the Fortune Chesterfield family's power and influence.

She placed the empty bottle in the sink and threw a
burp cloth over her shoulder as she walked toward the
door. Her legs grew heavier with each step, even though
she'd donned her favorite wedge sandals, a black-and-
white zebra-print pattern with sparkling crystals embed-
ded in the ankle strap. Alice didn't need the extra height
but somehow wearing heels always gave her a little jolt

of confidence. And she needed all the confidence she could get to face Charles again.

She opened the door slowly, mentally steeling herself for the sight of the tall, dapper Brit. Unfortunately, not even a superhero-level force field could protect her from Charles. Today he wore dark trousers and a crisp tailored button-down shirt. He looked amazing. She bit down on her lip to keep a groan from escaping, and he flashed a quick, almost uncertain smile.

"Hullo, Alice." That accent should be illegal for the things it did to her insides. But before the requisite melting could start, Flynn let out a burp that would make a drunken sailor proud. Nothing like a bit of baby reflux for an icebreaker.

She rubbed a hand along Flynn's back and stepped away from the door. "Come on in." Then she glanced at the throng of bags and packages gathered at Charles's feet. "Did you rob a toy store?"

He gave her another smile and adjusted his shirt collar. "I hope you don't mind. I picked up a few necessities for the boy."

Flynn belched again and this time she could feel something warm soak into the cloth over her shoulder. She dipped her chin to look at Flynn, whose cheek was now resting in a puddle of spit-up formula. "Let me just clean him up," she said quickly, noting that Charles's expression was an equal mix of amusement and disgust.

She turned for the nursery and made quick work of cleaning Flynn, who gurgled and gazed at her. She changed his outfit, ridiculously wanting her son to make a good impression with Charles this afternoon. She realized if Charles did indeed decide to be a regular part of Flynn's life, he'd have to get used to the dirty work of taking care of a baby. Still, for now she wanted things to be easy.

By the time she returned to the apartment's small living area, it appeared that half the room was filled with toys and space-guzzling baby contraptions. Alice had purchased the bare essentials when she was pregnant, both to save money and because her two-bedroom apartment in the trendy neighborhood west of downtown and close to her work had a lot of charm but not much room.

"Is that a T-ball set?" she asked, balancing Flynn in one arm as she pointed to a package that held an oversize baseball and plastic T.

"Baseball is the American pastime," Charles told her. "I thought Flynn and I could learn together."

She couldn't help her smile. "It will be a few years before he's ready for a ball and glove."

"I have time," Charles answered, his tone serious. "I want you to know I'm here for the duration, Alice. I'll admit I have no idea what I'm doing." He gestured to the mass of packages on the floor, looking hopeful and utterly irresistible. "But I want to try, if you'll give me a chance."

The good news was she'd gone a whole five minutes without melting into a needy, longing puddle at Charles's feet. The bad news was, with one sentence, he'd completely turned her to mush. She nodded, not trusting her voice at the moment.

She knew he was talking about trying with Flynn, but Alice couldn't stop herself from wanting more. For a year she'd been fine, proud that she'd risen to the challenge of having a baby by herself, resolved to raise Flynn on her own.

Charles made her long for things a woman like her

couldn't expect to have. What he was offering had to be enough. It was the right thing for Flynn, and that's what was important. As much as she'd tried to convince herself otherwise, a boy needed his father. Her own dad was sweet, if a bit distant and bumbling, in the role of grandpa, much as he'd been as a father to her. But Henry Meyers, tenured professor of history at the University of Texas at Austin, was never going to teach Flynn to play baseball or how to catch a fish or any of the things men other than her father seemed to know by osmosis.

Charles, for all his formal British mannerisms and expensive suits, was a man's man. She'd seen pictures on the internet of him horseback riding and fly-fishing, things she wanted her son to learn if he was interested.

"As soon as I discovered I was pregnant," she said quietly, "my baby became my whole world. I'd do anything for Flynn. I thought it was right not to tell you, Charles. I figured you'd be like the rest of my family and friends, who thought I couldn't handle being a mother. They said I was too fragile, that it took strength and hard work to raise a child alone." She pressed a cheek to the top of Flynn's downy head. "I needed to prove to them, and to myself, that I could do it."

"Alice."

She shook her head. "You say you don't know what you're doing, but many new parents don't at the beginning. Even if you think you're prepared, if you've read every child-rearing book and article ever published, if every weekend has been filled with classes and workshops, nothing prepares you for the moment you hold the baby. Nothing truly prepares you to take that tiny bundle home, knowing you're responsible for another life.

I've learned a lot in just four months, and here's the one thing that can't be taught."

She took a deep breath, cleared her throat. "It's how to love someone. The reason parents work so hard is love. A life-altering, fierce and potent love for your baby that makes all the sleepless nights and fear and doubt worth it." She stepped closer, watched Charles's blue eyes widen as he glanced between her and Flynn. "You said your father was wonderful, and I know you come from a close-knit family. You know how to love, Charles. I don't expect it to happen overnight, but I know you'll make a good father. I believe Flynn is lucky to have you." She smiled and held the baby toward him.

Charles didn't realize how much he needed to have someone believe in him until Alice said the words out loud. This woman, whom he barely knew, seemed to see into the heart of him, past his superficial facade and the walls he'd constructed that everyone else assumed made him who he was. She slew him with her honesty—a unique mix of vulnerability and strength.

He reached for Flynn, even as he wanted to scoop up Alice, too. His fingers itched to pull them both close and hope some of her goodness transferred to him. He settled for the baby, aware that Alice had let him into her life for the sake of the boy.

Supporting Flynn's body in the crook of his elbow, he placed a hand on the back of the baby's head and lifted him. Flynn's deep blue gaze focused on Charles, glancing from his nose to his mouth, then finally settling on his eyes. They watched each other for a moment before Flynn squirmed and his tiny, rosebud mouth curved into a small smile.

Charles hitched in a breath, knocked for an emotional loop at how much one tiny smile could mean to him. "I think he has gas," he muttered.

Alice laughed. "He's smiling at you. He's a happy baby, Charles." She stifled a yawn. "Not much of an overnight sleeper, but very happy."

He stood there, transfixed by the baby in his arms. "What do I do now?"

She laughed again. "Talk to him. Bounce him. He's just like your niece and nephews."

"He's different," Charles whispered. "He's mine."

Alice sank to her knees on the floor. "Is there anything in this generous pile of gifts that he can use before he's a toddler?"

Right. The toys. The reminder snapped Charles out of his reverie. "We should be able to find something. What do you think, Flynn?" He lifted the baby closer, blew a tickling breath against his neck and was rewarded with a gurgling laugh. It was the best sound he'd ever heard.

"Try that," he said, pointing to one of the larger shopping bags. He lowered himself next to her, turning Flynn to sit on his forearm, the baby's back and head resting against Charles's chest. "I got an activity gym. The colors are glaringly bright, but the saleslady assured me it's top-of-the-line and perfect for a four-month-old." He glanced at her. "Unless you have one already?"

"Not yet," Alice said with a shy smile. She reached for the bag but stopped as Flynn let out a determined grunt.

Charles glanced down at the boy, whose face turned bright red. "I think he's digested the bottle," he told Alice as he quickly held out Flynn with two hands. The baby kicked and gurgled some more, but there was no mistaking the smell radiating from his back end.

"Let me," Alice said quickly, scrambling to her feet. "We'll be back in a minute."

Charles let out a relieved breath as she disappeared into a bedroom with Flynn. Twenty-four hours a dad, and Charles wasn't sure he was quite ready for nappy duty. Instead he pulled the activity gym out of the box and fastened the toys to the arches that crisscrossed over the soft mat. By the time Alice returned with a fresh-scented Flynn, Charles was just putting batteries into the motorized mobile piece of the play set.

Alice crouched down and lay Flynn on his back under the arches. The boy immediately kicked his feet and swatted at the dangling toys with his hands.

"He's got the hang of it already," Charles said proudly. "Smart lad. Takes after his…" He paused as Alice arched a brow. "Both his parents."

"Of course," she agreed with a grin.

He loved making Alice smile and was surprised to find himself content to watch Flynn play with the toys, entranced by the joyful noises the baby made. Alice settled on the floor, stretching her legs in front of her, her back resting against one of the chairs in the small family room. Charles wished he could pull her to his side, tuck her up against him and feel her breathing, but he also knew what he wanted from her was less platonic than simple companionship.

He moved to the far side of the activity gym and traced one finger along the leather strap at her ankle. "I love these shoes," he told her.

"Me, too." She flexed and pointed her foot a few times. "I'd have a lot more savings in my retirement account if I didn't love shoes so much."

"You don't have to worry about a retirement account

any longer," he said. "I'm going to take care of you and Flynn."

Immediately she moved, drawing her feet up underneath her. "That's not what I was suggesting. You don't owe me anything, Charles."

"You're the mother of my child, Alice. Do you really think I'd ignore that?"

"I didn't seek you out for financial support."

"Which doesn't change the fact that I have it to give."

She bit down on her lip, moved closer to Flynn and softly stroked one of his tiny feet. "Are you going to try to take him away from me?"

"No," Charles answered immediately, taking her hand in his. "Alice, look at me."

She glanced up, her gaze wary.

"Why would you think that?"

"Because you're rich and powerful and British. Texas isn't your home. I know that."

He chuckled softly. "It's quickly becoming my second home, especially since most of my family lives here now."

"But you'll return to England at some point."

He nodded.

"I can't be separated from Flynn. He's too young. He's all I have."

"That isn't my intention, Alice." As much as he'd loved making her smile, Charles equally hated that he'd caused the pain he saw in her eyes now. "I've changed my plans so I'll be in Austin for three weeks. After that, I'll need to figure out the next step. But I'm not going to take Flynn from you. I promise, Alice."

She gave a shaky nod, swiped under her eye. He

shifted closer to her and traced the pad of his thumb along her moist cheek. "No tears, sweetheart."

"I'm sorry," she said automatically. "I'm tired and…"

"No apologies, either." He dipped his head until his lips barely brushed hers. "We're in this together. The three of us are a team."

"A team?" she said, the husky note in her voice making him nip the corner of her mouth.

"Team Fortune Chesterfield," he whispered, and pressed his lips to hers. Her mouth was soft and yielding, molding to his without question. The taste of her was new and yet familiar, and all the memories of their night together came flooding back to him. The way she'd touched him, her innocence the most erotic thing he'd ever encountered… His fingers trailed through her hair, which was soft as spun silk. He remembered how it felt to have those thick, blond waves fanned out across his chest as she slept. Her tongue touched his, hesitantly, as if she wasn't sure whether he wanted the kiss to deepen.

There were no words for what Charles wanted from Alice. His need was so elemental, the potential ramifications so jumbled in his mind that he could barely form a coherent thought. His body grew heavy with desire. Desire he understood. Then he felt something in his heart, a slight shift from normal, and a skipped beat that had him tearing his mouth away from hers. In all Charles's many interactions with women, his protected heart had never come into play. No one had ever come close to breaching his defenses.

Until now.

Until Alice.

"I have to go," he said as he lurched to his feet. "There's a… I need to… I'll call you tomorrow."

She stared up at him as if he had just sprouted a horn from his forehead. Her fingers pressed to her mouth like she couldn't believe it had, moments earlier, been crushed under his. What the hell was wrong with him? Alice told him she believed in him, gave him a chance to be a father and first thing out of the gate he practically mauled her. So much for his legendary charm and experience. He felt like a randy schoolboy with his first crush.

"Thank you for the gifts," she said after a moment.

"Of course." He ran a hand through his hair even as he backed toward the door of her apartment. "I can bring more. If there's anything you need—"

"No." She glanced at Flynn, who was now dozing under the activity gym, and then stood. "You've done more than enough, Charles." Her hands were clenched at her sides in tight fists. If he had to guess, she was trying hard not to physically push him from her home. That was no less than what he deserved.

"I'll call you," he repeated, and turned for the door. But before opening it, he swung back, dropped to his knees and reached for Flynn's chubby hand. "Goodbye, little man," he whispered. "Sweet dreams."

Chapter Five

Alice stood under the shade of an elm tree in front of her building the next afternoon, watching as a sleek Mercedes sedan pulled to the curb. True to his word, Charles had called that morning and asked to see her and Flynn again, suggesting he bring lunch to her apartment.

Unfortunately, Alice didn't trust herself alone with the handsome Brit after yesterday's kissing fiasco. Yes, she wanted a father for her son. But could she and Flynn ever be enough for him? She'd told herself at the start of all this that her needs were secondary to those of her son, but she was having trouble convincing her body. It had felt so right when Charles touched his lips to hers, and she'd wanted to sink into him and revel in the feel of her body thrumming back to life.

It had been silly to believe that Charles would want anything more from her than access to Flynn. What could someone like her possibly offer a man like him? The same doubts had plagued her during her pregnancy, contributing to her long list of reasons for not contacting him.

If she'd had any hopes about him wanting her in that way, they'd been shattered when he'd broken their embrace like she'd tried to eat him alive and he had one chance for escape. She'd gone for more than two decades without a man before Charles, and over a year since their night together. Maybe that's why her need for him seemed to overpower her.

Although she was rarely alone, with Flynn to look after, motherhood added a level of isolation to her already quiet life that she hadn't expected. Still, she had no intention ruining the fragile bond Charles had with Flynn just because she was the modern day equivalent of a dried-up spinster.

With that in mind, public outings with Charles seemed the most prudent course of action. But they still needed to maintain some level of anonymity. According to Charles, most people believed he'd gone to Horseback Hollow, as was his original plan. That gave them some time, but although Austin wasn't as overtly overrun with cowboys as Dallas or Houston, Charles didn't exactly blend in as a local. Alice hoped to remedy that today.

"Tell me again where we're going," Charles said as he approached her on the sidewalk. He wore a fitted black sweater, even though the temperature was hovering in the midseventies, and dark, tapered trousers. Even before he uttered a word, anyone within a block could tell he wasn't American.

"To the mall," she said. She held Flynn's infant seat

between them, needing every bit of physical distance she could manage.

"As in a shopping mall?"

Alice almost laughed at the words rolling off his tongue in that crisp accent. "Barton Creek Square isn't far from here, and you need a new wardrobe."

He ran a hand over the front of his sweater and arched an eyebrow. "Is there something wrong with my clothes?"

"Not if you want to constantly be recognized while you're in Austin," she told him. "You dress like you're British."

"I *am* British."

"Which is why we're going to turn you into an American for a few weeks." She smiled and stepped away from the building. "Trust me, Charles."

"I'm not wearing Wranglers," he mumbled, and she did laugh.

"No Wranglers," she agreed. "But at least one ten-gallon hat."

He shot her a horrified glance.

"I'm kidding." Alice found that she enjoyed teasing Charles. "Austin's fashion style is fairly casual and, because of the college and the music scene, it's less 'cowboy' than a lot of places in Texas. You'll be fine." She started for the walkway next to her building. "My car's in the lot around back."

"We can take mine."

"You don't have a car seat base."

He flashed her a proud smile. "I do, and I had it installed at the fire station the hotel concierge recommended."

She sucked in a breath, trying not to let her heart

be influenced by the thoughtfulness of that gesture. He lifted the car seat out of her hands, their fingers brushing.

"Hullo there, little man," he said to Flynn as he tipped back the sunshade. Flynn gurgled in response.

"I need to grab his stroller from the trunk of my car." She shrugged at Charles's questioning glance. "There's not a lot of room in the apartment, so I keep it in the car when I'm not using it."

He considered that for a moment. "A boy needs a yard to romp in, Alice."

"Flynn has a while to go before the 'romping' stage begins."

"If you'd let me—"

"My apartment is fine." She held up a hand. "One step at a time. Please."

"One step at a time. Let's drive around back to your car." He hit the remote start on the key fob and then clicked the infant carrier into the base waiting in his back seat. This was the first time she'd gotten in a car with her son and not been driving since her father brought her home from the hospital after Flynn's birth.

Charles held open the door and she slipped into the buttery leather seat, stowing the diaper bag at her feet.

"Do you always wear heels?" he asked, leaning over the top of the door.

"Whenever possible," she admitted. "These are low for me." Today she'd gone casual with a pair of polka-dot espadrilles with a stacked one-inch heel.

"I like them," he said simply, but the intensity in his eyes as they raked over her body made awareness whisper across her skin.

"Thanks," she murmured as he shut the door.

She concentrated on breathing as he came around the

front of the car, but that didn't help her muddled senses. The Mercedes was new, but the barest hint of Charles's scent lingered in the air. It wound around her brain until she felt like she might lose control, a feeling that only intensified when he climbed in and curled his long fingers around the steering wheel.

"Are you hot?" he asked, reaching forward to adjust the temperature control on the dash.

Alice almost choked on her own tongue. Was she hot? If he knew what she was feeling right now, he'd dump her and Flynn on the sidewalk in a minute. "Fine," she managed to reply in a normal tone.

They pulled around back and retrieved the stroller before heading toward Barton Creek Square. The upscale shopping center was only about ten minutes from her apartment.

"Of all the times I've visited the States," Charles said with a wry grin, "I've managed to avoid stepping into an American mall."

"Until now."

He winked at her. "Only for you, Alice."

She actually laughed at the absurdity of that statement. Now that she was becoming used to Charles being in close proximity, she began to relax. Driving to a mall was far less intimate than sitting together in her small apartment, even if it gave her the mistaken sense that somehow the three of them were a real family. Putting those dangerous thoughts aside, she pointed the edge of the mall out to Charles. "There's an underground parking garage near Nordstrom. That's a central starting point."

He nodded. "Even I've heard of Nordstrom."

"What do you normally do during your visits?"

"I see friends and my family. Texas is relatively new

for me. Before my mother discovered she was a Fortune, I'd spent most of my time on the coasts."

"Was being part of the Fortunes a big adjustment?"

"In some ways." Charles steered the sedan down the ramp of the multilevel parking structure. "But we've always been a big family, so having more cousins has been nice. None of us enjoy the additional notoriety that comes with the Fortune name, but we can deal with it."

"I heard that Kate Fortune is still in Austin. I saw a picture of her on the local news last week. She certainly is a walking advertisement for her youth serum."

His gaze was hooded as he glanced over. "I haven't met her yet."

"It's probably just a matter of time," Alice offered, wondering why she felt the need to placate Charles on the subject of Kate Fortune.

"We'll see." He pulled into an empty spot near the elevator on the second level and shifted the car into Park. "My sister Lucie told me Kate has been meeting with members of the Fortune extended family because she's looking for the right person to take over her company when she retires."

"That makes you a candidate?"

He shook his head. "Not yet. I've been in Austin almost a week and I've heard nothing from her. Not that I want to run a cosmetics company…"

"But you want the chance to say no."

One side of his mouth curved. "I'll admit, it pricks my ego not to be considered. Foolish, right?"

"Not at all." Alice understood how it felt to be overlooked, and as hard as it was to believe she had that in common with this handsome, dashing man, she knew that the pain of Kate Fortune's disregard went deeper than simple ego. "You'd be an excellent choice."

"Honestly, I have no desire to work with Fortune Cosmetics." He paused, tapped one hand on the steering wheel, then turned to her. "But what makes you think I could do it?"

She gave him a genuine smile. "You're smart and great with people. You have sharp instincts and I think you'd be a good manager."

He snorted. "I can barely manage my social calendar."

"That's what you want people to believe," Alice answered, shaking her head. "Because it's easier than admitting that you care. But you do, Charles. I watched you at the conference last year."

"I watched you, too, Alice." His voice was pitched low and she realized he was trying to distract her.

"Stop," she said, poking him in the arm. "This is serious."

He blinked at her. "I try to avoid being serious whenever possible. Everyone knows that about me."

"That's your mask, but there's more to you. No one can be as carefree as you act and still be successful without working very hard at it. You knew exactly what to say at the conference to put people at ease. You listened to what they wanted in a vacation and understood how to talk about England in a way that made it personal to each of them."

She hefted the diaper bag onto her lap, needing a distraction to stop thinking how personal she'd gotten with Charles after the conference. "Those were tourism professionals," she couldn't help but add. "They're practically immune to a sales pitch, even a very good one. But no one is immune to you, Charles."

He stared at her for several long moments and the nonchalance so often in his eyes dropped away for a moment, revealing a different man than the one the public knew. A man Alice could easily fall for if she wasn't careful.

"Not even you?" he asked.

She gave a startled laugh. "I'm a mother now. I don't count." Before he could weigh in on that pronouncement, she opened her door and climbed out. "We should get moving. Flynn will need to eat in about an hour and he usually gets fussy before that."

The air in the parking garage was sticky and stifling, and Alice quickly unfastened the car seat as Charles pulled the stroller out of the trunk. He didn't say anything as they walked toward the entrance of the mall, a burst of cool air greeting them when the automatic doors opened. Alice babbled on about the layout of the stores, the best options in the food court and the wonder that was the Nordstrom shoe department.

Charles listened but most of his attention was focused on maneuvering Flynn's stroller through the clusters of shoppers. Sunday afternoon was prime shopping time, and Alice wanted to find him some new clothes before he was spotted. The last thing she needed splashed across the local paper was a picture of Charles pushing Flynn's stroller.

"Here we are," she said as they came to a small storefront.

Charles squinted up at the sign. "This isn't Nordstrom."

"It's better if we start here. Marc & Cross is a Texas chain. They have stores in Austin, Dallas and San Antonio."

He glanced at the burly mannequins in the window, dressed as if they were going on some kind of hip cattle drive, then back at Alice. "You do a lot of shopping here?"

"No," she said around a giggle. "But I have friends who do."

"Boyfriends?" Charles's eyes narrowed.

She shook her head. "Friends who are guys."

"What's the difference?"

"I never… We didn't…you know." She wrapped her fingers around his upper arm and immediately regretted it. His biceps was hard and she could feel the warmth radiating from his skin.

"I'm certain they wanted to," Charles said, stubbornly staying right where he was. She tugged again. "I bet you had men lined up around the block."

"Hardly." She let go of his arm to walk into the store. He followed with the stroller. "I was such a late bloomer, I may have missed my chance entirely." She thought about her miserable love life before Charles and the condom that had languished in her purse for almost two years. The whole reason she now had Flynn. "We're not here to talk about me. We're getting clothes for you." She started for a rack near the front of the store, but Charles grabbed her wrist, sliding his fingers down her hand until they laced with hers.

"If that's the case, the men in Austin are complete prats." He grinned when she squinted. "Fools. They are complete fools, Alice."

"All of them but you," she whispered, then clasped a hand over her mouth. She hadn't meant to say the words out loud.

Charles's grin widened. "All of them but me," he

agreed. "Now what would you pick out that doesn't make *me* look like a prat?"

She started with a couple pairs of jeans, one a dark wash and another more faded. Both were boot cut, which Charles thought was ridiculous since he didn't own boots.

"Next stop is the Nordstrom shoe department," she informed him.

"My credit card is trembling with anticipation," he retorted.

She also picked out several shirts, both long and short sleeved, and a few pairs of shorts, since the temperature was going to only get hotter as spring progressed. One of the salesclerks took the clothes to a dressing room, and Alice couldn't help but notice the way the woman's eyes lingered on Charles. He seemed oblivious, and Alice figured basking in female attention was a daily occurrence for this far-too-attractive Fortune.

He shuddered as she handed him a baseball cap. "You can't possibly expect me to put that on my head."

"It's better than a cowboy hat, and it's good cover." She stepped toward him. Despite her height, she needed to stretch onto her tiptoes to place the hat on his head. She adjusted it, then brushed back the hair that curled at his neck.

His blue eyes darkened and he bent his head toward hers. So much for being safe in public. The bill of that baseball cap bumped her forehead at the same time Flynn let out a hungry squawk from his stroller.

Alice jumped away from Charles, knocking into a display of logo T-shirts. "You need shirts," she said, and blindly grabbed a few, shoving them toward him. "And Flynn needs to eat."

Charles took the shirts but watched her as she un-strapped the baby and lifted him from his carrier. "Do you need help?"

"I've got instant formula in the diaper bag." She hefted the sack in one arm, balancing Flynn in the other. "You try on everything. The food court is just across the way. We'll wait for you there."

Charles moved in front of her, lifted the diaper bag off her shoulder. "I'll get you settled first," he said, dropping a gentle kiss on the top of Flynn's head. It was a sweet gesture but also brought him close enough to whisper into her ear, "Unless you'd like to join me in the fitting room?"

"I…no," she blurted, and squeezed Flynn tighter. The boy let out a cry and the corners of his mouth turned down in a trembling pout that Alice knew indicated a full-blown wail wasn't far behind.

"Someday," Charles said smoothly, and turned for the back of the store.

Two weeks ago it would have seemed impossible to Charles that he could spend a thoroughly enjoyable af-ternoon in a temperature-controlled, fluorescent-lit shop-ping mall. But everything about being with Alice and Flynn shifted his preconceived notions about life. He had a suspicion that any activity done in the beautiful blonde's company would make for a better time than he'd had in years. Of course, the activities Charles most wanted to partake in with Alice weren't fit to even think about while he was bouncing his son on his knee, but he couldn't seem to stop his mind from wandering to thoughts of kissing her again.

After the first store, she'd convinced him to change into a pair of jeans and the Texas Longhorns T-shirt he'd purchased. The baggy denim and soft cotton felt foreign against his skin, but he had to admit he blended in better with the other men being led around the mall by their wives and girlfriends. He'd even gotten a pair of round-toed Western boots at Alice's beloved Nordstrom. He actually liked the weight of the shoes and was tempted to take a picture of himself to send to his siblings in Horseback Hollow. They wouldn't believe Charles dressed as an American.

His reward had been buying a pair of the sexiest shoes on the planet for Alice. She'd refused at first, but as soon as he saw the pair of strappy heels he'd wanted to see Alice in them. The more time he spent with her, the better he understood how men for so long had overlooked her.

Her pale blond hair and delicate features were gorgeous, but she had the ability to almost become invisible when other people were around. Her natural reserve and shyness made her shrink in on herself to the point that no one noticed her. Charles would have found it difficult to believe, since he could barely take his eyes off her, but in every store today the salespeople looked past her to him. She seemed to expect it, and the more it happened, the more Alice retreated.

The juxtaposition of the timid woman and the overtly sensual heels drove Charles crazy. The fact that he was the only man on the planet who knew that, underneath her shy exterior, Alice was just as passionate as the shoes would suggest just about sent him over the edge. He'd insisted she try on the red satin heels. The straps that wound around her ankles gave the impression that her feet were a tantalizing gift to be opened. Even with her wearing a crisp white T-shirt, and jeans rolled to her calves, her legs in those shoes were the most arousing thing he'd ever seen.

"They're too much," she argued, glancing at the price on the box.

"You're getting them." He jiggled Flynn on his knee, both hands supporting the baby, for Flynn's sake as well as to ensure that Charles didn't grab Alice and ravish her in the middle of the department store.

"I don't have an occasion to wear them." She sighed. "Since Flynn, my minuscule social life has become downright nonexistent."

"We'll find a place." Charles smiled at the salesclerk. "I'll take the heels and the boots," he told her, and handed over his credit card. When the woman walked away, he pointed at Alice. "Admit it, you love them."

She wrinkled her nose but grinned. "I do. I may just walk around the house tonight in my pajamas and heels because I love them that much."

"Any chance your pajamas are silk and lace?"

"Plain cotton flannel," she said with a snort, slipping her feet back into her espadrilles. "Not interesting at all."

"Invite me over," he coaxed. "I'll be the judge of that." Flynn waved his hands and kicked his feet. "Even the lad agrees."

Her face softened as she looked at Flynn. Charles could watch Alice watch their son for hours, marveling at the love shining in her eyes. Did all fathers feel this way about their child's mother? He was pretty sure Sir Simon had about Josephine. But his parents had been in love, and Charles barely knew Alice. It couldn't be anything more than the novelty of their situation.

"Charles—" she began, but broke off when his phone rang.

She scooped up Flynn as Charles pulled the phone from his pocket and glanced at the screen. His brother

Brodie. He sent the call to voice mail but a moment later the phone rang again. This time it was Jensen. Even as the phone rang, his text message alert sounded. "Damn," he muttered.

"Emergency?" Alice asked.

"To some people," he replied. In the midst of the barrage from his other siblings, Lucie texted to apologize for letting slip the news about Flynn and Alice. So much for his sister's ability to keep a secret. "I should probably deal with this." Charles held up his phone.

"No problem," Alice said immediately. "Flynn and I can walk—"

Did she really think he'd just desert her? It made him all the more frustrated at the intrusion when the result was Alice feeling insecure around him. "I'll drive you home first."

"I don't want to be a bother. If—"

"Alice, you aren't a bother." He realized his tone was harsher than he'd meant when she flinched. What was a bother were his nosy siblings. He took a step toward her. "I want to be with you and Flynn," he said gently. "Our son is my priority."

For some reason, his words made her hold the baby a little tighter to her chest. Charles wanted to question her but his phone rang again. "I'm silencing this thing until we're out of here. Let me sign the receipt and then we'll head for the car."

"I need to see to Flynn's diaper," she told him, looking almost apologetic. "There's a family restroom on the first floor."

"Then I'll bring the car from the garage and pick you up out front."

She nodded and placed the baby back in his carrier.

Charles watched her walk toward the elevator before finishing his purchase, collecting the shopping bags and starting for the car. He could feel the continuous vibration of his phone against his hip. His irritation grew by the second.

Whatever this was with Alice was too new to share with his family, as much as he loved them. He certainly didn't welcome their opinion on what kind of father he'd make. He could imagine what they'd have to say about that.

He pulled the car in front of the mall entrance and then helped Alice with the car seat and stroller. They were both silent on the way to her apartment, and Charles wished he could get back the cozy playfulness of the afternoon.

She practically jumped out of the sedan as he parked in front of her building. "I'm sorry for my foul mood," he told her as he took the stroller from the trunk. Where was his gift for charm when he needed it? "Let me walk you upstairs."

"It's fine." She clicked the car seat into place on top of the stroller. "You don't owe me an explanation, Charles. You don't owe me anything."

That might be true, but it wasn't what he wanted. His phone vibrated again. "Bloody hell, they're persistent." He scrubbed his palm across his jaw. "I've got to head out of town for a day. I'll see you when I get back." He bent his knees so he could look her in the eyes. "Right?"

Her rosy lips pressed together. "I don't expect—"

"No." He held a fingertip to her mouth. "I can't hear one more time that you don't expect anything from me. It's a refrain in my life that grows more tiresome by the hour." He leaned forward and replaced his finger with his mouth, giving her a kiss that he hoped promised her what he couldn't put into words just yet. "I'll see you soon, Alice."

She nodded, an adorable blush coloring her cheeks.

"Be good for your mum, little man," he said to Flynn, then climbed back into his car. He waited until he'd turned the corner from Alice's street, then pulled over to the curb. He quickly sent a group text to Brodie, Oliver, Jensen and Amelia.

Enough with the sodding messages. I'll be at the Horseback Hollow Cantina tomorrow at noon. Anyone with questions can meet me there.

Only a few seconds passed before the messages flooded in. Looked as if there would be a crowd of British Fortunes at lunch tomorrow.

Chapter Six

Alice didn't bother knocking on her parents' front door that night. She'd had Sunday dinner at their house every week since she'd moved out during her pregnancy.

At the time, both her mom and dad had begged her to stay. Although it had been a shock, her mother had taken the news of Alice's pregnancy better than her father. Lynn Meyers had mostly seemed worried that Alice wouldn't be able to keep herself and the baby safe and healthy if she went to live on her own.

She couldn't exactly blame her mother for worrying. Alice had lived at home all her life, even through four years at the University of Texas and once she started working for the tourism board. None of her friends had believed she was content to remain in her childhood bedroom, but Alice hadn't been motivated to leave until Flynn. Once she'd felt the baby move inside her, she'd started to resent her mother's well-meaning suggestions. Alice had needed to prove that she was strong enough to raise Flynn on her own, so she had put down the deposit on her small apartment two months before he'd been born.

Her father hadn't said a word when she moved out, which wasn't much different than how he'd been most of her life. Henry Meyers loved her, but he was far more interested in the details of the history of American immigration than his daughter's life. He hadn't questioned her story about the pregnancy being a result of a one-night stand, even though her mother continued to dig for more details about the father's identity.

There was no way she was going to reveal Bonnie Lord Charlie as Flynn's father to her parents. Meredith had a difficult enough time believing Alice could have caught the eye of the handsome Brit. Even if her mom and dad accepted the news, she wasn't ready to disclose her connection to Charles.

Her mom scooped up Flynn from his car seat as soon as Alice walked into the kitchen. Lynn cooed and cuddled the baby and even Alice's father fussed over him. It gave Alice a bit of confidence to remember that even if Charles didn't remain an active presence in Flynn's life, she had a family who loved her boy.

They ate the spaghetti dinner her mother had cooked and then Alice cleared the table while her mom fed Flynn a bottle and her father headed for his study.

"It feels like he changes every time I see him," Lynn said as Flynn's fingers curled around one of hers.

"He was almost sixteen pounds when I took him in for his four-month checkup last week." Alice stacked bowls and plates in the dishwasher as she spoke. "The doctor said he can try cereal before the end of the month."

"I wish you were still living here," her mother said gently. "I could help so much more. You look tired, sweetie."

Alice felt her fingers tighten around a glass. "I'm fine, Mom. He still isn't sleeping through the night. The pediatrician thinks solid food might help."

"I worry about you, Alice. Between work and caring for Flynn, there's no time for you. If you didn't have to work so many hours—"

"I love my job," Alice said, vigorously scrubbing the pasta pot before setting it on the dish drainer to dry. "And I love Flynn. I'm balancing the two of them the best I can. It's not an option to work less or else I can't pay for the babysitter and my apartment. You know that."

"But if you lived at home—"

"Not going to happen."

"Or had a husband…"

Alice dried her hands on a towel and went to sit at the table. Flynn had just finished his bottle and nuzzled his grandmother's shoulder as Lynn patted his back.

"Mom, I'm doing okay. Really."

"I know," her mother answered with a tender smile. "I'm proud of you, Alice. You're handling the responsibility of being a single mom better than I could have imagined. But it's hard for me to see you alone through all of this."

Alice thought of the time she'd spent with Charles in the past couple days. Being with him made even the mundane chores of parenting seem fun. Yes, she wanted more of that, but…

"There's something you're not telling me," her mother said suddenly, narrowing her eyes.

Alice blinked and tried to school her features. "No. It's nothing."

"It's a man," Lynn whispered.

"How do you..."

"Call it a mother's instinct," she continued, clearly perking up at the thought of a man in Alice's life. "Have you reconnected with Flynn's father?"

"I told you, I don't have a relationship with Flynn's father."

"At the time I believed you." Flynn burped and Lynn wiped a bit of spit-up from his chin. "But I can tell it's different now. Something, or someone, is on your mind. You were distracted during dinner. You listened to your father's thoughts on the instability of early colonial society without once suggesting that he start living in the present."

"It doesn't matter," Alice said quickly, but knew her mother could read through the blatant lie. Charles did matter, far more than she'd expected him to in such a short time. She wanted to believe him when he told her he'd be part of their son's life for the long haul, but it was difficult to discount his playboy reputation. "He's... Flynn's father is not the kind of man to commit to anyone."

"But he's the man you want?"

Alice sighed. "Nothing is going to come of it, Mom."

Lynn snuggled her grandson against her chest and Flynn's eyes drifted closed. "You're young, Alice. Just because you're a mother doesn't mean you don't have needs of your own."

"What I *need* is to take care of my baby." Alice stood

and lifted a sleeping Flynn from her mother's arms. "He's everything to me."

"You should have someone to take care of *you*, sweetie." Lynn stood and pressed a kiss to Alice's cheek and then Flynn's. "I'm not going to make you tell me who this man is, but I want you to know that I'm here if you need to talk. I know that your father and I were overprotective, and I probably still am, but you're a big girl now and I'm proud of you."

"Thanks, Mom." Tears pricked the back of Alice's eyes. "A baby might be exhausting, but it's a lot simpler, you know?"

Her mother gave a soft chuckle. "Life is complicated, relationships especially. Whoever this man is, if he could commit, do you see a future with him?"

Alice wanted a future with Charles with a longing that made her weak in the knees. But she was too practical to believe there was a chance of that happening. She couldn't hold a candle to the women he was used to, and the mundane reality of raising a child would never maintain his interest. "No," she whispered, and squeezed shut her eyes to keep from crying.

Immediately she was wrapped in a tight, motherly embrace. "I'm sorry, Alice." They stood in the kitchen for several minutes, Alice drawing strength from her mom until her breathing was back to normal.

Lynn drew away, ran a finger across Flynn's chubby cheek. "Whoever this man is, he's missing out on quite a prize."

Alice didn't have the heart to explain that Flynn's father might be keen on the baby, just not her. It felt weak and pathetic, when she should be thrilled and grateful that Charles was taking an interest in his son. That had been her goal from the first, and she couldn't let her feelings for Charles make her lose sight of that.

"We'll be fine." She had to believe that was true. Charles had gone to Horseback Hollow, so she had time to regain her emotional equilibrium before he returned. So far her intention of keeping her heart out of the mix had been a total failure, but she had to try harder.

Flynn was her whole reason for being, so how hard could it be to keep her interactions with Charles focused on the baby? Maybe she'd let things get too close too fast. Charles wanted to get to know Flynn, but there was no need to rush things. Maybe if she put the brakes on the time she spent with Charles, it would be easier to remember that the only reason he was in her life was the son they shared.

She was busy and tired, so it would probably make sense if she limited their contact to the weekends. Alice was a master at compartmentalizing her life. That seemed like a perfect solution to her trouble with Charles.

She kissed her mother goodbye and gave her father a hug, packed Flynn into her car and headed for home. She and her baby were a team. Team Meyers, not Team Fortune Chesterfield. Even if her team made her feel empty, it was best for everyone that she go it alone.

By the time Charles walked into the Horseback Hollow Cantina Monday afternoon, he was hot, tired and completely irritated by his siblings' interference in his life. It was nearly a six-hour drive from Austin to the quaint town that had become home to so much of his family. He'd left before sunrise and before he was halfway there had grown weary of the endless view of sky, livestock pastures and fields.

The long car ride had been somewhat productive, as he'd spent much of his time on the phone with his solicitor in London, working out the details of both a trust for Flynn and arrangements to take care of Alice's future.

There was a decent lunch crowd in the restaurant when he arrived, but he quickly spotted his brothers, Oliver, Brodie and Jensen, and his sister Amelia waiting at a large table near the back. A rush of love for his family rose to the surface, competing with his annoyance as he joined them. He was happy that his brothers and sister had found love in this small Texas town, but it wasn't easy having his close-knit family living an ocean away.

Amelia stood and greeted him with a fierce hug. "I'm so happy for you, Charles," she said in her soft voice. "Clementine is over-the-moon excited about having another cousin, although she wishes someone could provide her with a girl cousin." She arched an eyebrow at her three other brothers.

"Maybe Charles can go for a girl the next time around," Oliver said, shaking his head. "Or perhaps there's another little Fortune he has yet to discover."

"Oliver, stop," Jensen said, his tone reproving. "We agreed to hear Charles's side of the story."

"Whose side have you heard so far?" Charles asked, sinking into the chair between Jensen and Brodie. Amelia and Oliver sat on the opposite side of the table.

"Lucie's," Brodie said with a grin.

"She was supposed to keep the news a secret." Charles took a drink of water from the glass in front of him. "I thought she was an expert at secrets."

"Only her own," Amelia clarified.

A waitress approached their table, looking a bit dazed at the prospect of taking orders from so many British

Fortunes. She'd regained some of her composure by the time she got to Charles. "You're the royal one," she said, after he had ordered a burger and fries.

Charles pointed to Jensen. "He's the one they call 'sir.'"

The woman darted a brief glance at Jensen, then focused her attention back on Charles. "But you give the royal treatment, right?"

Charles cringed at having the embarrassing ad campaign mentioned in front of his siblings. The way the woman phrased the question made him sound like some sort of British stud for hire.

His brothers snickered. "Oh, he gives it all right," Brodie offered, laughing until Amelia swatted him on the arm.

The waitress smiled and scribbled something on the bottom of her order pad. "If you're in town for a spell and want some good ole Texas hospitality, give me a call." She ripped off a strip of paper and tucked it under the edge of the ketchup bottle in the middle of the table. "Don't have to be a royal to know how to have fun."

She turned from the table toward the kitchen, her hips swinging as she walked.

Oliver shook his head. "I forgot that sort of thing happens everywhere you go, Charles."

"It's disgusting," Amelia murmured.

Brodie grinned. "But a bit impressive."

Charles moved the ketchup bottle to cover the phone number. "I hate it."

"Since when?" Jensen asked.

Since Alice, Charles wanted to answer, even though he'd grown weary of his reputation and the attention that went along with it before that. But being with Alice had made it hit home how much he wanted something more from his life.

"Our Charlie Boy is a father now," Amelia said, when he didn't answer his brother's question. "That changes things."

"Has it, Charles?" Brodie asked.

"Flynn has changed everything," Charles said, absently running his hand through his hair. "But I'm still me and I'm damned scared of mucking up the whole thing."

His siblings greeted that pronouncement with silence.

"This is the part where you tell me I can do it," he muttered. "Words of encouragement and all that rot."

Oliver blew out a breath. "As in, hurrah, Charles, congratulations on getting a potential gold digger pregnant and saddling yourself with a lifetime of responsibility when you can barely remember to change your socks and underwear each day." As the oldest of Josephine's two boys from her first marriage, Oliver had always been protective of his brothers and sisters, and the blunt words stung. In truth, the dig at Charles's own character was easier to stomach than the implied insult to Alice.

"She's not a gold digger," he growled. "I won't hear you say a word against her, Oliver." He pointed a finger at each of them. "Not one word from any of you. Yes, the baby was a shock, but Alice is a wonderful mother and she's worked hard to support Flynn on her own. She hasn't asked me for anything."

"But you've offered," Brodie suggested.

"Of course I have," Charles snapped. "He's my son, she's his mother and I—" He broke off, unsure how to finish the sentence when he could barely wrap his own mind around his feelings for Alice and Flynn.

"You care about her," Amelia suggested in a gentle tone.

Charles took a deep breath. "I do."

The waitress brought their food at that moment and the table was silent as they were served.

"That changes things indeed," Jensen said, when the waitress was gone.

"Have you talked to Mum?" Amelia asked.

Charles almost choked on the french fry he'd popped into his mouth. "Bloody hell, no. And I don't want any of you to, either. I know what she'd say about all of this."

Amelia leaned forward. "She'd tell you to marry her." His three brothers nodded. "Perhaps that idea is worth considering," his sister added. The brothers shook their heads.

"That's a terrible idea," Brodie said around a bite of club sandwich. "You can't possibly marry her."

"Why not?" Amelia sounded offended on Alice's behalf.

"Because it gives her the power," Brodie said, as if the answer was obvious.

"Shall I tell Caitlyn you said that?" Amelia retorted.

Brodie blanched. "No way."

"You need to get custody of the baby." Oliver adjusted the cuffs of his expensively tailored shirt.

"Joint custody?" Jensen asked.

Oliver considered that for a moment. "Sole custody."

"Don't be daft," Charles snapped. "I would never try to take Flynn from Alice."

"Do you have a picture of him?" Amelia asked, clearly trying to diffuse some of the tension at the table. Charles loved his siblings, but he'd forgotten that they could each have strong and very differing opinions.

He wiped his hands on a napkin and pulled out the cell phone from his pocket. He clicked on his photo stream and passed the phone across the table.

"He's beautiful," Amelia said with a sigh as she scrolled through the pictures Charles had taken yesterday of Flynn.

"The girl is beautiful, too," Brodie added, looking over Amelia's shoulder. He glanced at Charles. "Not your usual type."

"You don't need to scroll through all of them," he said, reaching for the phone.

Jensen grabbed it first and studied the photos, his eyebrows raised. "This one looks like she actually has a brain inside that lovely head."

"Alice is smart, funny and kind, in addition to being beautiful." Charles sighed. "I highly doubt she'd want anything to do with me if it weren't for Flynn."

"You look happy with them," Amelia said, taking back the phone and holding it aloft for all the brothers to see. The picture had been taken at the mall's food court. Charles had been snapping pictures of Flynn, and a few of Alice when he could sneak them in. A woman at the table next to them had offered to take a photo of "the whole family." Both he and Alice had been embarrassed by the attention but had posed for the camera. Now that Amelia pointed it out, Charles saw that he looked not only happy but also relaxed in the photo, something utterly foreign to him in the past few years.

"Why are you wearing a baseball cap with a longhorn silhouette on it?" Oliver asked as he tipped the phone closer. "And why does it look like you're in a shopping mall?"

Charles grabbed the device and shoved it into his pocket. "I want to spend time with Alice and Flynn but can't take the chance of anyone recognizing me. She took me shopping for a more American wardrobe."

Jensen looked intrigued at this bit of information. "You mean this girl isn't trying to exploit her connection to you?"

"Not at all," Charles confirmed. "Alice is even more worried than I am that the tabloids will discover I'm Flynn's father. We want to have time to figure things out between the two of us before anything goes public."

"So why go out at all?" Brodie asked. "Can't you simply visit her at her home or have her to your hotel suite?"

Charles thought about being alone with Alice and sighed. "It's complicated."

"He wants to sleep with her," Oliver said with a laugh.

"No," the other three siblings said at once.

"It will mess with her head," Amelia exclaimed.

Brodie pointed a fry at him. "It will mess with *your* head."

Jensen nodded. "Whatever you do, don't sleep with her."

It was the one thing his brothers and sister all agreed on, making Charles smile. He had no plans to take Alice to bed again, except he couldn't seem to stop his longing to touch her. Maybe if they were together again, he could get it out of his system. No. Even he was smart enough to realize that once more with Alice wouldn't possibly be enough.

"Agreed," he said, meaning the word as he spoke it. "I'm going to take the next couple of weeks to get to know Alice and Flynn better and figure out how to make things work between us."

"But…" Amelia prompted.

"But I will not sleep with her," Charles added, and his siblings smiled.

Chapter Seven

Alice tried to focus on her computer screen Thursday morning but still felt like she was in a fog, despite three cups of tarry black swill from the office coffeemaker. Flynn had woken several times the previous night and she'd given up the hope of sleep around 4:00 a.m. It hadn't helped that anytime she closed her eyes, Charles's face popped into her mind.

He'd texted on his return from Horseback Hollow Monday afternoon, but she'd texted back that she and Flynn had plans and they could get together over the upcoming weekend. It was an outright lie, but she'd wanted time to shore up her defenses before she saw him again. Unfortunately, that could take a lifetime, and she knew Charles was losing patience with her.

He'd left two messages and texted several more times on Tuesday but she hadn't responded. She tried to convince herself that she was doing the right thing, that taking it slow would be better in the long run for all of them.

The truth was, she missed him. She missed the way he made her laugh and the fact that she could tease and flirt with him. She missed the way he looked at her like she was the only woman on the planet, one more reason he was dangerous to her heart. She'd seen enough photos and online videos of Charles to understand he gave every woman with him the same smoldering gaze.

Alice wasn't special, and the fact that he made her feel that way was something she was having trouble overcoming. So her plan to compartmentalize her relationship with him seemed like the best option.

"Are you ready for the marketing meeting?" Meredith peered over the top of the cubicle. "Oh, my. You look awful."

"Thanks," Alice said, and patted her palms against her cheeks, hoping to encourage a little color in her sallow, tired complexion. "I didn't get much sleep last night."

"I gather it wasn't Bonnie Lord Charlie keeping you awake until the wee hours."

She huffed out a laugh. "Hardly."

"Aren't you pitching the new international tourism campaign today?"

"Yes." Alice stood and straightened her dark gray suit jacket. She'd dressed up today to look the part of a seasoned tourism professional rather than a haggard new mom. She wore a tailored suit and a pair of patent-leather sling backs that she hoped would distract her bosses from the bags under her eyes. "I've been rehearsing since early this morning, but now I can't seem to finish a sentence without…" she paused as her mouth stretched open of its own accord "…yawning."

"You can do this," Meredith said, but her tone wasn't convincing.

Alice took a deep breath and one more fortifying gulp of coffee. "I can do this," she repeated, although she didn't sound any more certain than her friend.

She followed Meredith to the conference room at the end of the hall, holding her notes and handouts tight to hide the trembling in her fingers. Maybe she should have switched to decaf for that last cup of coffee. She desperately wanted her boss to green-light her idea for a new campaign. This was an opportunity to be seen as something more than a researcher and data cruncher for the tourism board. She knew she was good at her job, but she wanted a chance to prove she could handle her own campaign.

She plastered a smile on her face as she walked into the conference room, then ran smack into Meredith's back as her friend came to a sudden stop in the doorway. Alice peered around Meredith and her smile froze in place.

Charles sat in the chair next to Amanda Pearson, Alice's direct supervisor. Several other board members sat around the large table. There were two empty seats, one at the far end and one on the other side of Charles.

"Ladies, don't stand there gawking," Amanda said with an airy laugh. "I believe you both know Charles Fortune Chesterfield."

Meredith continued to stare until Alice poked her in the back. "Sit down, Mer," she said with a hiss.

"Did you know he was going to be here?" Meredith whispered.

Alice gave a sharp shake of her head. "No, but act normal. I don't want Amanda to guess anything."

Meredith moved forward. "Lord Charles," she said, giving an exaggerated curtsy.

He stood, pulling at the cuffs of his crisp white dress shirt. "Please call me Charles," he said, bestowing on Meredith his most charming smile. "I don't actually possess a title, despite what the tabloids would have you believe." He took Meredith's hand in his, and Alice could see her normally flirty friend's mouth drop open. Alice had started to think of the way women responded to him as "the Charles Effect."

Alice was determined to be immune to the Charles Effect today.

"It's nice to see you," Alice said, keeping her voice neutral. She took a step toward the far end of the table, but Charles held out the chair next to him.

"Please sit here, Ms. Meyers. I'm looking forward to hearing what you have to say this morning."

Meredith scooted to the empty chair at the end, leaving Alice to drop into the seat near Charles. Somehow she knew he was referring more to an explanation of why she'd blown him off the past few days than her campaign proposal.

"Charles is interested in working more with our office," Amanda explained, "and for whatever reason, Alice, he knows you from last year's conference." Her boss looked baffled as to why a man like Charles would remember Alice.

"It was your research," Charles said smoothly. "The figures you presented to support the impact of global tourism on the Texas economy were impressive."

He dropped his voice so low that only she could hear. "Everything about you impresses me, Alice."

Her gaze crashed into his for a second. That was all

the time she needed for the Charles Effect to kick in. Alice shook her head, trying to keep it clear.

"I thought it would be a good idea for Charles to attend this meeting, since he's in Austin for a few weeks." Amanda gave Alice a pointed look. "I hope he won't be disappointed."

"That seems unlikely," Charles added.

"Are you okay, Alice?" her boss asked. "You look pale."

"Fine." Alice wasn't sure she could say more than that at the moment. She was too busy trying not to react to Charles sitting so close to her. Her presentation and handouts were clenched in her fists, and she felt Charles lightly touch her wrist.

"Take a breath, Alice," he whispered. "You can do this."

She stood suddenly, wrenching her hand away from his. "The title of the campaign," she announced, clearing her throat when her voice came out in a squeak, "is It's Texas to Me, and while it fits into the larger scheme of the official state tourism campaign, it's also specific to the international market." She walked around the table as she spoke, placing a handout that showed a print ad mock-up in front of each person. "In our research we've discovered that a large percentage of first-time travelers to the United States from other parts of the world visit New York or California. Typically, they add Texas to the itinerary on subsequent trips, but we want to make the Lone Star State a first-run vacation destination."

She moved back to her place at the table but continued standing. It was easier to keep a bit of distance between herself and Charles this way. "The idea is that we'll showcase real people from other countries who have vacationed in the state and what Texas means to them. We'll show them with people from here—iconic cowboys, musicians, celebrities who call Texas home."

Several of the board bigwigs nodded as she made eye contact, bolstering her confidence. "We'll focus on what's special about each region, from the beaches of South Padre Island to the quaint shops of the hill country to the music scene in Austin. The goal is to give it a personal flavor and help travelers feel they have a connection to Texas before they even leave home. To make them think of Texas as their top-choice destination for an American vacation."

Amanda held up a hand before she could continue. "I think we've heard enough, Alice." The woman's smile was brittle and Alice realized she'd been right in suspecting that her boss hadn't really expected her to succeed. "That was—"

"Brilliant," Charles interrupted, quickly applauding. The rest of the attendees followed suit, and Amanda's smile froze in place.

"It was a good pitch," the woman allowed. "Perhaps I wouldn't go as far as brilliant."

"I agree with Charles," David McAvoy, the president of the tourism board, chimed in.

Alice felt her face flush as she sat down again. Charles gave her knee a friendly squeeze under the table. "I want to be involved," he told the group. "The ties I have to Texas have recently become more personal." He shot Alice a veiled glance. "And I can leverage my international contacts and the Fortune name here in the States to draw famous faces to the campaign. It has a universal enough appeal to be used in other countries, as well. I imagine the British Tourism Council might be keen on an It's Britain to Me campaign to run here in the States." He unleashed one of those killer smiles on Amanda. "If you're willing to allow Alice to lend me her expertise."

"Of course," Amanda told him, and for a moment Alice wondered if Charles was part vampire or some other nonhuman creature, given his ability to dazzle everyone he met with just a dashing grin.

"I have a lunch across town," David announced, "but get me a budget and time frame for the campaign by tomorrow morning, Alice. I'm going to put It's Texas to Me on the fast track."

"Thank you, sir," Alice said quietly. She stared at Charles while everyone else left the conference room.

"You surprised me today, Alice," Amanda said from the doorway.

Alice met her boss's steely gaze. "I surprised myself."

"I hope you can handle everything managing a campaign involves."

"I will."

Amanda took a step forward. "I've been thinking about a change in title for you, and this seems like the right time. I'm going to move you from travel research associate to tourism research manager."

Alice swallowed. "Thank you."

"Let's meet tomorrow morning to discuss new job responsibilities and a salary bump."

"Sounds good, Amanda."

"Charles, do you have lunch plans?" Amanda asked, running a hand through her thick hair. "I'd love to hear your thoughts on some of our other upcoming campaigns."

"Thanks for the lovely offer," Charles said smoothly, stepping forward. "But I do. I'd like to get a few more details on Alice's plan, but will stop by your office before I head out."

Her boss, who Alice knew had gone through a divorce late last year, wasn't deterred. "How long are you in town?"

"That depends," he answered.

"Give me a call," Amanda said in a soft purr Alice had never heard before. "I'd be happy to show you around Austin."

"I appreciate that. It's a marvelous city."

"They say everything's bigger in Texas." Amanda winked. "But there's plenty that's also better—like the women."

Charles chuckled, while Alice tried not to gag. Amanda was flirting with him as if Alice wasn't even in the room. And while the line was cheesy, she knew Charles probably heard a half dozen like it every time he left his hotel. It felt like every woman in the state was vying to be the next notch on Bonnie Lord Charlie's belt.

But not Alice. She was immune to the Charles Effect. Totally immune.

As Amanda left, Alice walked around the table, straightening chairs with a little more force than necessary. "Are you going to go out with my boss?"

"Of course not." Charles looked offended. "I'd like to go out with you if you'd ever return my messages and texts."

"I've been busy," she answered, gathering her notes from the table.

"You have a four-month-old baby."

"Who keeps me busy."

"Who goes to bed early each night," Charles countered.

"Me, too."

"A tempting thought," he said in a low whisper.

Alice closed her eyes and concentrated on stomping down the butterflies fluttering across her belly. "Why are you here, Charles?" she asked, when she felt safe looking at him again.

"For you," he answered, his gaze darkening.

And just like that, her defenses crumbled into a pitiful pile around her ankles.

She searched for a way to quickly rebuild them. "How was Horseback Hollow?"

"Have lunch with me."

"That didn't answer my question."

He grinned, but it was different than the one he'd given both Meredith and Amanda. This one seemed genuine, less practiced, as if her prickliness amused him. "Have lunch with me and I'll tell you all about it."

"You told Amanda you had plans."

"I do." He held out a hand. "With you."

"I haven't said yes. Maybe I already have a lunch date."

"Say yes, Alice."

She sucked in a breath and opened her mouth to refuse him. If she was going to have any chance of surviving the next eighteen years of her son's life, she had to set boundaries with Charles that wouldn't end with her heart being broken.

But he looked so hopeful waiting for her answer, as if he really wanted to be with her and not Amanda or Meredith or any other of his usual bevy of beautiful women. And despite what she tried to tell herself, Alice wanted to be with Charles more than was smart or safe.

She'd spent most of her life being prudent. The one

time she hadn't been, she'd ended up pregnant. But Flynn was the best thing that had happened to her, so maybe a bit of recklessness thrown into the mix wasn't so bad.

"We can't be seen walking out of the office together," she told him. "It would seem weird to everyone."

"Why?"

She shrugged. "Because men like you don't take women like me to lunch."

"This man does."

Her heart hammered in her chest. "Do you like Indian food?"

"I'm British," he said, as if that was an answer.

"What does that mean?"

"A real curry is almost as popular as fish and chips in London." He grinned again. "Yes, I like Indian."

"Good, because no one but me in this office does. There's a restaurant called Indian Palace around the corner from the building. You can order for both of us, and I'll meet you there in fifteen minutes."

His smile widened. "Cloak and dagger. I like it."

"Charles, be serious. You know we can't be seen together."

He nodded, but the smile remained. "If you really want privacy, my hotel is only a few blocks away."

"No hotel," she said, her voice coming out a squeak.

He laughed. "I'll see you in a bit, Alice." He stepped into her space before she could protest, traced his lips against her ear. "You really were brilliant today, love."

Alice's whole body heated and she grabbed hold of a chair to steady herself as she watched him disappear out of the conference room.

So much for guarding her heart against the sexy Brit.

* * *

Fatherhood was making him crazy. There was no other way for Charles to explain his actions today. He'd promised his siblings he had no intention of bedding Alice again, and he'd meant the words when he'd said them.

Then he'd proceeded to race back to Austin from Horseback Hollow with the hopes of spending more time with her. With Flynn, he corrected himself. He wanted to see his son. That was true, but not the whole truth. He'd missed both the boy and Alice during his short trip north to Horseback Hollow. The fact that Alice hadn't welcomed him back with open arms both irritated and intrigued him.

Women never avoided Charles. Never. Her reluctance to see him had made him only more intent on being with her. He'd tried to rationalize that he wanted to keep a friendly relationship with Alice for the sake of their baby, but that was ridiculous. He'd felt desperate to check in with her, to make sure he hadn't done something to cock up their tenuous bond.

Or maybe he just imagined a connection between them. Perhaps Alice wanted space to give him the subtle message that their relationship was simply two unattached parents working to raise their child. But he couldn't have forced himself to stay away from her even if he'd tried. From the moment she'd walked into that conference room, the anxious buzzing in his head had quieted and he'd felt an emotion strangely akin to contentment settle over him.

It had been impulsive to make a play for her at the tourism board office. He knew it was imperative they keep their ties to each other private, yet Charles couldn't resist the opportunity to see her, and working together would provide the most innocuous cover for doing so.

She walked into the restaurant at that moment, and all his doubts disappeared. She was as stunning in her business suit as she had been dressed for her role as mom, and Charles realized that he wanted to know more about every aspect of her life. Thanks to his famous family, his life was an open book. Now he wanted details about Alice and what made her tick.

He stood as she approached the booth he'd chosen in the far corner of the restaurant. A small smile played at the corner of her mouth, and he had the almost irresistible urge to brush his lips against hers again. But this wasn't her apartment or his hotel room, and while the half-empty restaurant appeared safe, he had to be careful whenever they were out together.

"Tell me about you," he said as she scooted into the booth across from him.

She seemed to stiffen under his regard. "There's not much to tell. Not everyone can be a jet-setting playboy."

He waved away the comment. "Old and boring news."

"No one thinks you're boring, Charles," she answered with a laugh. "Especially not women."

"There's only one woman I'm interested in, Alice."

She took a long sip of water. "You shouldn't say things like that."

"It's true."

She considered him for a moment. "I'm an Austin native. My father teaches American history at UT and my mom worked part-time as a teaching assistant at my elementary school."

"What were you like as a girl?" He leaned closer. "How will Flynn take after his mum?"

"He won't, I hope."

"You don't mean that. You're lovely, Alice. He'd be lucky to inherit your sweetness, not to mention your intelligence. Everyone on the board was blown away by you today."

She bit down on her lip as if his compliments made her uneasy. He started to ask her why, but the waiter brought the food.

"Chicken tikka masala, saag paneer and vindaloo," he said, placing the steaming dishes on the table. The young Indian waiter turned to the busboy who'd followed him to the table. "We also have basmati rice and naan for you to enjoy today."

"Thank you," Charles told the two men. "It looks delicious."

Alice's features relaxed as she looked at the food. "No one else I know likes Indian," she said, rubbing her palms together. "Sometimes I get it as takeout, but this is so much better."

Charles spooned a portion of each dish onto their plates and watched Alice take her first bite. Her eyes drifted closed, as if to better help her savor the taste, and she gave a soft moan.

"It's so good," she said with a sigh, her cheeks flushing when she opened her eyes to find him staring at her. "Silly to have that reaction to food, I know." She dabbed a napkin at the corner of her mouth.

"It's charming." Charles tore off a piece of naan, the bread warm between his fingers. "There is an amazing Indian place a couple of blocks from my flat in London. This is good..." He dipped the naan into the deep orange-red masala sauce. "But that restaurant takes it to a whole new level. We'll go there one day."

Her eyes widened, and the fork she held dropped to the table with a clatter.

"No pressure, Alice," he said quickly. "I know you want to take things slow."

She picked up the fork again and gave him a sheepish smile. "I don't even have a passport."

"You've never traveled abroad?"

"I've barely been out of Texas. My family went to California for a week when I was a girl because my dad had a conference there. And my grandparents retired to southern Colorado, so we'd drive to their cabin every summer. Otherwise…" She shrugged, as if apologizing. "You must think I'm a total country bumpkin. You're sophisticated and have traveled all over the world. I've been nowhere."

"You may live in Texas," Charles told her, reaching for her free hand, "but your taste in shoes definitely makes you more than a country girl."

She laughed at that and it made him enormously glad to be the man to put a smile on her face. "I do own cowboy boots," she told him.

"I can't wait to see them. Knowing you, they're something special." He laced her fingers with his. "I don't care that you haven't traveled." It was strangely appealing to think that he might be the one to introduce her to some of his favorite international destinations. Charles traveled so much for his work with the British Tourism Council, he'd become jaded, his senses dulled to the exotic locations and cosmopolitan cities. He wanted to see the world through Alice's eyes. "Where you've been doesn't matter to me. It's where we're going that counts."

"With Flynn," she said quickly, pulling her hand away.

"Of course," Charles agreed, tamping down the niggling sense of disappointment that curled through his gut. Alice was a fantastic mother, and he should be glad that their son was her first priority. Charles was, but it didn't stop him from wanting more. "When can I see him again?"

"He's usually tired and a little cranky in the evenings at the end of the workweek." She smiled. "Both of us are."

"I'll take tired and cranky," Charles told her. "From both of you."

She studied him for a moment, as if trying to determine if he really meant that. "I don't want to take him out tonight, but you could come over for dinner. Or stop by later if you have other plans."

"No other plans, and I'd love to come for dinner. I'll pick up a pizza. Everyone in America likes pizza, right?"

She laughed at that. "Not everyone, but most of us. A pizza would be great. Thank you."

"Two dates in one day." Charles saluted her with his water glass. "I'm a very lucky bloke."

Chapter Eight

Alice had just slipped into a pair of loose yoga pants when the doorbell rang. She glanced in the mirror and immediately regretted her decision to change from her suit into more comfortable clothes. At least dressed for work, she looked a bit put together. In her T-shirt and sweatpants she was the quintessential exhausted new mom. That couldn't be appealing to someone like Charles.

She pulled out the elastic band that held back her hair, letting her blond waves curl against her cheeks. Her hair might be a mess, but at least it falling in her face might camouflage her wan complexion.

The doorbell buzzed again, and she lifted Flynn from where he lay on her bed and went to answer it.

Unlike Alice, Charles looked totally put together, even in his casual jeans and T-shirt.

"Delivery," he said, holding up the cardboard pizza box.

She laughed and stepped back to let him into her apartment. "If all delivery guys looked like you, every single woman in America would be eating pizza seven nights a week."

"You have it all wrong, love. Tonight I'm a ubiquitous Austin pizza guy," he told her in an over-the-top American accent. "I like blending in." He leaned forward to press a gentle kiss on Flynn's forehead. "Hullo there, my wee man."

Alice caught a whiff of Charles's shampoo over the tangy scent of the pizza and bit back a groan. Inviting him to dinner had seemed like a good idea a few hours ago, but now she remembered why she'd insisted on spending time with him in public locations. Even as exhausted as she was, Charles made her body hum to life. The soft cotton T-shirt stretched across the muscles of his back and the jeans fit him in a way that made her mouth water.

"Shall I hold him?" he asked, setting the box on her coffee table.

Alice blinked, trying to gain control of her raging need. She wanted to beg Charles to hold *her*, wanted to press against all that strength and forget about her exhaustion and stress. She wanted to lose herself, and the unwanted thought that she was already losing her heart washed over her, an icy dose of reality.

"Sure," she said, careful not to let herself touch Charles as she deposited the baby in his arms. "I'll get plates. Would you like a beer or glass of wine?"

"Beer, please."

Charles balanced the baby in his arms, and Flynn rubbed at his eyes, letting out a tired cry.

"I'm sorry," Alice said automatically. "I know you probably don't want to deal with him fussy."

"I'm his father," Charles said, quirking a thick brow. "I'd venture to guess this isn't the worst I'm going to have to handle in the next few years."

Years. Alice gripped the pizza box tight in her hands. She'd have years to wallow in her unrequited lust for Charles. The only positive she could see was she'd save tons of money on hot water as she imagined many cold showers in her future.

She set two plates and napkins on the small table in her dining area, then grabbed a couple bottles of locally brewed beer from the refrigerator. "I can take him while you eat," she told Charles, opening the box he'd brought. The pizza was covered with fresh mozzarella, basil and tomatoes. Her stomach growled in response.

Charles chuckled. "I'll hold him while *you* eat." He bounced Flynn gently and the baby let out another cry, but slowly settled into the crook of Charles's arm with a yawn.

"He needs his last bottle before he falls asleep."

"I think I can manage a bottle."

"I'll make it," Alice offered, but Charles shook his head. "Tell me what to do."

She thought about arguing. Alice was so used to doing everything on her own that it was hard to delegate tasks related to Flynn.

"Alice, let me help." Charles's voice was low and coaxing.

She felt ridiculous tears prick the back of her eyes. She wanted to, but was afraid to depend on him, then be left on her own again. It was irrational and probably a result of being so tired. Sometimes she felt that if she

actually stopped moving, working, struggling—even for
a few minutes—she'd crumple under the weight of her
life and never surface again.

But Charles was Flynn's father, and she'd sought
him out. She owed him a chance to be a real part of
her baby's life.

"There's a machine in the corner of the counter. Take
a bottle from the cabinet above and put it under the spout
like a coffeemaker. Hit the red button and the formula
and heated water will mix. Just make sure you screw the
cap on tight before feeding him." She smiled. "I made
that mistake once and ended up with formula all over
both of us."

"Got it." Charles held out a chair. "Sit down, Alice.
Enjoy a beer and a slice of pizza. I'll take care of Flynn."
He winked at her. "You can supervise."

"Supervise," she murmured, dropping into the chair.
"I'll work on that." She bit into a piece of pizza, amazed
at how much better it tasted when she could actually
take a moment to enjoy it. These days she scarfed down
most of her meals while caring for Flynn, or at her desk
at lunch so she wouldn't be late picking him up from the
sitter's. Two meals in one day with Charles, and she'd
felt pampered at both of them. It was embarrassing how
easily she could get used to the sensation.

"This is like an espresso machine for formula,"
Charles said as the machine whirred.

"It was a splurge," Alice admitted. "I used some of
the gift cards I'd gotten for his shower. With his nighttime sleeping patterns, it's made things much easier."

"I'm all for easier," Charles said as he balanced Flynn
in one arm and tightened the cap. He sat in the chair
across from her and tipped the bottle into Flynn's mouth.

The baby's eyes drifted closed even as he gulped down the formula. "It's like he's asleep but still eating." Charles smiled at Flynn. "An impressive lad, indeed."

"I'm going to start him on cereal this weekend," Alice said, taking a sip of beer. "If you want to be here…"

"I wouldn't miss it."

Alice watched the two most important men in her life for a few minutes. There was a quiet intimacy to the three of them sitting in her small apartment, Flynn's contented gurgling as he ate the only sound. She wished it could be like this all the time, then mentally kicked herself for entertaining the thought. They weren't a family, and pretending they were would only lead to heartbreak. "I can take him now, if you want pizza before it gets cold."

"I'm fine," Charles told her, still looking at Flynn. "I can't get over having a mini me running around in the world."

"Being carried and pushed by stroller through the world, you mean."

"He'll be running soon enough." Charles shot Alice an apologetic glance. "If Flynn is anything like me, he'll keep you on your toes. My mum was constantly having to bail me out of scrapes and misadventures when I was a boy. She said I had enough energy for twins."

"Good to know." Alice huffed out a laugh and took another drink of beer. "I bet you got away with a ton because you were too cute to stay mad at for long."

Charles grinned. "It still works that way."

Flynn had finished the bottle and was now dozing in Charles's arms. Lucky baby. "I'm stuffed." Alice stood and placed her plate in the sink. "I'll change him and put him down for the night." She took the baby from Charles. "Thank you for the help and for dinner."

"My pleasure on both counts."

She put Flynn into a fresh diaper and his pajamas and then settled him in his crib. He snuggled against the soft sheet with a sleepy sigh. Alice stifled a yawn. Flynn always went down without a fuss, although staying asleep for the night was a bigger challenge.

By the time she returned to the kitchen, Charles had loaded the dishwasher, put the leftover pizza in the refrigerator and was wiping the table.

"Are you always this perfect?" she asked, leaning against the door frame.

"Hardly ever," he said with a grin. "You seem to bring out the best in me." He hung the dishrag over the faucet and turned.

They watched each other for several moments, awareness ricocheting through the small space. Charles crossed his arms over his chest, the muscles of his arms bunching in a way that made Alice want to…

Nope. Not going there.

"I should probably go," he said, but didn't make a move to leave.

"Do you want to watch a movie?"

One side of his mouth curved. "Can you stay awake for a whole movie?"

"How about a TV show?" she amended. "Not that you have to stay. I guess with Flynn asleep there's no reason…"

"I'd love to stay." Charles crossed the room to her, tucking a lock of her hair behind her ear with one finger. "Would you believe in all my travels to the States, I've never watched American television other than in an airport waiting area?"

She rolled her eyes. "Because you normally have way more exciting things to do."

"Nothing excites me more than you, Alice." His voice was pitched low and that familiar melting sensation started in her belly. His head moved closer, just inches, but Alice felt his breath tease her cheek. She waited for the touch of his mouth on hers, but instead he straightened. "Well, then," he said, clearing his throat. "What's on the programming menu tonight?"

"Reality TV or crime dramas." She forced herself to take a step back so she wouldn't be tempted to plaster herself to the front of him.

"You're not planning to subject me to any type of housewives?"

She laughed and they moved toward the overstuffed couch in her family room. "How do you feel about surviving the Alaskan wilderness?"

"Better to watch than experience it firsthand."

She turned on the lamp that sat on the end table next to the sofa, then grabbed the remote. "Let your introduction to the other side of American culture begin."

Charles had to admit he found the program about life on the frozen Alaska tundra fascinating. But it wasn't half as riveting as the beautiful woman curled up next to him. Alice had fallen asleep before the first commercial break, but Charles hadn't woken her.

He knew if he did, she'd be embarrassed and apologetic and most likely make him leave. The last thing he wanted was to return to his luxurious hotel room. In truth, the only thing he wanted was to stay in this tiny, simple apartment with Alice tucked in the crook of his arm. For all the years he'd spent partying and traveling, his old lifestyle held no appeal now.

He felt useful with Alice, needed in a way that filled his soul. It had always seemed like a sign of weakness that even in a crowd of fun, fancy people he could feel so alone. But now he understood it was the connection to another person he'd been missing. The motivation to be something more than anyone expected.

The monitor that sat on the coffee table crackled and Flynn gave a small cry. Alice stirred, made a sweet, snuffling noise, then snuggled closer to him. As gently as he could, Charles turned down the volume on the monitor and rearranged Alice so her head was on a pillow instead of his shoulder.

Nerves danced across his skin as he quietly walked into the baby's bedroom and flipped on the low-wattage lamp on the dresser. It was ridiculous to be nervous at the thought of going in alone to his son, but until now all his interactions with Flynn had been under Alice's watchful eye. That's how Charles had wanted it. The easy way. A week of being a father and he could already feel himself falling into the pattern of popping in when it suited him, armed with toys or goodies, but disappearing again if there was real parenting work to be done.

It made sense to leave that to Alice. She was far more comfortable in her role as mother than he feared he'd ever be as a dad.

But he wanted to try.

He approached the crib as if Flynn might pop up, jack-in-the-box style, at any second. Another silly thought, since the baby couldn't even sit up on his own yet. As Charles peered over the crib railing, Flynn lay on his back, staring up at him even as he continued to cry.

"What's wrong, little man?" Charles reached out a hand and placed it on the baby's rounded belly. Flynn took a few shuddered gulps of air and opened his mouth, seemingly poised to let out a true wail. Not wanting to wake Alice, Charles gathered the boy into his arms and started bouncing. The baby's cry cut off and he reached out, poking his fingers at Charles's face.

"See now," Charles crooned. "Everything's fine. Did you have a bad dream or—" He broke off as the smell of something rotten hit his nose. It was putrid and rank, making Charles want to gag. Flynn smiled, then squirmed in his arms. Charles could imagine whatever it was in that diaper being ground into the baby's soft bottom. Even he knew that wasn't good.

He'd never come close to changing a diaper. Not for his niece or his nephews. Hell, nappies were as foreign to him as braiding hair. He glanced at the door to the family room and thought about fetching Alice. As with most things related to Flynn, dirty diapers were her area of expertise.

So much for Charles's valiant effort at parenting through thick and thin. He'd meant "thick" in a hypothetical way, not scraping a baby's bottom.

Then he looked again at Flynn blinking up at him, lashes wet with glistening tears. The boy shoved his fist in his mouth and loudly sucked, observing Charles with a thoughtful stare as if measuring his worth as a father.

Charles did *not* want to be found lacking.

"We can manage this," he said out loud—to himself as much as Flynn. The changing table was situated next to the crib and seemed equipped to handle a veritable army of baby bums. A stack of diapers were arranged in a basket on the shelf under the changing pad, along with a container of wipes, several tubes of lotion and cream, and a toy that looked like a psychedelic bumblebee.

He lay Flynn on his back on the pad and connected the straps that hung on either side across the baby's belly. "First things first," Charles whispered, and handed him the bee to play with. Next he grabbed the wipes and a diaper, then began unsnapping the footed pajamas the baby wore. As soon as Charles opened the front of the sleeper, another wave of nasty nappy stench hit him. He realized he probably should have turned on the overhead light so he could actually see what he was doing. At the same time, he didn't really want to see in too much detail.

"You must be a chip off the old block," he told Flynn, "because you've certainly made a royal mess." Although the room was cool, Charles felt sweat drip down the side of his face. He wiped it on his shoulder, then took a deep breath, holding it as he undid the diaper and opened it.

"Bloody hell." He blinked, cringed and began grabbing handfuls of wipes to clean up the mess. Flynn patiently gummed his toy and then kicked his legs.

"Stop," Charles yelled, before he thought better of it. Flynn's rosebud mouth turned down in a pout. "Sorry, chap," Charles said, forcing his voice to be cheerful. "But you don't want to step in it when we've almost got you cleaned up."

Unfortunately, the *almost* seemed to last far longer than it should. Charles wiped and wiped but couldn't seem to remove all the mess. "How does your mum do this every day?" he asked the boy.

"Believe it or not, it gets easier with practice."

Charles glanced behind him to see Alice coming through the door.

"I didn't want to wake you," he said.

"You didn't." She nudged him to the side. "Mind if I take over?"

"Please," he muttered. "I'm utter rot with nappies."

"You're trying," she said, and gave him a sleepy smile. "I woke up and the monitor wasn't on, so I came looking for the two of you."

"Flynn had a postdinner explosion."

"He's not crying." Alice deftly finished the job of cleaning the baby and putting on a new diaper. She placed the dirty one and all the wipes into a garbage can next to the changing table. The diaper pail whirred when she snapped the lid shut.

"I hope that thing's rated for hazardous materials," Charles commented.

"I've heard it gets worse when he starts solid foods." She rearranged the sleeper, pried the toy out of Flynn's hands and picked him up off the pad. "Did you give your daddy a big mess to handle?" she cooed to the baby, snuggling him close.

Daddy. Charles preened at the word. Okay, maybe he hadn't handled the diaper change like a pro, but he'd tried his best. As a daddy would.

"Do you want to put him down again?" she asked, smiling up at Charles.

"Sure." He took the baby from her, Flynn burrowing against his chest. "Your mum needs a break, little man. How about you stay asleep until morning?"

Flynn didn't answer, but he also wasn't crying in protest, which Charles took as a win. He leaned over the crib and placed him on the sheet. The baby kicked and swatted at the air, but almost immediately his eyes drifted shut. "Good night, little one," Charles whispered.

Alice was watching them from where she stood near

the dresser. She flipped off the light and Charles followed her to the kitchen sink.

"You did good in there," she said as she turned on the faucet and handed him the soap.

"I've never seen anything like that," he said with a small shudder.

"Like you said, he's an *impressive lad*."

Charles laughed at the way she mimicked his accent and they finished washing hands in a companionable silence.

"I'm sorry I fell asleep," she said as she led him back into the family room. "This must be the most boring night you've had in years."

"Hardly," he said, tapping one finger to the tip of her nose. "Boring is being stuffed into an uncomfortable monkey suit in a room full of pompous strangers, counting the minutes until you can make a polite exit."

"Right." Alice made a face. "Sipping expensive champagne and surrounded by beautiful women. You're not fooling me, Charles."

"Sincerity isn't one of my best traits," he admitted, "but I mean every word of it. I can think of no place I'd rather be than here with you and our baby."

She stilled at his final words. *Our baby.* He wondered if she regretted inviting him into her life. There was no doubt she wanted him to have a relationship with Flynn, but Alice was the first woman in his life he couldn't seem to read. The only woman who'd ever really mattered romantically.

He forced himself to take a step away from her, to give her the space he guessed she needed. "I should let you get to bed, too."

Something in her hazel eyes flashed. "Because I'm a tired wreck?"

He pushed his hands into the front pockets of his jeans. "Because I'm trying to be a gentleman here."

She stared at him for another minute, then tugged her bottom lip into her mouth. Desire shot through him like a cannon and he took another step toward the door. He was about to turn and grab the handle when Alice closed the distance between them and pressed a gentle kiss to the corner of his mouth.

So much for being a gentleman.

Chapter Nine

Alice didn't want Charles to be a gentleman, and she wasn't about to let him leave without kissing him. She knew it was reckless, but she couldn't manage one more second without being close to him again.

The need had been building inside her all night, despite her exhaustion. Who could blame her? Charles was a fantasy for women around the world. But it was watching him fumble in the dim light of Flynn's nursery that had pushed her over the edge. There was nothing more important to her than her son, and for Charles to be making an effort to truly support her as a father was about the sexiest thing she'd ever seen—even if he had no idea what he was doing.

He tasted as amazing as she remembered, spicy, refined and just a touch exotic. He could wear American clothes all day long, but he was British upper class to his core. More importantly, he was a man.

Right now he was hers.

He gathered her into his arms and framed her face with his hands. His kisses were gentle and slow, like he was savoring her. Although inexperienced, Alice had always thought of a kiss as a prelude to what came after. But Charles pressed his mouth to hers like this was the main event. He was in no hurry to race to the next stop. His tongue traced the seam of her lips, coaxing them open, and she felt her knees give way. Talk about melting.

Without breaking the kiss, Charles turned, pressing Alice's back to the door as he deepened the kiss. His fingers trailed through her hair and as his kisses grew hotter and more demanding, Alice heard herself moan. That small sound seemed to spur him on and he circled her hips with his hands, pulling her hard against him.

"Charles," she whispered, her body tingling from head to toe, "I want…" She didn't quite know how to ask for what she wanted from him, but in the end it didn't matter.

Her voice seemed to yank him out of the moment. He pushed away from her, leaving Alice sagging against the door, her breath coming out in strangled gasps.

"I'm sorry, Alice," he said, his own voice strained.

"Don't—"

He held up a hand. "That shouldn't have happened. I can't…" He ran a hand through his hair, met her gaze with a crooked smile. "You're a lovely girl, but we can't go there." His tone had gentled, and Alice couldn't help but think she wasn't the first woman to be brushed off with that soothing accent.

"Why?"

He blinked at her direct question, and even Alice was

surprised at her own bluntness. Apparently sexual frustration made her bold.

"Well…" His blue eyes roamed over her. "It would complicate things between us."

Alice laughed, pressing the back of her hand to her kiss-swollen lips. "Because they're so simple now?"

His smile faltered. "Sleeping together would muddy the waters. I need to… We need to keep our focus on the baby."

Alice understood the sentiment, but it felt like a rejection nonetheless. Maybe Charles hadn't enjoyed kissing her the way she had him. Her desire felt one-sided, a little pathetic and a whole lot embarrassing.

She grabbed for the handle of the door, stepping back as it opened. "I understand," she whispered. "Good night, Charles."

"Alice—"

"Good night," she said again, more firmly. She forced herself to meet his gaze, to prove to him she wasn't breaking apart inside.

He lifted his hand but she gave a sharp shake of her head. "Don't. Please."

He looked as miserable as she felt. "I'll call you tomorrow."

She wanted to tell him no, to cut Charles out of her life for good. But he was the father of her son, and she would do right by Flynn no matter what.

"Tomorrow," she agreed, and shut the door behind him.

But Charles didn't call the next day. Instead he showed up for her late-morning meeting to finalize dates on the new campaign. Looking at him in his tailored suit and crisp white dress shirt, his hair still damp at the ends, made Alice's lungs stop working for a second. She tapped her chest with her knuckles, reminding her body to do its job and her lungs to keep pumping air in and out.

He was attentive and charming to all the women from the research and marketing departments in the conference room. More importantly, he was respectful of Alice and her ideas about It's Texas to Me. It was difficult to hold on to her anger in the face of his overt kindness. It was almost as if he was trying to make up for what he wouldn't give her last night. Even if he wasn't attracted to her, she knew Charles genuinely cared for her as Flynn's mother. Somehow that would have to be enough.

Of course, it wouldn't be easy to spend the rest of her life comparing herself to the type of woman who would interest Charles. He was seated next to her boss. Amanda, flipping her shiny blond hair and decked out in a bright red power suit that showed off her curvy figure, fawned over him and made a show of inviting him to lunch after the meeting. Alice tried not to pay attention until she realized Charles had declined Amanda's offer and was turning to her.

"We're still on for lunch?" he asked.

Alice felt her mouth drop open and quickly snapped it shut.

"Remember, we'd planned to discuss my ideas for tweaking the campaign to make it appropriate for several of the countries involved with the European Tourism Board, and how I could help with my contacts."

"Sure," Alice stammered, and glanced at her boss, who was glaring at her from the far end of the table. "I hope you don't mind."

"Of course she doesn't," Charles said, before Amanda

could answer. He flashed her a brilliant smile and took Amanda's hand, brushing the barest kiss across her knuckles. "You understand, love?"

"Of course," Amanda agreed with a giggle. Alice rolled her eyes. Cue the Charles Effect.

Meredith leaned close to Alice's ear as she stood from the table. "He wants you bad."

"We have a child together," Alice whispered. "That's all there is between us."

Meredith gave her a funny look but didn't argue.

Alice grabbed her purse from her cubicle and went to find Charles. He was waiting for her in the lobby, the tourism board's longtime receptionist watching him as he stared out the window.

"The phones are ringing," Alice said, tapping on the desk as she walked by.

The receptionist jumped, then threw Alice a cagey smile. "How anyone in England gets work done when that man is around is beyond me."

He turned as Alice approached and she had to agree with the other woman's assessment.

Charles smiled, almost tentatively, and took a step toward her. "About last night," he began, but Alice shook her head.

"I don't want to talk about it, and especially not here." She glanced over her shoulder to where two other women from the office had gathered at the receptionist's desk. Charles was like some rare object on display—the elusive British bachelor. Right now, she wasn't in the mood to entertain a group of prying eyes. "Let's go." She grabbed his arm and dragged him out the door.

The noonday sun was almost violently bright, and she shoved her sunglasses onto her nose. "What are you doing showing up at my office again?" She started down the busy sidewalk, releasing Charles as they jostled through the crowd. But when she turned to look at him, he was gone, only to pop up again on her other side.

At her questioning gaze, he shrugged. "A gentleman always walks on the street side when with a lady."

"In case she wants to shove him into traffic?"

He smiled. "Among other reasons."

"Is that a British thing?"

"I'm not sure. It's something my father taught us." He looked down at her as they stopped at a crosswalk. "I'll teach Flynn one day."

An immediate tingle coursed through her. The ladies at her work might be susceptible to the Charles Effect, but her feelings for him were far more dangerous. "You didn't answer my question."

"I came to talk about the campaign," he said, placing his fingers on her elbow as the light changed and she stepped off the curb. "Plus I wanted a chance to spend time with you and not feel it necessary to hide out."

"Why?" she couldn't help but ask. "I assumed you said everything you needed to last night."

"Hardly. I want to be your friend, Alice. The connection we share is powerful."

She drew in a shaky breath at his words, even as she understood he was talking about their baby. "Based on what I've seen in the papers, you have plenty of friends."

"Acquaintances," he clarified. "Not the same thing at all."

She had to hide her smile at the knowledge that this dashing man had chosen her. Even if she wanted more, she had to find a way to be satisfied with friendship.

He glanced around as she guided him toward another intersection. "Where are you taking me?"

"The best lunch place in Austin," she said with a grin.

"You like food," he observed, and she glanced up at him again. He wasn't wearing sunglasses and his eyes were almost the same color as the spring sky.

"Last time I checked, eating is pretty essential to a person's survival."

He pushed her hair off her forehead with the tips of his fingers. "It wasn't an insult, Alice. But I'm used to women who are more concerned with moving the food around on their plates than with actually taking a bite."

"I bet they eat a lot of salad, too."

He nodded. "Most seem partial to lettuce, yes."

She couldn't help but laugh. "Maybe the lifestyle of the rich and famous isn't all it's cracked up to be." She led him down a path that intersected the sidewalk near the park's entrance. "Because I'm about to blow your mind, Mr. Fortune Chesterfield."

Chapter Ten

Charles wanted to tell Alice she'd already blown his mind on so many levels. It went way beyond making him a father, as shocking as that revelation had been. Alice seemed unimpressed with his reputation and the trappings of his fame, a wholly unfamiliar experience for Charles but one he'd quickly grown to appreciate.

Case in point was that they now stood in front of a brightly painted recreational vehicle, a new Texas experience for Charles. He was used to dining at steak houses and trendy bistros, but took his place in the short queue behind Alice.

"A food truck?"

"The best tacos in Austin." She pointed to the large chalkboard hanging from the side of the truck. "They have daily specials, but my favorite is the Chicken Sink."

"Is that supposed to sound appetizing?" He cocked a brow, earning a laugh.

"It's a chicken taco with everything but the kitchen sink thrown in."

"I'm sure there is an American cultural reference I'm missing, but…"

Her grin widened. "It means there's a ton of stuff on top of the chicken." She held up her hand, ticking off ingredients with her fingers. "Guacamole, green chili, sour cream and *queso*, plus salsa and a bit of shredded lettuce. They don't use a ton of any one item, but you get a mix of all the different flavors."

"It's delish," the woman standing in front of them said, looking over her shoulder. Her gaze caught and held on Charles. "Wow," she murmured, then threw an apologetic glance at Alice.

"No worries," Alice told her. "Happens all the time. Eventually you get used to him."

"I'll take your word for it," the woman answered, and turned back around.

"What happens all the time?" Charles didn't begin to understand the exchange between the two women, but was quite curious.

"The Charles Effect," Alice said, before a blush rose to her cheeks. It was as if she hadn't meant to share those words with him. The line shifted and one of the servers beckoned them forward. "Saved by the taco," she muttered, before turning to Charles. "Do you know what you want?"

"What is the Charles Effect?" he asked.

"I'll order for both us." She ignored his question and requested a sampling of menu items from the clearly popular food truck. Charles handed the man a few bills before Alice could pull her wallet from her purse. "I dragged you halfway across downtown in the midday heat," she protested. "I can pay."

"Call me old-fashioned," he drawled.

As they shifted to the side to wait, Alice began to babble about the vast array of food trucks that could be found throughout Austin's various neighborhoods. "That should be one of our features for the ad campaign. Food is a big draw for vacationers, and my research shows that almost half will drive up to thirty miles from their intended destination to try a popular restaurant." She paused to catch her breath, then started to speak again, but Charles held a finger over her lips.

"Explain the Charles Effect."

"It's…you know…how women react to you."

"You mean the fact that women like me."

She barked out an indelicate laugh. "They more than *like* you, Charles. You mesmerize them."

"But not you?"

The man at the food truck called her name and she hurried forward to grab the paper sack. "There's a hidden park bench around the corner near the fountain. It's usually empty."

"Are you going to answer my question?" Charles asked as he followed her.

She kept her attention on the food, divvying up the foil-wrapped tacos after taking a seat on the bench. "Our friendship gives me immunity to your charm."

"Is that so?"

"Yep." She peeled back one corner of the foil and took a small bite of taco. "You need to eat. I only have an hour for lunch."

"Your boss won't mind if you're with me."

"David might not, but Amanda certainly will." Alice

dabbed a napkin at the corner of her mouth. "She wants you for herself."

"She can't have me." Charles bit into the taco and nodded. Both the food and his lunch companion made him happy. He was happier spending time with Alice than he could remember being in ages. "I like this kitchen sink."

"I told you," she said with another quick smile. "Do you have food trucks in London?"

"We do. You see them most often at festivals or in open-air markets. You need to get a passport, Alice. There's so much to see in the world."

She shrugged. "I've got a job and a baby. That doesn't leave much time for traveling."

"Or dating?"

She coughed wildly, and Charles thumped her on the back.

"That came out of nowhere," she said, as her breath returned to normal.

"We talk a lot about my social life, but I've heard almost nothing of yours."

"There isn't anything to share," she answered.

"So no dates since..." He trailed off.

She blushed again as those hazel eyes darkened to a deep green color. "Nope. No time. No inclination. No... just no."

"Are you really immune to me, Alice?"

"I am."

He leaned closer. "Could I change your mind?" His tone had gone low and silky, like the luxurious sheets she remembered from her one night in his hotel room.

"You won't try." She jumped up from the bench, walked to a nearby trash can and threw away the taco wrapper before turning back to him. "You were the one who said we could only be friends, Charles. I don't care how much you trifle with other people. You care about Flynn, and you aren't going to do anything that will mess this up." She walked back slowly, watching the emotions play across his face. "I trust you. I believe you'll do the right thing by your son."

She wished the right thing for both of them was being together, but Charles had already made his thoughts on the subject clear. The only reason he was toying with her now was because she posed a challenge. Even though he acted the part of the irresponsible rake, she knew he wouldn't willingly hurt Flynn.

"Damn," he muttered. "You certainly know how to set a high bar." He stuffed the rest of his uneaten taco into the bag and wiped a sleeve across his forehead. For the first time since she'd met him, Charles didn't look cool and in control. He seemed almost panicked at the idea of someone having expectations of him that didn't involve a drink and a laugh.

"There's an outdoor concert tonight at Zilker Park, on the lawn in front of the botanical garden." She sank down on the bench and nudged him with her elbow. "I'm going to take Flynn. It would be good to have a *friend* to go with us."

"Certainly," he said without hesitation, but Alice wasn't even sure he'd heard the invitation.

"We'll figure this out," she told him, resting her head on his wide shoulder. "Team Fortune Chesterfield and all that."

"Team Fortune Chesterfield," he repeated, and wrapped an arm around her waist.

They sat there for a few more minutes and she felt Charles slowly relax. Alice kept her breathing normal,

even as awareness skittered across her skin and through
her body. She tried to ignore it as best she could. Sexual
frustration notwithstanding, it was nice to have a friend.
If nothing else, Charles was her partner in parenting. It
gave Alice more comfort than she cared to admit that
she was no longer alone.

"I need to go," she said eventually, hating to break
the connection between them. She lifted her head and
Charles stood.

"We haven't discussed the campaign." He held out a
hand to her and she slipped her fingers into his.

"Let's talk on the way back to the office."

He nodded but didn't let go of her hand. He threw
away the rest of the trash from lunch, and she led him out
of the park. Despite the necessity of it, she wasn't ready
to return to her office and he didn't appear in a hurry to
let her go. They talked about the campaign and he asked
for a list of her favorite things in Austin. He seemed truly
interested in what made it Texas to her. She started to
rattle off the typical list of live music, food and the ubiquitous Western spirit, then changed her mind. Alice had
always been more interested in the parts of Austin that
could best be described as hidden gems.

She told him about the local graffiti park, the natural swimming hole at the Hamilton Pool Preserve and a
few museums and galleries that weren't on most tourist
itineraries. "Does that make me seem weird?" she asked,
after promising to take him to one of the quaint neighborhoods she liked outside of town. "My job is all about
the things that make Texas popular, but those aren't my
favorite spots."

"On the contrary," he answered, taking her elbow as
they crossed a busy intersection. "It's something we have

in common. The places in London I prefer are the ones I can go to without fanfare—a bookstore tucked down a cobblestone street across from the British Museum in Bloomsbury, or a family-owned Italian restaurant on the outskirts of the theater district. I'd like to explore the places in Austin that appeal to you, Alice." Goose bumps rose on her skin at the way he said her name. "I want to discover them with you as my guide."

She forced herself to keep walking, when she wanted to stop and kiss him in the middle of the crowded street. It was disconcerting to find they shared this penchant for the unique. Charles was a man she could so easily love. What had started as a one-night stand had turned into much more.

But he'd offered her friendship, and that had to be enough.

Too soon they were at the entrance of the tourism board office. "I'm terrified of the woman who answers the phones," he said, glancing past Alice into the plated glass door. "She looks at me like she wants me for her next meal."

"I'd think you would be used to that look from women by now," Alice said with a laugh.

"Yes, but she looks hungrier than most."

Alice shook her head and laughed again. "I'll see you tonight, Charles."

He nodded and started to walk away, then turned back. "Until tonight, love," he said, and dropped a light kiss against her hair. The implied intimacy of the gesture made her heart squeeze.

She was quickly discovering that regular life was more exhilarating than she could have imagined with this man at her side.

* * *

Alice pushed Flynn's stroller through the crowd gathered in Zilker Park later that evening. She'd texted Charles to meet her on the lawn in front of the botanical garden, knowing it would be easier to walk than to deal with traffic and parking before the popular concert series.

Flynn made a noise and she pushed down his shade cover, not paying much attention to the people she passed on the sidewalk until a man stepped in front of her, blocking the path.

"Excuse me," she said, then glanced up into a pair of familiar blue eyes. "Charles, it's you."

"I take it my disguise is working," he said with a laugh, and bent forward to kiss Flynn's downy hair.

"You look like a Texan," she admitted as he fell in step beside her, "but the accent gives you away."

"Then I'll have to work on being the 'strong silent type.' I can channel my inner John Wayne."

Alice hid her smile. He definitely had the strong part down, with his broad shoulders and long-limbed gait. Although Charles wasn't dressed in his usual dapper British garb, her body still reacted to him. His fingers brushed hers as he took over handling the stroller, and warmth and desire spiked through her. He'd changed into a faded pair of jeans and an orange Texas Longhorns T-shirt, quintessential Austin fashion for a man in his late twenties. He wore a dark blue baseball cap and the work boots he'd bought when they were together.

"How did you break in those boots so quickly?" she asked, pointing to the scuffed toes.

"Would you believe I did some work on my brother-in-law's ranch?"

"Not for a second."

"You know me too well, Alice Meyers." He ruffled her hair. "The truth is, I gave them to the concierge at the hotel. His son is my size and works in construction." Charles laughed when she gaped at him. "Turns out the Four Seasons really is full-service," he said.

"Only you, Charles." She waved her hand toward an area near the top of the hillside. "Is that spot okay? It's far enough away from the stage to be safe for Flynn's ears. Plus he won't bother anyone if he gets fussy." She glanced around the crowded lawn. "Although there's not much shade on the hill. Maybe we could—"

"How about there?" Charles pointed to a clump of trees about halfway up the hill. Under the shade of the branches were two lawn chairs, with a blanket spread across the grass in front of them. A wicker picnic basket sat to one side with a galvanized-steel bucket next to it.

Her mouth dropped open. "Did the hotel take care of that, too?"

He shook his head. "I had some time on my hands this afternoon and wanted you and the baby to have a good spot for the concert."

"I don't know what to say… Thank you."

"I believe in full service, too."

She let him lead her to the picnic area, feeling like the luckiest woman on the planet. Well, she'd feel even luckier if this was a real date. How was any man going to measure up to Charles?

She brushed away the thought, rationalizing that she'd be too busy raising her son to worry about a man in her life.

She lifted Flynn from the stroller and set him on the soft

blanket. His gaze immediately caught on the leaves fluttering above him and he seemed as content as Alice felt.

"We have a selection of sparkling water or lemonade for the evening," Charles told her, making a comically gallant gesture toward the ice bucket.

"Lemonade, please," she said as she sat next to Flynn. Charles handed her a cold bottle, then lowered himself to the blanket on the other side of the baby. He pulled the picnic basket closer and took out a plate of cheeses and a box of gourmet crackers.

"This is perfect," Alice said with a sigh, stretching her legs in front of her. She saw a few people glance their way, but no one seemed to recognize Charles.

"To a perfect night," he agreed, and held up his can of sparkling water for a toast. They shared the cheese and crackers as the sun dipped behind the trees. Despite her awareness of him, Alice found it remarkably easy to talk to Charles. He asked her more questions about her childhood and shared stories of his brothers and sisters growing up in England.

As an only child with very little extended family, Alice loved the thought that her son would grow up knowing aunts, uncles and cousins. Of course, that thought was immediately followed by the worry that Charles would want to take Flynn off to either Horseback Hollow, or worse, England, and Alice would be left alone and missing her boy.

She was afraid to broach the subject and ruin the mood of this lovely evening. Charles had told her over lunch earlier that his family solicitor was finishing up the papers that would ensure Flynn was provided for, so Alice decided she could wait to talk about custody as part of that discussion.

Despite the noise around them, Flynn drifted off to sleep. Alice pulled a blanket from the bottom of the stroller and covered the baby.

As she glanced up at Charles she found him staring at her shoes. At first glance, these were relatively simple tan pumps. But the inside edge of the shoe was a band of lace, with corresponding lace panels on either side of her heel. They were demure but at the same time gave a glimpse of skin that made Alice feel quite sexy. It was no accident she'd chosen them for her evening with Charles. She might have agreed to be his friend, but that didn't mean she wouldn't tempt him when she could.

She stretched her foot forward, pointing her toe.

"More remarkable shoes," he murmured, shifting down the blanket, "but each pair makes me more intrigued about what's hiding underneath."

"Y-you've seen my feet," she stammered when he reached for her ankle. He slipped off the shoe, cradling her heel and pressing his thumb into the arch of her foot.

A moan escaped Alice's lips before she could stop it. As much as she favored fancy heels, they did often leave her feet sore. "That feels nice," she whispered, closing her eyes to enjoy the sensation. His hands felt like heaven as they massaged, the touch alternately soft then firm.

He finished with one foot, then took off the other shoe. Alice tried not to think of his touch as foreplay, imagining his hands on other parts of her body.

But before her daydreams had time to overtake her, Flynn let out a sharp cry.

She jerked away from Charles.

"He's hungry," she said, as she scooped up the baby, embarrassed at how husky her voice sounded.

"I'll get the bottle," Charles offered, without missing a beat.

She stood with Flynn in her arms, not bothering to put on her shoes. Charles shook up the formula, uncapped the bottle and handed it to Alice. She was careful to take it without touching him, not sure she could handle the contact with how sensitized she felt at the moment.

The baby guzzled happily, and Charles cleaned up the remnants of their meal.

"I can do that when he's finished."

"It's not a problem," Charles told her with a smile. "Think of it as your very own royal treatment." His grin was so cheeky she couldn't help but return it.

As Flynn finished the bottle, the band appeared on the stage. They were a bluegrass quartet. The lead singer played the banjo and was accompanied by a fiddle player, upright bassist and drummer. The crowd applauded, several couples near the front surging to their feet to dance to the spirited music.

"They're good," Charles said, putting the lid back on the picnic basket.

"Most music in Austin is good." Alice lifted Flynn to her shoulder and patted his back. "We're famous for it."

"This is Texas to me," Charles said softly, and reached out a hand to her.

Shifting Flynn to a more secure position in one arm, she lightly placed her fingers in Charles's. He spun her slowly, then gathered her close. The three of them danced together, swaying to the music as the band launched into a ballad, the fiddle player taking the lead with a resonating melody that tugged at her heartstrings.

Pale streaks of pink and orange colored the sky above

them, and Alice could just see the faint outline of the moon beginning to rise behind the stage.

"You're barely breathing," Charles whispered against her ear.

She pulled back. "I seem to have forgotten how," she said, and sucked in an almost painful gulp. "It's the music." She laughed and moved off the blanket, clutching Flynn to her chest. "The fiddle gets me every time."

Charles lifted a brow as if he knew too well that she was lying through her teeth. "Of course. The fiddle." He didn't move closer but tapped his toe in time to the music. "I like it here, Alice."

She brushed a light kiss across the top of Flynn's head. "I like it with you here, Charles." She turned away as soon as the words were out of her mouth, embarrassed at how much they revealed. This was temporary, she reminded herself as she swayed to the music with Flynn. Charles had made no promises, and she didn't expect him to. Her only connection to him was through her son, even if it felt like more every time they were together. She kept her attention focused on the band until her emotions were under control.

"Do you want to hold him?" she asked, turning to Charles after the next song finished.

He gave her a searching look, as if he wanted to say something, but in the end only nodded. "Certainly." He took the baby carefully, balancing an alert Flynn on his forearm.

"You look like you're holding a football," she told him as she slipped back into her shoes.

He made a face. "It's a rugby hold. A football is something you kick with your feet."

Alice made a show of glancing around. "You'd better

not let anyone in Texas hear you say that. We take our American football seriously around these parts." She purposely put an extra bit of twang in her tone. "They'll run you out of the state quicker than you can say 'God save the queen.'"

"Don't listen to her, young man," Charles cooed at the baby. "Stick with Daddy and I'll teach you what's what with sports." He looked up at Alice and winked. "He's quite awake for it being so late."

She couldn't resist taking a step closer and reaching out to trace a finger along Flynn's soft cheek. Her wonder at her son never waned, no matter how tired or stressed she felt. But being here with Charles, it was easy to forget all those troubles. "He likes watching you," she murmured.

"Or maybe it's the fiddle," Charles said, and she could hear the teasing note in his voice.

She crossed her arms over her chest and tapped a finger against her chin in mock seriousness. "Yes, we've established that the fiddle is thrilling."

"Thrilling," he repeated.

She nodded. "In a *friendly* sort of way."

He let out a bark of laughter that made Flynn jump. The baby's face contorted as he let out a wail. "I mucked that up," Charles said.

Alice automatically reached for the baby, but Charles shook his head. "Mind if I try to quiet him?"

"Sure." She watched, emotion wrenching her heart as he rocked the baby to the beat of the music. Charles might blend in with the crowd in his American clothes, but to her he still looked like the British playboy she'd read about for years in the tabloids. He was someone who had every advantage that money could buy, but here he was, trying to fit into her world—her son's world—even as he was so clearly out of his depth.

How could she resist falling in love with him?

At the thought, Alice stumbled back a step. This was the worst of all possible outcomes for her time with Charles and a secret she would take to her grave. But it wasn't the Charles Effect or his charm and natural affinity with women that had done her in. It was these small moments of sweetness and authentic emotion when he wasn't relying on his reputation. She saw Charles for who he was, flaws and all, and that was the man she loved.

But he was still the man she would never have.

Despite how she'd tried to guard it, her heart splintered into tiny pieces at the thought.

Chapter Eleven

"Have you lost your handsome British mind?"

Charles paused midbite to glance at the black-and-white photos thrown onto the table before him. He'd stopped in the hotel restaurant to grab a quick breakfast before heading over to the Texas Tourism Board office.

It was a bit disturbing how much he wanted to see Alice, especially after having spent most of the previous evening with her. Despite her protests that she was fine, he'd insisted on walking her and Flynn home from the concert, then had taken a cab back to his empty hotel room.

She hadn't invited him in, and he didn't blame her. He'd been the one to throw down the "friend" gauntlet, but no matter how he tried to convince himself it was for the best, he hated it. It was easier to think that was why he craved being close to her—she was an itch that he hadn't been able to properly scratch.

But what if that wasn't the whole story?

Normally Charles tired of women quickly, and not just in the bedroom. Alice was different. He was crazily attracted to her, but even without acting on that desire, Charles enjoyed being with her. She talked to him like he was a real person. She teased him and flirted without even realizing what she was doing. Flynn was a huge motivator, as well, and Charles wanted more time with both of them. For a man who'd done his best to avoid commitment for most of his life, all he hoped for now was that Alice would give him a chance to prove he could change.

Because he could, except...

"What the hell is the meaning of this? Did you have me followed?" His voice was stiff and dripped with contempt as his gaze shot up from the pictures. As much as he loved the image of the three of them as a happy family, this was a violation of the worst sort. But it wasn't a slimy paparazzo or tabloid reporter who stood in front of him.

The woman who stared down at him regally from the other side of the table was the epitome of class and style. She was clearly older, although nary a wrinkle marred her porcelain complexion. It was as if she had refused to allow something so trivial as the passage of time to mark her. There was an air of power around her that few would defy, but Charles had never been one to cower when faced with an outright challenge.

"Kate Fortune," he said with a practiced smile, placing his fork on the white tablecloth. "I was wondering when you would grace me with your presence."

"You can save that suave charm for one of your high-society groupies, Charles." She tapped a manicured finger on the table. "If my people can so easily deduce your identity, despite your American disguise, it won't be long until your secret is out."

Charles pressed his lips together. "I want privacy while I'm in Texas," he said through clenched teeth. "There's no secret to discover beyond that."

She arched one fine brow. "Are you going to invite me to join you?"

"Of course," he said, standing and pulling out the chair next to him. "Please have a seat, Ms. Fortune. Would you like a menu? The waffles are quite good."

"No waffles," she answered with a small chuckle, her expression softening a bit. Lucie had told him Kate had remained in Austin longer than she'd planned because she'd fallen ill and the doctor suggested her recovery would be easier in Austin than at home in Minneapolis during the brutal Minnesota winter. As Charles studied her, he noticed her silk suit seemed to be too big for her tiny frame.

"I'm still strong enough to manage both my company and my own affairs," she told him, as if reading his mind.

"And your family?" he asked.

"Cheeky boy," she muttered.

"That's what my mother always told me."

Kate draped the cloth napkin across her lap and signaled the waiter for a cup of coffee. "I like you more than I expected."

Charles tilted his head, acknowledging the compliment. "Then I'll strive to continue to exceed your expectations."

"From what I understand, that would be a rare feat for you."

"Were you this charming with the rest of the Fortune offspring?"

She smiled at the question. "Certainly not. I tailor my conversation to each individual."

"You spoke with Lucie recently," he observed.

"Your sister is a lovely girl. She takes after your mother."

"Indeed she does."

"I wonder if you are very much like your father."

Charles felt himself stiffen and had trouble keeping his gaze neutral. "What do you know of Sir Simon?"

"I know he was a good man and an even better father. I've done my research on all branches of the Fortunes, and you British lot have spent so much time in the spotlight that it's easy to gather facts on you."

"The tabloids often don't tell the whole story, if any portion of it."

One side of her mouth curved as she sized him up. "Does that mean you're not a charming rake with a raging Peter Pan complex who skated by on your looks and family name for the better part of your life?"

"I… It doesn't… There hasn't been… I don't have a Peter Pan complex." Charles broke off as he struggled to keep his breathing normal. He darted looks to the tables on either side of them, but it appeared no one had overheard Kate's scathing assessment of his worth. He wasn't sure whether to be outraged, embarrassed or some combination of the two, since this virtual stranger had concisely summed up his existence in a well-placed verbal attack.

Kate paused as a cup of steaming coffee was set in front of her. She added a scant dollop of cream and stirred, then carefully removed the spoon, setting it neatly on the saucer. Charles got the impression that Kate Fortune was methodical about every move she made, and it was no accident that she'd sought him out after discovering his connection to Alice and Flynn. The thought made an unfamiliar wave of protectiveness roll through him, crashing through his shored-up defenses like a river breaching a dam.

Before he could voice his concerns, Kate held up her hand. "I'm not going after you, Charles." She flipped the pictures over so the images were hidden from view. "My goal is to secure the future of Fortune Cosmetics. I need someone who can work with me to learn the business and dedicate him- or herself to the company the way I have."

Charles pushed his plate to the side, his normally hearty morning appetite ruined. "That isn't me."

"Are you asking or telling?" Kate retorted.

"A bit of both, I suppose. I'm not interested in running your cosmetics company, and you don't think I have it in me to dedicate myself to the business."

She studied him over the rim of her coffee mug. She clearly wore lipstick, skillfully applied like the rest of her makeup, but not a trace had bled onto the white porcelain of the china cup. Everything about Kate Fortune was perfect. "As I said, I've done my research. You are actually quite an asset to the British tourism industry. Despite outward appearances, I think you take your role as an unofficial ambassador very seriously."

Charles released a breath, relieved that the formidable cosmetics maven hadn't skewered him again.

"But," she continued, setting the cup back on the table, "I wonder if you truly understand the value of family and the commitment it takes to maintain ties with the people nearest to you."

"I'm committed to my son," he said, gripping the edge of the table so hard his knuckles turned white. "Since I found out about Flynn, I've been more dedicated to him than I have with anything or anyone before in my life. Arrangements have been made for his future, ensuring that he will always be taken care of no matter what. I put my own plans on hold to stay in Austin and spend time with him. I plan to be a part of his life going forward." Charles forced himself to relax his fingers, running a hand through his hair. "I may never measure up to Sir Simon, but I'm bloody well going to be the best father I can to that boy. No matter what you or anyone else thinks about me."

She reached out and patted his hand, as if placating a small child. "Don't get all riled up on my account. I'm not talking about your son. It's easy to love a baby."

Charles nodded. It had certainly been simple to become enamored of his son. And as for Alice—

"But family connections through the generations are just as important," Kate continued, before he could fully wrap his mind around his feelings for Alice. "They aren't always neat or easy, but it's essential to maintain those ties."

He focused on her words and on what Lucie told him had been developing within the Fortune family. "Do you include the Robinsons in those family ties?"

Kate's eyes widened a fraction. "That's a complicated situation."

"Indeed, but in the name of family, they are just as important as any of the rest of us."

She frowned, as if considering that. "My sources tell me that Ben Robinson has tracked down Jerome Fortune's mother."

"I've heard that, as well." Charles didn't volunteer any of the other information Lucie had shared.

"Jacqueline Fortune, Jerome's mother, insisted that her son is dead." Kate's expression was carefully neutral.

"Do you believe that?"

Kate shook her head. "I don't. Do you?" She leaned forward, her eyes narrowed, waiting for his answer.

"No," Charles said after a moment. "But as you say, it's complicated. I realize how lucky I am to have had the father I did. Not all children have that, and from what I understand Gerald Robinson was not the easiest man to have as a parent." Charles didn't know much about the scion of Robinson Tech and had met only a couple of the Robinson children at a charity function the previous year. Lucie had become friends with Vivian Blair, who was now engaged to Wes Robinson, who was in charge of research and development at the powerful computer company. His sister had wanted to pepper him with details about the relationships within that family, but Charles had too much going on in his own life to worry about a different branch of the Fortunes.

"He won't admit that he's really Jerome," Kate said, her mouth thinned to a worried line.

"But his children are convinced he is," Charles said softly. "They have reason to make a claim on the Fortune name beyond wanting to know the truth."

"The Fortune name holds a lot of weight in many areas."

"So does the Robinson name," Charles countered. "They don't need the money and it can't be easy to go up against a man as complicated as Gerald."

"Jerome," Kate corrected.

Charles nodded. "We're in agreement on his true identity."

"Perhaps we agree on more than just that," Kate murmured.

"Like that I'd be a terrible choice to take over your business."

She laughed, a throaty chuckle, and her eyes sparkled in enjoyment. "You really are a scamp, Charles Fortune."

"A lovable one, I hope."

She arched one sculpted eyebrow. "I've heard that, as well." Kate reached for her purse and pulled out a small velvet pouch. "I have something for you. It's been in the Fortune family for many years."

Charles automatically shook his head. "I can't take—"

"You can take what I offer to you," Kate said, her tone as regal as any aristocrat Charles had met. "And be grateful."

"Yes, ma'am," he said, quietly chastised.

She slid the velvet case toward him. "Open it."

He gently pulled out a glittering emerald engagement ring with brilliant smaller diamonds surrounding the center stone. It was clearly vintage, in an understated art deco style, and he'd guess it was worth a small fortune, to use the word in the literal sense. There was a bit of filigree outlining the top edge and he could see the letter *F* in the design. "It's beautiful," he told her with a half smile, "but not quite my size."

"It's not for you," she said with an eye roll. "But you'll need it."

An image of Alice popped into Charles's mind and his heart lurched in response. But just as quickly, a wave of fear and dread rose in his throat, almost choking him. A ring was a level of commitment he'd never imagined himself making, mainly because he knew he would disappoint the woman wearing it. If that woman was Alice and he messed up enough that she tried to deny him access to Flynn... Well, that would never work.

"I don't think so," he said, adjusting the collar of his Turnbull & Asser hand-stitched shirt. He snapped shut the pouch and pushed it in Kate's direction.

"A word of advice," she said, pushing it right back to him.

"Just one?" he quipped.

Kate smiled. "Your hair is about to catch on fire from how hard you're thinking. Keep the ring, Charles, even if you never use it. But don't think too much about it. Some things are better when they're spontaneous. Rely on your instinct."

He shook his head. "My instincts are horrible. Ask anyone who knows me."

"Alice Meyers is not your usual type," Kate said, slowly rising from the table. "Have your instincts about her been wrong?"

He stood, as well, grabbing the small ring pouch. As his fingers closed around it, the strangest thing happened. Instead of thrusting it toward Kate as he'd planned, he shoved it into his pocket.

That earned him a wide smile from the commanding cosmetics mogul.

"Just because I don't look my age," she told him, "doesn't mean I'm not wise beyond my years." She offered her hand to him.

"Ms. Fortune, it was a true pleasure," Charles said with his most courtly bow. Instead of shaking her hand, he bent over it and brushed his lips across the paper-fine skin of her knuckles.

"A scamp," she repeated, but her eyes were dancing.

"Good luck with your search for a successor," he told her as she gathered her purse.

"Thank you, Charles." She turned for the restaurant's exit, walking slowly even as the rest of the customers watched. He supposed Kate Fortune was more used to being the center of attention than he was. "Good luck with your new family," she called over her shoulder.

New family.

He mulled the words over in his mind and decided that they had a nice ring to them. Patting his pant pocket where the pouch was tucked, he sat back down to enjoy the rest of his breakfast, his appetite suddenly restored.

"I can't do this anymore." Alice dipped her french fry into a puddle of ketchup, then pointed it at Meredith. "I've gained three pounds in two weeks from stress eating."

It was Friday, the end of the workweek, and Alice had convinced her friend to go to lunch.

"It does no good to avoid him," Meredith said, forking up a bite of Cobb salad. "He keeps coming to see you, and Amanda's starting to get mad that you aren't paying enough attention to our Bonnie Lord Charlie."

"Why can't he understand that it will look suspicious if we're seen together all over town?"

"Not really," Meredith observed, "since he's working on the ad campaign with you. Julie in graphic design told me he actually has some decent ideas about the staging for some of the It's Texas spots, and that he's called in favors from every famous Texan he knows."

"That's true," Alice admitted. "He has much more insight into trends in the global tourism industry than anyone gives him credit for." She bit the tip off her fry and chewed. "But working together doesn't justify taking me to lunch every day and hovering around my cubicle at the end of the day so he can walk me to my car."

"Right." Meredith pointed her knife at Alice. "Heaven forbid someone treat you like a gentleman." She made a pretend slashing motion across her throat. "The despicable cad...off with his head."

Alice rolled her eyes. "You know what I mean, Mer. Men don't pay attention to me."

"Because other than those fancy heels you wear, everything about you screams 'Don't look, don't touch.'"

"I do not scream that," Alice protested. "Do I?"

"Why do think that condom languished in your purse for so long?"

"Because when I'm out with you, guys don't notice me."

"Charles notices you," Meredith said, her tone turning wistful. "Sometimes when we're in a meeting and someone else is talking, I'll catch him staring at you and it's..."

"What?"

"It's hot. Like the Texas plains in summer hot. Like you're a cold glass of water and he's been in the desert for months. Like—"

"Enough." Alice choked out an embarrassed laugh. She could feel her face growing warm at the thought of Charles watching her. "I get your point."

"Are you sure?" Meredith arched a brow. "Because from the circles under your eyes and the fact that you're crabby most of the time, I couldn't tell."

"I have a four-month-old baby."

"And you're sexually frustrated."

Alice clamped a hand over her mouth to stifle a gasp. "I can't believe you said that out loud," she whispered, ducking her head and glancing around to make sure no one had overheard her outspoken friend.

"It's true," Meredith said, but thankfully lowered her voice. "Charles wants you, and you're a fool not to take him to bed again."

"It's complicated," Alice said with a heavy sigh. "And he doesn't want more complications. You know limiting what's between us to friendship was his idea." She took a long drink of her sweet tea. "I need to honor that."

"You need to tempt him more."

"I need to respect his wishes." Alice shook her head. "If something happens between us and it affects his relationship with Flynn, I'd never forgive myself."

"Do you really think you'll be able to live like this for the next eighteen years?"

"I have to," Alice said, dropping her head into her hands. "It will get easier."

"In your dreams." Meredith popped a cherry tomato in her mouth. "Is he coming to the cocktail party tonight?"

"Yes," Alice mumbled. The Texas Tourism Board was hosting an event to celebrate the start of the summer vacation season. They'd rented an up-and-coming art gallery in a trendy neighborhood east of downtown. Many of Austin's prominent businesspeople and civic leaders would be attending. Charles, of course, was on the list.

"Will he be wearing a tux?"

"Probably."

"Then it sure won't get easier anytime soon." Meredith winked. "That man is lethal in a tux."

"You look lovely, sweetie," Lynn Meyers said as she took the diaper bag from Alice and carried it down the hall toward the kitchen. The cocktail party was set to start in an hour, so Alice had driven out to her parents' place to drop off Flynn for his first sleepover.

Alice followed with the baby carrier, and Flynn happily sucking his binky.

"Thanks for keeping him tonight, Mom. Are you sure this is okay?" Anxiety sat heavy in her stomach. "I'm sure I can pick him up later without waking him."

"Don't be silly. Your father and I are excited to have our grandson all to ourselves for the night." Her mom set the diaper bag on the kitchen table and tapped Alice's father on the shoulder. "Isn't that right, Henry?"

He started, then looked up from the book he'd been reading. "The baby's staying here? For how long?"

Lynn shook her head. "Just one night. I told you about it last week."

"Right," he mumbled, then glanced at Alice with a sheepish smile. "Sometimes I forget to pay attention."

"It's okay," she said, and bent forward to kiss his cheek.

"I hope you're going to put a sweater on over that getup," he said, eyeing her bright red dress. "You've got too much skin on display."

Alice settled Flynn's car seat on the table and glanced down at her fitted but relatively demure dress. It was a classic boatneck sheath with a red lace overlay. "The only skin anyone can see is my arms," she told her father.

"You should cover them," he said. "It gives men ideas."

"Ideas," her mother said with a scoff. "Don't be old-fashioned, Henry." Lynn unstrapped Flynn and lifted him out of the car seat. "Alice is beautiful."

"I know she's beautiful," Henry countered. "That's the problem."

"I promise it's not a problem, Dad." Alice reached for the diaper bag. "Men aren't that interested in me."

Her father pushed away from the table and stood. "At least one man was," he said, hitching a thumb at Flynn. "I may be an old geezer, but I'm aware of how babies are made."

Alice darted a pleading look at her mother.

"Henry, will you set up the portable crib I bought for Flynn? The box is in Alice's old bedroom upstairs."

"I'm on it," her dad answered, but first turned to his grandson, who was balanced in his wife's arms. "How do you feel about Civil War documentaries?" he asked, tickling Flynn's little toes.

The baby gurgled in response, making her father laugh. "Good point. We'll start with the Revolutionary War."

He stepped toward Alice and gave her a gruff hug. "Wherever you're going tonight, I have no doubt you'll be the most beautiful girl in the room."

"Thanks, Dad," Alice whispered, emotion making her voice catch. Her father might be the epitome of the absentminded professor, but she knew he loved her.

He shuffled toward the hall, then called over his shoulder, "Put on a sweater."

Lynn gave Alice a gentle smile. "He means well."

"I know."

Her mother shifted Flynn up to her shoulder. "He's also right. You *are* a beautiful woman. I can't help thinking there's something going on in your life that you aren't sharing with me."

Alice automatically shook her head. "It isn't worth mentioning."

"Has anything changed in the situation with your young man?"

"I don't have a young man, Mom."

"But there is one you want."

Alice wanted a particular one with every fiber of her being. "I want Flynn to be happy more than anything else." She pulled a piece of paper from the diaper bag's front pocket. "Here are instructions for tonight. He gets one more bottle before bed." She reached out and placed a hand on Flynn's back. "I hope he sleeps for you. He was up twice last night."

"We'll be fine," her mother assured her.

"I could come back here after the reception is over," Alice offered quickly. "You don't have to stay up, but that way I can deal with him when he wakes."

Lynn shook her head. "I can handle a night with him, Alice. Go home after your event and sleep. You're a wonderful mother, but even the best parents need a break."

"Thanks, Mom." Alice wrapped an arm around her mother's thin shoulder. "What would I do without you?"

"You'll never have to find out," Lynn whispered, returning the hug.

As excited as she was about the thought of a full night of sleep, Alice still had trouble leaving Flynn at her parents' place. She reviewed the contents of the diaper bag twice, checked that her father had set up the crib right, insisted on changing the baby's diaper and generally fussed as much as her mother would allow. Lynn finally pushed her out the door with a gentle nudge.

Alice knew Flynn was safe with her parents, and as she drove back toward downtown Austin, some of her anxiety disappeared. She even switched on her favorite radio station, cranking the volume and singing along with a catchy pop tune. A night off might be just what she needed to recharge and bring some much-needed emotional order back into her life.

By the time she arrived at the event venue, she was even mentally prepared to see Charles. Although she'd avoided him for most of the workday, she had sent a text that they should probably keep their distance at the party, so as not to attract attention or suspicion about their relationship. Every day Alice saw more of Charles in Flynn, from the boy's laughing blue eyes to the set of his chin when he was upset. If she and Charles were seen together too often, it was only a matter of time before the truth of the connection they shared would come out. She understood it would happen eventually, but Alice wanted to remain in her safe bubble with just the three of them as long as she could.

Charles hadn't responded to her text, and he wasn't at the party when she arrived. Maybe he'd grown tired of her vacillating between wanting to be with him and needing space. She certainly had. At least she'd gotten sick of the needing space part, even though she continued to tell herself it was better for all of them in the long run. Charles wasn't known for his long attention span, and she still expected him to move on to his next conquest at any time.

She'd dropped her car back at her apartment and then taken a cab to the event, so she accepted a glass of champagne from one of the passing waiters and then hung at Meredith's side as they made their way through the party. The fizzy liquid made her feel like she was drinking bubbles, and helped her relax. She even noticed a few of the men throw glances in her direction. Perhaps Meredith was right and the reason Alice didn't date, even before Flynn, was because she was too guarded when it came to men.

She looked in the mirror and still saw the shy, gangly book nerd with thick glasses and a mouth full of braces. But motherhood had changed more than her sleep patterns. It gave Alice a confidence she didn't have before. The knowledge that she was making it work, despite the difficulties of being a single mom, helped her see herself in a different light.

It was time she let other people see more of that light. She left her friend and approached the bar, squeezing in next to an attractive man who had earlier smiled at her across the room. He turned when her arm brushed the sleeve of his coat, his eyes crinkling at the corners. They were nice eyes, a warm coffee color, but nothing like the vivid blue of Charles's gaze.

"Can I buy you a drink?" the man asked, one corner of his mouth tugging up.

"The drinks are free tonight," she observed, then shut her eyes for a moment. That was his opening line, she realized, and she'd already messed it up. But the man only grinned at her.

"Then can I order you a drink tonight and buy you dinner tomorrow?" He held out a hand. "I'm Troy, and those are the most fantastic shoes I've ever seen."

She glanced at the red, strappy heels Charles had bought her and felt a pang of longing that had nothing to do with the guy standing in front of her. "Thanks," she answered. "My...they're new. I'm Alice." She placed her hand in his, expecting to feel at least a semblance of the sparks that always lit across her skin when she touched Charles.

Nothing. She ignored the disappointment that spiked through her.

"It's nice to meet you, Alice. What are you drinking?"

Alice felt a hand clamp down on her arm. "Nothing that you're ordering for her." A clipped British accent spoke from behind her.

She whirled to find Charles glowering at the man next to her.

"Charles Fortune Chesterfield," Troy said, his dark eyes widening a fraction. "Your reputation precedes you."

Charles's expression grew stonier. "As does yours, Warner." He tugged on Alice's arm. "If you'll excuse us."

"Stop," Alice sputtered, as Charles pulled her away. But before she took two steps, Troy grabbed her by the other wrist.

"Maybe she doesn't want to be excused," he said, his drawl growing more pronounced. Alice knew what that meant for a Texan. The thicker the accent, the quicker trouble was brewing.

Charles had called him "Warner," which meant that she'd been asked to dinner by Troy Warner, heir apparent to one of the largest privately held oil companies in the state. The firm was headquartered in Houston, but the Warner family were longtime supporters of the state's booming tourism business. They owned a sprawling guest ranch in the Texas Hill Country and were stakeholders in several of the state's professional sports teams.

She glanced around to see a number of people near the bar staring at them, and realized she was literally being pulled in two directions by these very different—

but very alpha—men. Stepping out of her shell was one thing, but being made a public spectacle was quite another.

"Enough," she whispered, shaking free from both of their grasps. "This is *not* a competition."

Troy leveled a look at Charles. "Are you sure about that, sweetheart?"

"Positive," she muttered as she caught Amanda's eye from the other side of the bar. Her boss's brows rose so severely they almost hit her hairline. Alice needed to defuse this situation as quickly and quietly as she could. "I'm going to walk away from both of you to powder my nose. I suggest you shake hands or do some backslapping or whatever men do when they're finished with a ridiculous display of egos."

Plastering a smile on her face, she turned first to Troy and leaned in for a polite but distant hug. She was pretty sure Charles growled in response, but she ignored the sound. "Thank you for the dinner invitation," she said softly, "but I have to decline."

"It's a pity, sugar," he said as she moved away. "My loss, I'm afraid."

Next she wrapped her fingers around Charles's muscled arm. To a casual observer it would look like a friendly squeeze, but Alice did her best to surreptitiously dig her nails into his custom-fitted tux jacket. She looked into his clear blue eyes, the sweet smile never leaving her face, and whispered, "I hope you understand why I'm going to kill you."

His opened his mouth to speak but she shook her head. "Going to powder my nose," she repeated, loud enough for the people around them to hear.

Then, with her face burning and her knees knocking, thanks to the curious stares she received, Alice hurried across the room as fast as her wobbly legs would carry her.

She bypassed the restrooms and pushed through the heavy steel fire door that exited out on the alley behind the building. The evening air was still warm, but not nearly as stifling as the atmosphere of the party.

What the hell had Charles been thinking? As far as anyone at the event knew, they were coworkers. A public scene would raise questions Alice didn't want to answer.

There was no way to avoid returning to the party, however, and she'd just about caught her breath when the steel door whooshed open. She straightened as Charles appeared in the alley, his gaze wild as it landed on her.

He stalked toward her and she started to speak, but before she could get a word out, his mouth clamped over hers. All thought dissolved under the pressure of that wholly demanding and utterly intoxicating kiss.

Chapter Twelve

Charles pulled Alice tight against him, wanting to feel every part of her. Needing to claim her. Desire, anger and frustration swirled within him, an electrifying mix only heightened by the feel of actually having Alice in his arms. His hands roamed up and down her back and hips, wanting to feel her curves, wanting to rip away the gorgeous dress and get to the beautiful body underneath.

He was tired of ignoring the passion he felt for her. Her text today suggesting in a few curt words that they feign indifference to each other at the party had settled under his skin like an itch he couldn't quite reach. Charles wasn't used to limits or boundaries and he wanted to rip through hers like the windstorms he'd read about that battered the Texas coast, leaving nothing standing in their wake.

But he respected her, cared for her. His emotions were

so mixed up he could hardly define them. All he knew was that he'd walked into the party with every intention of giving her the space she seemed to need.

Then he'd seen her at the bar with Troy Warner. Charles didn't know the oil scion well, but had seen him around town enough to know that Troy surrounded himself with beautiful women, and lots of them. Much as Charles had.

At least until Alice.

She belonged to him, and not just because they had a child together. Charles had spent a long time avoiding commitment, and he hadn't offered anything to Alice to give her reason to believe he'd changed.

But he had. Because of her. For her.

Everything else had faded away at that moment. He'd ignored the greetings of people he knew and the curious stares from those he didn't. His only goal was getting to Alice.

Now he had her, and while he wasn't planning to let her go anytime soon, he realized mauling her in a deserted alley wasn't the best plan of action for winning her heart.

He gentled the kiss, eased his hold on her, but even as he pulled back, she wrapped her long arms around his neck, her fingers tangling in the hair brushing his collar.

Her response enflamed his need all over again and it was several minutes before he thought about breaking the kiss.

In the end, Alice pulled away, her wide hazel eyes staring up at him with a need that quickly transformed to anger.

Charles didn't need his brother Oliver's gift with finances to know that didn't add up to anything good.

"I'm so mad at you," she said, smoothing her fingertips over her lips as if she could wipe away his kiss.

"I'm sorry," he offered automatically. In his experienced, a well-timed apology worked wonders with an angry woman.

Alice, however, didn't appear mollified. If anything, her expression darkened. She placed her hands on her hips and glared at him. "For what?"

He was momentarily distracted by the way that red dress hugged her curves. "Excuse me?"

"Why are you apologizing?"

He ran a hand through his hair and tried to think of an answer that would make her happy. "For what I did to set off your temper."

She rolled her eyes. "Which was?"

"Being an ass."

"That's a given." Her laugh was tight. "Can you be more specific? Or does it normally work to simply throw about placating words in an effort to get out of the doghouse?"

"Yes, actually," Charles admitted, running a finger under the collar of his starched tuxedo shirt. "I'm a bit of an expert at dodging trouble."

She continued to stare at him, the toe of one sexy-as-hell red heel tapping on the cracked pavement.

"Those shoes are amazing."

"Don't change the subject, Charles."

"Right." He took a breath, blew it out slowly and flashed her his most charming smile.

No response except a slight narrowing of her eyes.

"I'm sorry," he said again, "for making a scene when you'd asked me to act casual at the tourism event. But you should understand—"

She held up a hand. "No. No excuses. I'm finally getting a chance to prove myself at work, and I won't let you jeopardize it. It may not matter to you, Charles, but my career is important to me."

"Slow down, Alice," he said, stepping toward her. "It matters to me. You matter to me. I don't want to muck up anything, but it killed me to see Troy Warner flirting with you. I'd wager no man at that party could take his eyes off you tonight and I've never been good at sharing. You can ask my mum about that."

"I doubt every man was riveted by me," Alice said with a shake of her head. "That's silly."

"I was riveted," he said softly, taking her hand in his and lifting it to his mouth. "I still am. I can't think of anything else but you, Alice. I want to make you laugh and listen to you talk and kiss you senseless." He turned her hand over and pressed a kiss to the delicate skin on the inside of her wrist. "I want you in my bed again."

She swallowed and then licked her lips, the motion making heat weight his body. "You said we should just be friends."

"I'm a bloody idiot," he answered without hesitation.

She rewarded the comment with a half smile that made Charles feel like he'd just been awarded his own knighthood. "I don't want anyone knowing about us. It's better for Flynn that way." She paused, then added, "For all of us."

Charles wasn't sure he agreed, but there were more critical points to clarify right now. "Is that a yes?"

"I don't remember you asking a question."

"I know Flynn is with your parents tonight. Will you spend the night with me, Alice?"

He held his breath as he waited for her answer. "Yes," she whispered finally, and he reached for her again, lift-

ing her into his arms and spinning as their mouths met.
Nothing he'd ever done meant as much as hearing her say
that one word. Alice wasn't the type of woman who gave
herself casually. It meant something that she'd agreed to
be with him. Despite his doubts and fears, he wanted to
mean something to her.

Something more than friends.

"My car is with the valet," he said, when he could
force himself to release her.

She laughed and shook her head. "We need to go
back to the party."

"You're joking, right?"

"If we both disappear at the same time, everyone will
know we're together."

"We *are* together."

"One hour." She leaned forward and whispered
against his mouth, "Please."

"Very well," he conceded. "But I'm going to need a
minute to collect myself."

She glanced down at the front of his pants, her eyes
widening.

"It's going to be the longest hour of my life," he said
with a groan.

"Sorry," she replied, the corners of her full mouth
pulled down.

He kissed her again, hating to see a frown on those
beautiful lips. "Never doubt that you're worth the wait,
Alice." He opened the heavy door and motioned her in.
"I'll meet you inside. One hour and then the real fun
begins."

Charles was right, Alice thought fifty-five minutes
later. This had definitely been the longest hour of her life.

She'd returned to the party and Meredith's side, shaking off her friend's questioning glance.

Amanda had tried to corner her in front of the buffet table, but Alice had managed to stay engrossed in conversation with various tourism board supporters, knowing her boss couldn't fault her for schmoozing with their clients and guests.

It was a wonder Alice managed to follow the thread of any conversation when her skin continued to prickle and butterflies danced across her middle each time Charles caught her eye. They stayed on opposite sides of the room. Physical distance was the only way to make it through the minutes they'd agreed to spend at the event.

She hadn't even minded when she'd noticed him talking to Amanda, her buxom boss giving off so many signals she might as well be wearing a neon placard that said Take Me Home. Instead Alice had felt the imprint of Charles's mouth on hers long after she'd reapplied lipstick and rejoined the party.

She might not be able to envision a future with the ruthlessly single Brit, but she knew he wanted her for tonight. There had been a moment when she'd considered denying his request to spend the night with him. Alice's heart was far more involved than she'd ever intended. The pain that was sure to come when Charles tired of her could affect not only her, but Flynn, as well.

But there was simply no way she could resist Charles, impending heartache or not. She didn't fool herself into thinking she could get him out of her system in one night, but she would take what she could get for now.

Live in the present moment and worry about the consequences later.

Of course, the last time she'd been with Charles, the consequences had changed her life.

Deep in thought, she started when a waiter tapped her shoulder.

"Ms. Meyers?" he asked.

"Yes, that's me. Is everything okay? Does Amanda need something?"

"I was asked to give this to you." He slipped a note-card into her hand and ducked away.

She unfolded the piece of paper and smiled at the words written in bold script inside.

"The longest bloody hour of my life is over. Meet me out front."

A smile curved her lips as she refolded the note and glanced around the crowded room. Meredith was laughing with a group of their coworkers, and Amanda sat at the bar next to Troy Warner, her hand on the attractive bachelor's arm.

Alice made her way out of the party and through the front door. A valet stood by a wooden stand. As soon as he saw Alice, the man pointed up the street. Charles's Mercedes sat a half block away, parked by the curb, the front passenger door open.

She took a step toward it, then looked back over her shoulder. "How did you know who I was?"

The older man grinned and tapped the brim of his valet cap. "Mr. Fortune Chesterfield told me to look for a beautiful woman in a red dress."

"Oh." Alice smoothed her hand over the red lace. "Well, thank you, then. Have a good night."

"You, too, ma'am."

Alice hurried toward the Mercedes and slipped into the rich leather seat. Charles smiled at her. "Hello, Alice."

"Hi," she said, her voice no more than a squeak.

"I would have waited for you directly out front, but I didn't want anyone to see us together."

"Good idea," she said as she fastened the seat belt across her lap. After a moment, she glanced at him. "Why aren't we leaving?"

He winked. "You might want to shut your door first."

She giggled. "Of course." She reached for the door and closed it. The interior of the car felt suddenly intimate.

Charles reached for her hand. "You don't have to be nervous, Alice. Nothing is going to happen tonight that you don't want."

"That's why I'm nervous," she answered. "Because I want everything."

His grin widened. "In that case," he said, revving the luxury car's powerful engine, "we'd better get going."

It took only a few minutes to drive to the posh hotel where Charles had a room, the same hotel he'd stayed at during their last encounter. One of the Four Seasons' valets opened Alice's door after they pulled to a stop under the portico that shaded the front entrance. Charles was around the car in a few seconds. He took her elbow and began to steer her inside.

Alice felt stiff and unsure, suddenly nervous about not only the wisdom of spending the night with Charles, but whether she could live up to his expectations. One night with a virtual stranger, even one as handsome as Charles, had been nothing compared with the pressure of being with someone she truly cared about. A man she loved.

As if sensing her mood, Charles spun her toward him before they'd taken two steps. His kiss was soft and coaxing, filling her senses until she felt almost boneless with desire. She melted into him, holding on to his broad shoulders for support. After a minute he lifted his head, those blue eyes gone stormy gray. "Better?" he asked, with one last kiss to the corner of her mouth.

She nodded. "I want this to be good, Charles, and—"

"It will be perfect, Alice, because it's you and me." He laced their fingers together and led her into the hotel lobby. "Will you trust me? Trust us?"

She gave another jerky nod, unable to speak around the emotion in her chest. Instead, she took in the interior of the hotel. The last time she'd been here with him it had been late at night, and she'd had enough to drink that she'd barely noticed the beautiful decor.

The walls were an antique beige with expensively patterned wallpaper, dark mahogany trim giving the impression of a classic country club. Everything about the space screamed money and understated style. As in many exclusive hotels, the staff were professional and discreet, purposely not looking as Charles led her through the lobby toward the bank of elevators on one side. When she'd come here with him a year ago, Alice had felt like Julia Roberts in *Pretty Woman*, wholly out of her element in the posh surroundings.

But tonight, as she held tight to his warm, strong hand, Alice realized the feeling bubbling to the surface inside her was belonging. Whatever happened tomorrow, tonight she belonged with Charles—in his arms and in his bed.

They stepped into a waiting elevator and he punched the button for the top floor. He turned to her as the door slid closed, his gaze questioning as if he still didn't trust her decision to come with him tonight.

Before he could speak, she pressed her mouth to his,

putting all the things she wasn't ready to say into the kiss. He responded in an instant, turning her so her back was against the cool wall of the elevator. His mouth was frenzied, trailing kisses from her lips to the line of her jaw and lower to her throat. His fingers moved aside the sleeve of her dress and his palm splayed across the top of her breast.

She sucked in a breath, arching into him, just as the elevator chimed.

"Just a few more steps," he whispered, straightening her dress.

She was dizzy with need as she followed him down the hall. He fumbled in his pocket for the room key, and it bolstered Alice's confidence to see that his fingers trembled as he held it up to the lock.

He threw her a boyish smile. "You make me lose my mind."

"Good," she told him, and leaned closer.

Then the door was open and he hauled her into the room, claiming her mouth once more.

She wanted to touch him, to feel his skin under her hands. She pushed at his tux jacket as he tugged on her zipper. The result was a jumble of limbs that had them both laughing.

Charles moved back, his breathing ragged but a teasing light in his eye. "There's no hurry."

Alice shook her head, placed a hand to her pounding heart. "I'm kind of in a hurry."

"We have all night." He reached out a finger, pushed a lock of hair off her shoulder, the light touch magnified on her heated skin. "I don't want to rush, Alice. I'm going to make this perfect for you." He put his hands on her shoulders and turned her, reaching for the zipper of her red dress. She hitched in a breath as the cool air of the room whispered across her back, followed by his knuckles brushing along her spine.

Her nerves made her want to rush this before she lost her confidence. She didn't want to think about any of the other women he'd been with and how she wouldn't measure up to them.

"Only you and me," Charles whispered into the nape of her neck as he pushed the dress down her arms. It pooled at her feet, leaving her in only her bra, underpants and those red heels he'd bought for her.

She swallowed back her nerves and turned to face him. "Now you."

"I'm too busy enjoying the view," he said, his eyes roving all over her body.

"Charles, please," she said, feeling color rise to her cheeks.

His eyes darkened in response. "Your skin is so pale you blush all over. I can't wait another minute to touch you." He took a step toward her but she shook her head.

"Too many clothes," she said, pointing at him.

Immediately he tore off his jacket, then tugged at his tie and unbuttoned his shirt.

"You move fast when you're motivated," she told him as he shrugged out of his shoes, socks and pants.

"Hell, yes," he agreed, and a moment later, he was down to his boxers. She started to slip out of the heels, but he grabbed her around the waist, hauling her against his lean chest. "Not yet. I'm still enjoying them too much."

He kissed her, his tongue tangling with hers as he moved them toward the bed. He threw back the covers, then lowered her onto the cool sheets. He sat back and took one of her feet in his hands, slowly removing the red heel as he caressed her arch, then repeated the action with the other heel. He pressed his hands to the bed on either side of her hips, staring into her eyes as if searching for something. "Are you sure, Alice?" he asked, his voice unsteady. "Is this what you want?"

She almost answered "forever" because that was the truth, but she could never admit that to Charles. Instead she whispered a simple "yes," which must have been enough, because he kissed her again, his hands moving everywhere on her body. Her bra and panties were gone a minute later, followed by his boxers. He pulled a foil packet from the nightstand drawer and ripped it open with his teeth.

"Good idea for you to provide the protection this time," Alice said with a jittery laugh, suddenly feeling anxious all over again.

Charles brought his face inches from hers. "Everything happens for a reason, darling, and your sentimental condom was no exception." He kissed her long and hard, then thrust into her, making her gasp his name.

He gave an answering moan, then Alice lost all ability to think. Her body took over, moving with Charles as if they'd been together for years. He knew exactly how to touch her, what to whisper, the way she wanted to be held. When the pressure built and finally broke over them like a sparkling wave, like every bit of sunshine and light she'd ever felt, Alice knew she was ruined for any other man.

Whether her time with Charles lasted days or weeks, or even it was over after tonight, her heart would be his forever.

Chapter Thirteen

Charles lay wrapped around Alice hours later, after making love to her for a second time. He tried to calm his heart, which was pounding not because of exertion, but from the emotions tumbling around his chest like so many rocks spilling over the side of a mountain face. That's how he felt after being with Alice again—as if he were standing on a sharp precipice, about to free-fall off the edge. Adrenaline was pumping through him, and he didn't trust himself to speak, afraid of the words that would pour out of his mouth. Words that would make him seem needy and desperate, and expose the soft underside of his heart that he kept locked away.

This was sex, he reminded himself, and he'd done the same thing too many times to count, with more women than he should admit. Being with Alice should be no different.

Except it was. And that scared the hell out of him.

He wasn't willing to let her go, but he'd have to eventually. Kate Fortune had accused him of having a raging Peter Pan complex. As offensive as the idea was, Charles hadn't ever given much thought to settling down and being responsible. His reputation, career—his whole life—was based on being the Fortune who refused to grow up. As much as he wanted to live up to his father, Charles hated the idea that he might fail. It had always been easier not to try, and the consequences of his actions hadn't mattered.

But they would to Alice. He knew he could be a part-time father and a halfway decent one, but a woman like Alice deserved a man who could fully devote himself to her. Charles had always been afraid there was something inherently lacking in him—some ability to commit that had seemed to skip him in the family gene pool. If he was destined to disappoint Alice, wouldn't it be better if he never tried in the first place?

She snuggled closer and he dropped a soft kiss on her bare shoulder as he sifted her spun-silk hair through his fingers.

"Thank you for tonight," she said softly, and he could hear the sleepy smile in her voice.

He made what sounded even to his own ears like a Neanderthal grunt. Where had his gallant polish gone now that he needed it most?

Her whole body stiffened when the silence drew out between him. "Should I go?" she asked, clearly interpreting his inability to form a coherent sentence as disinterest.

Yes, he wanted to yell, *go before I mess this up or hurt you or reveal so much that you hurt me.* He was so wrapped up in his own doubts that he didn't register that she'd moved out of his arms until the bed shifted. He grabbed her before she stood, and pulled her back onto the bed, lifting himself above her.

"Stay." His tone was too gruff, he knew, and she turned her face to the side.

"It's okay, Charles. You don't have to say—"

He smoothed his hand along her cheek and tipped it until she met his gaze. "I should say so much more, but my brain appears to have been addled by the best shag of my life."

The corner of her mouth lifted slightly, but was enough to give him a glimmer of hope that he could make this right.

"The best?"

"If there was a better than the best, you would be it." He kissed the tip of her nose. "I'm sorry I made you feel anything different. Stay with me tonight, Alice. I want to wake up next to you tomorrow. I want to open my eyes and see your beautiful face."

Her smile broadened. "Okay."

"Tell me it was better than okay for you?"

She tapped one finger to her mouth. "I don't have much for comparison…"

He flipped onto his back and took her with him. "Maybe you need more to compare it to?"

"Maybe I do," she agreed, and kissed him. After that, all his doubts melted away in the heat and light of Alice.

Although he'd asked her to stay the night before, Charles expected to be ready to say goodbye to Alice once they woke up. He liked a solitary morning, usually needing to recover from his active nighttime social life.

But once again, being with Alice was a revelation.

He was not only happy to have her body curled around him, he wanted to spend as much of the day as he could with her. He watched her sleep, her breath easing in and out. She was on her side, facing him, the sheet bunched under her arms with just the tips of her breasts showing. She'd washed off her makeup sometime in the night and in the morning light he could see a faint dusting of freckles across her nose. He wondered if Flynn would have his mother's freckles and her sweet spirit. Charles couldn't wait to see how his son developed.

He also couldn't seem to wait for Alice to wake up. Charles trailed his finger along her collarbone, then down her chest, curling his fingertip in the sheet to tug it down.

Alice's eyes flew open as her hand clamped over his.

"Good morning," he said, bending his head to press his lips to the swell of her breast.

"Hi," she said with a small yelp of pleasure. "You're up early."

"Every day, love."

"Now I see where Flynn gets his sleep habits." She yawned, then yelped as Charles nipped at her skin. "I need coffee."

"I have something to wake you up faster than caffeine." He pulled at the sheet again. "It's going to be your best morning ever."

She stretched her arms around his neck, and his muscles heated in response. "Let's see what you've got."

After a leisurely breakfast ordered from room service and a shower, Alice insisted she needed to go back to her apartment to change and then pick up Flynn from her parents.

"I'll drive you," Charles offered, pulling on the Keep

Austin Weird T-shirt that was quickly becoming his favorite.

"To my apartment?" Alice asked, slipping on the red heels from the previous night. He wanted to buy her those shoes in every color and beg her to wear them for him each night. "Thanks, that would make the walk of shame I'm about to do less embarrassing."

"No shame," he told her. He paused, then added, "I could free up my schedule and take you out to your parents' house to get Flynn if you want."

The truth was, he had nothing on his calendar for the day. He'd taken to leaving it empty in the hopes that he'd get to spend time with Alice. It was easy enough to fill when he needed to, and most of his friends and family would be shocked to see him rearranging his plans for a woman. At this point, he didn't care.

But the look Alice threw him from across the room definitely wasn't encouraging.

"That's not a good idea."

"Why?"

"My mom and dad don't know anything about…" She squeezed her fists at her sides. "About Flynn's father."

"You mean me?"

"We agreed to keep this private, Charles."

"For how long?" he asked, grabbing his wallet and keys from the dresser and shoving them in his pocket. "My brothers and sisters know I have a son now. They aren't going to tell anyone outside the family. I assume your parents aren't going to phone it in to the tabloids."

"Of course not."

"Then why can't I meet them?"

She took a step toward him. "Because they would have expectations for you and me. I love my parents, but they're traditional. It was difficult for them to come to terms with me becoming a single mother. I can't just waltz in there and introduce them to some international playboy who also happens to be my...my baby daddy."

"That's an interesting term," he said through clenched teeth.

"I'm sorry, but it's the truth."

She looked as miserable as Charles felt, and he wanted to wrap her in his arms and tell her he'd make everything right for both of them. The problem was, he didn't know how.

"Give us more time to figure things out, Charles. Unless you have the answer for how all of this is going to work."

"I'm here now," he offered, even though it sounded lame to his ears. But he couldn't give her anything more. He wasn't ready, wasn't sure he'd ever be.

Alice gave him a tight smile. "I appreciate that, but I'm not prepared for you to meet my parents. Not yet."

"Whatever you want," he said, and forced his own smile. "Let's be on our way, then."

They rode in silence to her apartment, and Charles hated every second of it. He wanted to reach across the interior of the car and take her hand. He wanted to do something to renew the feeling between them, the one that made him itchy and uncomfortable and happier than he could ever remember.

But he didn't say anything. He didn't do anything. He pulled to the curb in front of her building minutes later. "Here you go, love."

She put her hand on the door handle. After a moment she turned to him. "After his afternoon nap, I'm going to give Flynn cereal for the first time. I know it's not the most exciting way to spend a Saturday." Her smile was hesitant but did wonders for his mood. "But I'd love for you to come over and help."

"I wouldn't miss it," he said, and her smile widened.

Alice finished changing Flynn's diaper just as the doorbell rang. She hurried to put a new outfit on the baby, then carried him out to open the front door.

Charles stood on the other side, holding a cardboard box that hit him midchest. On the side was a photo of a baby in a high chair.

"You didn't have to do that," Alice said, taking a step back to make room for Charles to enter.

"You said you hadn't bought a high chair yet." He lifted it easily, his arm muscles bunching under the casual T-shirt he wore. No matter how much he dressed like an American, Charles always looked like the perfect, dashing Brit to her.

"I haven't needed one yet," she told him. "And I'm a little short on space in here."

He beamed. "That's why this one is perfect." He flipped the box around and pointed to the picture on the other side. "The saleswoman recommended it for small spaces. It folds up to only eight inches wide so you tuck it into a corner when he's finished eating." Charles leaned forward and jiggled Flynn's foot. "Hullo, little man. Are you ready for some tasty porridge?"

Flynn looked at him and broke into a smile and happy gurgling that made Alice's insides clench. Looks like she wasn't the only one enamored with Charles. But she was determined to protect Flynn's innocent little heart, even if hers was already preparing for the inevitable ache.

"Thank you. That's very generous, Charles. You don't have to lavish us with gifts every time we see you."

"Who's lavishing?" he asked with mock solemnity. "This is only the tip of the iceberg."

She went to close the front door, but he held up a hand. "I'm not kidding, Alice. There are three more bags in the hall." He propped the high chair box against the back of the couch, then stepped around her.

Alice's eyes widened as he pulled several large shopping bags with a local toy store's logo printed on the sides into the apartment. "What more could we need?"

"According to the saleswoman, quite a bit. The developmental milestones come fast in the next few months, so I've got board books and teething rings and activity toys for every occasion."

Flynn watched Charles unload the bags with interest. Alice was still in shock. "You don't need to do this."

"But I want to." He reached for the big box again. "Let's get this thing set up so we can start our boy on some yummy…" He paused, flashing her a sheepish smile. "What is it he eats again?"

"Rice cereal."

"Sounds tasty."

Charles tipped the box flat on the floor, then lifted his arms. "I'll take him for a bit."

"Are you sure?"

"He can read the assembly directions to me."

Alice laughed but grabbed a small fleece blanket from the arm of the sofa and spread it onto the floor. "He's four months old," she said as she laid Flynn on the soft fabric.

"Then we'll have to wing it."

Flynn kicked his arms and legs as if he was excited by the prospect of helping his daddy with a project.

The flutter in Alice's heart as she watched her two boys together felt both familiar and sweet. Even if the scene before her wasn't entirely true. Charles wasn't hers, as much as it had felt like it last night. Yet he was here now, and Alice was becoming quite an expert at living in the moment and burying her deeper needs and desires.

She mixed together the dry cereal and water until it was the soupy consistency Flynn's pediatrician recommended. By the time she had turned from the counter, Charles was setting Flynn into the high chair.

"That was quick."

"Turns out they come almost assembled. There's one problem, however."

She took a step closer and smiled. Flynn's face was eye level with the high chair tray, his little head drooping to one side. "He may need to grow into it a bit."

"A bit," Charles agreed, and they shared a grin that she imagined parents all over the world could appreciate. It was the amusement of two people united in their love for a baby, which made even the littlest moments special.

She found a blanket to prop Flynn up, then adjusted the straps of the high chair until he looked comfortable.

Charles picked up the bowl of cereal from the table and stirred it a few times. "This doesn't look edible."

"It is for babies." She arched an eyebrow. "Unless you want to taste test it first?"

"That sounds like a dare, Ms. Meyers."

She pulled a spoon out of one of the kitchen drawers and pointed it at him. "Are you up for the challenge?"

With a cheeky grin, he took the spoon from her and dipped it into the cereal. "Only for you," he told her, then took a bite.

She couldn't help but smile as she watched him. How

many other people had seen this playful, casual side of Charles? Probably his mother and siblings. Maybe friends from school. But Alice wondered if he'd let down his guard with any other women before her. It wasn't something that came natural to him, so she doubted there could be many.

"Hey." He touched a fingertip to her nose, making her jump. "I'm the one supposed to be making faces here."

She shook off her musings. "How was it?"

"Not bad, but not good, either." He turned to Flynn, who was watching the exchange with wide eyes. "What do you think, wee man? Ready for a go at it?"

As if in response, Flynn slapped his palms on the plastic tray. Charles started to hand the bowl to Alice, but she shook her head. "Do you want to give him the first bite?" she asked.

"Are you sure?"

Every moment she'd had with Flynn had been on her own. She'd changed diapers, soothed him, witnessed his first smile and listened to his first baby babbling by herself. That's how she'd wanted it. She'd needed to prove to herself and to her parents and friends that she could manage things on her own. That she was more than anyone thought she was.

But that was just one more way Charles was different. He expected her to be the expert on parenting. And in many ways she was, although she was no longer alone. Even if it couldn't be as much as she wanted, she and Charles were partners and connected for life by their beautiful son.

So she was happy to let him take the lead on his "first" first.

She nodded and he turned to Flynn. "Let's make your

mommy proud, Flynn, my boy." He scooped up a small bit of cereal and held it out to the baby. Flynn opened his mouth automatically as the spoon got closer and Charles dipped it between his rosebud lips.

Immediately Flynn pulled back, scrunched up his face and shuddered.

Alice held her breath and Charles froze, waiting to see the rest of the reaction.

After a moment, the baby's features softened and he smacked his lips together, then opened his mouth for more. "Well done, lad," Charles said with a laugh, and fed him another bite.

Alice took over, and eventually Flynn turned away from the spoon, signaling he was full. She put the bowl and spoon into the sink as Charles lifted him out of the high chair. She watched Charles grab a wipe from the container on the table and dab it at Flynn's cheeks. Something about the way he held the baby made Alice melt even more than usual. It was late afternoon and she wanted nothing more than to grab Charles and pull him close, to lean into his strength.

That was dangerous. Heartache was one thing to deal with, but a complete break was too much. She would save that for when she was safely alone again.

"Do you want to do something fun?" she blurted before she passed the point of no return.

Charles rocked Flynn gently in his arms. "What did you have in mind?"

"Bats," she said.

Charles cocked a brow. "Bats?"

"They're a thing in Austin. The world's largest urban bat colony lives under the Congress Avenue Bridge downtown—over a million bats. They migrate down to

Mexico for the winter but come back each March. Every spring and summer night around sunset they take off for their evening feeding. It's pretty amazing to see."

He didn't look convinced.

She pointed to his chest. "You're wearing a Keep Austin Weird T-shirt. It's time to prove you believe it."

"Another challenge?" Charles grinned. "I like it. Lead on, my dear."

Alice was always surprised there were locals around town who hadn't ever visited the bats. Maybe her family was quirkier than most, but when she was a kid they'd packed a picnic at least once a month during the summer and come downtown for the evening display. She loved the nightly ritual and had watched it become a popular tourist attraction.

But Alice still remembered her dad's secret parking space near the bridge, and guided Charles to it. They parked, then pulled out the stroller and attached Flynn's infant carrier to the top. Joining the small crowd of people moving toward the bridge, she and Charles walked in comfortable silence. To passersby they were just another family on their way to witness one of the city's more unique attractions.

They found a spot just off the path near the edge of the bridge, near the place Alice had stood so many times with her parents. The sky was streaked with ribbons of pink and purple as the sun set behind the nearby buildings.

Above the noise of people they could hear a high-pitched chirping. "Bats?" Charles asked.

Alice nodded, then smiled as he tightened the sun cover over Flynn's car seat.

"He's safe," she said gently.

"No use taking chances," Charles answered, before wrapping an arm around her shoulder.

Just then the sound of fluttering wings filled the air, and a mass of bats flew out from below the bridge, black against the pink-and-purple sky as they streaked across it in an undulating pattern.

She heard Charles suck in a breath as he pulled her closer. "Amazing," he whispered into her hair, and Alice felt a wash of contentment roll through her.

Everything about this moment was amazing. Never, in all the times she'd been here with her parents, had she ever imagined standing in the same place with her own family. Temporary as it might be, she would remember it forever. The feeling of belonging with Charles was something she'd never be able to replace.

After the bats had flown off for the night, the three of them made their way back to her apartment. Flynn was asleep in his car seat, and she quickly changed him and put him to bed for the night. Charles was waiting by the front door when she came out, his hands stuffed in the front pockets of his jeans.

"That was one of the best evenings out I've had in a long time," he told her.

"You're lying," she said with a laugh, "but I appreciate it, anyway."

"It's the truth, Alice." He stepped forward and cupped her cheeks with his hands. "Anything we do together makes it the best." His mouth brushed lightly against hers, but when she stepped into him, he pulled away.

"I should go." He shoved his hands into his pockets again. "I'm sure you want some rest while the baby is down." He backed toward the door, a half smile curving his lips. "If I stay, I'm afraid you won't get much sleep."

She should let him leave but couldn't stand the thought of this night ending. She wanted to lose herself in him again. To continue what they'd started last night and claim as much time with him as she could.

"Sleep is overrated," she said, and reached for him.

His hand stilled on the doorknob. "You don't have to do this."

"I want to, Charles." She ran her palms up the hard planes of his chest even as his body remained like a statue beneath them. It was difficult for her to take the lead. Being assertive wasn't part of Alice's nature, but this man was worth the effort. Being a mother had changed her, and in some ways Charles had changed her, too. Although he didn't move, she knew he wanted her. Last night had been real and it gave her the confidence to thread her fingers through his hair and pull his face down to hers. "I want you."

Those three words seemed to release something in him, because the next thing she knew, Alice was in his arms and he was heading for her small bedroom. "Right now, my sole aim in life is to make you happy." He kissed her, running his tongue across the seam of her lips.

"This is a very good start."

Chapter Fourteen

The next morning, Charles sat at the small table in Alice's kitchen, Flynn in his arms. The baby had finished a bottle, let out a huge burp and was now sucking on his fist as he gazed up at Charles.

Alice set a plate with a toasted bagel and half a banana on the table. "Sorry I don't have anything more."

"This is great," Charles told her, and, surprisingly, he meant it. He lived out of hotels more weeks than not and was used to big breakfast buffets or ordering room service. But this quiet morning waking up with Alice and Flynn was the best he'd had in ages. So good, in fact, that he didn't want it to end.

"I've been thinking…" he said, as Alice sat across from him, her long fingers wrapped around a steaming mug of coffee.

"Should I be worried?" she asked with a small smile.

That was another thing he loved—the more time he spent with her, the less Alice seemed to feel shy around him. She had a playful, teasing streak that most people in her life didn't get to see. The fact that he did made Charles ridiculously happy.

"I want to bring Flynn back to London with me." Charles held the boy closer as he took a bite of bagel.

Alice stared at him a few moments, then asked, "For a visit?"

"Of sorts." Flynn fussed a bit, so Charles stood and rocked him until he quieted. "Would you like to live across the pond, Flynn, my boy? Romp about Kensington Gardens and visit the London Zoo?" Charles kept his gaze on the baby even as he spoke to Alice. "It's a brilliant plan, if I do say so myself. My flat has three bedrooms, so I can easily turn one into a nursery. It will be simple enough to have my assistant make the arrangements."

"Your assistant?"

"I haven't mentioned her?" He reached for a rattle and held it up for Flynn to grab. "Mary's been with me for years. She handles all my scheduling and basically runs my life."

"You need someone to run your life?"

Charles chuckled but kept watching Flynn. "It's a busy life, my lovely Alice."

"And you want to make Flynn a part of it?"

Something in her tone made him glance away from Flynn toward the woman now standing a few feet from him, arms crossed over her pink T-shirt, one toe tapping against the carpet. "You, too, of course," he answered quickly, wondering if that's what had made her temper spike. Because there was no denying the mulish set of her jaw.

What had happened to the Alice who had been pliant in his arms all night, or the one who had sweetly cuddled Flynn between the two of them early this morning? Hell, Charles would take almost any mood in place of her anger, especially as it appeared aimed directly at him.

"As I said, there are three bedrooms in the flat. I've dropped a few hints to Amanda about loaning you and your stellar research skills to the British Tourism Council for a few months."

"You've talked to my boss?" There was a sharp edge to Alice's tone that made Charles flinch. Even Flynn seemed to notice the change and began to whimper softly.

Charles rocked the boy more vigorously as he took a step toward Alice. "Just in passing. I thought it best to lay the groundwork—"

"For me to leave my life behind?" Her hazel eyes had gone hard as stone.

"Alice, you keep posing questions that sound more like accusations. I'm doing the best I can here. Being a father is new to me, as is thinking about someone other than myself."

"By 'someone,' you mean Flynn?" she asked, her mouth barely moving as she spoke.

"And you. I understand the two of you are a package deal. If you don't feel comfortable staying at my place, I can set you up with your own apartment in the neighborhood. It's a lovely area of London with—"

Flynn let out a sharp cry and Alice moved forward before Charles could react. She scooped the baby out of his arms and held him close. The boy immediately quieted and nuzzled against her shoulder. "It's a generous offer," she said, but her voice sounded hollow.

"I mean it." Charles knew he was losing ground, but couldn't figure out why, or how to regain his footing. "I've told you before, we're a team. I'll make sure you're comfortable and taken care of. Flynn won't want for a thing."

"A team," she murmured. "I take it your assistant is part of this team, as well?"

He shrugged. "In a manner of speaking. But I'm talking about you and Flynn. The three of us."

She gave a jerky nod. "When would you want to leave?"

"I have a meeting with the director of the British Tourism Council at the end of next week that I can't reschedule. If you need more time, I can go over first and get things ready."

"Can I have a few days to think about it?"

Charles felt himself frowning. "What's there to think about? Flynn is my son and I want him—both of you—with me. I want to take care of you." He knew he was mucking this up, that whatever he was saying was pushing her away instead of bringing her closer. He wanted to scoop her into his arms and kiss her until the distance between them disappeared.

"This is new for me, too, Charles. I don't even have a passport."

"I have connections that can expedite that process."

"You have a lot of things," she said, "but all I have is my baby and my family. I need time."

He sighed. Of course she did. This was not a rejection. Not outright, anyway. He shouldn't have assumed she'd be as excited about his plan as he was. But he had, because he thought she'd felt as much for him as he did for her. Maybe that had been just wishful thinking. He was Flynn's father, but that didn't mean Alice would want anything more than help with parenting. Yes, they'd shared a few nights of passion, but that could be a new mother needing to scratch an itch, with Charles being the most convenient outlet. The idea created a sick feeling in his chest. Charles had never had to work hard for anything in his life, and certainly not the affections of a woman.

The potential for failing made him want to turn and run, but then he glanced at Alice, who stood on the far side of the small family room, watching him as she cradled Flynn in his arms.

No.

He wasn't going to take the easy way out this time. Alice and Flynn were too important. If she needed time, he'd give it to her. More importantly, he'd find a way to convince her that he was worth taking a chance on.

"Take the time you need, Alice." He moved toward her, bent and kissed the top of her forehead. "I need to visit my family in Horseback Hollow before I return to England." He ruffled Flynn's hair. "I'll ring you in a few days, and we'll discuss our plans then."

He wasn't sure he could take another argument, so before she could offer one, he turned and left her apartment. It was time to become the man his father had believed he could be.

"He walked out on you just like that?" Meredith took a long pull on her beer and shook her head. "No fight? No declaration of love?"

Alice forced herself to laugh even as embarrassment

colored her cheeks. "He said he'd call in a few days. He needs to check in with his family." She glanced at the baby monitor that sat on the coffee table, almost hoping that Flynn would let out a cry so she could have an excuse not to have this conversation. Meredith had called shortly after Charles left, and Alice hadn't been able to hide her hurt at the way the morning had ended. Her friend had brought over carryout and beer from a local brewpub. While Alice was grateful for the company, she didn't want to revisit the humiliation of Charles's earlier offer.

Meredith sniffed. "After demanding that you leave your whole life behind and follow him to England."

"It's not much of a life," Alice said quietly. "He probably thinks he's doing me a favor. I could still work, and I'm sure I'd have more help with Flynn."

"But you'd be an ocean away from your parents."

"I want Flynn to know his father."

"Alice." Meredith scooted closer on the sofa and took Alice's hands in hers. "What do you want for yourself?"

Alice stared at her friend for a moment, finding it difficult to process the deeper meaning of the question. "I told you…"

"You are an amazing mother," Meredith said softly. "I know that no one believed you could handle raising a baby on your own. We underestimated you. All of us did. Your parents, everyone at work. Me."

"It's okay."

"No. It's not." Meredith shook her head. "Although you've proved us wrong, Flynn can't be your whole life." She held up a hand when Alice would have argued. "The best thing you can do for that baby is to be happy. What is going to make you happy, Alice?"

"Charles," she whispered, before she could stop herself.

"I knew it," Meredith shouted, and jumped up from the couch.

"Meredith, quiet. You'll wake Flynn."

"It isn't just for Flynn that you want to follow Charles, is it?" Her friend sank back down, tucked her legs under her. She'd lowered her voice, but her tone was animated.

"It's not that simple."

"Why not? You want him. He wants you."

"He wants me in the same way he wants his assistant. I make his life easier."

"Is that so bad?"

"I don't want easy." Now Alice stood, paced from one side of the room and back. "You all weren't the only ones who doubted I could handle motherhood. I never thought I could do it on my own. The past year hasn't been easy, but every difficult moment has been worth it. It's made me a better person. It's changed me. I don't want to go back to depending on someone. If I go with Charles, where does that leave me? Who will I be with him?"

Meredith frowned. "You'll be Alice. Flynn's mother."

"But what if Alice isn't enough? What if I have to watch him date other women? What if he meets someone he wants to marry, when I'm..."

"In love with him?"

Alice didn't bother to argue. "I told myself not to let it happen, but I couldn't help it."

"Of course not," Meredith agreed. "He's Bonnie Lord Charlie. Half the female population is in love with him."

"You don't understand." Alice ran a hand through her hair, thought of the way Charles had fanned the strands across the pillow early this morning. "I love him despite the way the world knows him. I love him for the parts of him that no one else sees. The pieces that he doesn't even see. He's a good man, more than most people ever imagine. I know he cares about me, but it isn't enough. If I've just discovered that I'm strong enough to stand on my own, how could I ever be satisfied with half a life?"

Meredith pressed her fingers to her temples. "Then you're not going to go with him?"

Alice shrugged. "I'm not sure I can let him go."

"Heartache either way."

"Heartache seems like a pretty good option at this point." Alice felt a tear track down her cheek. "It's full-blown heartbreak that scares me half to death." And swiping at the tears with her fingertips, she sank into her friend's comforting embrace.

Chapter Fifteen

"I've been wondering when you were going to grace me with your presence, Charles."

Charles smiled and dropped a kiss on his mother's soft cheek where she sat in the cozy study of her condo outside of Horseback Hollow. The house was small and relatively casual compared to the sprawling estate where Charles had grown up, but his mother looked as regal as if she were about to take high tea with the queen. Although Josephine May Fortune Chesterfield had spent most of her life in England, she'd adapted to life in this quaint Texas town like she was made for it.

It had been only a few years ago that Josephine had discovered she was the third triplet in a trio that included James Marshall Fortune, head of the powerful Atlanta company JMF Financial, and Jeanne Marie Fortune Jones, who had raised her brood of children in Horseback Hollow. The British Fortunes had first come to the tiny town for their cousin Sawyer's wedding to Laurel Redmond, but all of them, except Charles, had eventually returned to find love in Texas.

His mother enjoyed being near her children, grandchildren and extended family. She'd even found the beginning of a new relationship with retired pilot Orlando Mendoza. She'd cut back on her philanthropic duties overseas and spent more time working with local charities now. But even with her busy schedule, Charles knew she always had time to play the family matriarch, a role she embodied with compassion, caring and only the most refined and well-intentioned measure of heavy-handedness.

"So sorry, Mum," he said, as he dropped into the chair next to her.

"Sit up straight, Charles," she said quietly.

"Right." He corrected his posture with a wink. "The state tourism board has kept me quite busy the last couple of weeks."

Josephine raised one eyebrow. "Is that all?"

"Who told you?" He narrowed his eyes. "Was it Lucie? I made her promise…"

"The question is not which of your siblings mentioned your young lady to me," his mother said. "I'm wondering why I didn't hear the news from you." She held up a hand to stave off his explanation. "More importantly, when do I get to meet this woman and my new grandson?"

"It's complicated," he muttered.

"I wouldn't expect anything else from you."

He lowered his head into his hands and took a deep breath. Although he'd been worried about his mother discovering the truth about Alice and Flynn, now it felt like a relief. Josephine was the most loving, compassionate person Charles knew, and he would have felt that way even if she hadn't been the one to change his nappies when he was a babe. He hadn't realized until now how much he wanted her advice and perspective on the unholy mess that was his current life. "I'm sorry I haven't said anything to you about the baby."

"And the baby's mother? This woman who tracked you down to tell you after the fact that you are a father?"

"Don't judge her," Charles said immediately. "The way I left things after our time together…she had no reason to believe I'd be interested in the baby. You know how the tabloids paint my life."

"I understand. The fact that you're defending her means you've made peace with the way things happened."

He gave a small nod. "Her name is Alice Meyers. We met at a tourism conference last year and she's…different than my typical girlfriends."

Josephine pressed a manicured hand to her chest. "Thank heavens for that."

"I haven't brought her to meet everyone because she's shy and I think my lifestyle makes her nervous. She's happy with a quiet night at home and doesn't come from a big family. I know she likes me… I think she likes me…" He choked out a laugh. "I want her to like me."

"Charles, you are one of the most likable people in the world. If she can't appreciate that…"

He shook his head. "That's the thing, Mum. She doesn't seem to care about what makes me popular with everyone else. It's almost a negative that I'm famous. I don't have to try with her. She doesn't care about going out or being seen with me. It's…normal."

"Normal is underrated," Josephine said, nodding.

"Your father and I wanted to give our children a regular upbringing, but it was difficult with the British press hounding us so much of the time."

Charles stood and moved to the sofa next to his mother. "You and Dad were the best, Mum. It scares the hell out of me that I won't be even a tenth of the parent either of you were."

"You have a big heart, and you want to do the right thing by your son. That counts for a lot."

"That's what Alice tells me."

"I like her already. It's also obvious that you care about her very much." Josephine tilted her head to study him. "Perhaps that's part of your difficulty."

The thing about having an amazing mother was sometimes she was so perceptive, even when Charles didn't want her to be. "I can't remember ever feeling this way about anyone. Alice matters. But I'm afraid of handling it poorly. I haven't exactly had to work hard for most of my success."

Josephine gave a motherly *tsk*. "You sell yourself short. Have you told her how you feel?"

"I asked her to come to London with me. Along with Flynn, of course. I can turn one of the extra bedrooms into a nursery."

"What is Alice going to do in London?"

"I've arranged for the Texas Tourism Board to loan her to the British council for a bit."

His mother's eyes widened a fraction. "Did she agree to that?"

"Not exactly," Charles admitted. "But she will. She has to. I can't imagine not having her and Flynn in my life."

"But from how you've explained it, that's not what you told her."

"She knows it's what I meant."

"Are you certain?"

"Of course," Charles answered, even though he wasn't certain at all. "I want to take care of her and protect her. I'd never make that kind of an offer if I didn't care about her." He glanced at the framed photos of his siblings and their families that lined the cherry bookshelf. "What do I do now?"

Josephine gave him a gentle smile. "What do you want?"

"I want a family of my own. Alice and Flynn are it for me."

His mother shifted closer, leaned forward to pat his cheek. "Just make sure she knows that, dear." She glanced at her watch and stood. "And bring them to visit before you leave Texas, if that's indeed what you decide to do. I want to meet the woman who's captured your heart."

He shook his head. "I care about her, Mum. That's different than my heart being involved."

"If that's what you need to believe," she said. "I'm meeting Orlando for an early dinner with Jeanne Marie and Deke. Would you like to join us?"

"As much as I enjoy my aunt and uncle's company, I'll take a rain check." Charles stood, as well, and gave his mother a quick hug. "I'm going out to the ranch to visit with Amelia and little Clementine."

"You're staying in Horseback Hollow for a few days, then?"

He scrubbed a hand over his jaw, realized he'd forgotten to shave this morning. "Alice told me she needs a couple of days to think about her decision regarding London. If I'm in Austin, I won't be able to stay away from her. While I'm here I'm hoping someone can help me come up with a plan to convince her that leaving with me is best for everyone."

"What if you can't?"

"Not an option. This is the most important thing in my life, and I'm going to fight for Alice and Flynn. No matter what."

Josephine cupped his cheek in her elegant hand. "Your father would be proud, Charles."

Alice was in a meeting Tuesday morning when her phone started ringing. She normally kept it with her, set to vibrate, on the days her mother babysat Flynn, in case of an emergency. But the number that flashed on the screen wasn't one she recognized, so she pressed the button to send it directly to voice mail, and focused her attention back on Amanda, who was talking about an environmental tourism initiative at the front of the room.

A moment later the vibrating started again and Alice glanced down to see three more "unknown" numbers come through. Weird.

"Alice, are we keeping you from something important?" Amanda's clipped tone rang out in the quiet room, and Alice felt like a schoolgirl called out by a reproachful teacher.

"Sorry," she muttered, and turned her phone to Do Not Disturb mode for the rest of the meeting.

She pulled it out again as she walked toward her desk thirty minutes later. Before she had a chance to check the twelve new voice mails she'd received, she noticed everyone in the office staring at her. A prickly feeling started between her shoulder blades at the attention. What had happened to have her coworkers gaping at her?

Meredith was waiting in front of Alice's cubicle, a mix of sympathy and frustration in her eyes.

"What's going on?" Alice whispered as Meredith dragged her into the small space.

"Nothing to see here, people," her friend announced to the office as a whole. "Go back to whatever you were doing. She's still our Alice."

"Of course I'm still Alice. Why wouldn't I—" She broke off as Meredith shoved her into the desk chair. The computer monitor glowed bright with the front page of a popular online gossip site. The photo was the first thing that caught her attention. It was a picture of Charles, her and baby Flynn from the evening of the park concert. Alice was holding Flynn as Charles leaned over the two of them, his arm circling her shoulders. There was no denying the intimacy of the moment, and Alice felt her heart tug as she remembered the sweetness of that night and the passion she and Charles had shared after Flynn went to bed. Then her attention jerked to the headline above the photo, written in bold, black type.

Bonnie Lord Charlie's Love Child Living in Texas.

Oh, no.

Her gazed jerked to Meredith's. "Everyone knows."

Her friend gave a small nod. "It hit while you were in the meeting. Almost all the online tabloids have picked up the story. The office phone has been ringing off the hook and the receptionist called building security to stand watch at the front door." She shook her head. "The paparazzi are waiting for you outside."

Alice's chest constricted painfully and she bent forward, gasping for breath. "This is my worst nightmare, Mer."

"I know, sweetie. I'm sorry."

"No." Alice shot out of the chair, punched at the screen of her cell phone with trembling fingers, then grabbed her keys and purse. "Flynn is with my mom. I've got to get to my parents' house before the reporters do."

"Alice, we need to talk."

She glanced over her shoulder to see Amanda standing in the opening of her cubicle.

"I need to speak to you in my office. Now," her boss announced.

Alice gulped back the panic choking her throat. "I can't."

Amanda crossed her arms over her designer blazer. "Is it true? Is Charles your baby's father?"

"Yes," she whispered as she stepped forward.

"How did it happen?"

"I'll give you a lesson on the birds and bees later," Meredith answered for her. "Right now, Alice needs to get to Flynn."

Amanda shook her head and something besides panic welled in Alice. Determination. "I'll go through you if I have to," she said with more calm than she felt. "But I'm leaving to get to my son right now."

"Not out the front door." Amanda hitched a thumb over her shoulder. "The sidewalk is teeming with reporters. They'll never let you through."

Alice had parked in a lot around the corner from the tourism board office because it was cheaper than the covered garage attached to the building. "How am I going to get to my car?" she said with a desperate sob.

"Take mine," Amanda offered immediately, then

looked from her to Meredith. "No need to gawk at me. I'm not a total monster."

"I never thought you were," Alice told her honestly, "but thank you."

"Come on, I'll grab the keys for you." She ushered Alice through the office, and no one dared make eye contact, with Amanda leading the way. "I'm impressed," she said, as she pulled a key fob out of her purse. "I never thought you had it in you to nab a Fortune."

"That wasn't my intention," Alice said, knowing people around the world now thought of her as an ambitious gold digger. "I wanted my son to know his father. If it weren't for—"

"Enough." Amanda tossed the keys to her. "I was joking. No one who knows you would ever believe you were capable of being that opportunistic."

"Plenty of people who will think it, anyway."

"Forget them," Amanda advised. She took a tube of lipstick from her purse and reapplied it quickly. "I'm going to go out front and distract the paparazzi." She flashed Alice a calculated smile. "I've always wanted to be on camera. You hurry out to the garage before anyone catches on that you've left."

Alice nodded. "Why are you doing this?"

"I like to give you a hard time, but you're good at your job and I know you're a fantastic mother." She pointed at Alice. "There was also a spark so bright between you and Charles Fortune Chesterfield it could set fire to wet logs."

Charles. Alice knew he'd gone to Horseback Hollow to visit his family before returning to England. She'd asked for time to think about his proposal that she accompany him to London, and couldn't help but wonder if he'd changed his mind during his time away. After all, he was used to women falling at his feet, not questioning him. Had the press tracked him down in the tiny Texas town where most of his family lived? None of the Fortunes were fans of the paparazzi, and they wouldn't welcome the intrusion into their lives. How would they feel about the woman who'd caused it?

Her breath caught again, but she didn't have time to worry about Charles or the rest of the Fortunes now. She had to get to Flynn.

True to her word, Amanda distracted the reporters so Alice could escape. As she pulled out of the garage, she saw the mass of paparazzi crowded around the entrance of the tourism board office.

She called her mother on the way out of town, and then Charles, disappointment washing through her when his voice mail picked up on the second ring.

Nerves rocketed through her as she turned down her parents' street, followed quickly by relief when she saw the cul-de-sac empty of cars.

Her mother had the door open before Alice was halfway up the walk.

"Flynn," Alice whispered, scooping up the wide-eyed baby from Lynn's arms and cradling him tight to her chest.

"Alice, some of the women from my bunco group have been calling the house." Her mother's gaze was filled with worry. "They're saying—"

"I know," Alice interrupted, moving past her into the bright entry and then tugging on her arm. "Where's Dad? I need to talk to both of you."

They found her father in his study, staring at the computer screen behind his desk. He was watching a news clip from one of the most popular American gossip sites. Alice gasped as her face appeared. It showed her walking next to Charles on a city sidewalk. She was oblivious of the camera shooting footage of them, but there was no mistaking the dreamy expression on her face.

She looked like a lovesick schoolgirl.

It was mortifying to think that's how she appeared every time she looked at him. That while she was busy trying to be strong and independent, her face gave away everything she was feeling.

Her mother put a hand on her arm, as if offering support from the judgment and personal attacks aimed at her and Flynn from the tabloid report.

"Daddy."

At the sound of her voice, her father hit the mute button on the keyboard and turned in his chair.

She expected to see disappointment etched on his features, but there was only concern.

"Are you okay, Alice?"

Any other question and she could have held it together, but the reminder of how much her parents loved her in their own gentle way was too much. Tears blinded her and her mother helped her sink into the chair across from her father's desk. It was the one she'd spent hours in as a girl, reading her favorite books as he worked on syllabi and research papers.

She continued to clutch Flynn, but at his short cry she relaxed her hold on him.

"I'm fine, Dad," she lied, wiping at her cheeks. "I should have known that the story would break eventually, but I didn't want to believe it."

"So it's true?" Her mother's voice sounded dazed.

"Charles Fortune Chesterfield was your one-night stand?"

"Charles is Flynn's father," Alice said with a nod.

"It looks like more than a one-night stand from the footage they're showing of the two of you."

"I didn't tell him about the baby at first, but I realized he had a right to know his own son. Charles has been spending time with Flynn these past few weeks while he's been in town."

Lynn perched on the edge of the big desk and studied Alice. "And you, too?"

"And me, too," she whispered. "I…"

"Fell in love with him," her mother finished. "He's the man you told me you can't see in your future."

Alice pointed at the computer, where images of her still flashed, along with pictures of Charles's other girl-friends. "Look at me next to the other women he's dated. There's no comparison."

"You're right," her father agreed. "You are more beautiful than any of them."

"Not to mention you look like you have something between your ears besides air," Lynn added.

Alice sniffed, then smiled at the way her parents immediately came to her defense. "He's such a good man, much more than how he's portrayed in the press. I love being with him, love who I am when we're together. He's learning to be a great father to Flynn and I don't want it to end. But…"

Henry steepled his hands in front of him. "I don't like *but*s."

"He asked me to move to London with him."

"Oh." Her mother's shoulders slumped. "If that's what

you want, of course we'll support you. I can't imagine you and Flynn living so far away."

"I haven't heard a 'but' yet," her father said. "Is a transatlantic move what you want, Alice?"

"I don't know," she admitted quietly. "I want to be with Charles, but I'm afraid that he only asked me because of Flynn." The baby had fallen asleep in her arms and she smoothed a hand over his soft hair. "I know it sounds silly, but I want him to want *me*, not just the mother of his baby."

"That's not silly at all," Lynn told her.

"The boy would be a fool not to realize what a prize you are," her father added in his gruff voice.

"We just needed more time," Alice murmured. "Now that the story has broken—"

Lynn glanced at the computer screen and shook her head. "Turn that off, Henry. I've seen plenty from the tabloids." She looked back at Alice. "Have you talked to Charles?"

Alice shook her head in turn. "I haven't been able to reach him. He's visiting family in Horseback Hollow and I know at least one of his siblings lives out on a ranch. Maybe there isn't good cell phone reception where he is."

"So it's possible he doesn't know what you're dealing with here?"

That seemed hard to believe for a family who was so used to being tabloid fodder, but the alternative was that Charles was avoiding her. "I'm not sure. I guess so." She took a deep, shuddering breath. "The press was waiting for me outside of work today. What if they're already at my apartment? What if they come to your house?"

Her father leaned forward. "You're safe here, Alice."

"Why don't you spend the night?" her mother suggested. "You look exhausted and I don't want you to face the paparazzi on your own."

"I think I'll do that, Mom. Thank you."

"Of course, sweetie." Her mother reached for the baby as Alice stood. "You still have clothes up in your old bedroom. I'll take Flynn while you get changed, then we'll have dinner." She balanced Flynn in one arm and wrapped the other around Alice's shoulders. "We're going to get you through this."

Afraid she'd start crying again if she tried to speak, Alice simply nodded. She showered, then changed into a pair of pajama pants and a Longhorns T-shirt she'd left in her bedroom. She fed Flynn one last bottle, then put him down for the night before having a quiet meal with her mom and dad. They seemed to understand she wasn't up for more talking, and both kissed her goodnight after dinner.

She checked her phone once more before climbing into bed, but Charles still hadn't called. Instead her voice mail was full, and texts continued to pop up on the screen, with reporters and friends trying to contact her. It seemed everyone in the world wanted to speak with her, except the one person whose voice she wanted to hear.

Placing her phone in the nightstand drawer so she wouldn't have to see it continue to light up, she rested her head on the soft pillow. The sheets smelled like the detergent her mother had used for years, and the feeling of safety Alice always had in her parents' house gave her a little comfort. She turned on her side and watched Flynn through the slats of the crib set up in one corner of the room. In the glow of the night-light she could see his mouth work as he slept, unaware of the firestorm surrounding him and his mother.

She hated that he was going to grow up with reporters as part of his life. Had she compromised her vow to protect her son, by falling so hopelessly in love with Charles? What would it be like if she moved to London? Would the British press be part of her everyday life, and who would she have to protect her?

As doubts and fear careened through her mind in the silence of her childhood bedroom, her thoughts kept returning to Charles. Was he still in Horseback Hollow? Why hadn't he called her? Did the press coverage they were receiving change his plans? Had their future together been ruined before it had even begun?

Chapter Sixteen

"Hey, James Bond, do you mind taking it easy on the curves?" Charles's brother Jensen grabbed the handle of the passenger door of his oversize Chevy truck. "My truck has a lot of power but it doesn't exactly handle like an Aston Martin."

Charles saw the sign for the Horseback Hollow branch of the Redmond Flight School and Charter Service in the distance and instead of slowing down, pressed his foot harder to the gas pedal.

"You'll be no good to Alice and Flynn splattered all over the side of a rural Texas highway."

That pierced the panic swirling through Charles's mind and he forced himself to slow as he turned into the airfield. It was almost twenty-four hours since the story of Flynn's paternity had broken in the tabloids. Unfortunately, he'd been out on a ride with his brother-in-law, Quinn Drummond, when the news first hit, and had left his phone in the ranch's guest bedroom. They'd gone straight to dinner at one of the neighboring properties, and so far out of town, the reception was spotty at best.

By the time he'd gotten back to Amelia and Quinn's house, it had been almost midnight, but most of his family members were waiting for him, with various opinions on how to handle the media frenzy. The Fortunes in Horseback Hollow were somewhat insulated from the paparazzi, but Lucie had video chatted in from Austin, where an apparent media circus was raging.

He'd listened to Alice's three voice mails, her tone more desperate in each subsequent message. But he'd waited to call her back until this morning, not wanting to wake her or Flynn so late at night. That had been a terrible mistake.

Her cell phone had gone directly to voice mail each time he called, and he'd finally resorted to tracking down her parents' home number. It had taken a fair bit of convincing before her mother believed he was actually Charles Chesterfield, and when she did, Lynn Meyers wasted no time in expressing her disappointment in how he'd left Alice to fend off the tabloid press on her own. For someone known worldwide for his charm, Charles had an abysmal track record with the Meyers women.

He explained the situation as best he could, then resorted to begging for information on how Alice was dealing with everything that had transpired. The real panic had set in when Lynn informed him that Alice was planning to leave Austin to escape the press. She wouldn't tell him where her daughter planned to go, but did let him know that Alice was mostly ignoring her phone, since it was difficult to tell calls from the press from those of her friends and coworkers.

Charles's only thought was that he had to get to Alice before she left with Flynn. He was terrified that she'd disappear before he had the chance to tell her he loved her.

Because that's what had become clear to him in the midst of the tabloid furor. He didn't care if he never attended another society party again. He loved Alice and the life he had with her. She didn't need to fit into his world. He wanted to create their own perfect life together. He'd been a fool not to realize it sooner. A fact his siblings had been more than happy to point out over and over.

Even that didn't matter.

All he cared about was finding Alice.

He slammed on the brakes and threw the truck into Park, tossing the keys to Jensen as he climbed out. Charles had insisted on driving to the small airport, as he didn't trust his buttoned-up brother to get him there on time.

Orlando Mendoza, his mother's new love interest, had offered to fly him to Austin. The trip was only about an hour by air, as opposed to the six hours it would take him to drive. Six hours he didn't have if he was going to reach Alice in time.

The reality was that he could track her down even if she left Austin before he got there. But somehow in Charles's mind, getting to her first was an essential part of proving that he deserved another chance with her and Flynn.

"Thanks for your help," he called to his brother as he darted toward the small terminal building. "I'll call when I work things out."

To his surprise, Jensen caught up with him in a few steps. "I'm going with you."

Charles shook his head but didn't stop moving. "Don't be ridiculous. I can handle this."

"Believe what you want, but if you're determined to make things right with Alice—"

"I am."

"Then you need support."

"From you?" Charles paused outside the door of the hangar.

Jensen flashed a patently big brother smile. "From all of us." He pointed through the terminal's plate glass windows. Brodie, Oliver and Amelia stood talking to Orlando, next to a shiny single-engine airplane.

"You can't be serious."

"Lucie will meet us with a car in Austin."

"You don't even know Alice," Charles argued, shaking his head.

"All the more reason for us to come along for the ride. We want to meet her before you pledge your troth and all of that business."

"My troth?"

"Do you want to argue or shall we be off?" Jensen pushed through the double doors, leaving Charles no choice but to follow.

He was both annoyed with his siblings for intruding and touched that they were willing to put their own busy lives on hold to support him. But whichever emotion won out in the end, Jensen was right about one thing. Charles didn't have time to waste arguing.

He sat next to Orlando in the cockpit, not wanting to spend the flight listening to his siblings argue over how he should handle both the press and Alice.

It was a clear day, perfect for flying, and Orlando was a careful and experienced pilot. His salt-and-pepper hair was a contrast to the burnished tan of his face, and he still had the strong build of a much younger man. Charles knew Orlando was semi-retired and appreciated him arranging this trip on such short notice.

He told him as much, talking through the headsets to express his thanks. Orlando glanced at him, gave a brief nod, then focused on landing the plane on the short runway outside Austin.

As the plane touched down, Orlando finally spoke to him. "Good luck today, Charles. Your mother is proud of you for fighting for your baby and the woman you love."

"She was the one who taught me that love is worth fighting for." He flashed a self-deprecating smile. "Too bad I was never the quickest study."

Orlando returned his grin before his gaze turned serious again. "From everything your mother has told me about Sir Simon, your father would be proud of you, too."

Emotion welled in Charles's throat as he met the older man's steady brown eyes. His mother had said almost the same thing to him, but hearing it from someone who was a father to his own brood of grown children and who would have been close to Sir Simon's age made Charles feel like he was somehow gaining his own dad's blessing.

At the very least, Sir Simon would have respected Orlando, and Charles guessed the two men might have become friends. Although no one would ever take his father's place, Charles was suddenly grateful his mother had gotten another chance at happiness.

Just as he hoped to earn his own second chance with Alice.

As promised, Lucie was waiting for them behind the

wheel of an SUV large enough to fit them all, once they exited the terminal.

"How bad is it?" Charles asked. She gave him a quick hug, while Amelia, Brodie, Oliver and Jensen climbed into the back. Orlando had offered to wait with the plane so that his siblings wouldn't have to spend more than a day away from home. Charles only hoped he'd have a reason to stay in Austin.

"Have you reached Alice yet?" Lucie slid into the passenger side as he took the wheel. Charles was simply too nervous not to be in control of the driving.

He shook his head. "I rang her again as soon as we landed, but still no answer. According to her mother, she's quite upset."

"Of course she is." Lucie stared out the front window as they turned onto the main highway from the airfield.

Amelia leaned forward from the backseat. "We've grown up with the attention and it's still upsetting when a story hits. I can only imagine how that poor girl is reacting."

As could Charles, and it made his stomach turn with worry, anger and regret. He should have been more careful when they were together. He should have kept Alice and Flynn safe.

He stepped harder on the gas, ignoring Amelia's gasp as she flew back in her seat.

"No more talking," Charles growled. "If you all want to tag along, at least do me a favor and shut the hell up."

He heard Brodie bark out a laugh. "He's sounding more American by the moment."

"You'll be the first one left on the side of the road." Charles glanced in the rearview mirror. "So I advise you to close your piehole."

To Charles's amazement, that final bit of slang did the trick, and his siblings were quiet for the rest of the drive.

Alice was not surprised to hear the doorbell ring as she zipped shut her suitcase. Although most of the paparazzi had been waiting on the street in front of her building, a few had managed to sneak into the place when other residents entered. After opening her door to a microphone and camera shoved in her face, Alice had quickly learned to ignore the ringing.

She'd returned to her apartment from her parents' house early this morning under the cover of darkness. Flynn had dozed in his car seat, and Alice had sneaked into the back of her building without incident. But she hated sneaking through her own life, with the constant fear of being ambushed by the press.

The uproar over the discovery that Charles was the father of her baby would eventually die down, but their lives would never again be anonymous. There would always be an interest in Flynn. How did the Fortune family deal with that kind of scrutiny on a daily basis?

She wondered if the tabloid news had finally reached Charles in Horseback Hollow, and wished she could hear his voice. Maybe he'd called her by now, but Alice had been so frustrated with the texts and calls she continued to receive that she'd chucked her cell phone out the car window on her way home this morning. It had been impulsive and foolish, but she'd barely slept last night and wasn't thinking clearly.

The insistent knocking continued, and Flynn gave a sharp cry from his crib. Alice lifted him up, cradling him against her as she stepped into the family room and stared at the door. She'd made plans to visit an aunt who lived outside Dallas, but how was she going to leave with reporters at her door?

"Are you in there, Alice?" A crisp British voice clipped out the words. "Answer the door, love."

Her heart seemed to stop beating in her chest, and at the same time, relief washed through her. Charles would know how to handle the paparazzi. Charles would make the hell of the last twenty-four hours fade away.

Relief was followed quickly by a dizzying anger at the situation and a lingering disappointment in her handsome British playboy for not rescuing her sooner.

No.

Not rescuing.

Alice was not a woman who needed rescuing, no matter how much she'd wanted it.

Hadn't motherhood taught her she could stand on her own two feet? She was strong enough to fight for herself and her son. The question was, could she be strong enough to prove to Charles that *she* was worth fighting for?

She opened the door, planning to tell him everything she was thinking, but stopped short at the sight that greeted her. Charles wasn't alone. Two women and three men whom Alice immediately recognized as his five siblings flanked him on either side.

So much for the paparazzi. Alice was under siege by the British Fortunes.

All those aristocratic eyes staring at her were enough to make the thoughts in her head scatter.

"Alice, thank God you're still here." Charles's words had her attention snapping back to him.

"I'm actually on my way out," she said, proud that her voice remained steady despite the emotions swirling through her chest. "Flynn and I are going to visit my extended family until the worst of the attention blows over."

"You can't leave," he answered immediately, something close to panic flashing in his blue eyes.

"Why?"

One of the women, a tall, hazel-eyed beauty, leaned forward. Alice recognized her as Lucie, Charles's younger sister, who was most recently the focus of a tabloid storm centering on her secret marriage to Austin native Chase Parker. "Well, unless you have an invisibility cloak tucked away somewhere, there's a media circus on the sidewalk downstairs," she said.

Alice straightened her shoulders. "I won't let the paparazzi hold me prisoner in my own home." Even though that's exactly how she'd felt the past day.

"She's got mettle," one of the men commented, nudging Charles in the arm. "I like her already."

"It's obvious you don't deserve her," the taller man on Charles's other side muttered. "So you'd better make this good."

"Make what good?" Alice asked, a hysterical giggle rising in her throat as her gaze darted between the various Fortunes. It really was too much to have them all crowded in the hallway staring at her. She managed to tamp down both the laughter and panic, holding on to her baby like he was her anchor in a fierce storm.

"I'm not making anything good," Charles snapped.

"Clearly," the second sister, Amelia, murmured, and reached out to run a finger across Flynn's soft cheek. "He's a beautiful boy."

"Thank you."

"Charles said Flynn gives you some trouble sleeping." Amelia offered a gentle smile. "Clementine was the same way and I often wondered—"

"I'm wondering if the rest of you will be quiet," Charles practically growled, shooting angry glares at his brothers and sisters, "so that Alice and I can have a conversation."

Immediately, Amelia stopped speaking, and along with the rest of the Fortunes, looked expectantly at Charles.

"You can't leave," he repeated in a ragged whisper. "You're going to London with me. I can take care of you there. You and Flynn."

She gave a small shake of her head. "I never agreed to that, Charles. I told you I'd think about it but—"

"You have to, Alice. What's happened here proves it. You need me."

She swallowed. "I need you?"

He looked baffled that she would question him. "Flynn needs me."

At that moment, the baby let out a small cry. Alice looked between her baby and Charles.

"Let me," Amelia offered, holding out her arms. "I'll take care of him."

"Flynn is staying with me. I'm his mother." Alice wrapped her arms around the baby and stepped back into the apartment. She wasn't handing over her baby to anyone, no matter how well-meaning Charles's sister appeared.

The truth was, the Fortunes were better equipped to care for the baby, with all the demands the press would make. They were a strong family with plenty of resources to ensure that Flynn would be protected. But Alice loved Charles, and she knew it would be too difficult to be a part of his life and not have her feelings returned. Despite the valid reasons he'd given why they should be together, never once had he mentioned love.

She took a deep breath, looked him in the eye and whispered, "No."

Charles felt his chest constrict as Alice uttered that one syllable. He could hear the collective sigh from his siblings.

"You'll be a wonderful father," Alice told him, tears shining in her eyes. "And I want you to continue to spend time with Flynn, of course. But I need more."

More. How could he give her more when he was ready to offer everything he had? Everything he was.

The only answer was that *he* wasn't enough.

He started to back away, to give her the space she obviously wanted, when Lucie elbowed him hard in the ribs. "You've told her, right?"

Charles glanced at his sister. "Told her what?"

Jensen flicked him on the side of the head. "That you love her, you dunce."

Charles smacked away his brother's hand. "Stop. Beating. On. Me." He turned and threw each of his siblings a pointed glare that they seemed happy to return. "She knows I love her," he shouted.

"You love me?"

He whirled to face Alice again. "I asked you to move to another country with me. Why else would I make that offer?"

"To take care of Flynn," she answered immediately.

He felt a poke at his back. "Tell her," Lucie chided.

Of course he loved Alice. How could he not? But he suddenly realized he'd never said the words out loud.

He'd never said those three words to anyone. Maybe to his mother when he was a boy, but never as a man would say them to a woman. Not to any of the girls he'd dated. Not either of the times he'd been engaged.

Alice had already told him no. His gut told him to cut his losses and turn around before he made a bigger ass out of himself, and with the additional humiliation of his brothers and sisters to bear witness.

But another voice—one that sounded suspiciously like his father's—reminded him that he'd promised to fight for the woman standing in front of him. To prove himself worthy of her. To be a man who would make his parents proud. Even if he wound up heartbroken, he had to risk everything. Alice deserved the best he had to give.

He wanted to push her into the apartment and shut the door on his siblings. To gain a bit of privacy. But no. This had to be done here and now. No more hiding.

"I love you," he said, and bent so he was level with her beautiful—if wary—gaze. "I think I started falling in love with you that first day on the park bench."

One corner of her mouth curved as her eyes turned watery. "Really?"

"I never really understood the concept of a North Star until I met you, Alice. You are my guide in the night when I can't see anything else. You're the person who inspires me to make better choices in my life. You've shown me that I have more potential than I ever thought possible." He shot another glare over his shoulder to where his siblings stood huddled against the far wall of the corridor. "That there is more to me than anyone believed."

"You're already that person, Charles," she said softly, and his heart expanded even more.

"Only with you." He leaned in and brushed a soft kiss across her lips. "I want to take care of you, but not because you can't take care of yourself. My father taught me that one of the highest expressions of love is to take care of the people who mean the world to you. I also need you, rather desperately, I'm afraid, to care for me. To be patient, because I'm liable to make mistakes at every step."

He heard one of his brothers cough and mutter something that sounded like "not good." He shook off the distraction and focused on Alice.

"But I'll work hard to fix every one. To make you happy. To be the man you and Flynn deserve. Please give me that chance."

"What exactly are you asking, Charles?" Emotion danced in her eyes. Love for him. Devotion. Patience. It made all his fears and doubts fade away.

An image of Kate Fortune popped into his mind. He reached into his pocket for the velvet pouch that held the ring she'd given him. He'd brought it to Horseback Hollow to show his mother, and still carried it.

Without hesitation he dropped to one knee and pulled out the delicate gold band.

He heard a gasp, then a rather loud sniff behind him. Lucie, no doubt. He ignored it, continuing to stare into Alice's wide hazel eyes.

"Alice Meyers, would you do me the great honor of becoming my wife?"

"Yes," she whispered, and adjusted Flynn so that Charles could slip the ring onto her left hand. "I love you, Charles. So very much."

"Want me to take the baby so you can kiss her properly?" Jensen offered with a brotherly nudge.

"I can kiss both of them perfectly well with no help from you," Charles muttered, then folded both Alice and Flynn into his embrace. The baby laughed as Charles kissed Alice, Flynn's chubby fingers poking at each of his parents' cheeks.

His siblings let out a rousing cheer.

"Team Fortune Chesterfield," Alice said against his mouth.

"Team Us," he answered, and kissed her again. This was his future…his family. Charles intended to hold on to Alice and Flynn with every piece of his heart.

Epilogue

"Are you nervous?" Alice asked as she watched Charles take another deep breath.

They stood on the sidewalk in front of her parents' house three days after Charles had declared his love for her. In that time, the media circus that surrounded them had begun to fade, spurred by Charles's very public declaration of love for her and the announcement of their engagement.

His sisters, Lucie and Amelia, had coached Alice on how to handle the tabloid press when she did encounter them. Knowing she had the support of the Fortune family made Alice feel far more confident in her ability to cope with the public aspect of Charles's life. But right now her handsome Brit was the one who looked distinctly uncomfortable.

He balanced Flynn's infant carrier in one arm and ran

his free hand through his hair. "Of course I'm nervous. I'm about to be introduced to your parents."

She laced her fingers with his and led him up the paved walk. "You've met heads of state, Fortune 500 CEOs, celebrities from all parts of the world. My mom and dad are an ordinary couple from the suburbs of Austin." She shook her head. "Why would they make you nervous?"

He stopped, tugged on her hand until she turned to him. "Because they're important to you, Alice. They love you and I love you, so it would help if they at least liked me." He made a face. "Our courtship didn't follow the prescribed timeline. Meeting your parents after we've had a baby together and gotten engaged takes the phrase 'putting the cart before the horse' to a whole new level."

Alice laughed. She couldn't help it. Charles looked almost comically stricken. Then she brushed a light kiss over his lips. "They want me to be happy," she whispered into his mouth. "You make me happy."

She felt a little of his tension ease as he rested his forehead against hers, grounding himself in her. Since that afternoon in her apartment, Charles had become even more affectionate with her. Saying the words *I love you* out loud had freed up something in him, fragmented the last of his defenses so that now every moment they were together his touch conveyed the fact that he was well and truly hers.

It made her heart swell until it felt almost too big for her body to contain.

A throat cleared discreetly behind her and she turned to see her parents standing in the doorway. She knew Charles had nothing to worry about from Henry and Lynn Meyers.

He held out a hand as they approached. "Mr. and Mrs. Mey—"

Her mother cut him off, enveloping them both in a warm hug. "Call me Lynn," she said. "I'm so glad our Alice found you, Charles. I know you'll take good care of her."

Alice could see that her mother's faith in him bolstered Charles's own confidence. "Every moment of my life," he promised as he returned Lynn's hug. "Your daughter is a precious gift. One that I'll treasure and guard each day."

"Oh, well. That's perfect, then." Her mother took a step back, her hand pressed to her chest as if she was having trouble gathering a breath.

"The Charles Effect strikes again," Alice murmured, making him smile at their private joke.

She hugged her father, and Henry shook Charles's hand, clearly not as quickly won over as his wife but approving in his own quiet way. "I'd like to know what you Englishmen are taught about the Revolutionary War," he told Charles.

"I'd be honored to discuss that with you, sir," Charles answer, earning a small smile from Henry. At that moment Alice was certain her Fortune would fit in just fine as part of their tight-knit family.

Flynn made a small sound from his carrier, and her mother led them into the house. An hour later, Charles came into the kitchen, where Alice was helping her mother set the table for dinner.

"Everything all right?" she asked. Her father had dragged Charles off to his office soon after they'd entered, and she hoped her dad had limited the conversation to details of American history and not grilled Charles about their relationship.

"Fine," he answered, but ran a hand through his hair at the same time. His nervous tell. "Can I speak to you outside for a moment, Alice?"

Her mother glanced up from the vegetables she was chopping for a salad. "We still have fifteen minutes until the roast is ready. I can handle things in here."

Her heart suddenly beating a funny rhythm in her chest, Alice picked up Flynn and followed Charles out the French doors onto the covered patio of her parents' backyard. "Is something wrong? Did my father—"

"He loves you," Charles interrupted, taking her hand and raising her fingertips to his lips. "Both your parents love you and Flynn so very much." He smoothed his other hand over the baby's soft skin. "I can't imagine taking you away from them."

"My home is with you now," she assured him, reaching into the back pocket of her jeans. "This came today." She held up a shiny new passport. "I have one for Flynn, too, so we can leave for London as soon as I get my apartment packed." She shut her eyes for a moment as emotion threatened to overtake her.

Alice meant what she said. She had no doubts about moving to England to be with Charles, not when she was so sure of his love. But it was still difficult to think about leaving behind the life she'd built for herself. She was proud of the woman she'd become in the past year, but even more excited about creating a future with Charles.

She opened her eyes to find him looking at her with such tenderness it made tears threaten. "I'm fine," she whispered. "I promise."

"I have something to show you, as well." He took his

phone from his pocket and lifted the screen so she could see. "What do you think?"

It was a photograph of a gorgeous two-story brick house, not quite a mansion, but definitely larger than anywhere Alice had ever lived. There were oversize gables, a midnight blue slate roof and copper gutters that gave the home a timeless air. The photo must have been taken at the height of summer because a colorful flower garden was visible to the side of the house and a large elm tree provided shade for the inviting wrap-around porch.

"It's beautiful," Alice told Charles, covering his fingers with her own. "But I don't need an English manor to make me happy."

"That's a good thing, love." He leaned in to kiss her. "Because this house is right here in Austin."

Alice felt her jaw drop, and Charles ran a finger under her chin to tip it closed. "I may never wear a ten-gallon hat, but I'm not going to separate you and Flynn from your family. Or mine, for that matter," he added with a grin.

"Charles, thank you." Alice threw her arms around his neck and he folded her into his strong, safe embrace.

"Thank *you*," he whispered against her hair. "For making me whole. For being my home. My everything. I love you, Alice."

"I love you, Charles. With all my heart."

Flynn gave a great belly laugh as Charles held them closer, and Alice knew she had found her home.

* * * * *

Don't miss the next installment of the
Mills & Boon continuity

THE FORTUNES OF TEXAS:
ALL FORTUNE'S CHILDREN

Zoe Robinson refuses to believe she's a secret
Fortune, but she can't deny the truth—she's falling
for Joaquin Mendoza! But can this Prince Charming
convince his Cinderella to find happily-ever-after
with him once he uncovers his own family secrets?

Look for
FORTUNE'S PRINCE CHARMING
by
Nancy Robards Thompson

On sale May 2016, wherever
Mills & Boon books are sold.

MILLS & BOON®

Why not subscribe?
Never miss a title and save money too!

Here's what's available to you if you join the exclusive **Mills & Boon® Book Club** today:

- ✦ *Titles up to a month ahead of the shops*
- ✦ *Amazing discounts*
- ✦ *Free P&P*
- ✦ *Earn Bonus Book points that can be redeemed against other titles and gifts*
- ✦ *Choose from monthly or pre-paid plans*

Still want more?
Well, if you join today, we'll even give you
50% OFF your first parcel!

So visit **www.millsandboon.co.uk/subs**
to be a part of this exclusive Book Club!

MILLS & BOON®

Helen Bianchin v Regency Collection!

MILLS & BOON®

Cherish™

EXPERIENCE THE ULTIMATE RUSH OF FALLING IN LOVE

A sneak peek at next month's titles...

In stores from 7th April 2016:

- **The Billionaire Who Saw Her Beauty** – Rebecca Winters *and* **Fortune's Prince Charming** – Nancy Robards Thompson
- **In the Boss's Castle** – Jessica Gilmore *and* **The Texas Ranger's Family** – Rebecca Winters

In stores from 21st April 2016:

- **Rafael's Contract Bride** – Nina Milne *and* **James Bravo's Shotgun Bride** – Christine Rimmer
- **One Week with the French Tycoon** – Christy McKellen *and* **The Detective's 8 lb, 10 oz Surprise** – Meg Maxwell

Available at WHSmith, Tesco, Asda, Eason, Amazon and Apple

Just can't wait?
Buy our books online a month before they hit the shops!
visit www.millsandboon.co.uk

These books are also available in eBook format!